I0419020

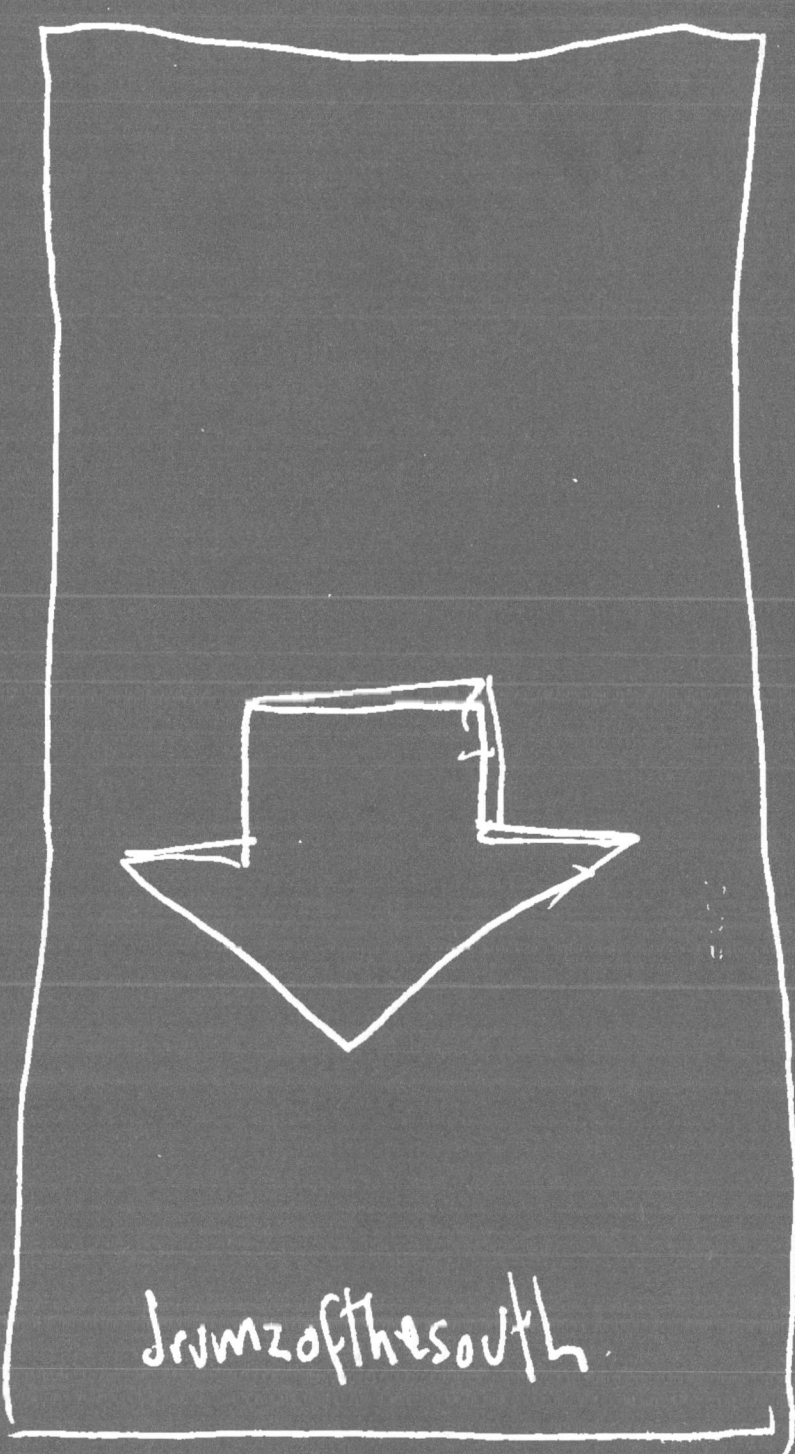

First published in 2021 by Georgina Cook.
This version published in 2024 by Velocity Press
velocitypress.uk
georginacook.net

Printed and bound in Poland by Interak
Editor - Georgina Cook
Design - Felix Luke felixluke.co.uk & Alfie Allen alfie-allen.com
Photography - Georgina Cook
Words - Georgina Cook, Emma Warren, Martin Clark,
Charlie Dark, DJ Flight, Jason Goz

Georgina Cook has asserted her right under the Copyright,
Designs and Patents Act 1988 to be identified as the author
of this work

All rights reserved. No part of this publication may be
reproduced, in any form or by any means, without permission
from the publisher

Copyright © Georgina Cook

ISBN: 9781913231668

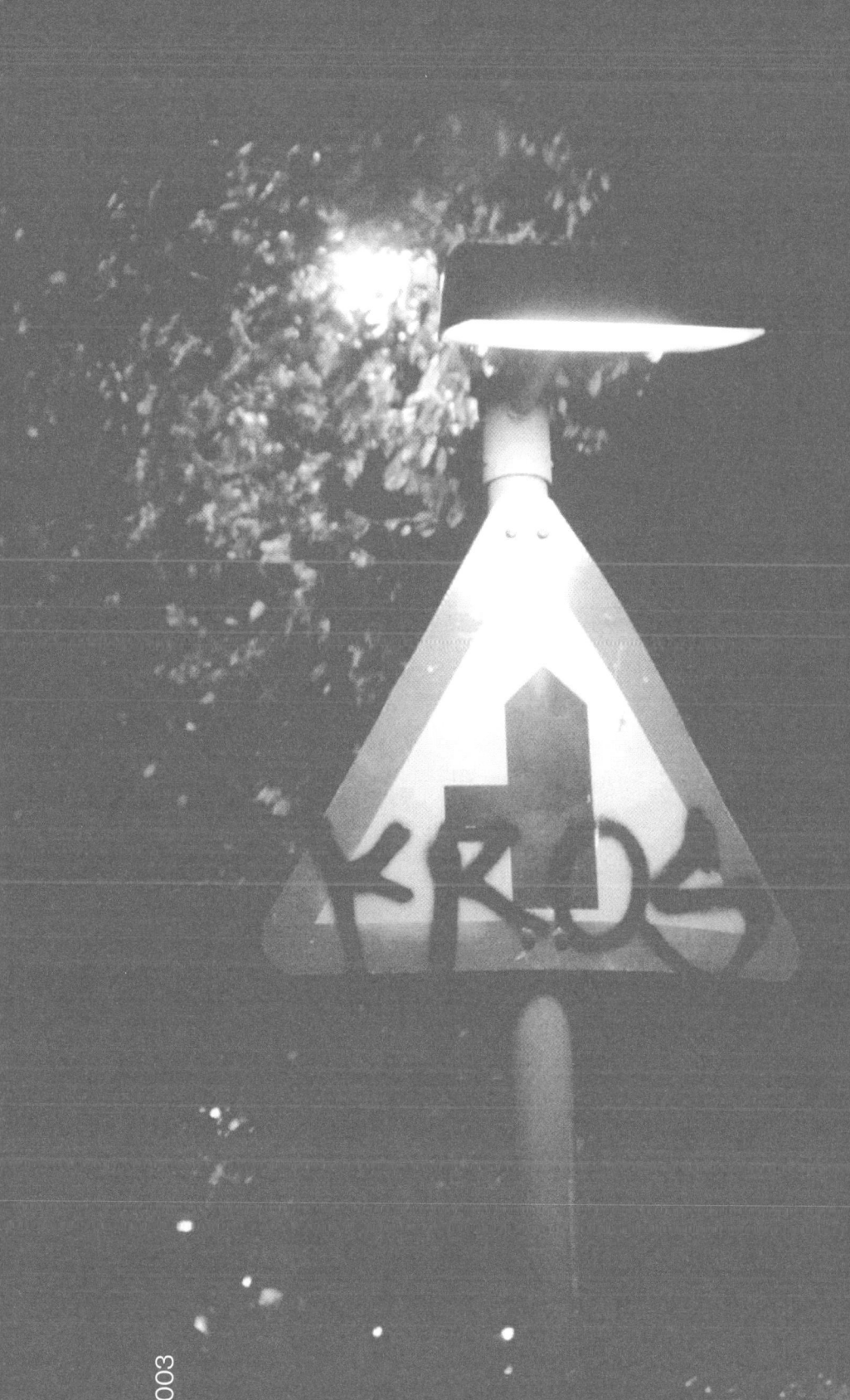

Foreword by Emma Warren

Most nightclub photographers focus on the dancefloor, as if it exists in isolation. Georgina Cook opens this book with sunset over South London, with a telegraph pole radiating wires in all directions like a partially-constructed spider web. She photographs the dancers but she also photographs the interconnected locations that feed into and out of the club: in her case, the journeys required to get there and get home again; the hand-written notices pinned up on the wall at Rinse FM; mugs of tea in Loefah's flat. I've even seen photographs she took of people clearing up after DMZ, the room empty apart from a couple of security and a lone staff member, dancing solo.

The secret to Georgina Cook's work as a writer, publisher, podcaster and photographer is that she was – and is – on the dancefloor. She hasn't parachuted in once or twice. She was there in the early years of dubstep, week in and week out, and luckily for us, she also took photographs, even though no-one had commissioned her to do so. Like much citizen-generated culture, the early iterations of the music that became dubstep operated like a community of contribution, with people bringing what they had. Instead of getting on the mic or DJing, Georgina got behind the lens.

I met her on the dancefloor at one of the monthly DMZs in 2006, when I began my own deep immersion in the music and the culture being built by Mala, Coki, Loefah and SGT Pokes at DMZ, and by Sarah 'Soulja' Lockhart and crew at FWD>>. 15 years of friendship and occasional collaboration means I can tell you something else about Georgina Cook: she sees more clearly than most people. Most people stop looking at some point, out of self-preservation. But she keeps looking and looking and looking, sucking up all the information and finding ways to condense and express what she sees.

The photographs in this book were taken through the lens of a battered Nikon D600. It replaced another camera which was stolen at another London club called Cargo, an incident which prompted Seckle from the Dubstep Forum to set up a proto-crowdfunder for its replacement. She looks on behalf of the community and the community looks after her.

What do I see in her rare photography? Red lights at night, inside the place and back outside again, in the rain. Landlines, Nokia charger wires and battered dubs. Residential TV aerials and pirate radio studios. Burial's night bus, without any night bus appearing on these pages – although there are some of her iconic shots that accompanied his earliest releases. Empty train stations and graf on the train journey uptown, which draws a line between her work and the work of another storied photographer, Martha Cooper, who also shot around her subject. An orange halo around the queue outside Mass, before DMZ, where Loefah did the guest list.

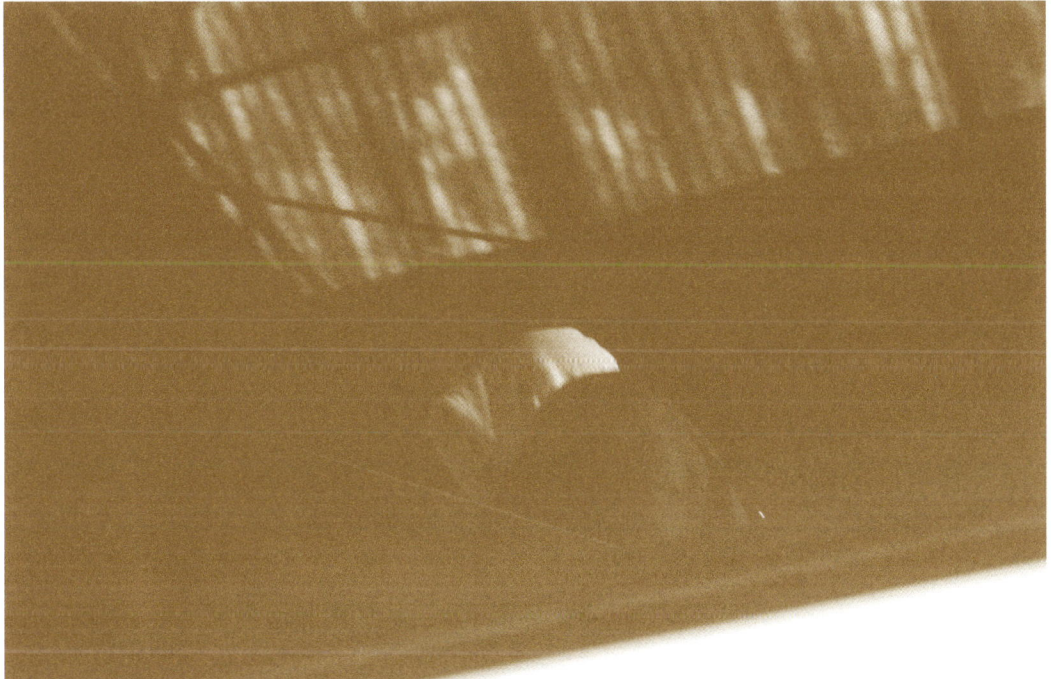

The visual effect that she calls 'amber glow' tells us something else about her work, which is also true of any work that captures the ongoing present of culture. It shows us how things have changed, and therefore, something about how things are now. The smoking ban arrived in 2007, around the end of the period covered in this book. This meant that clubs lost the visual presence of overhanging vapour, even if it saved our lungs some. The period also coincided with the end of diffused sodium street lighting, which began disappearing in 2005-6, when Croydon replaced some of its lighting. In 2011 the borough and neighbouring Lewisham began replacing 38,000 street lights, substituting the old SOX lights with bright white LED.

Georgina Cook makes light, or the lack thereof, her friend: street lighting; the white penlight that allows the DJ to see the decks in a dark club; smears of red light bulbs. She also makes condensation her friend, using fine aerosol rain like a filter and doing the same with the body-induced humidity in clubs where the energy levels are so high that people are not just banging the walls, they're banging the monitors that hang from the roof in front of the DJ booth. Long exposures give us a hint about what was happening, in the half-step space between the beats, in the moments before the bass returned and made the inside of your cheek bones vibrate.

What else? There's Mala and Coki in the studio, shot from above, mid-joke. Kode9 behind the decks, smiling. Appleblim pointing, stamina crew. Heads down, knees up, leaning forward. Red Stripe and Guinness, spillages and carnage. A slumped one, at DMZ. Functional clothes and girls not having to dress up. Smokers on the dancefloor. Evidence of a crowd reload.

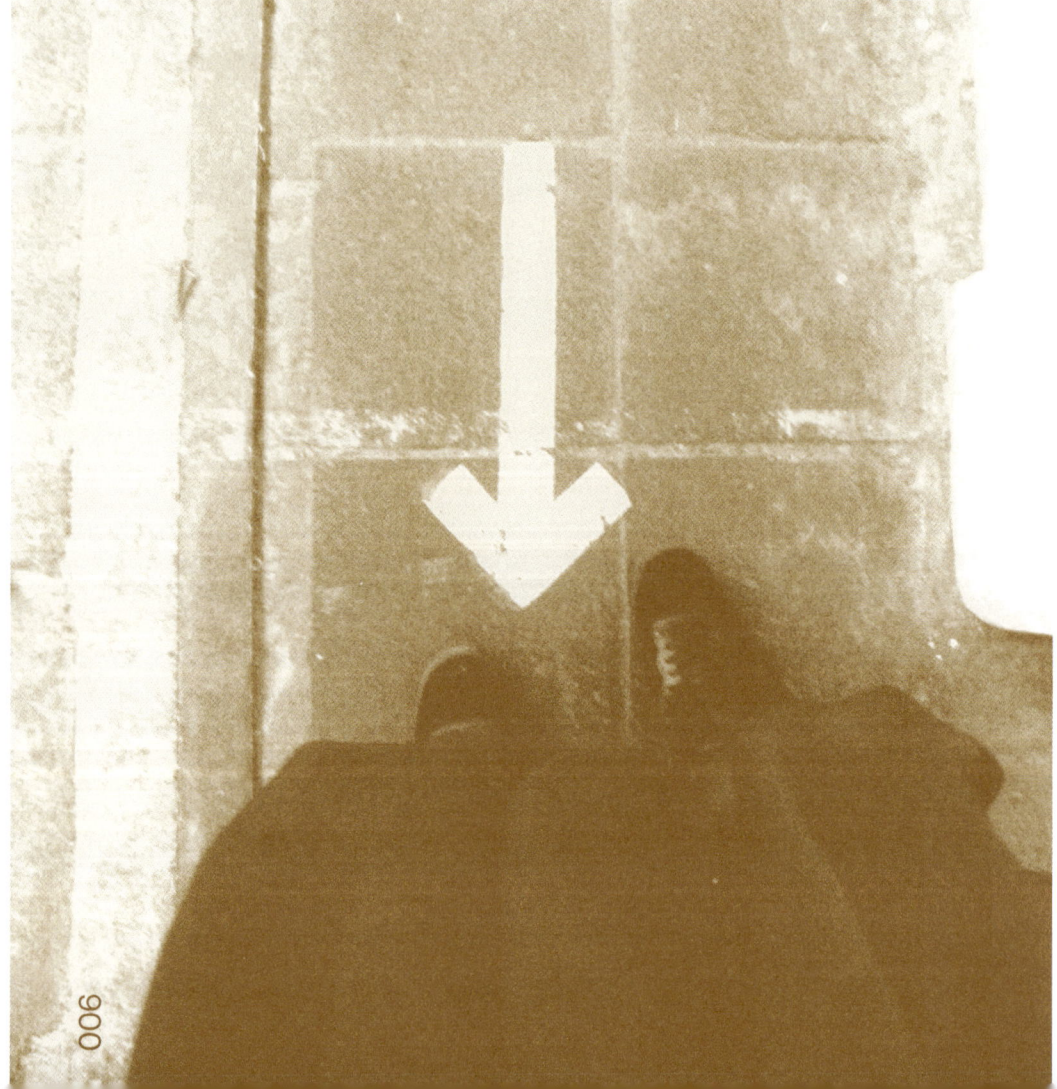

separated isolation. At this point, some elements of dubstep overlapped with garage – see that shot of Benny Ill, who if he wasn't DJing was often somewhere at the back. Some of it overlapped with grime. Some of it pointed to what would come next. The layering of communities and musical histories is evident in that shot of Wiley, Jammer and JME front left at FWD>> during a Mala set, as he's dropping Midnight Request Line. Skream's tune is about to destroy the room and create another moment of connection between the two communities. You can see him in the left hand corner of the shot, hand on mouth, looking tense, as his tune is about to be tested in front of grime's dons. Writer and producer Martin 'Blackdown' Clark is standing next to him, confident in what is about to happen. Wiley's looking out of shot and JME is laser-focused on the rotating dub. Jammer's already got his lighter out. Tubby – another person who linked both styles of music – is leaning in, anticipating what will happen next and SGT Pokes has already transcended into the moment of coiled-up calm that precedes the most lemony bass face. All that information is contained in this one frame. Skepta later remixed the tune, and grime MCs were still freestyling on it right into the late 2010s when Novelist jumped on it during a live set at Worldwide FM. It's a lot.

Whenever I read or hear the word 'forward' – or in this case 'foreword' – I hear it in the voice of Crazy D who'd MC the club of the same name. He was a minimalist MC, drawing on the rich histories of soundsystem mic men: sometimes just bending the word 'forward' into three parts, other times drawing for his key phrases: 'warm and easy' or 'deeper and darker we go'. The new edition of this book goes backwards into the past, but it goes forward too, as a brilliant example of how to contribute to culture, how to record what happened from within, and how to publish it.

Forward, always.

Preface

Astonishingly, this is the second edition of Drumz Of The South, in book form. The first arrived in 2021, as a result of crowdfunding (which over 500 people from around the world contributed to), and resulted in over 1000 copies being flown around the world from my very own desk. Attempting to distribute the book myself meant I ran into obstacles sending it to places that are a relative stones throw away from my home on the south coast of England. This was in part due to the impact of Britain's exit on trade and customs, which suddenly made sending things to Australia easier than sending them to France, Belgium and Germany. A fukkery, as my friend Breezy (and Amy Winehouse) would say. SO, while Drumz Of The South has been for everyone since it's early form as a blog and Flickr account, this edition, three years later, is particularly for all of you that couldn't get hold of the first.

Somewhat beautifully, this edition with Velocity Press, arrives around the time of Drumz Of The South's 20th birthday. Happy Birthday to us. And knowing what I know about music and youth culture, through collaboration with great people like The Museum of Youth Culture for example, 20 years is generally the cycle in which cultures and fashions come around again. Testament to this is my nephew who is also 20 years old. Last Christmas, I gave him a copy of Burial's Untrue and I derive great pleasure from seeing him post tunes and photos related to some of the artists in this book. Like many of you, he knows about this stuff through relatives who were there when it was happening, the multitude of Instagram accounts dedicated to sharing it, and through labels like Deep Medi, Wheel & Deal, Hyperdub and GD4YA whose sonic offerings stretch between eras.

I guess dubstep and grime are as inspiring to you as jungle and garage were to me at the age of 20. Lots of you around this age even go as far as researching and writing about elements of it as part of higher education. I know this because I am frequently contacted with questions about it. Some of these questions are at the basis of the reflections in this book - the texts sandwiched between the photos.

The first edition of this book has taken on its own life since it was published. It's often taken onto the dance for different artists in the book to sign for example. I've even had a few people contact me referring to it as "the bible," which causes me to smile and cringe in equal measure. It's also sometimes the catalyst for my involvement in exhibitions and talks.

Here I feel the need to point out that Drumz Of The South was and still is only ONE perspective of the early dubstep scene in and around South London. If you haven't already done so, I urge you all to seek out accounts by others who were there - some of whom have contributed to the written reflections in this book, but also photographers like Shaun Bloodworth, Ashes57, Hark1karan and Grumpy Claire. History, like community I feel, is created by the many, not the few.

Introduction by Georgina Cook

From the age of 14, I lived in a modest part of South London called South Norwood. I lived with my family in a cul-de-sac on a relatively leafy hill upon which buses screeched.

South Norwood is in a borough called Croydon, named after the town of cement and ill-repute. People in the area largely didn't have much good to say about Croydon. But for younger people into music, it offered bars and record shops like Big Apple and Wax City. Most Croydon venues were of the "No Hats No Trainers" ilk, with the exception of a couple of spots like The Black Sheep Bar, a small venue with a big, eclectic vision.

I found myself there aged 19 reviewing DJ Grooverider for The South London Press newspaper. I was well into dnb so the opportunity to travel 20 mins to photograph a Metalheadz legend was pretty special. He was playing as part of a night called Spectrum, whose resident DJs were Andy Skopes, Mek (aka Dave Deoke), Raid + Logik, Louis Krystal and SGT Pokes.

SGT Pokes is a key character in this story. As a member of "The Sheep" team, he had pushed the venue to program electronic and bass music. He's also key because our journey with dubstep practically started together, with me driving him to his first dubstep line-up at The End. Often rolling with Pokes was Mala, another key character in the Drumz Of The South story, plus Loefah and Coki.

The highly musical community facilitated by The Sheep, plus my love for South London and its wider music scene, was the initial

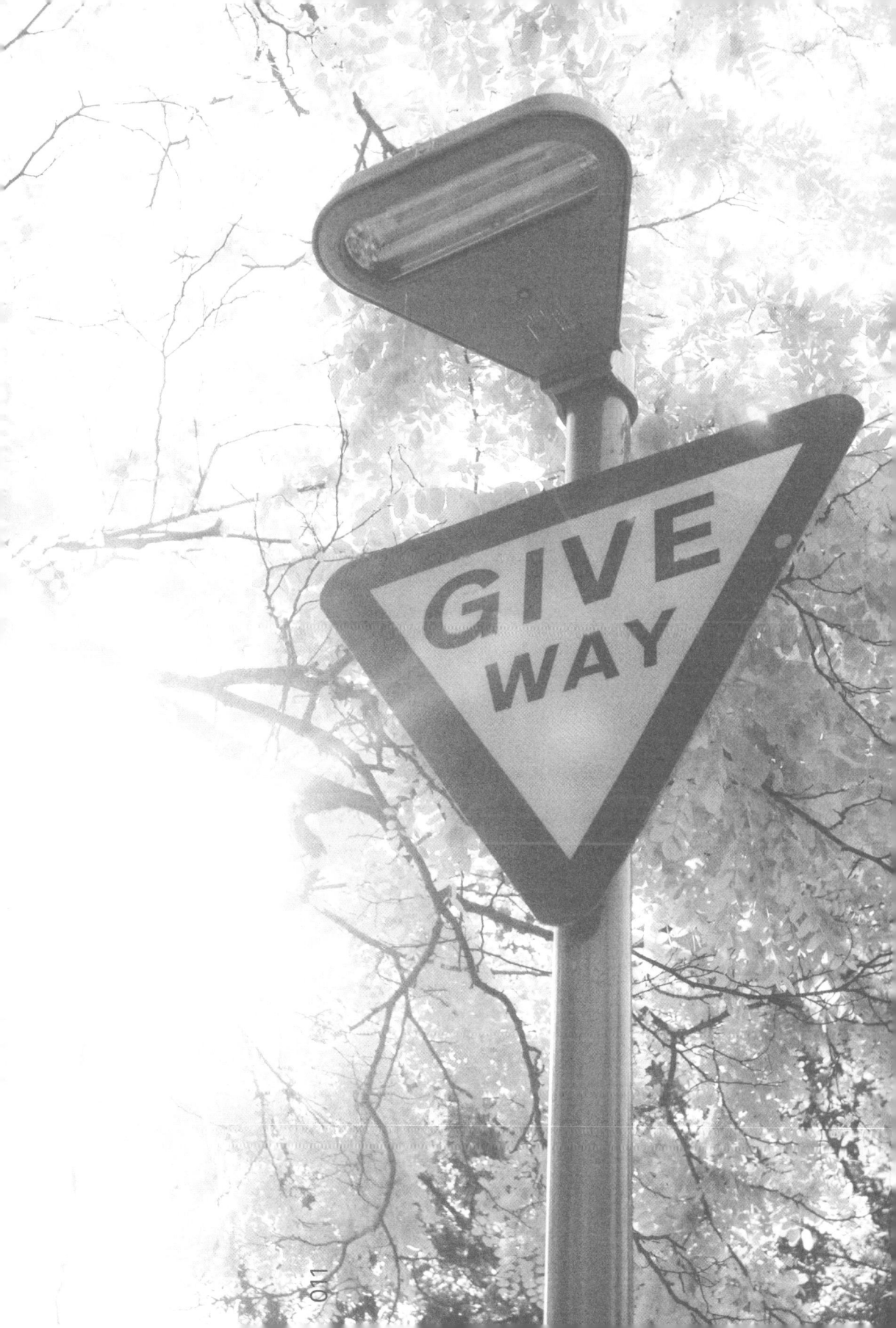

inspiration for Drumz Of The South. It was born in 2004 as an A4 paper newsletter, before quickly becoming an online blog, that allowed me to share my photos and words with the world.

One day I organised the blog into chapters. What you've just read is a summary of the early days of Drumz Of The South, which led to Drumz Of The South: The Dubstep Years (2004-2007). Or in other words, this book.

The first time I heard dubstep was in Mala's car outside The Black Sheep Bar, in 2004. He played me a track called B, made with his musical partner Coki, under the name Digital Mystikz.

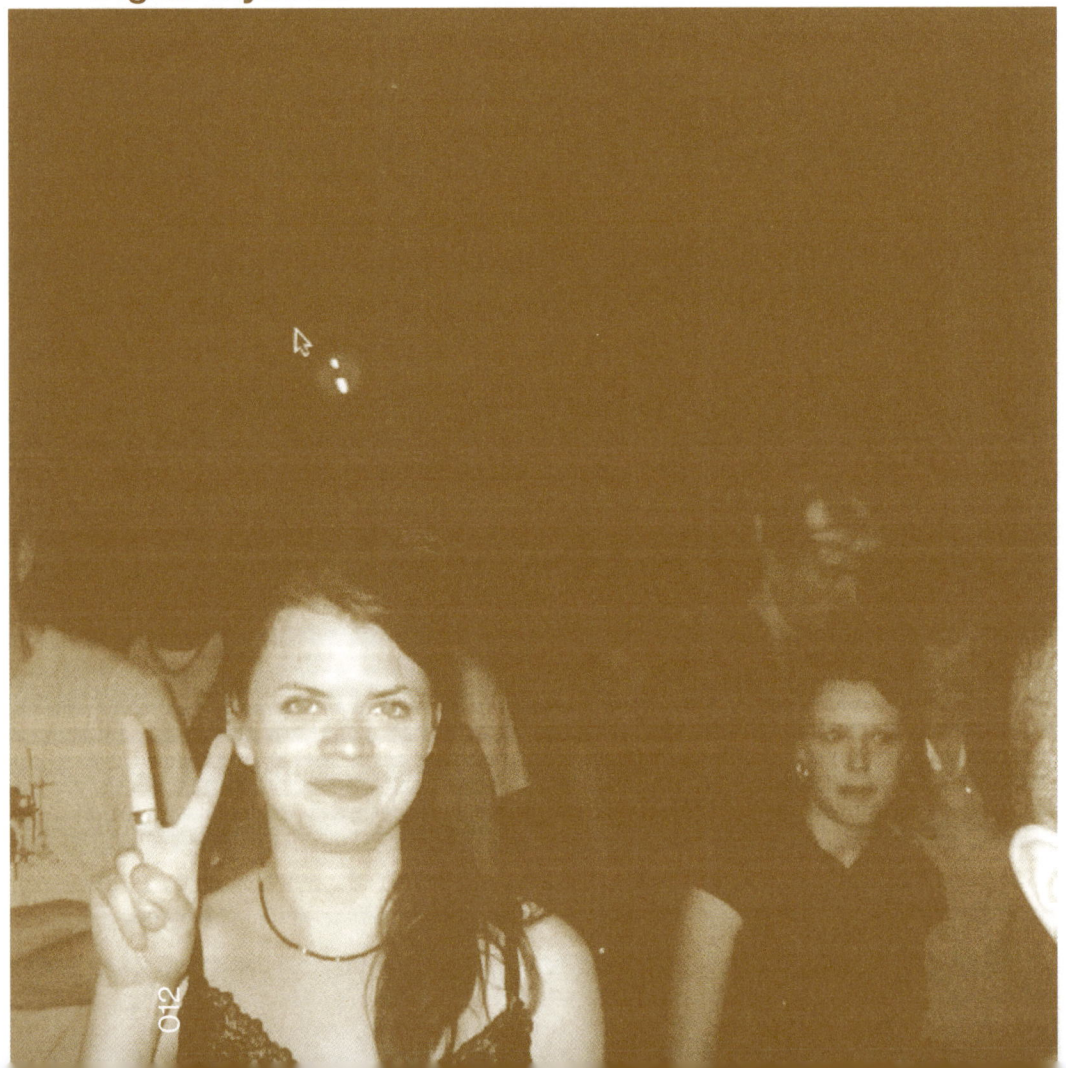

B has a rolling bassline that gives weight to a breathy vocal which repeats B. It has a tension and beauty that all the best jungle and dark garage tunes had. I'd never heard anything like it, yet it was completely familiar at the same time. Mala told me that people were calling it dubstep. I knew I had to get involved.

My involvement started with weekly trips to FWD>> at Plastic People in Shoreditch. I tuned into Kode9 and Youngsta on Rinse FM and attended pretty much every event that Mala, SGT Pokes, Loefah, Coki, Skream, Hatcha, Crazy D, Plastician, Chef, Horsepower, N-Type, Walsh and other DJs from the ends were playing at.

These nights came to be the focus of Drumz Of The South, which by then had the tagline "Music is a journey, life is just something that happens along the way" - credited to my friend and artist "X", formerly known as BLT.

I took photos at most events, trying to photograph scenes that I thought would inform history in years to come through smokey pitch-black darkness, without killing the vibe with my flash. Additionally, I often took photos to and from events, of London's streets and trees. To me, they said as much about the music, as the gestures and movements of the dancefloors.

Following an event, I would be up into the early hours editing and uploading my images, writing, and posting it all up on the Dubstep Forum. As the scene and the sound grew, so did the blog, which received messages from places like Poland, Germany, the U.S, Brazil and Australia. Many said that my photos allowed them to "see" the music for the first time.

Music is a journey, and in 2021, 17 years after first hearing B, Drumz Of The South became a book. In August-September 2021, I ran a crowdfunding campaign to print the first edition.

A combination of things led to this happening, but mostly, it sprang from a desire to create something to honour that special time and everyone involved, many of whom appear in the following pages. Note - if you don't appear, either you eluded my camera or I'm not happy with the photo(s) that I took of you, which is my bad. But I hope you know you're in here, in spirit, and you're appreciated.

"For all the past, present and future communities that make good things happen."

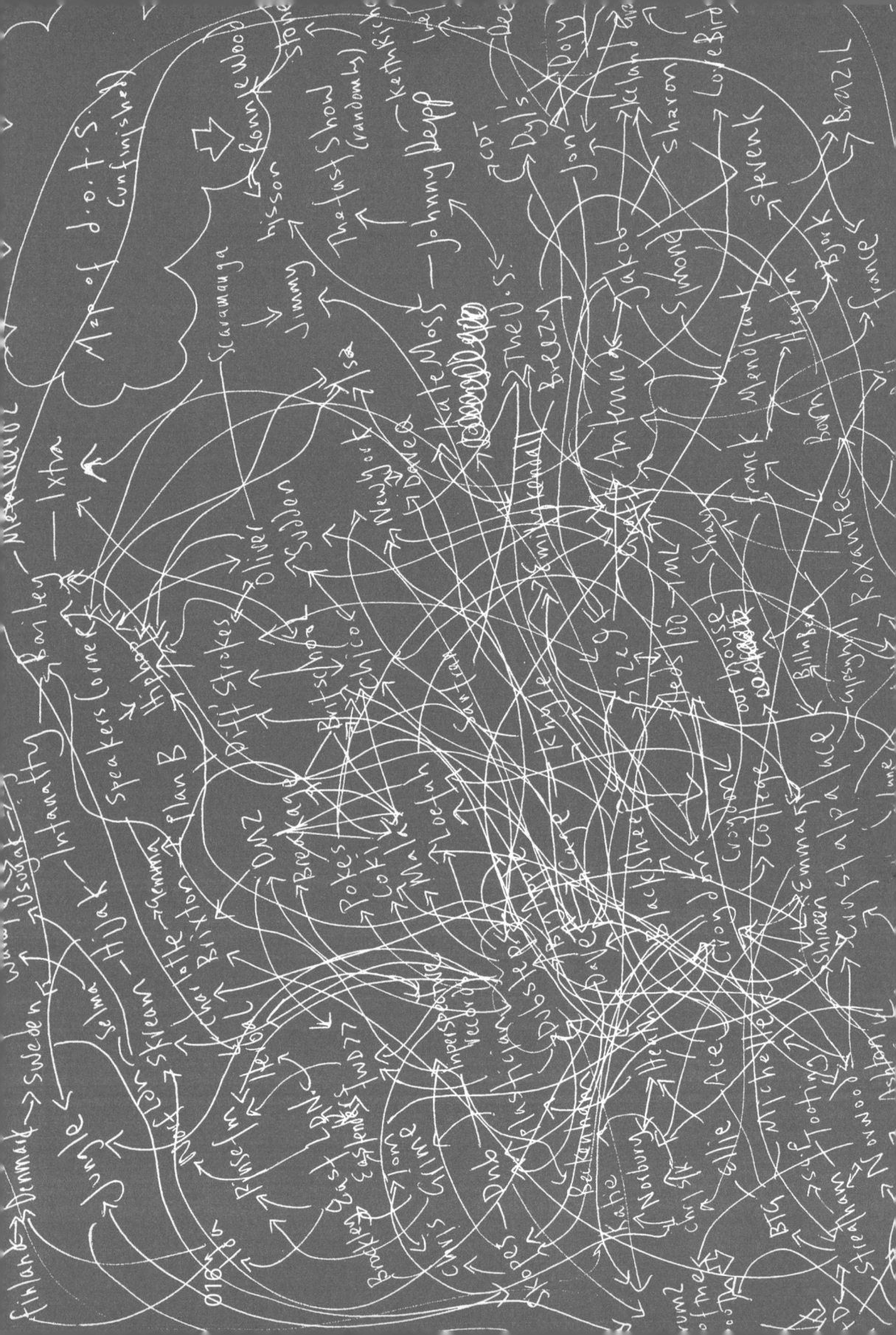

The Dubstep Years:

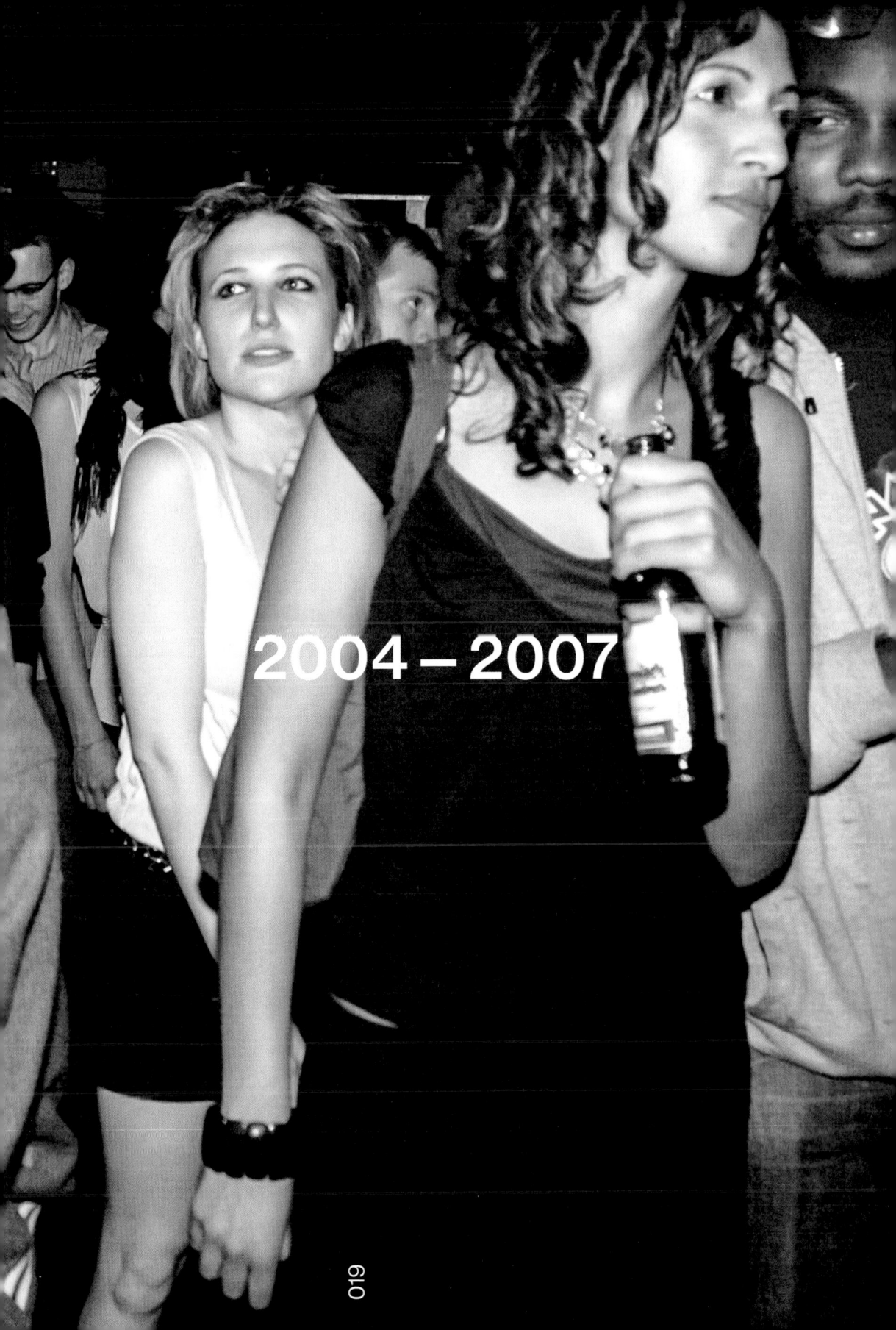

2004–2007

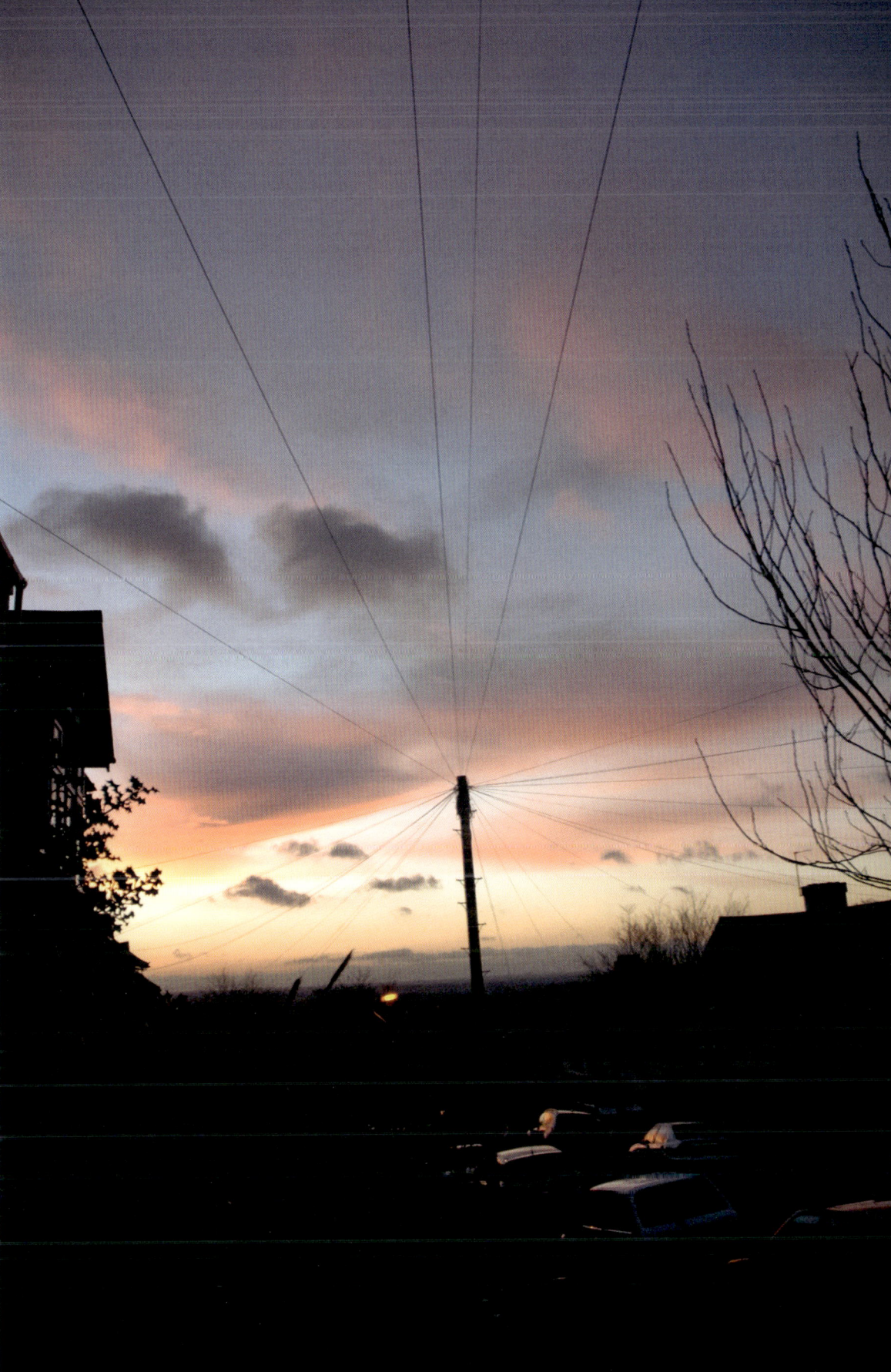

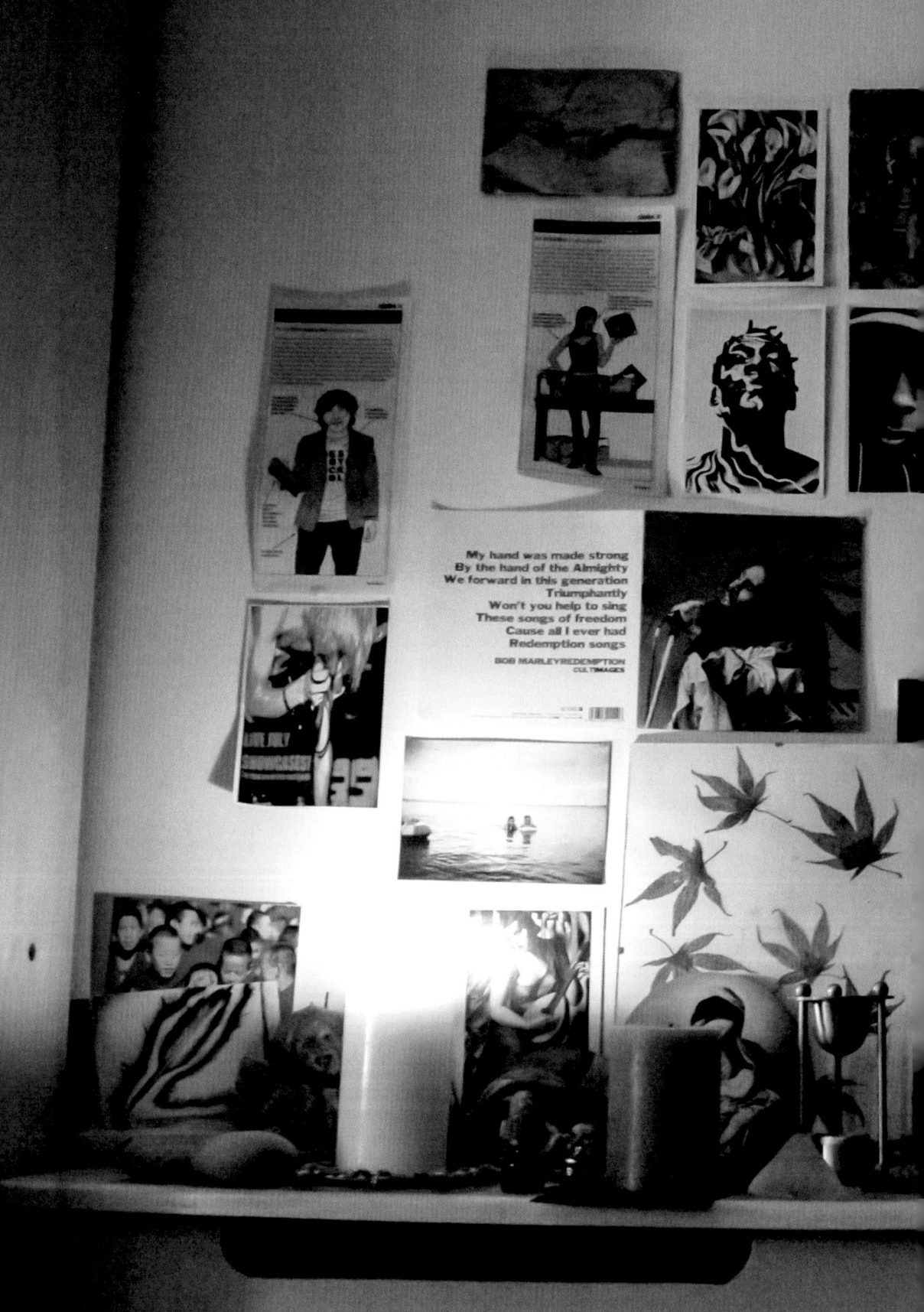

My hand was made strong
By the hand of the Almighty
We forward in this generation
Triumphantly
Won't you help to sing
These songs of freedom
Cause all I ever had
Redemption songs

BOB MARLEY REDEMPTION
CULT IMAGES

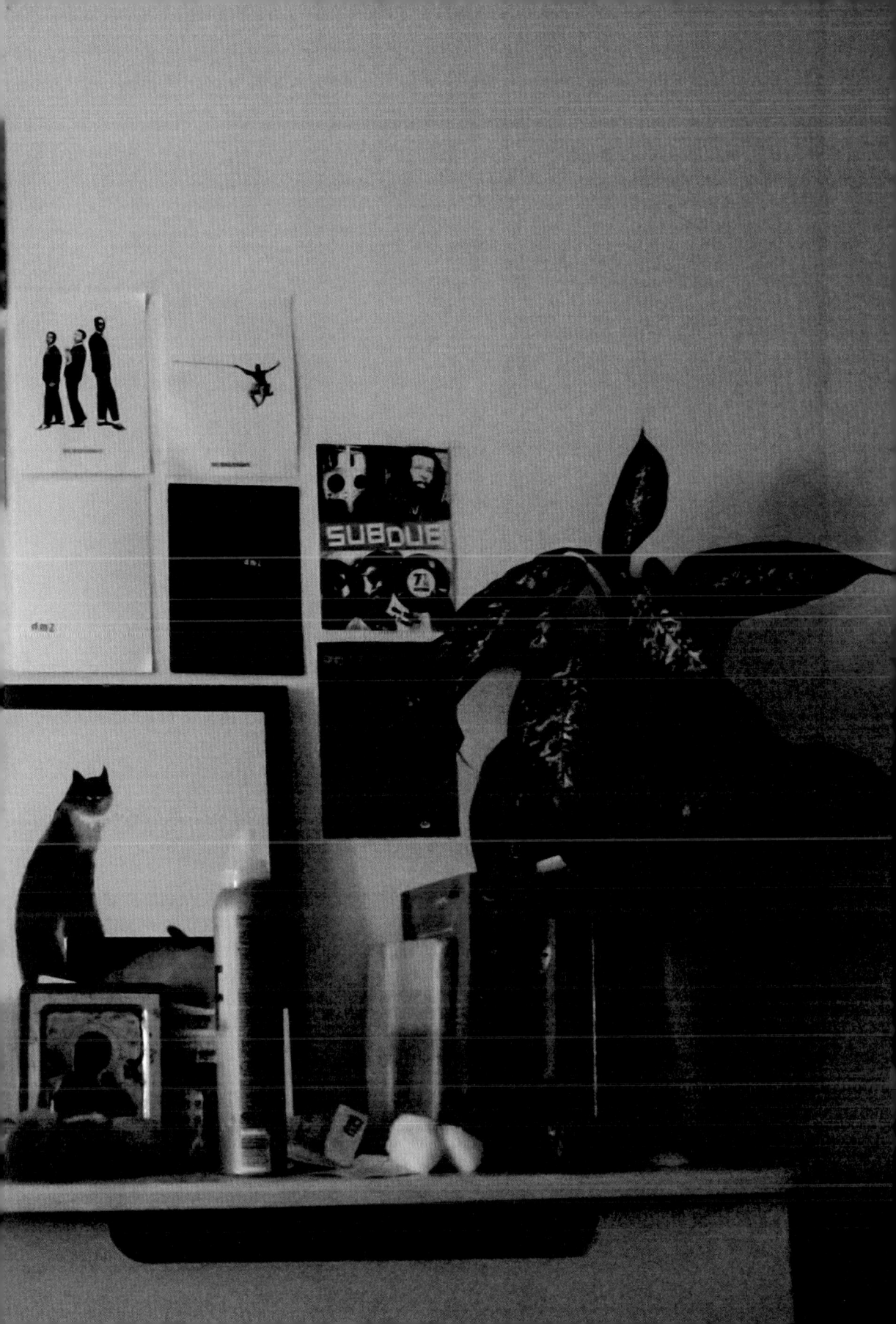

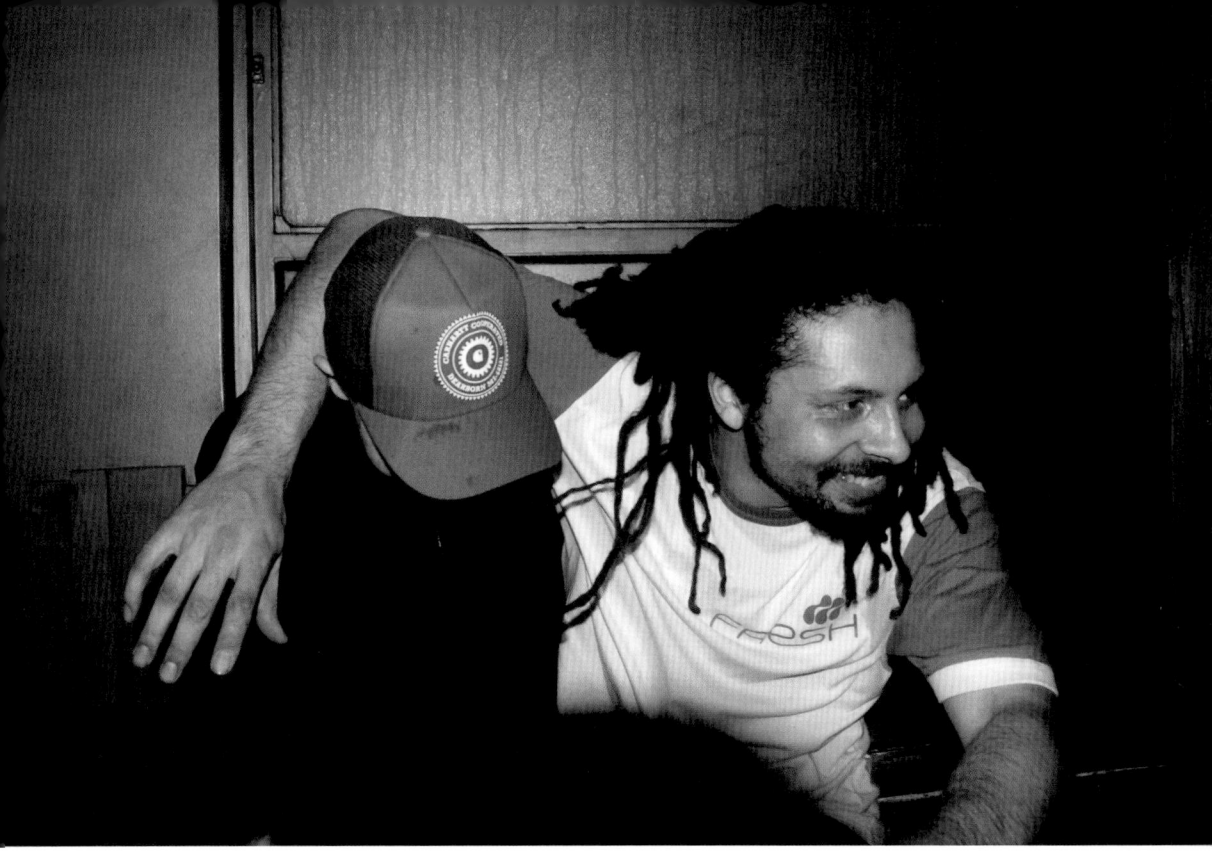

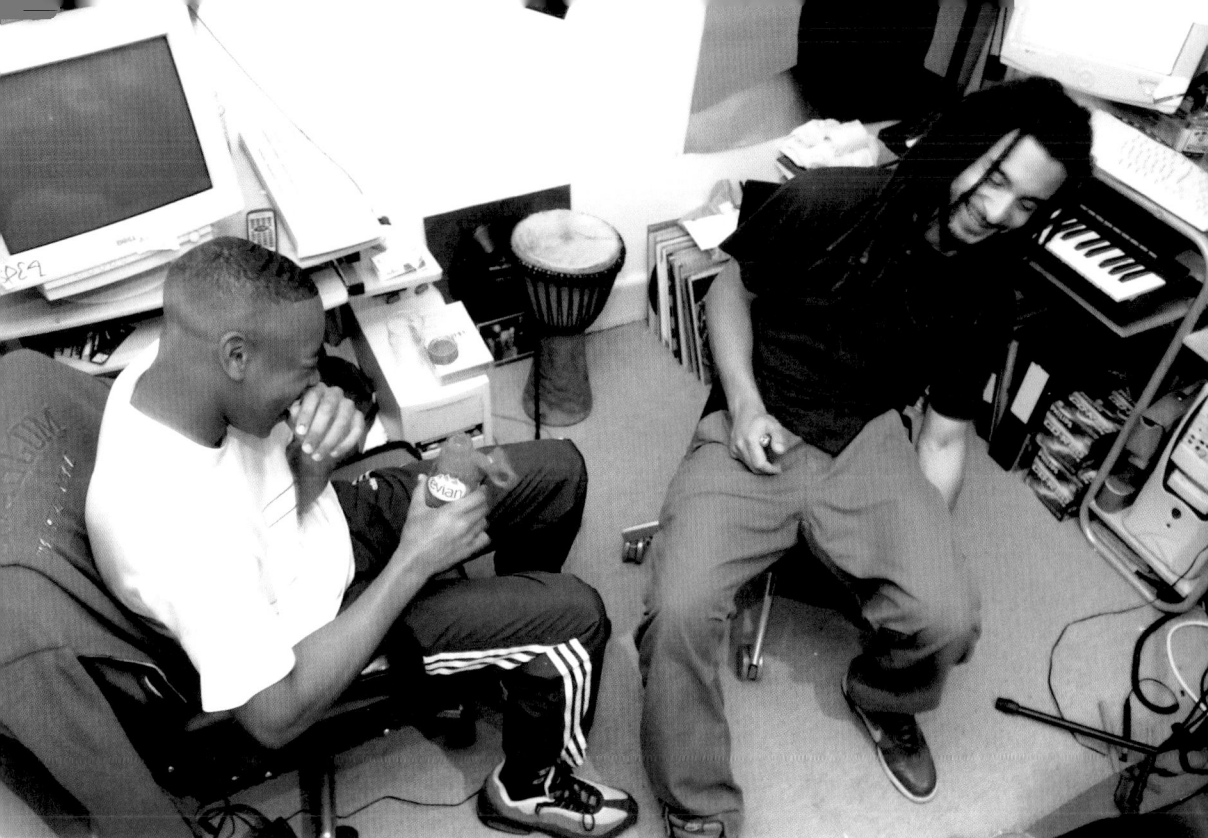

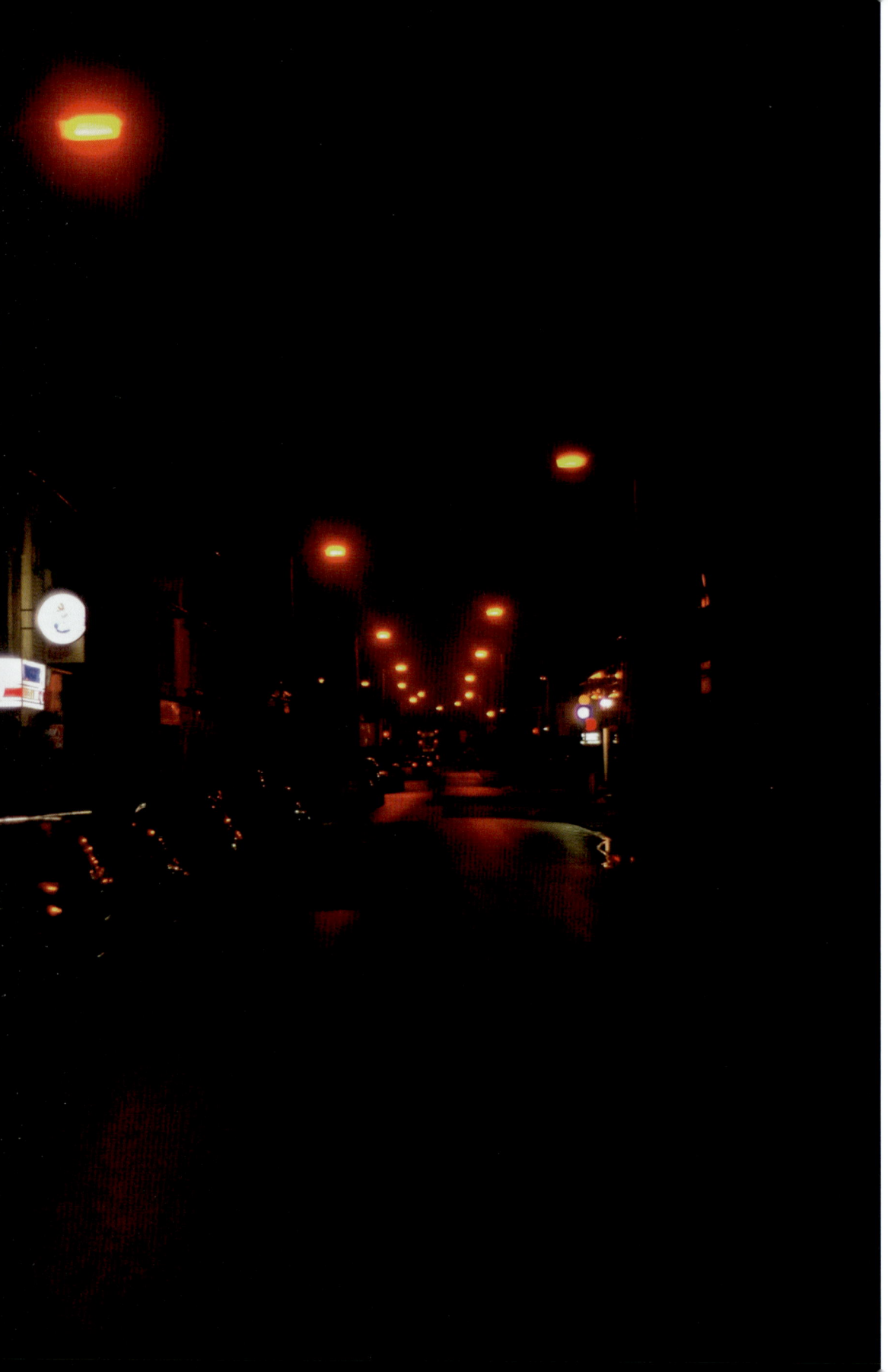

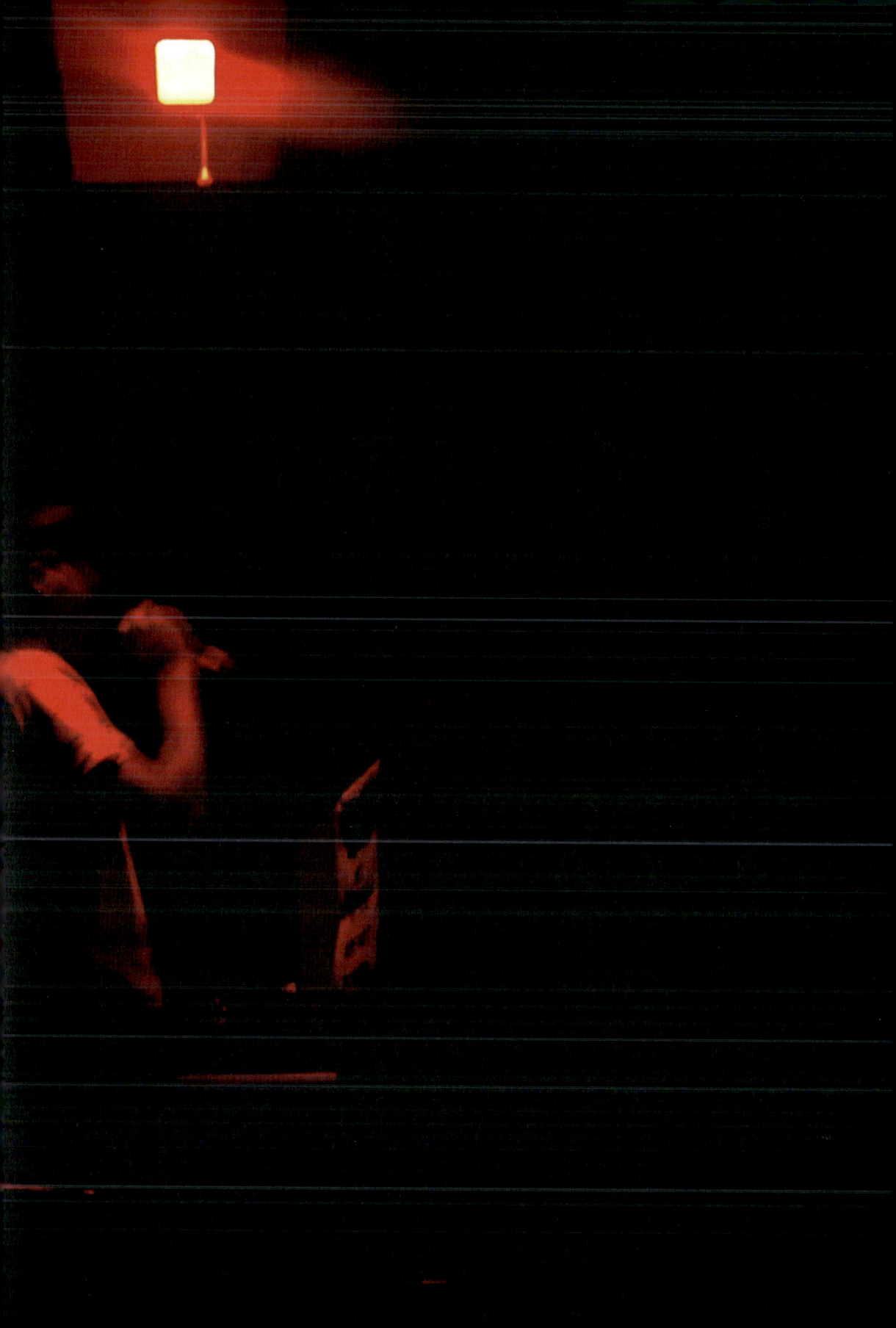

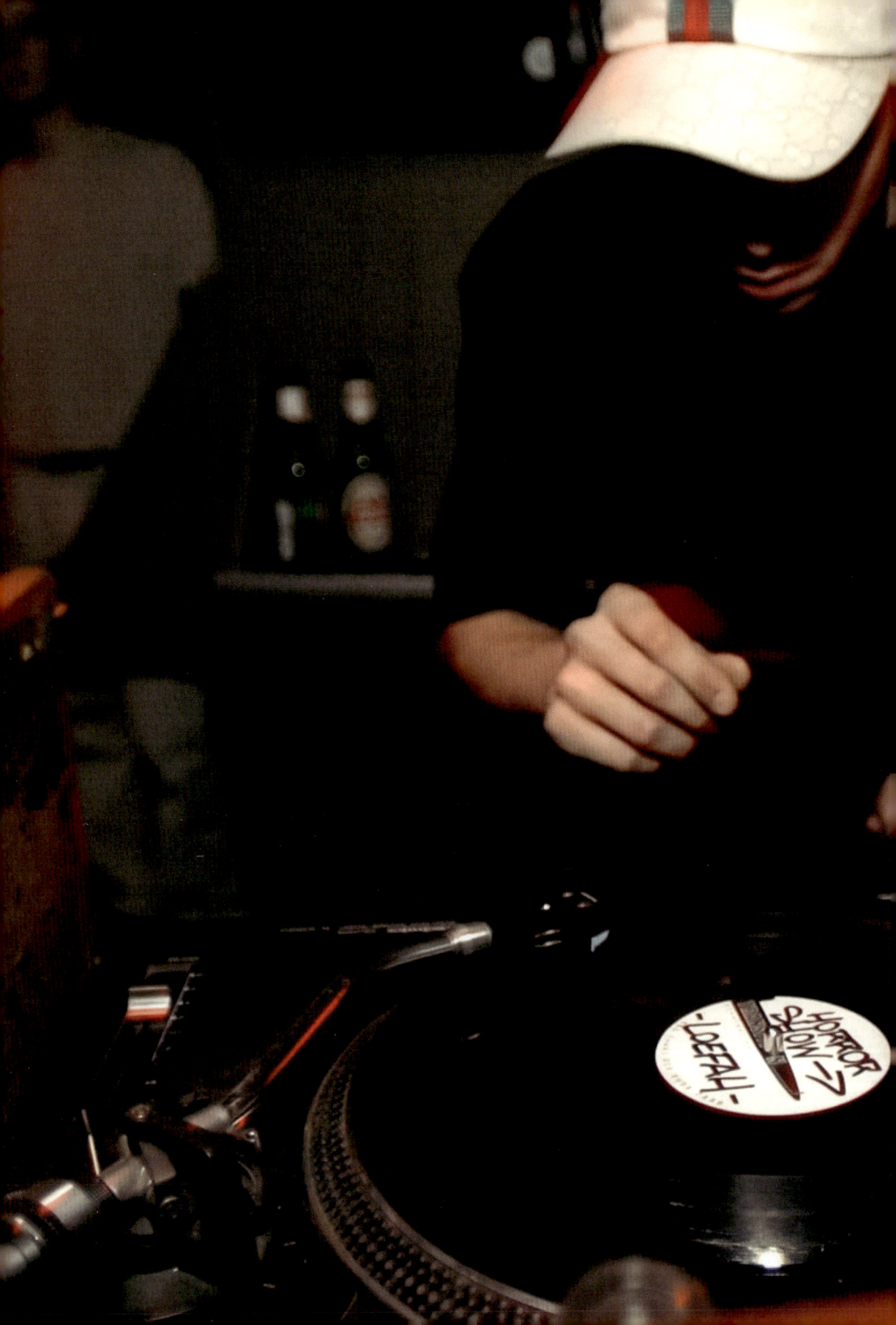

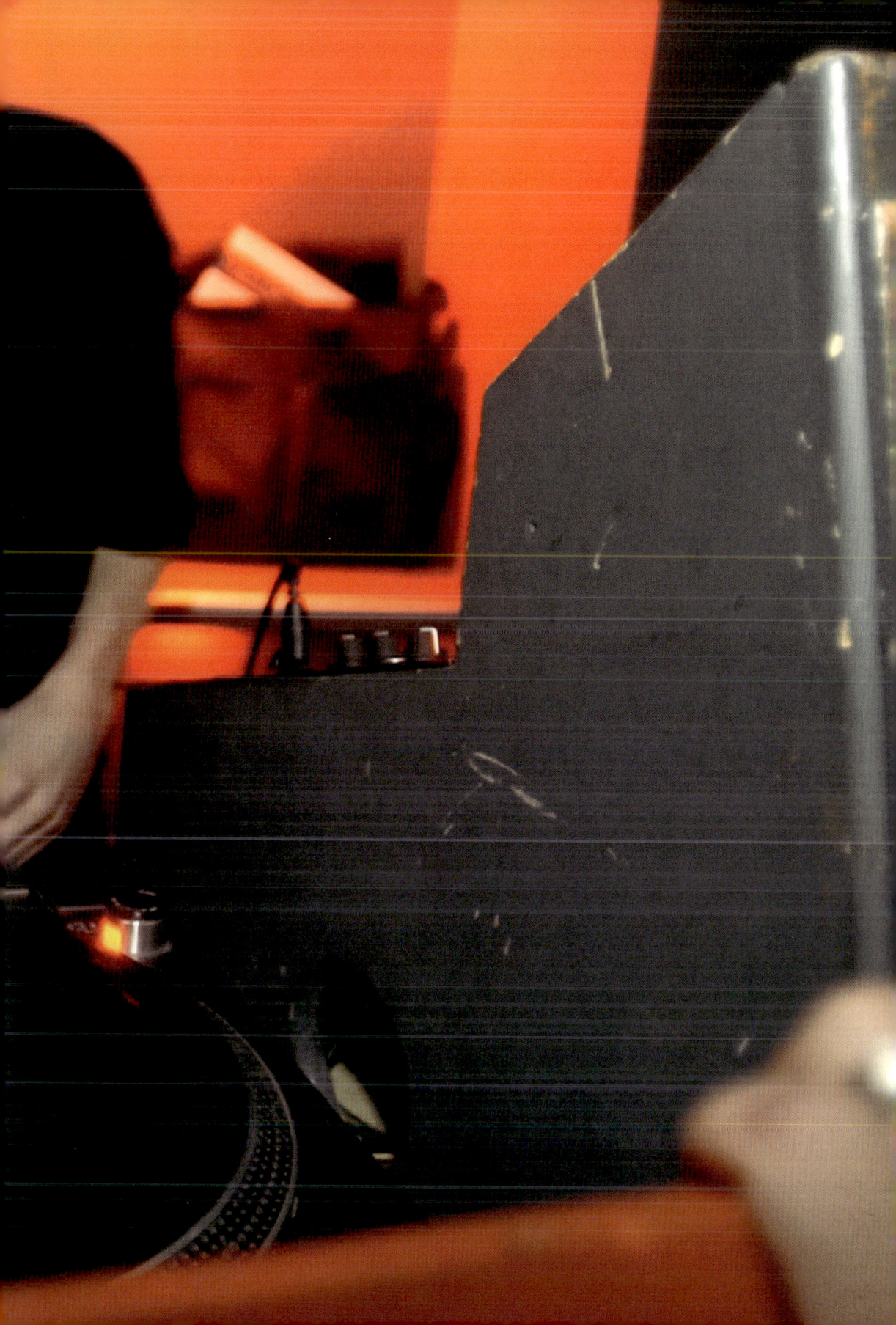

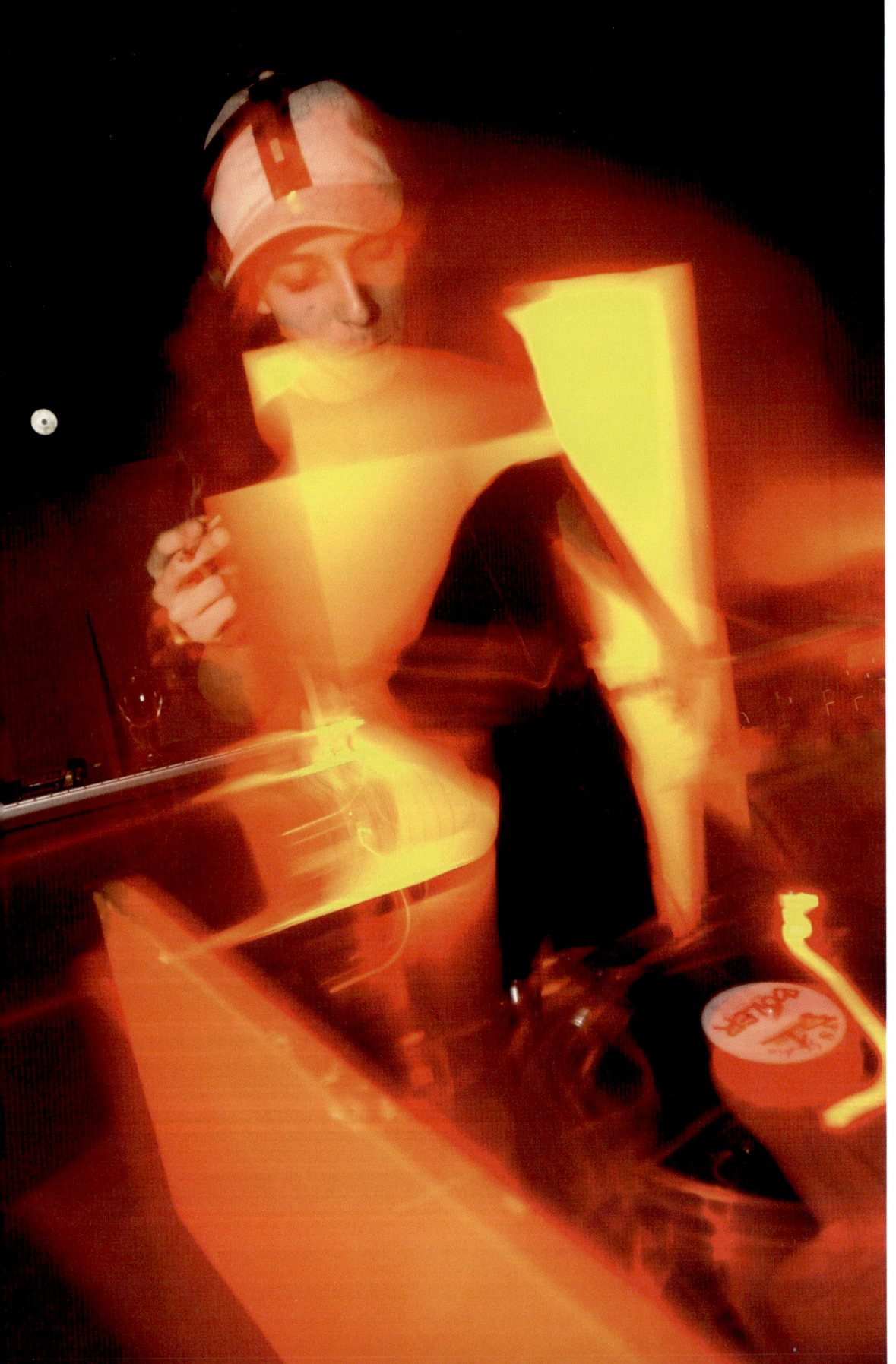

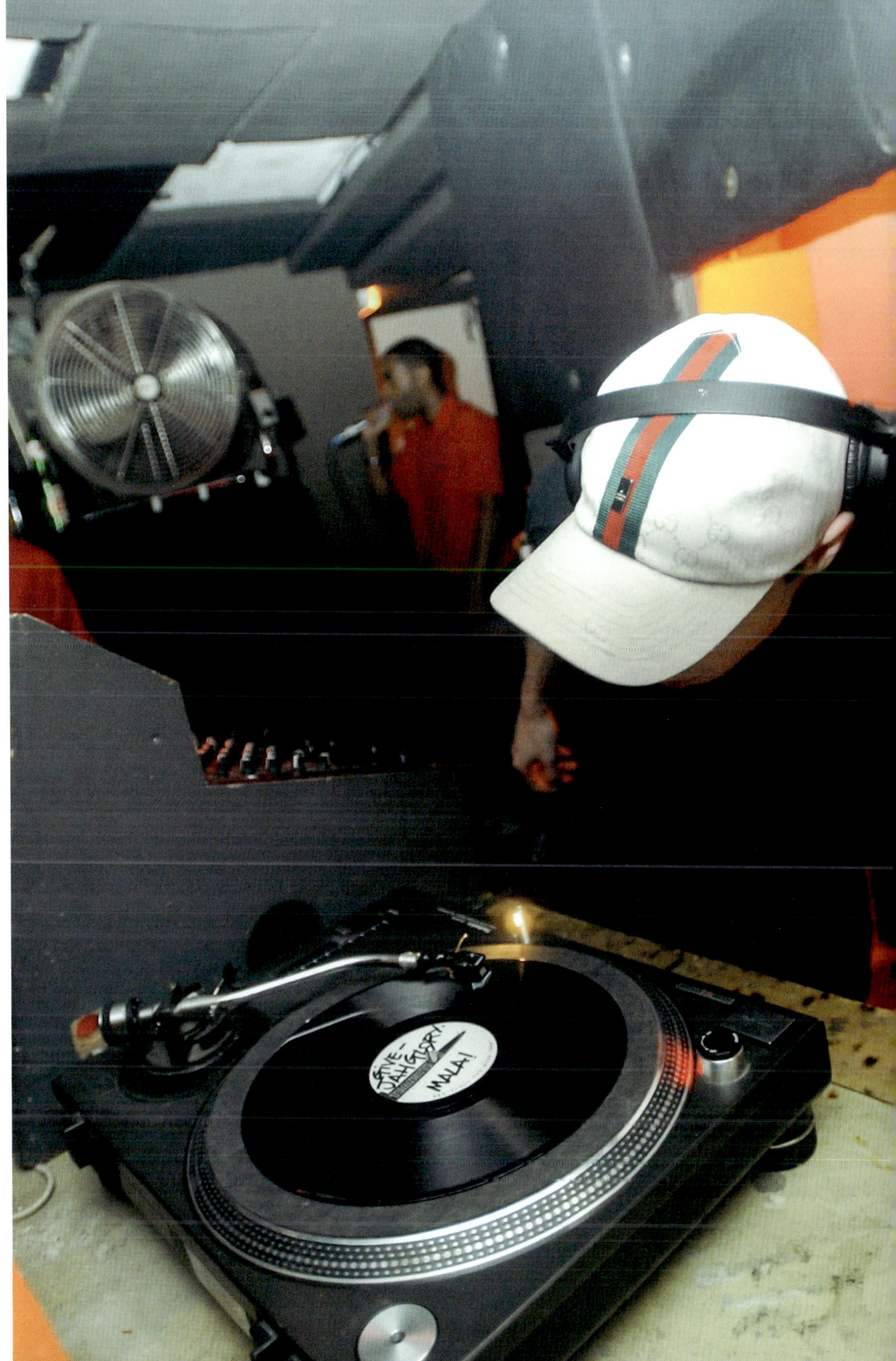

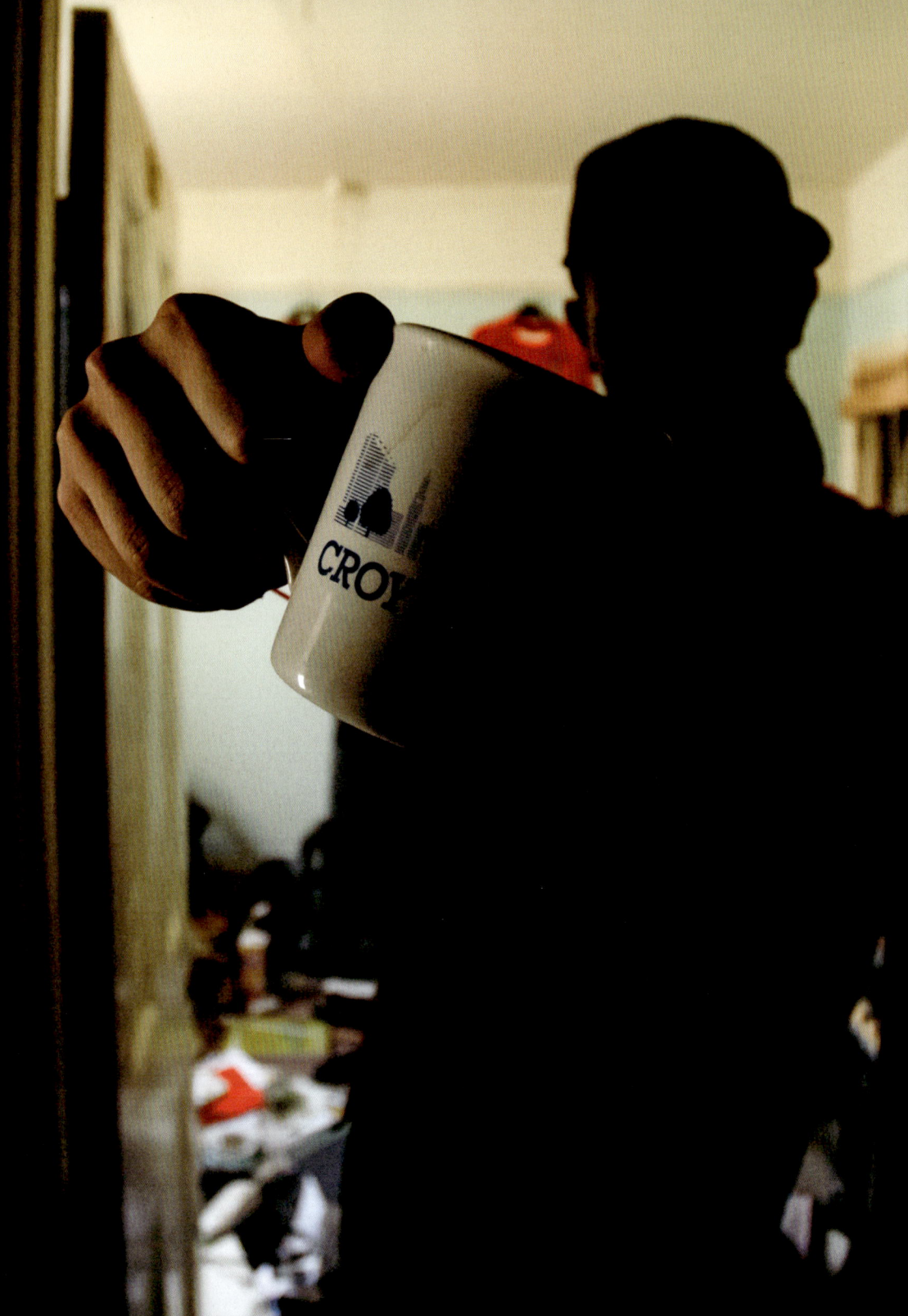

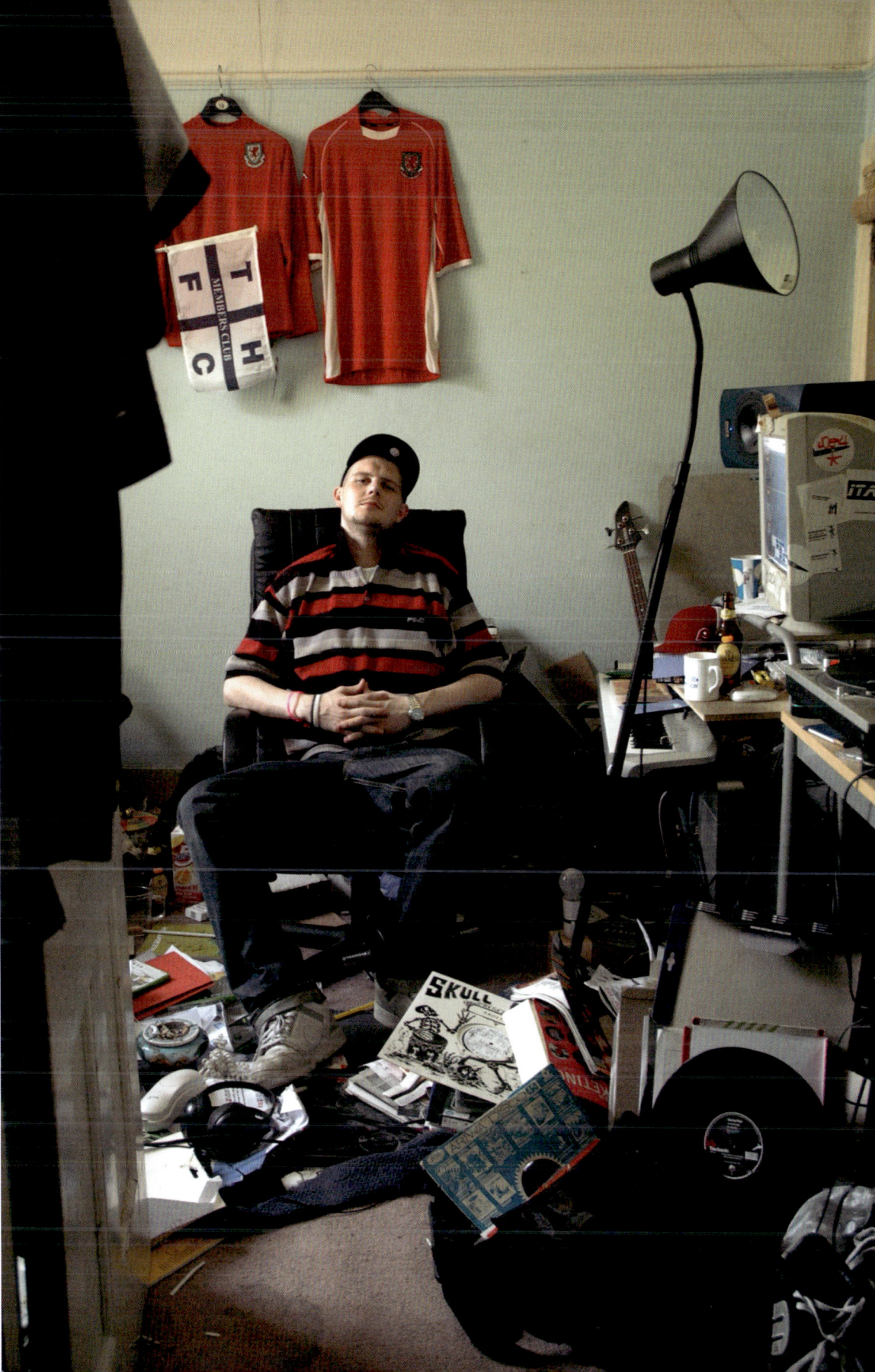

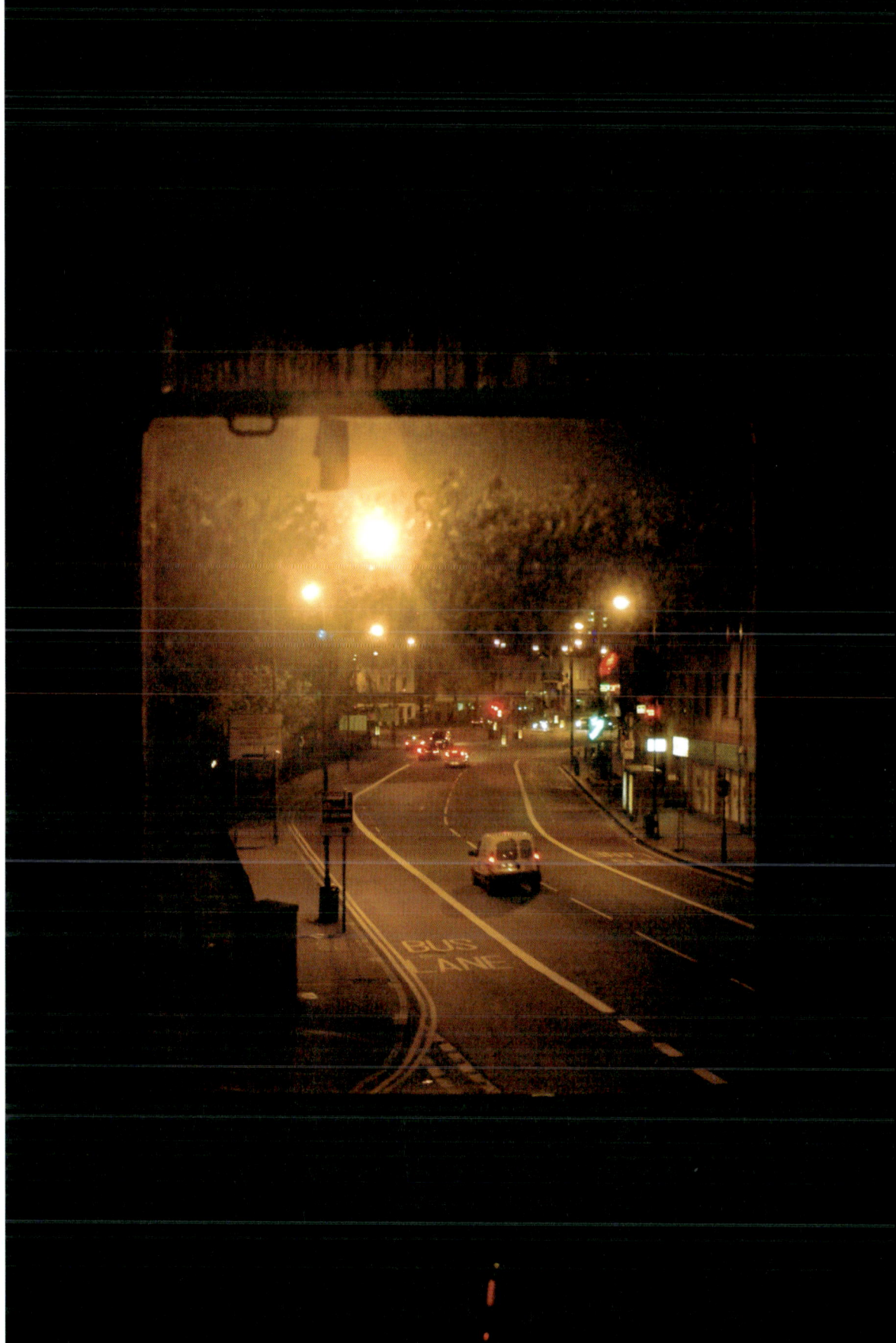

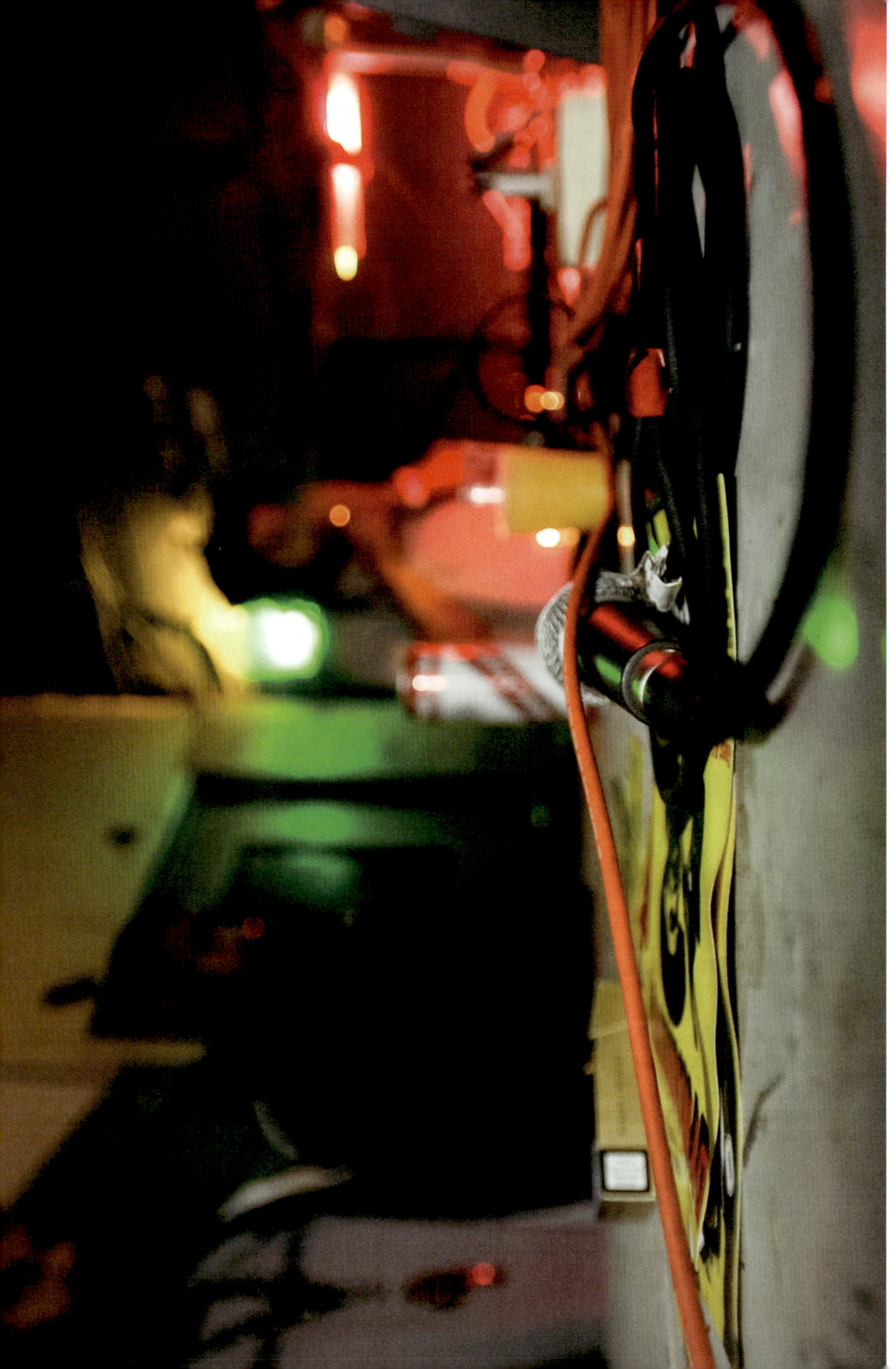

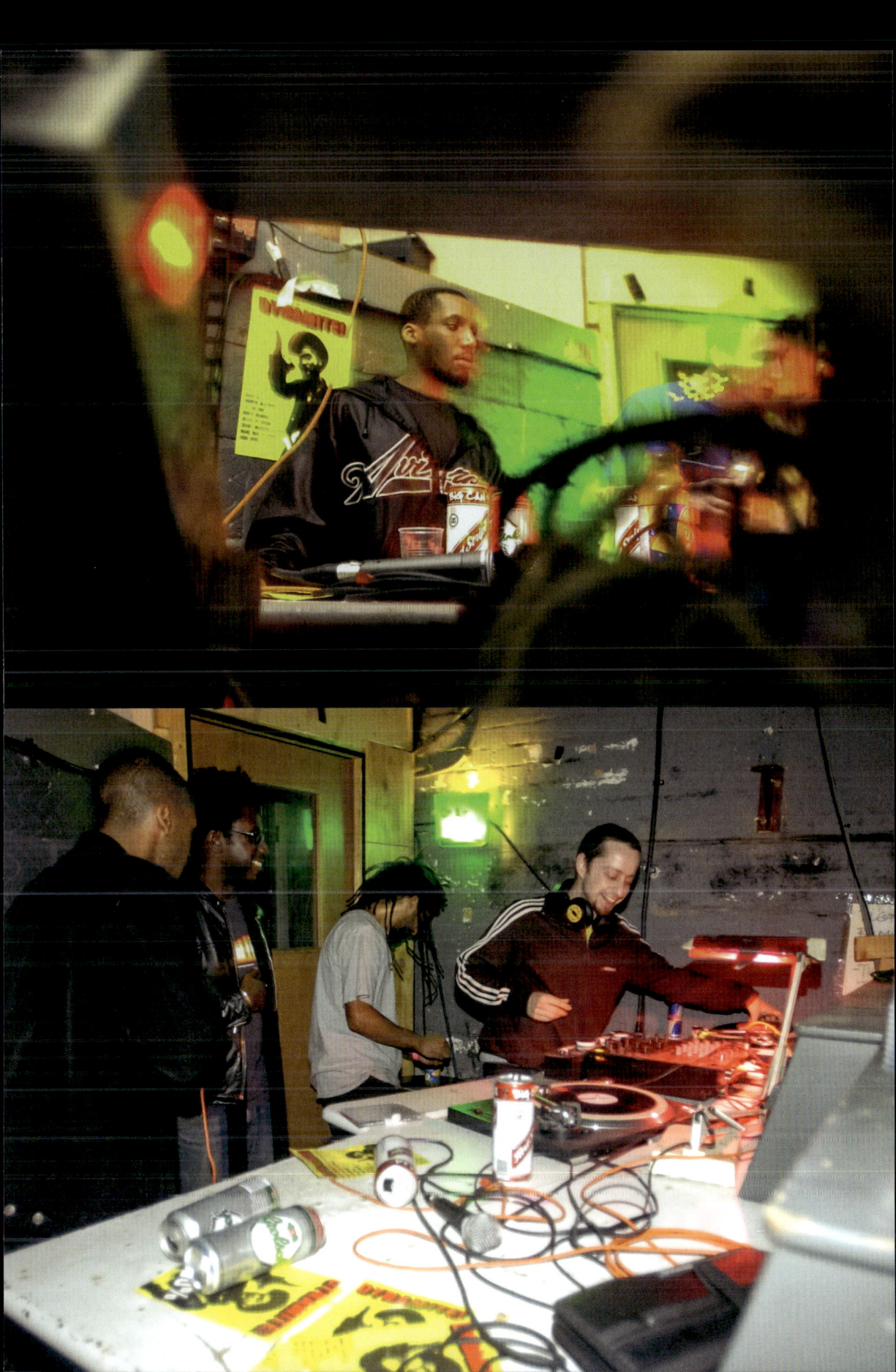

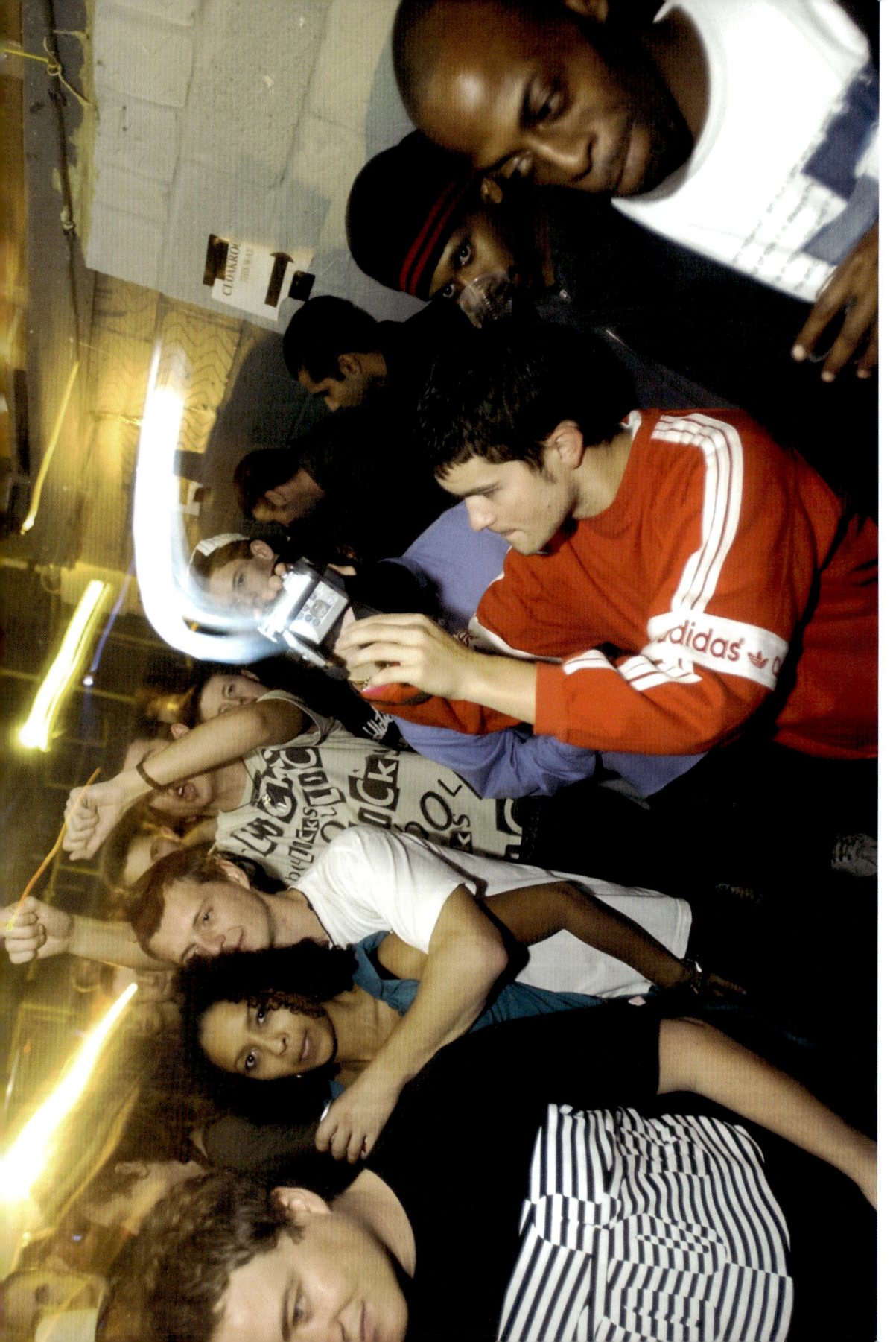

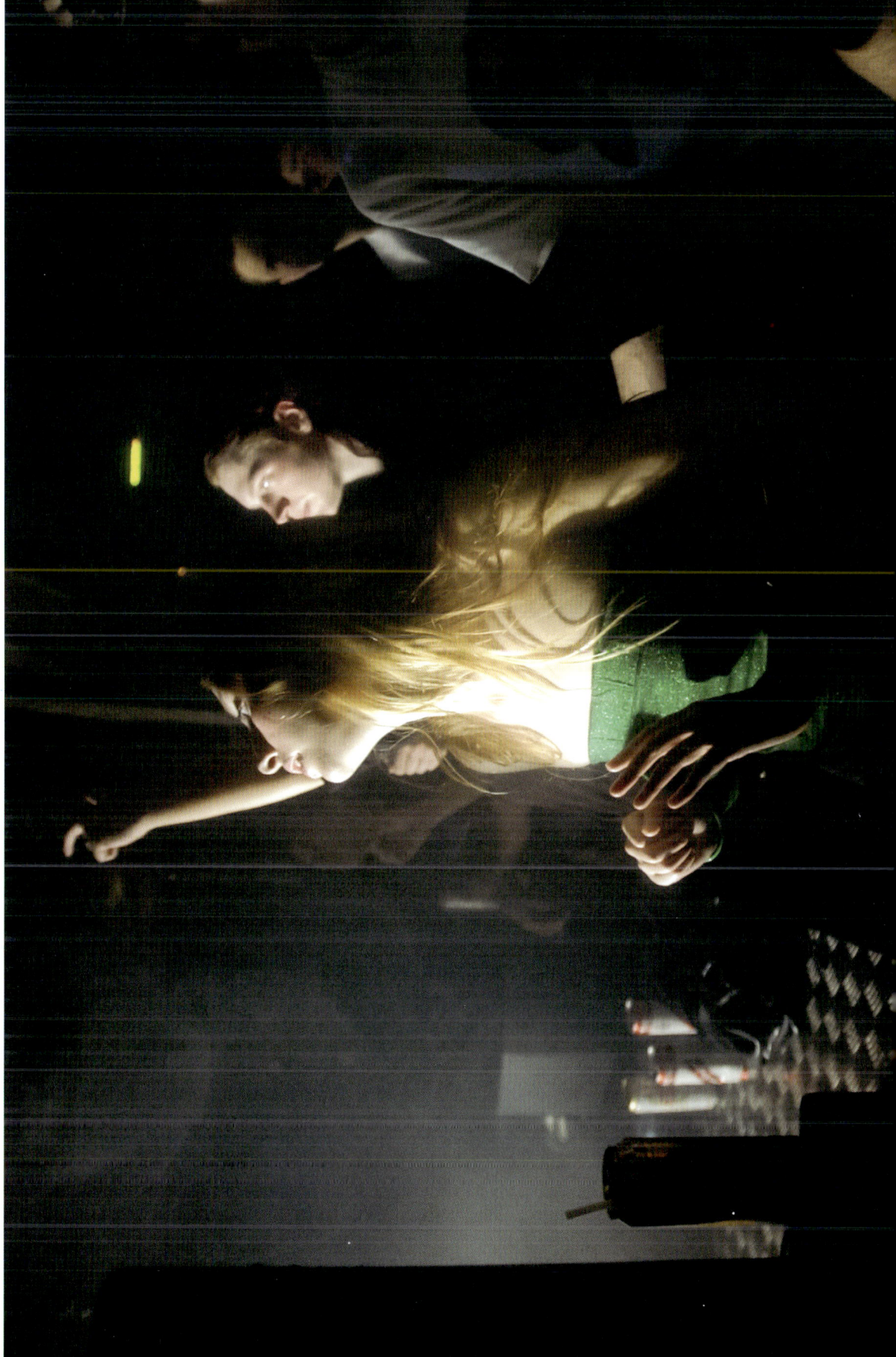

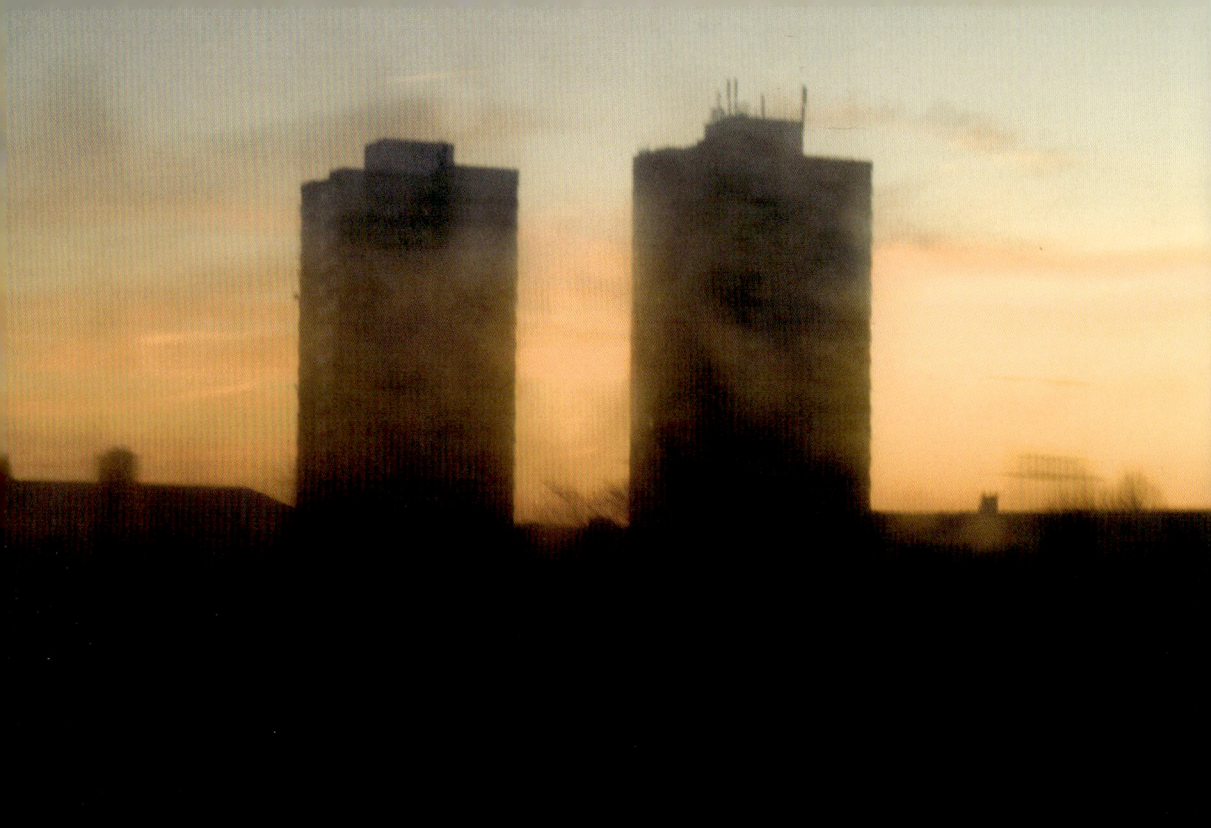

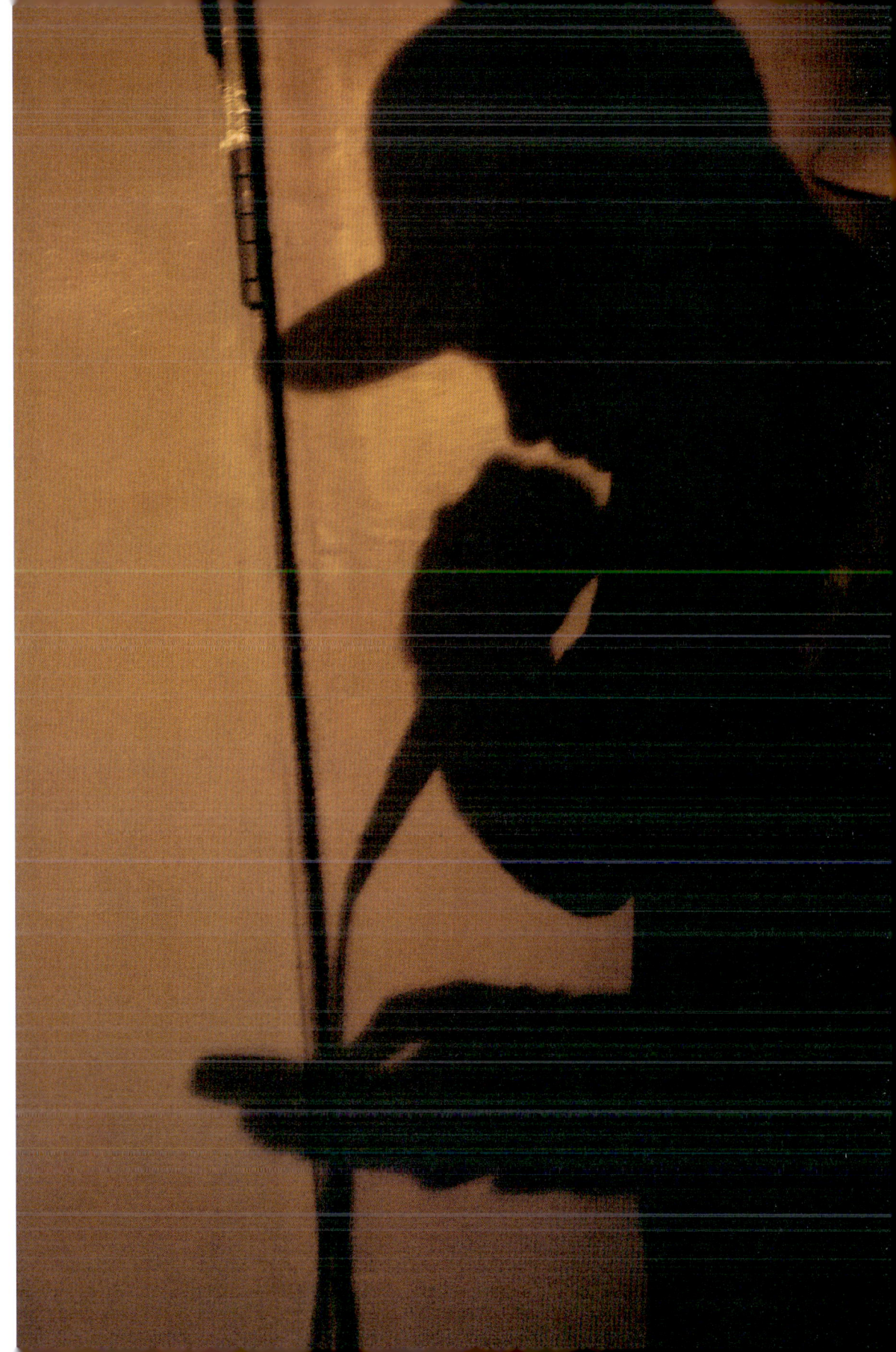

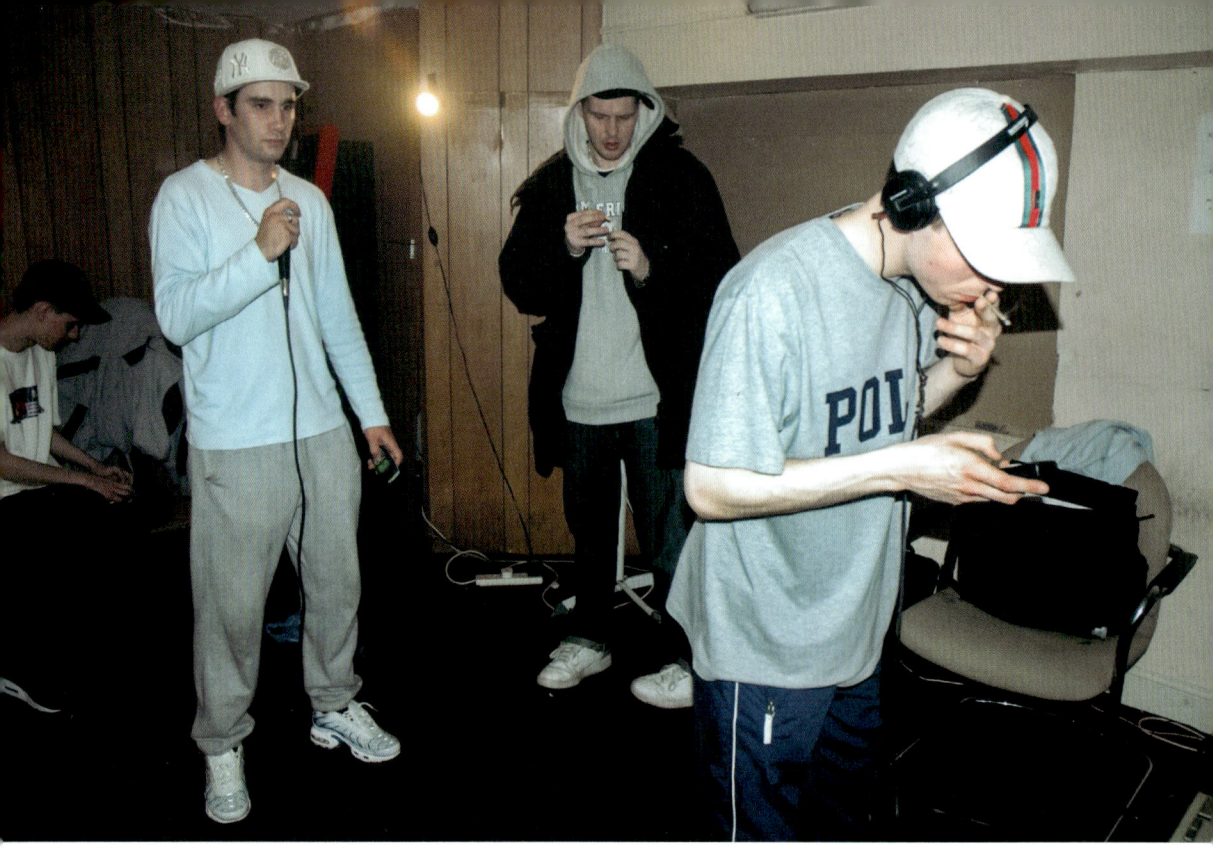

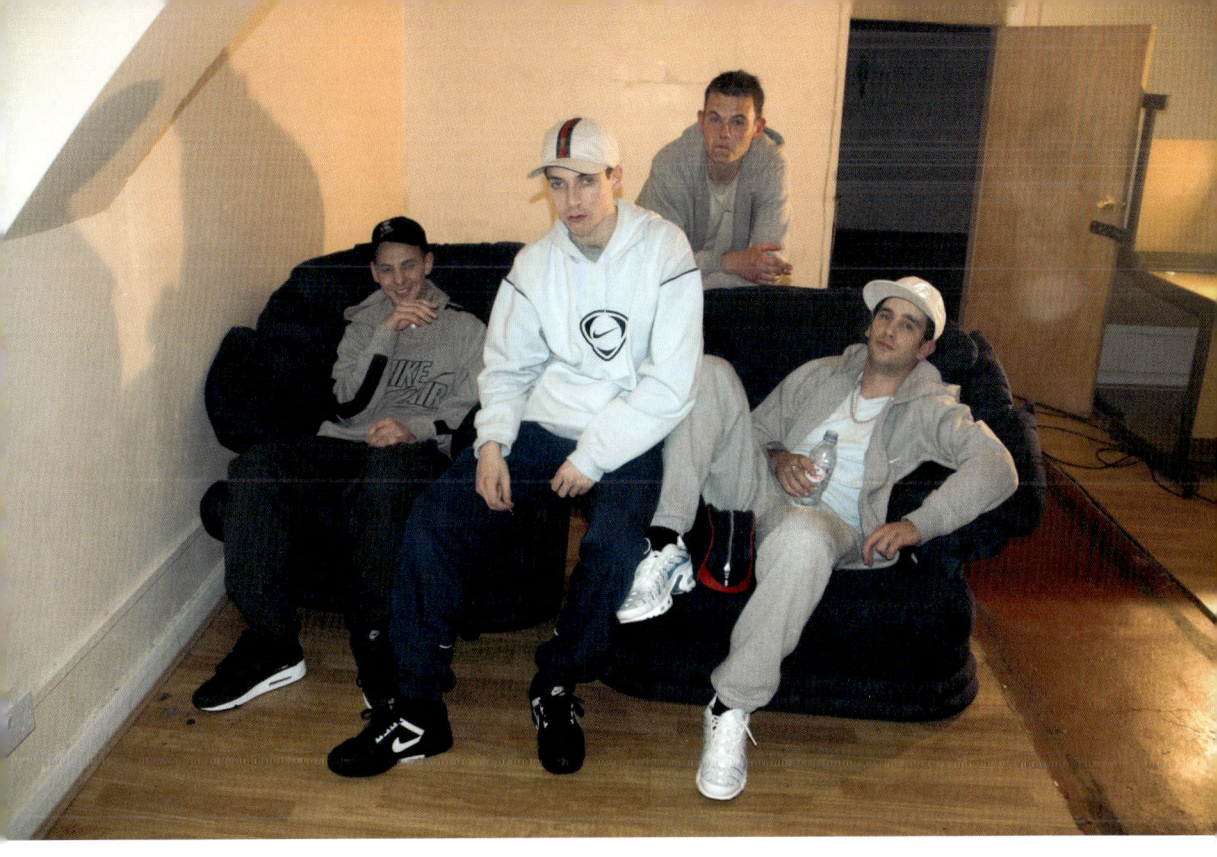

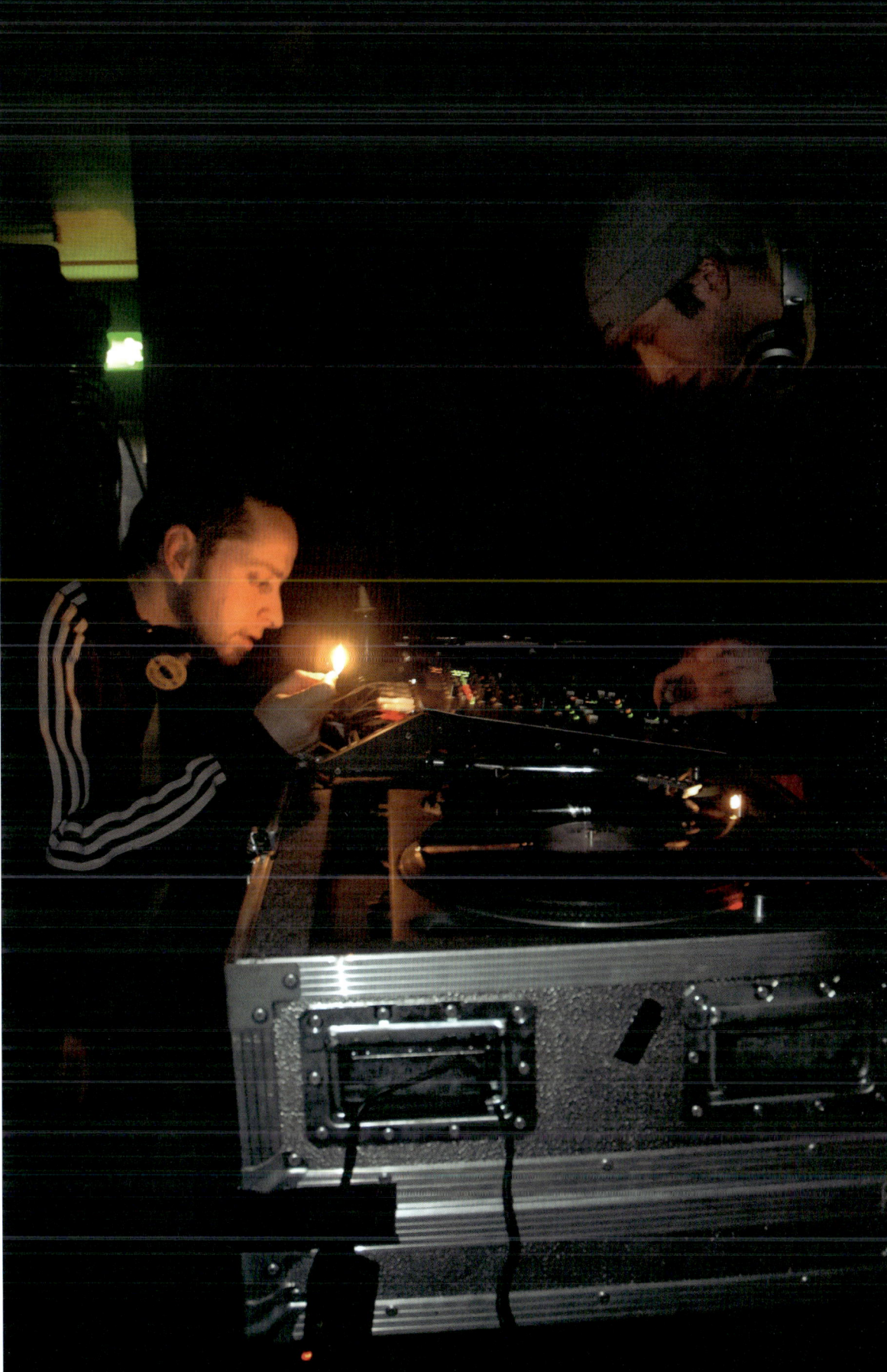

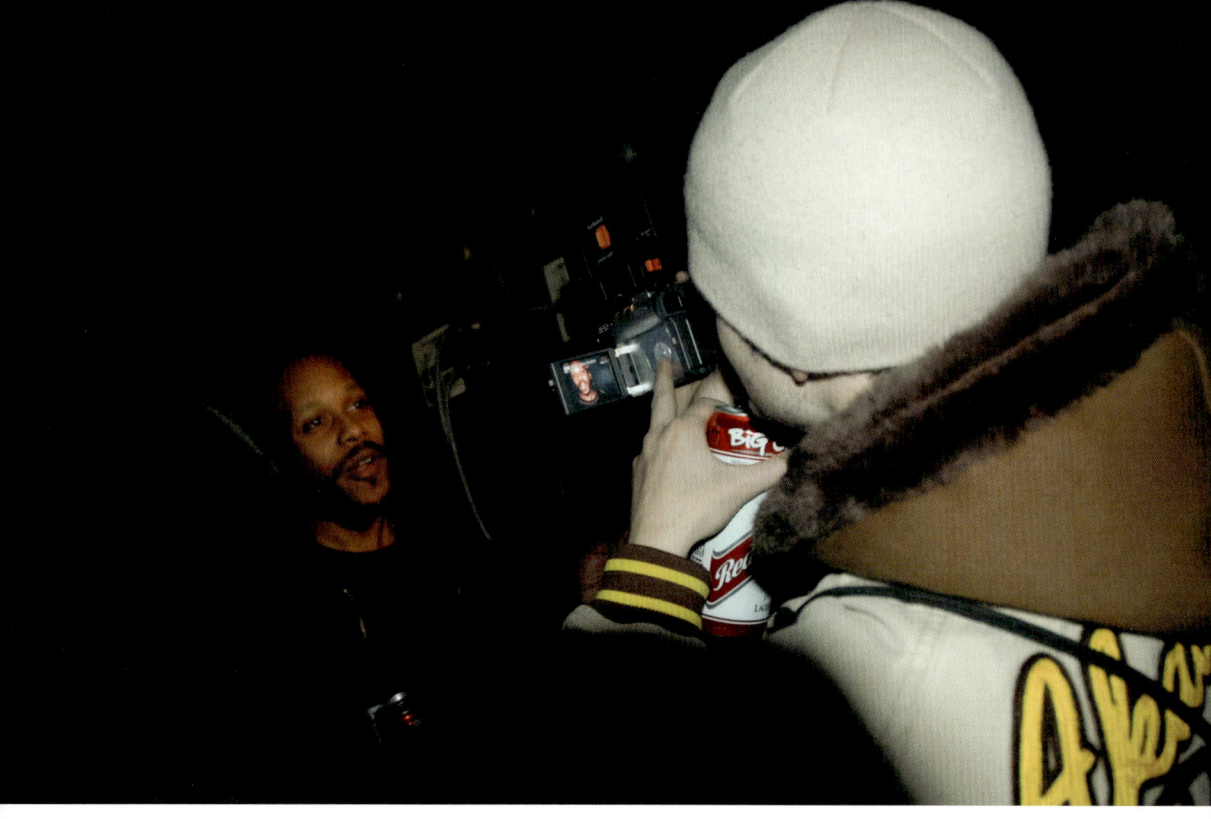

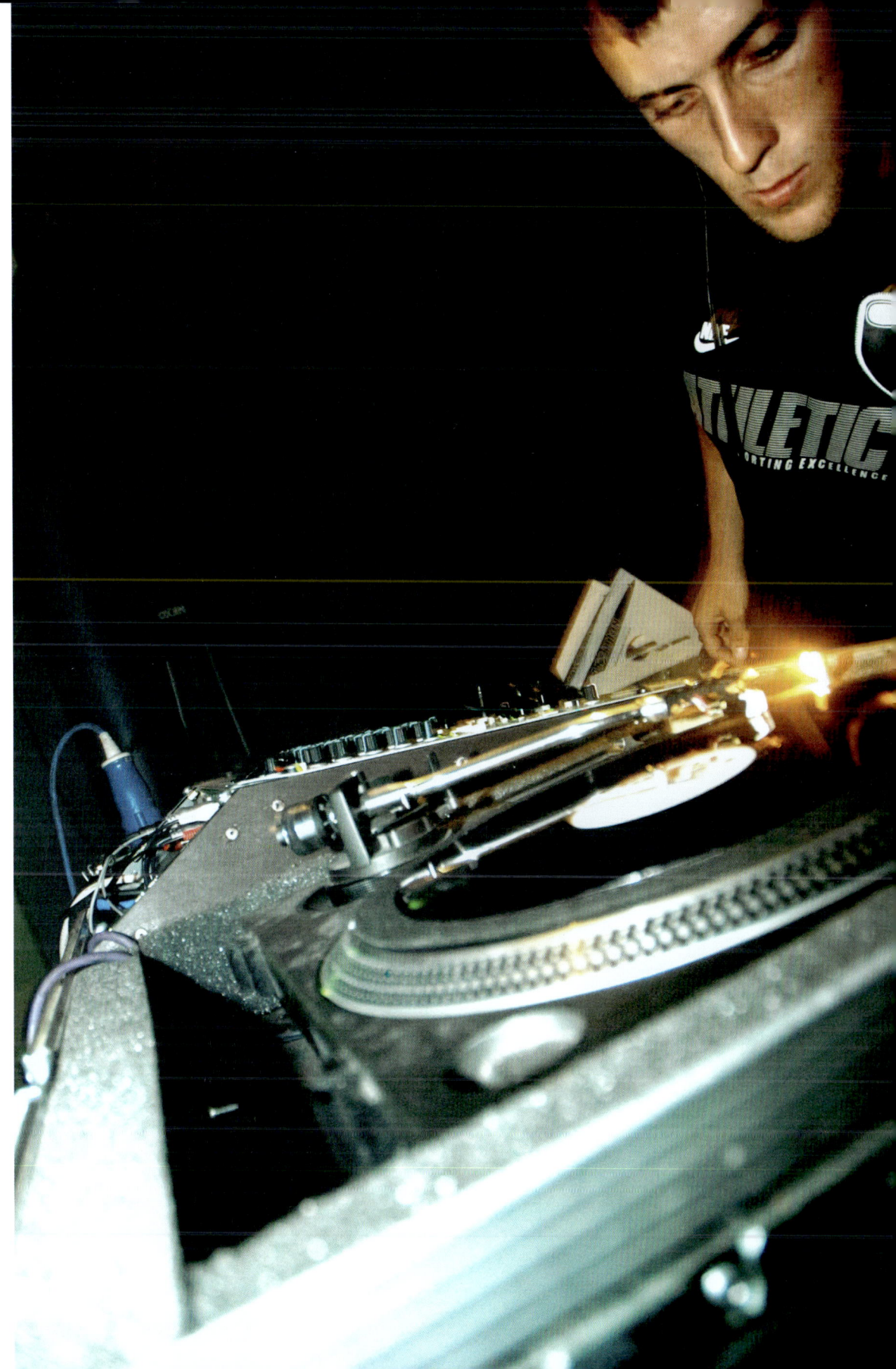

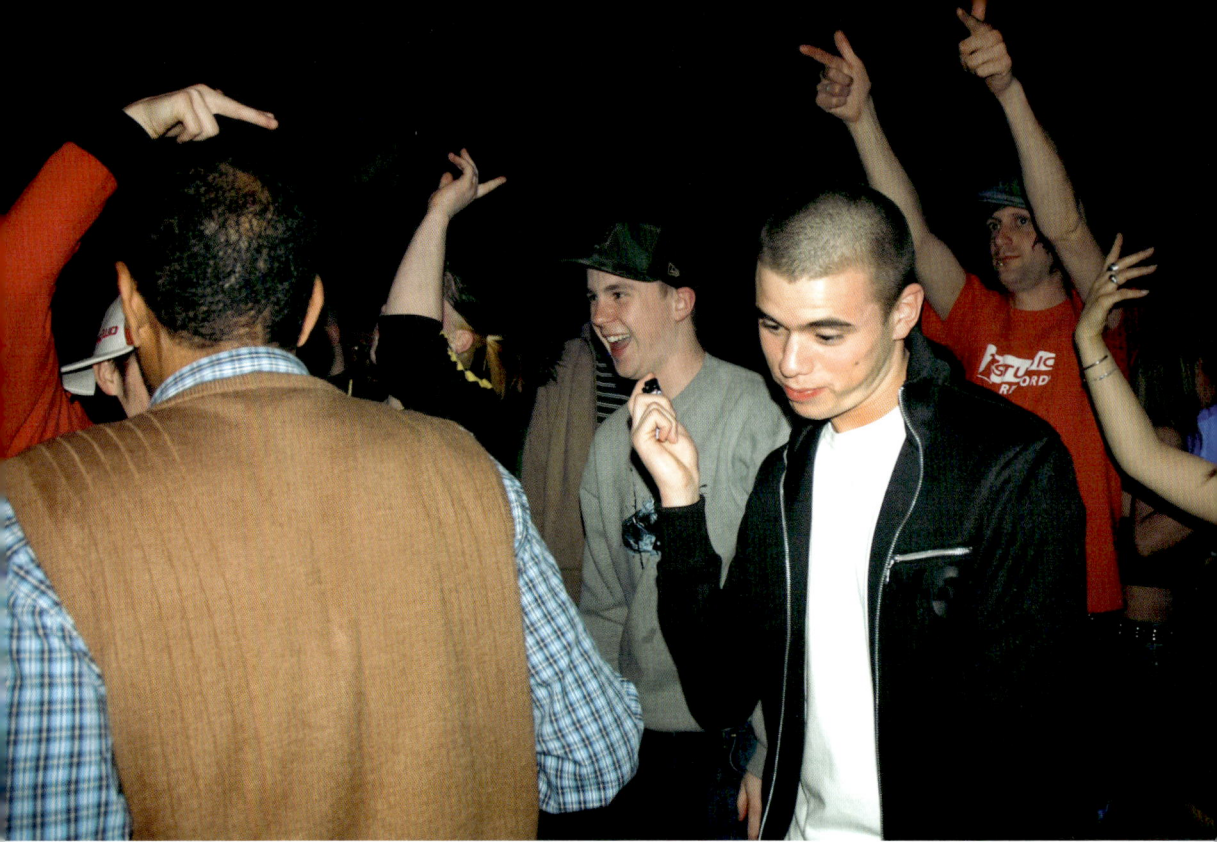

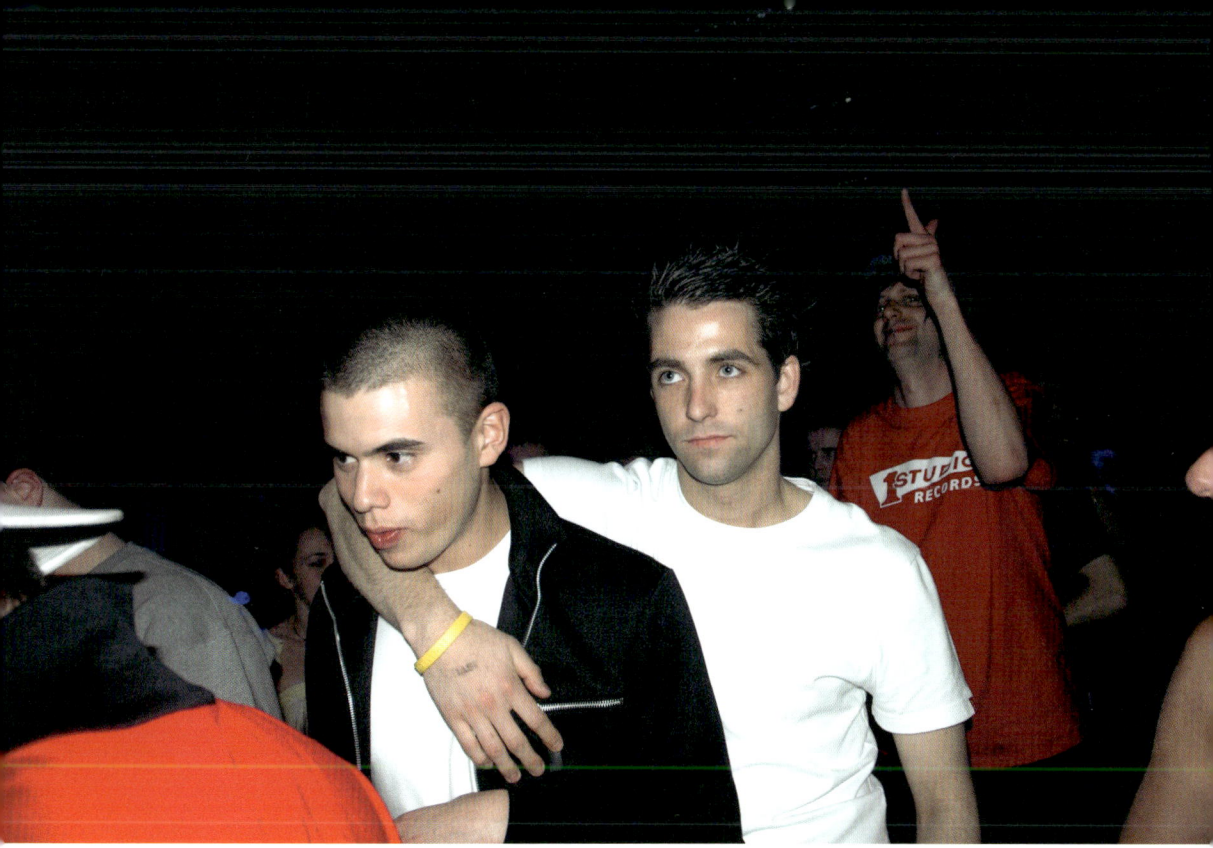

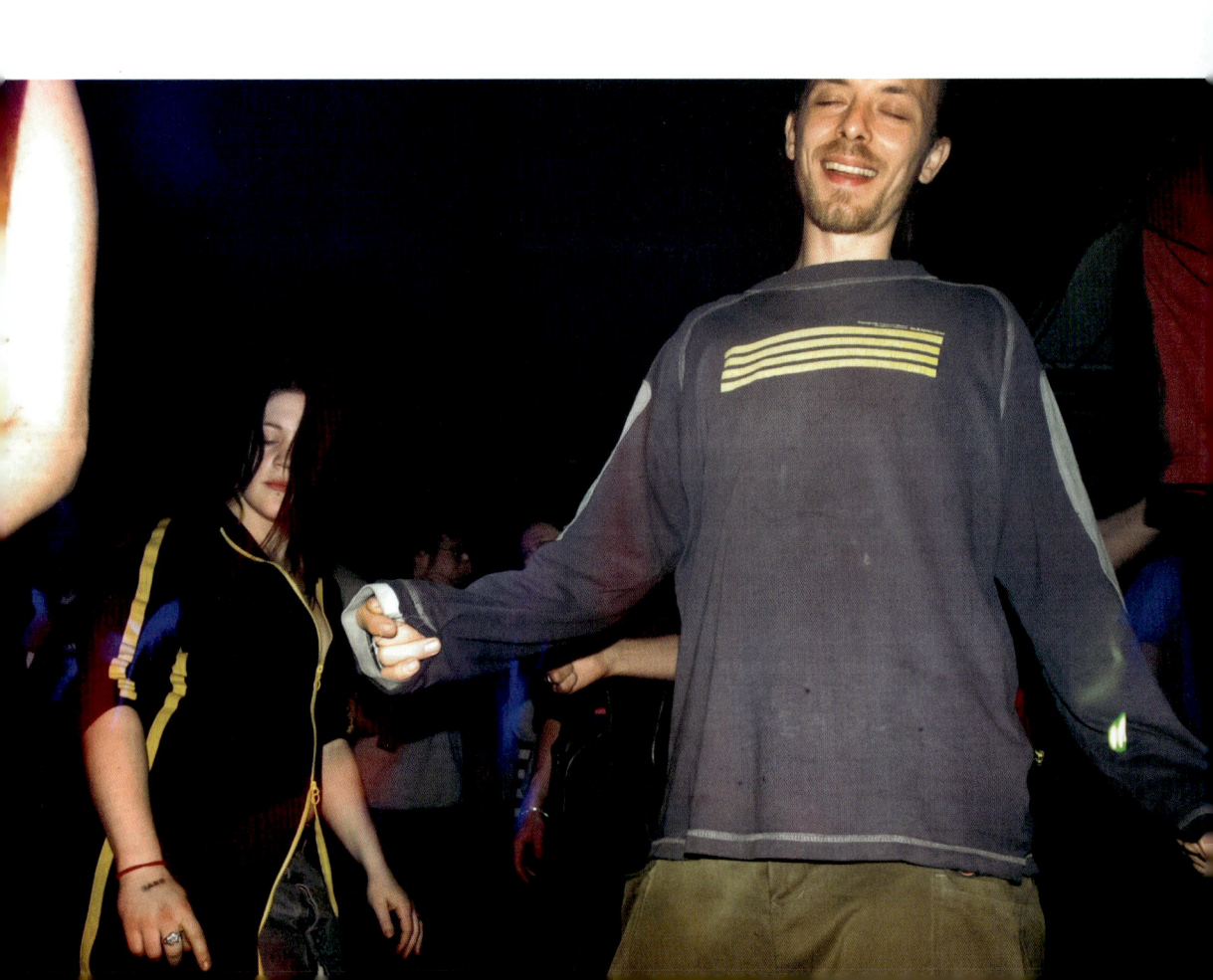

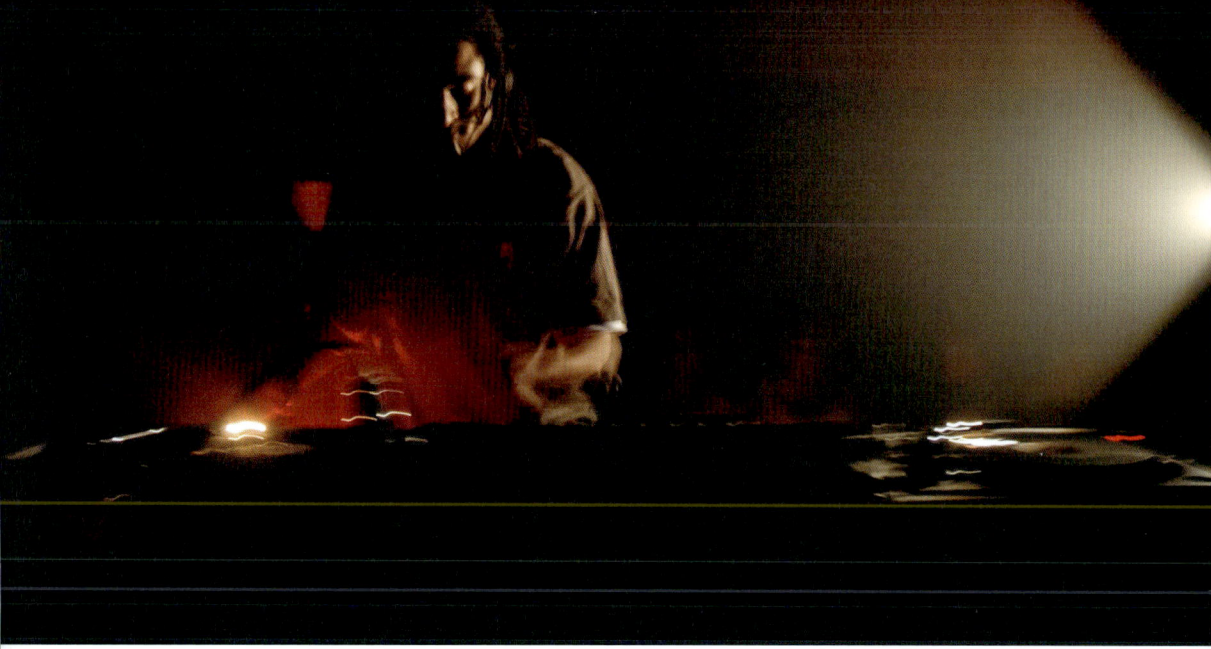

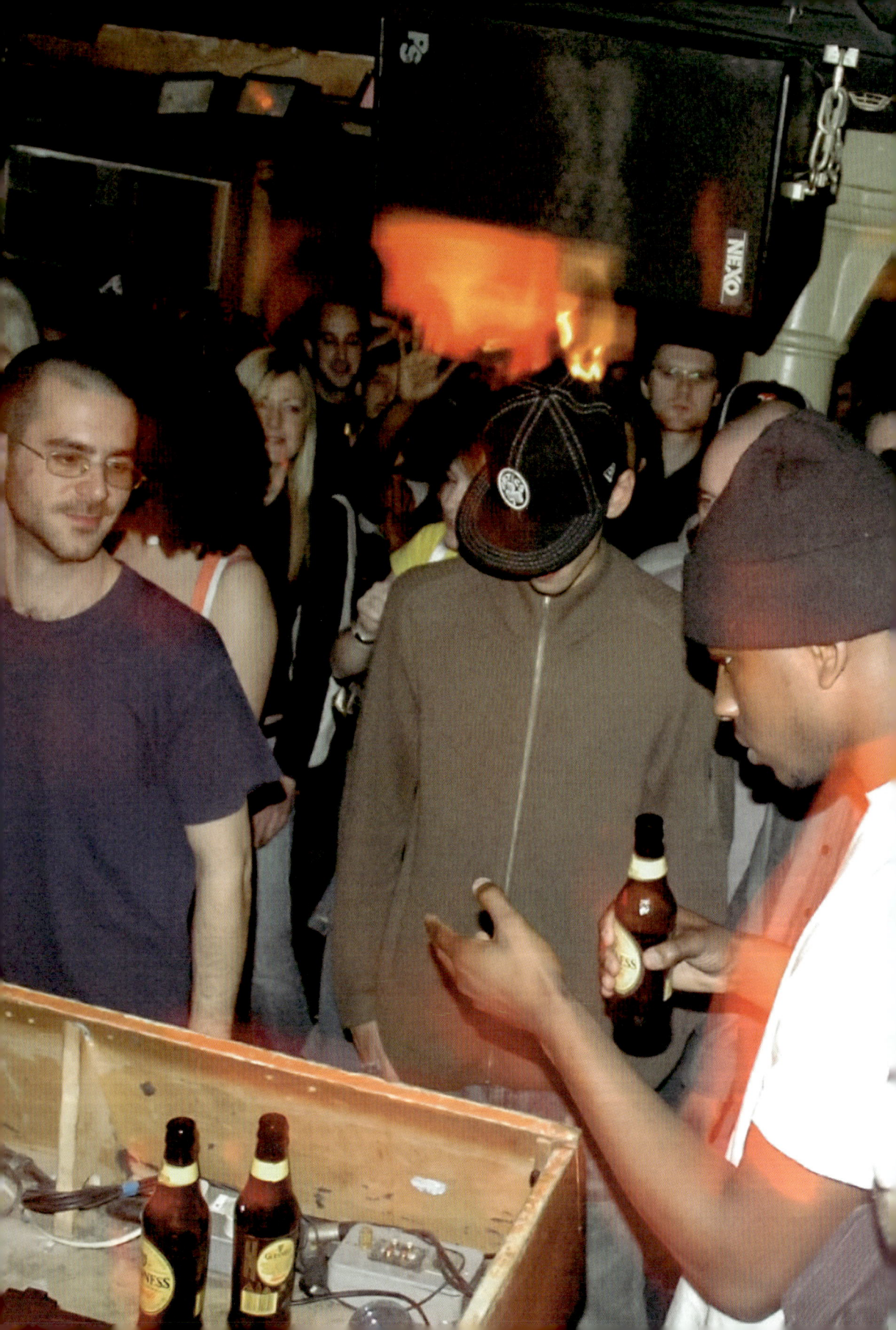

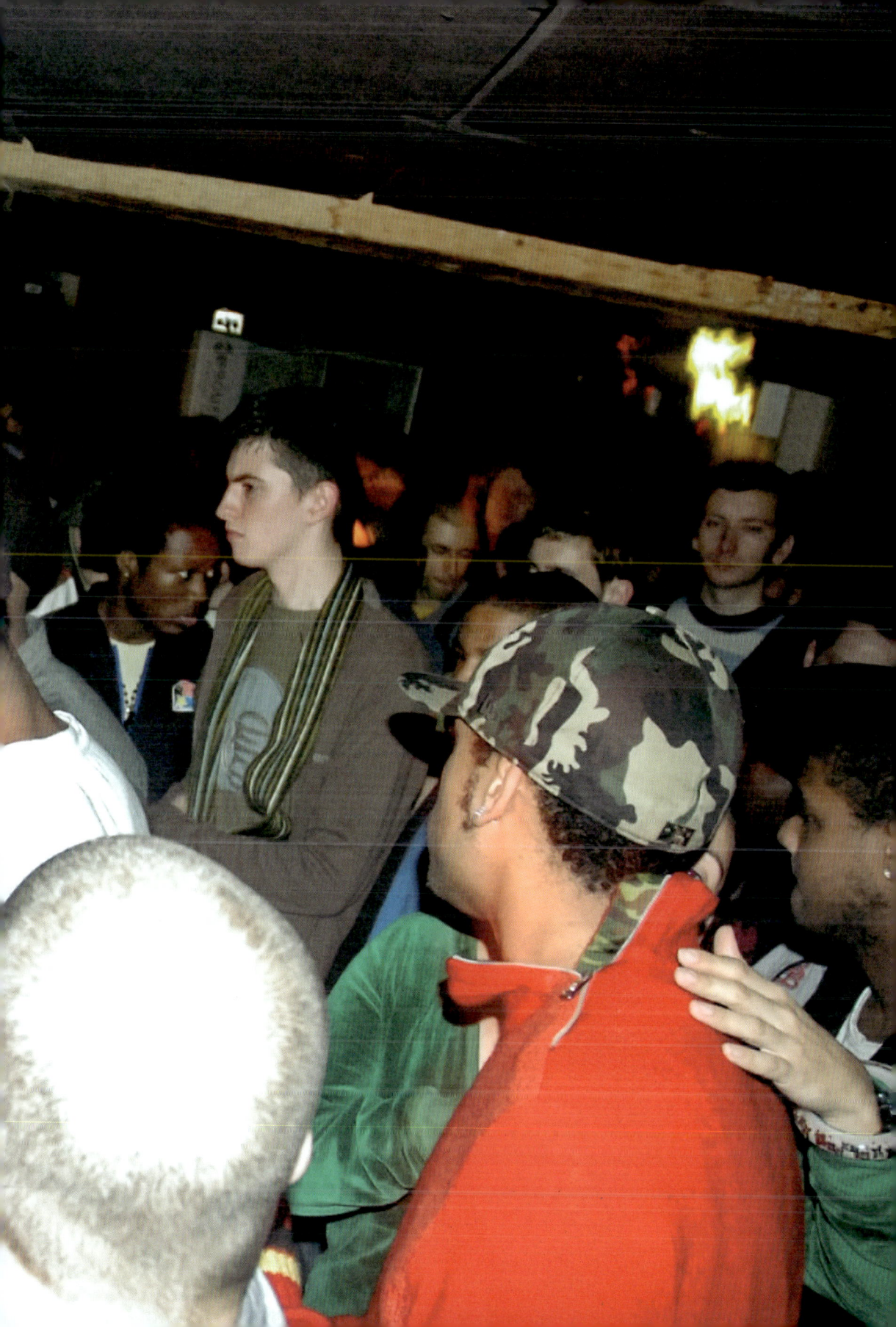

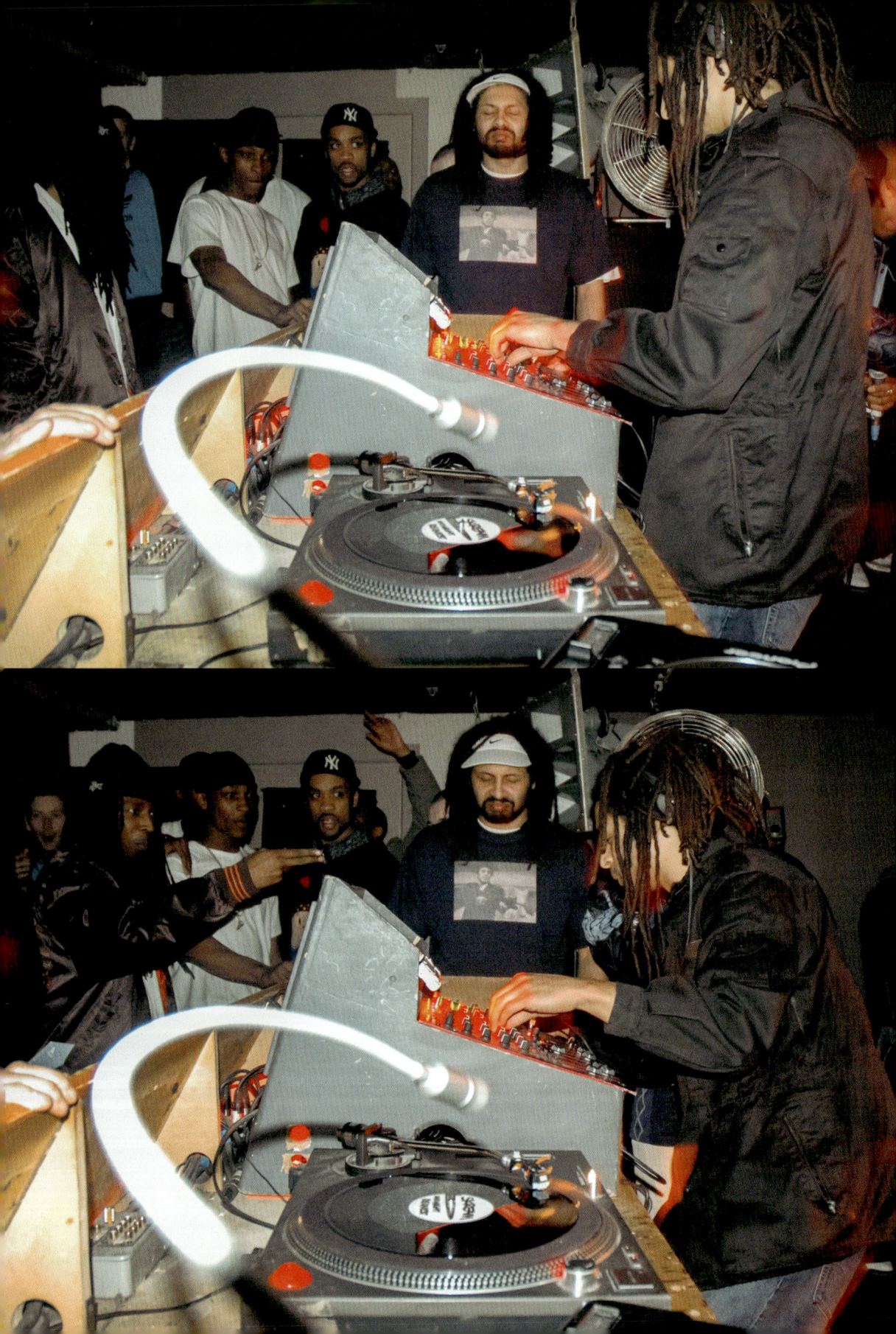

"Are We On Air? Yes We Are."
Martin Clark aka Blackdown on Midnight Request Line.

Setting the scene

First the fundamentals: this is a run of shots taken by Georgina in Plastic People at the club night FWD>> circa 2005(?). It was dark, it was loud, it was exhilarating & it was unfolding in real-time.

From left to right in the main shot there's: Skream, Jammer (Nasty Crew, BBK, Mas Tiempo), me, JME (Roll Deep, BBK), Jackie from Leeds' Steppa zine, Wiley (Roll Deep), MC Pokes (DMZ), Mala (DMZ), MC Crazy D (FWD>>) and DJ Tubby (Braindead, Newham Generals).

Mala's about to finish his set; Roll Deep are about to go on the decks next. The photo, at least privately to Georgina and I, has since become known as "Martin's moment" because shortly before it was taken, I yelled at Georgina across the rib-deflectingly loud dancefloor to catch the fleeting intersection before it was gone.

Why? Mala & Wiley were at the peaks of their creative powers, with outsized influence on shaping the new and flourishing dubstep or grime scenes respectively. So even at the time, even in the moment, the intersection of two of the most influential British musicians - and heroes of mine - felt like history being made in real-time.

Musician's see things differently

If you look closely to the left of the shot, you'll see Skream with his fingers pensively held to his face. His eyes reach the camera but his thoughts are towards the deck, where his anthem "Midnight Request Line" is being dropped by Mala. What does he see in this scene? It's an inflection point in his life, in dubstep and - with much of grime's giants standing literally in front of him - in the relations between dubstep & grime themselves.

Whereas fans of different scenes often see their camps as very distinct, musicians see sound in a different way. When Skream opens a digital audio workstation like Fruity Loops 5, whether he's thinking about dubstep or grime he'll see the same thing: kicks, bass, pads or FX. It's music's common component parts that are visible, not scenes or genres. "I started it as a grime tune..." he told me in August 2005 in relation to the dubstep anthem. "There's a formula to it. I've been trying to study it. But I can't get it."

Skream saw something different in that workstation and built an anthem in one style that blew up another. Initially championed by Youngsta in dubstep, and then Skepta & DJ Maximum in grime, by the time Ricardo Villalobos and Laurent Garnier could fit it into their visions, the vista was expanding from one corner of Plastic People to beyond the known horizon.

"-hello, are we on the air?"

"yes we are."

- "Hello Mum, I'd like to hear a new beat on the request line."

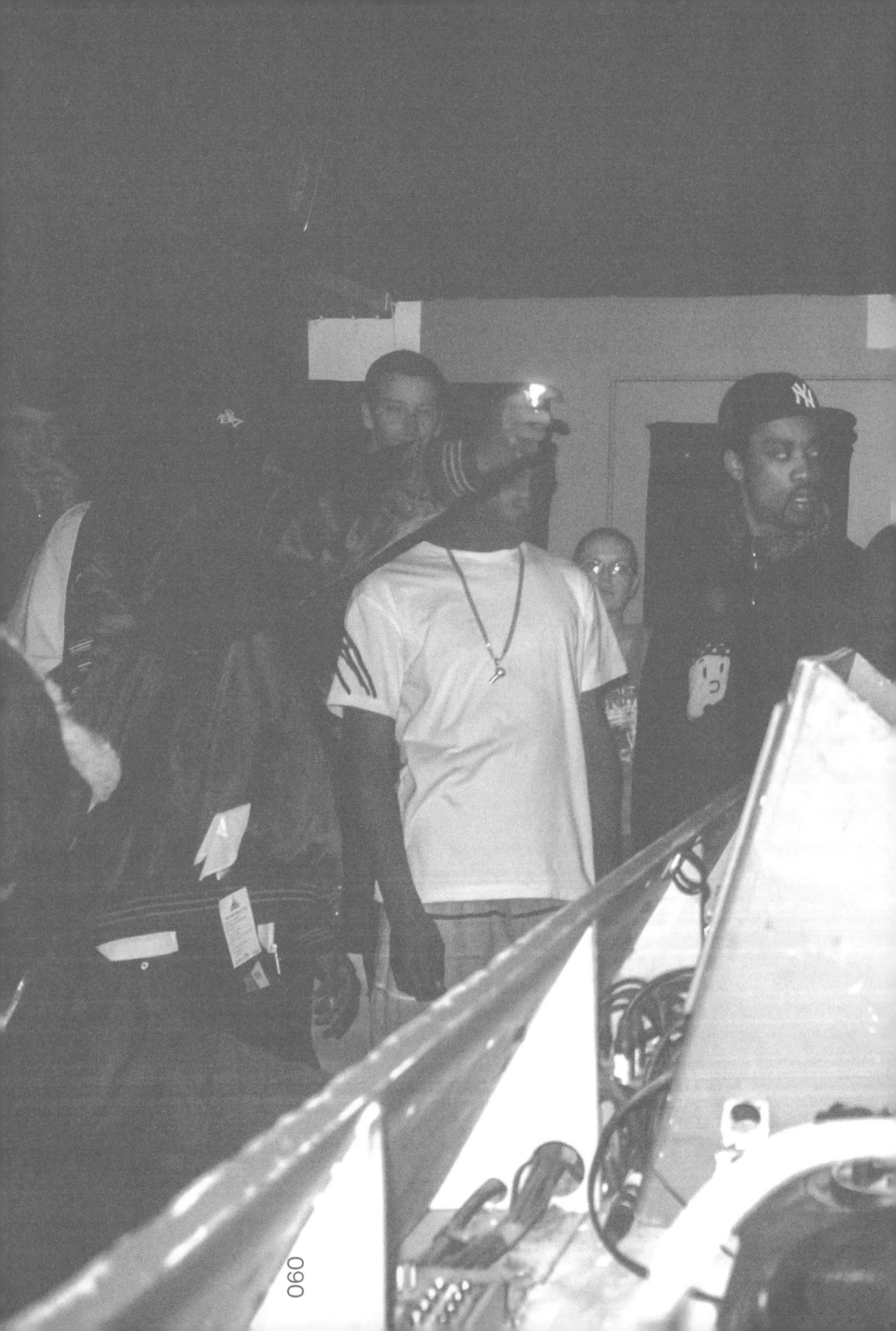

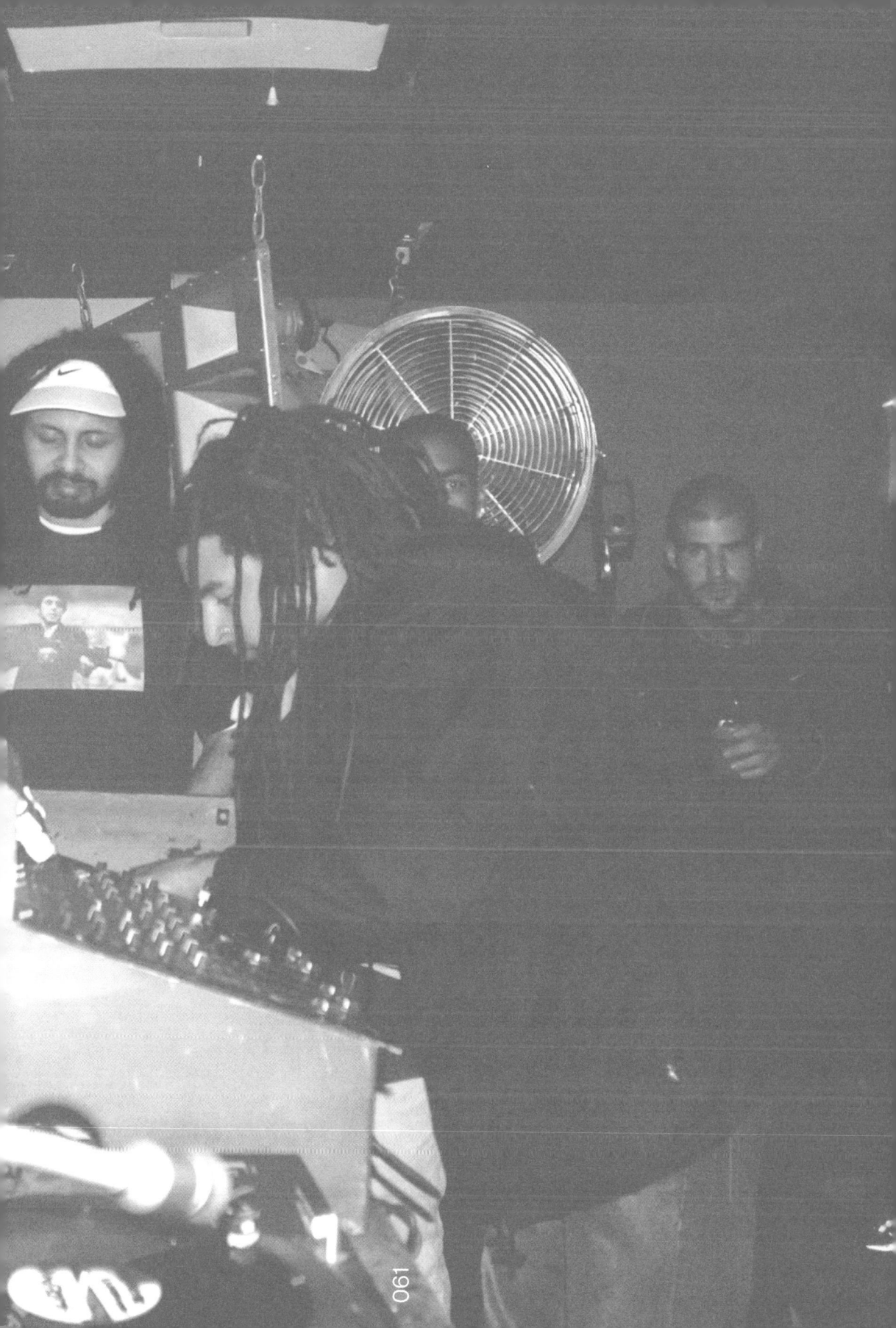

Hearing then, now

So that's the fundamentals, framed: sonic history was captured in chromatic chemistry to an SD card. And lots has been written, either at the time or since, about how the dubstep & grime scenes.

But what does the photo tell us about now? Especially as seminal labels do their 15-years-of, 20- or even 30-years-of revival parties designed to give ravers now a taste of then, what does the photo have to say about how history could be made again, today? What are the cultural & musical fundamentals, if any, that can keep things moving FWD>>?

If you like music, focus on the sound

Let's start with the obvious: Plastic People's sound system was incredible. Loud, physical, immersive and never harsh. DJing on it, as I was lucky enough a few times, was like wrestling with a violent storm. But sound like this is the exception, not the rule. Most venues are built around their business model, aka selling you drinks. So if you do find somewhere that sounds incredible where communities can try and fail creatively: support it with your feet, your wallet and your heart. History tells us they're influential but highly fragile.

But there's a second nuance to the proposal to "focus on the sound". While Georgina's photos illuminate the scene with flash, Plastic People's dancefloor was pitch black dark. If you like music, as in... really like music, seek out venues that deprive your visual senses to enhance your auditory ones. We live in an era where the default unit of cultural currency is video: a story or a reel, real or AI-generated. But our brains absorb music differently, using much older more fundamental parts in conjunction with the sections that access memory in real time. If so, if there are opportunities to immerse yourself in sound with little light: take it. It hits differently.

History is like beef: nothing but timing

Survivor bias is a thing: for every lauded musician who gets to tell us how history was made, there are thousands who didn't have the cultural impact. For those that did survive, one thing is fairly common: they had great timing - and I'm not talking about an exceptional sense of tempo.

Maybe knowing this is useless, as who can change when they're born? That's fair comment. But time does have some lessons to teach us, like a refix of the Wiley line "beef ain't nothing but timing." Firstly very little musical history comes from rehashing or faithfully reviving the past. Fun? Yes. Happiness? Yes. Togetherness, like that last song at a wedding? Yes. But musical history: no. So if you're looking for history being made, seek out musicians and communities who are writing their own, not reviving someone else's.

A second lesson is around your own timing. Optimism is a powerful force: if you believe you can begin to build, but if you don't you won't even start, so we remain optimistic about what we can all nurture, build or create throughout our lives. But experience also tells us some endeavours are just easier at certain phases of our lives. In our teens and early 20s our brains are making new connections making us the most open to new sounds and memories. This often coincides with times when we have the most degree of freedom in our lives. So my message here is if you see an opportunity early, go for it: press the button, take the shot. It's doubtful you'll regret it later; It's likely harder to come by later too.

Follow your hunches; treasure your expectations

Let's double down on optimism. Music is sonic patterns that create emotion in our brains. Do we really think we've seen every permutation that can exist already? Of course not. What this means then, if you're looking for the writing of musical history, is that it's there to be found, made and supported.

Great, it's there. But where? As someone who's been up close when three happened (drum & bass, dubstep, grime) and at decent proximity to three others (UK funky, deep tech, amapiano/afrohouse) my tip is this: follow your hunches; treasure your exceptions. Listen to music in new places, from new people. Something makes you feel a certain way? Follow that hunch. Something feel a bit different? Treasure that exception.

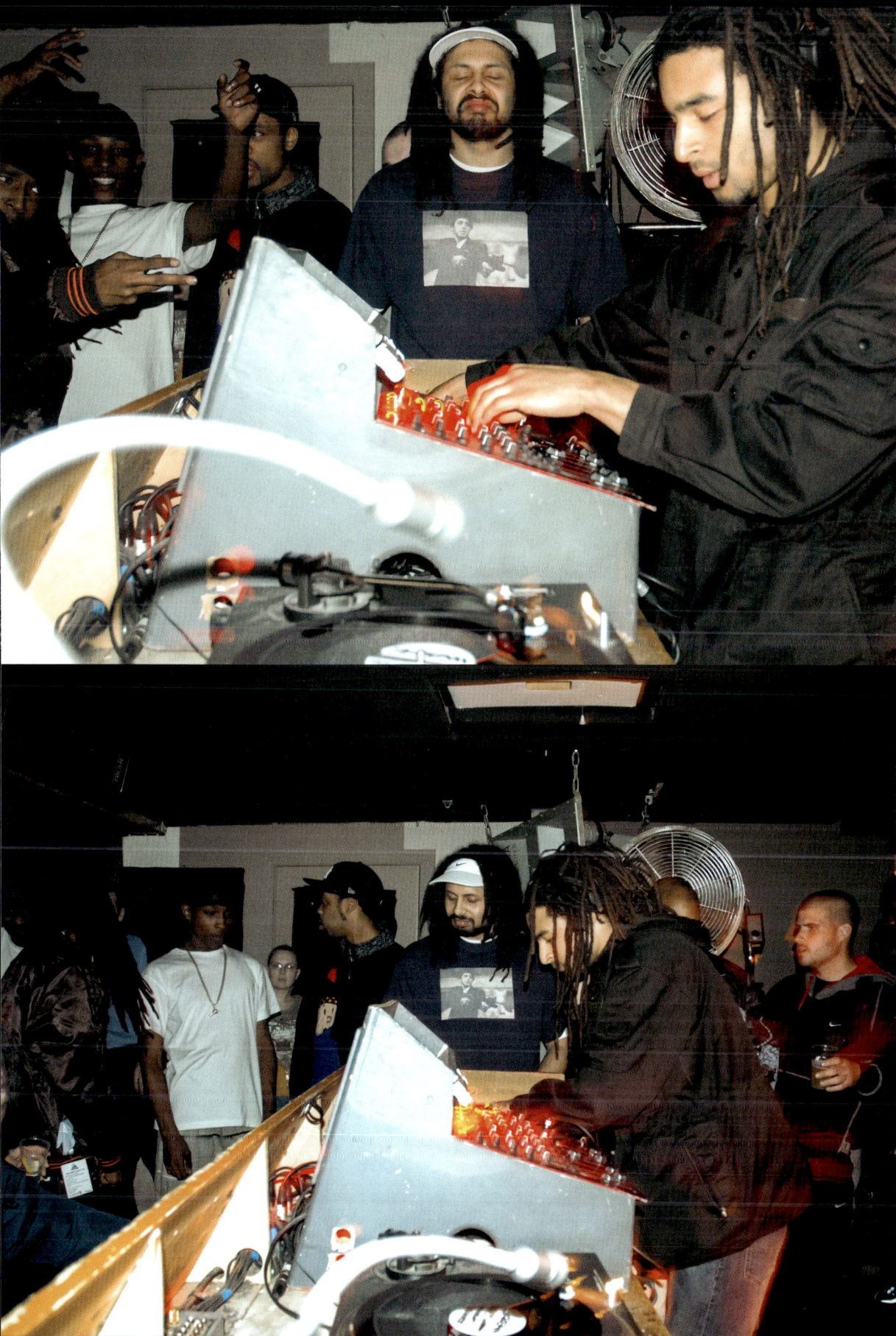

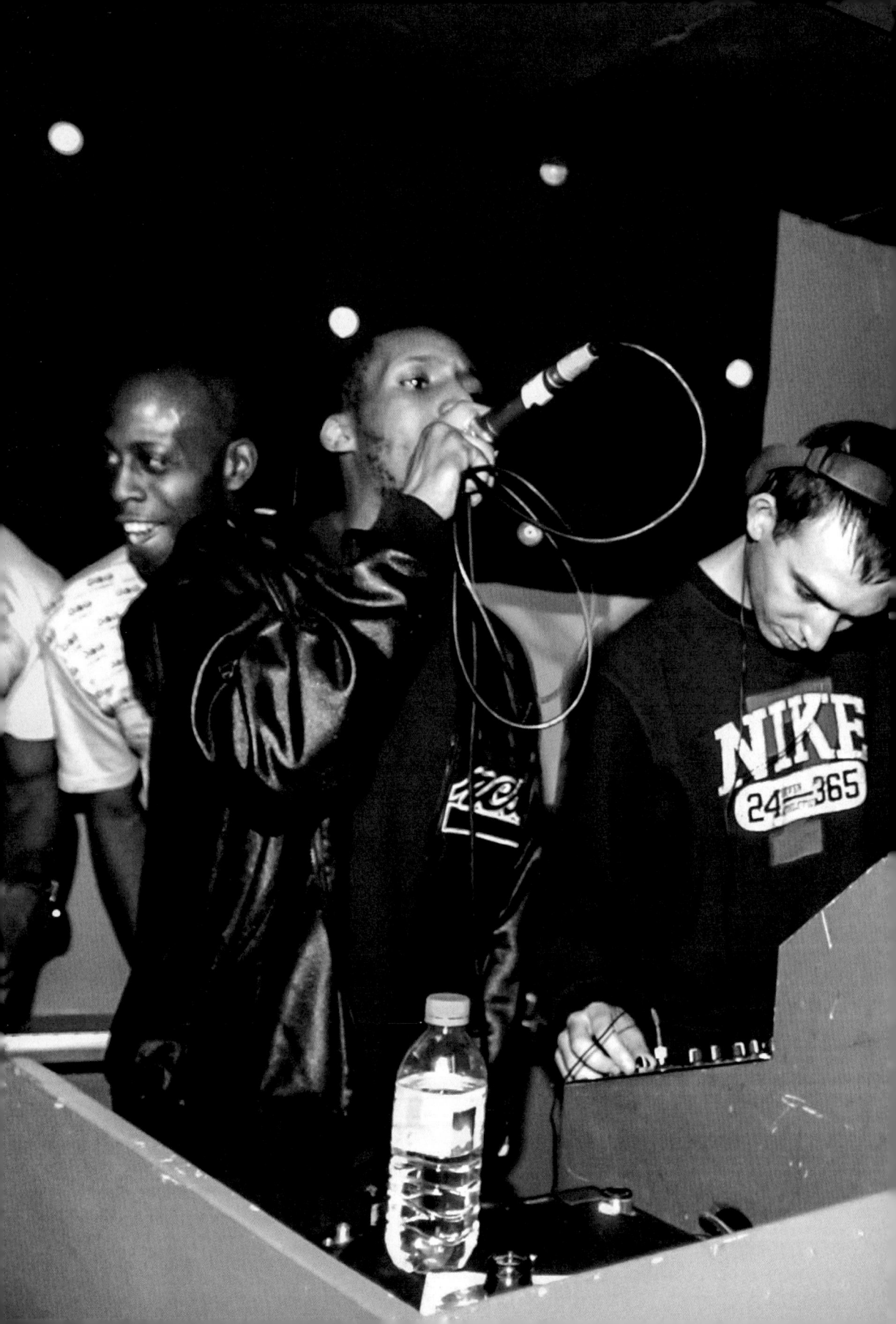

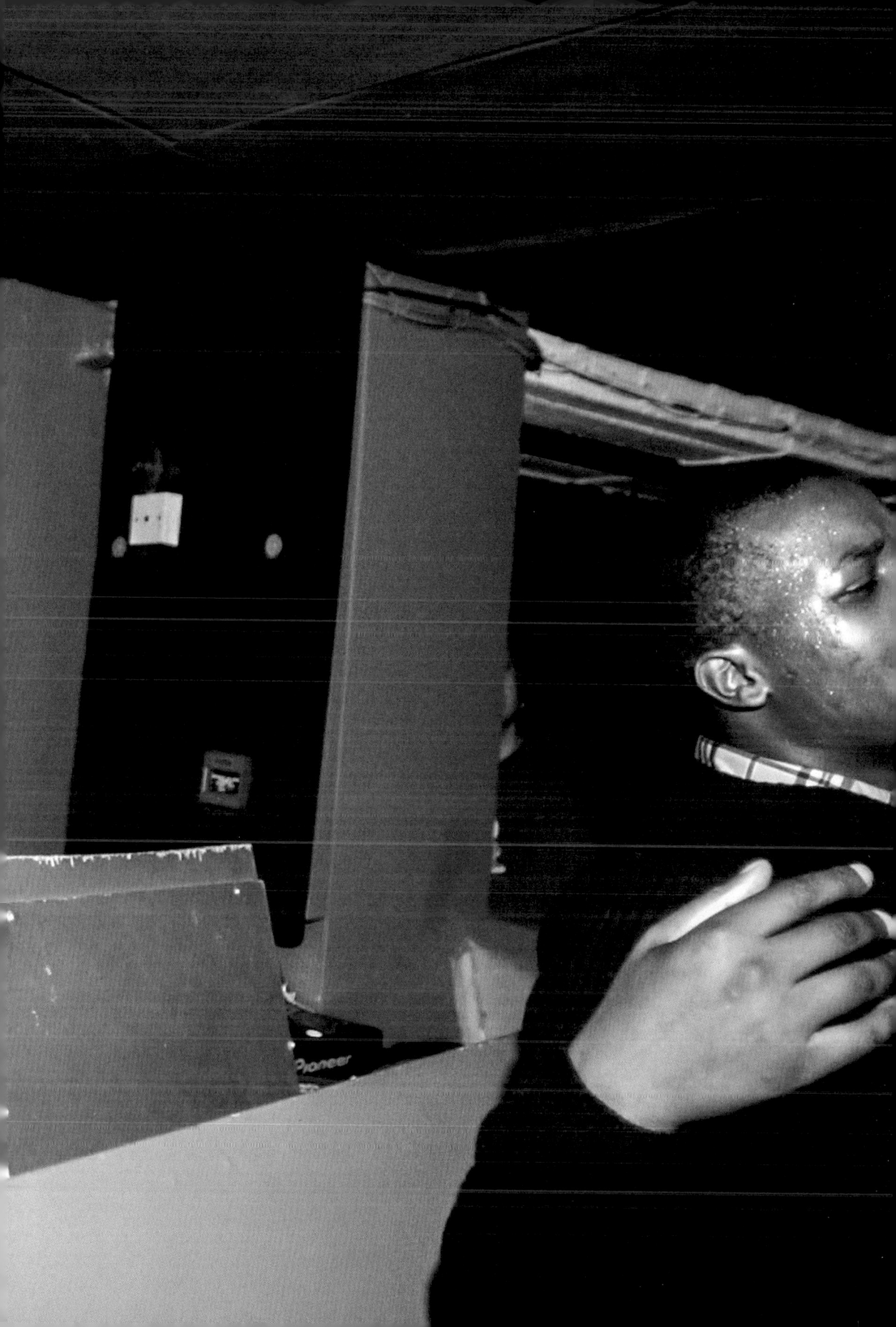

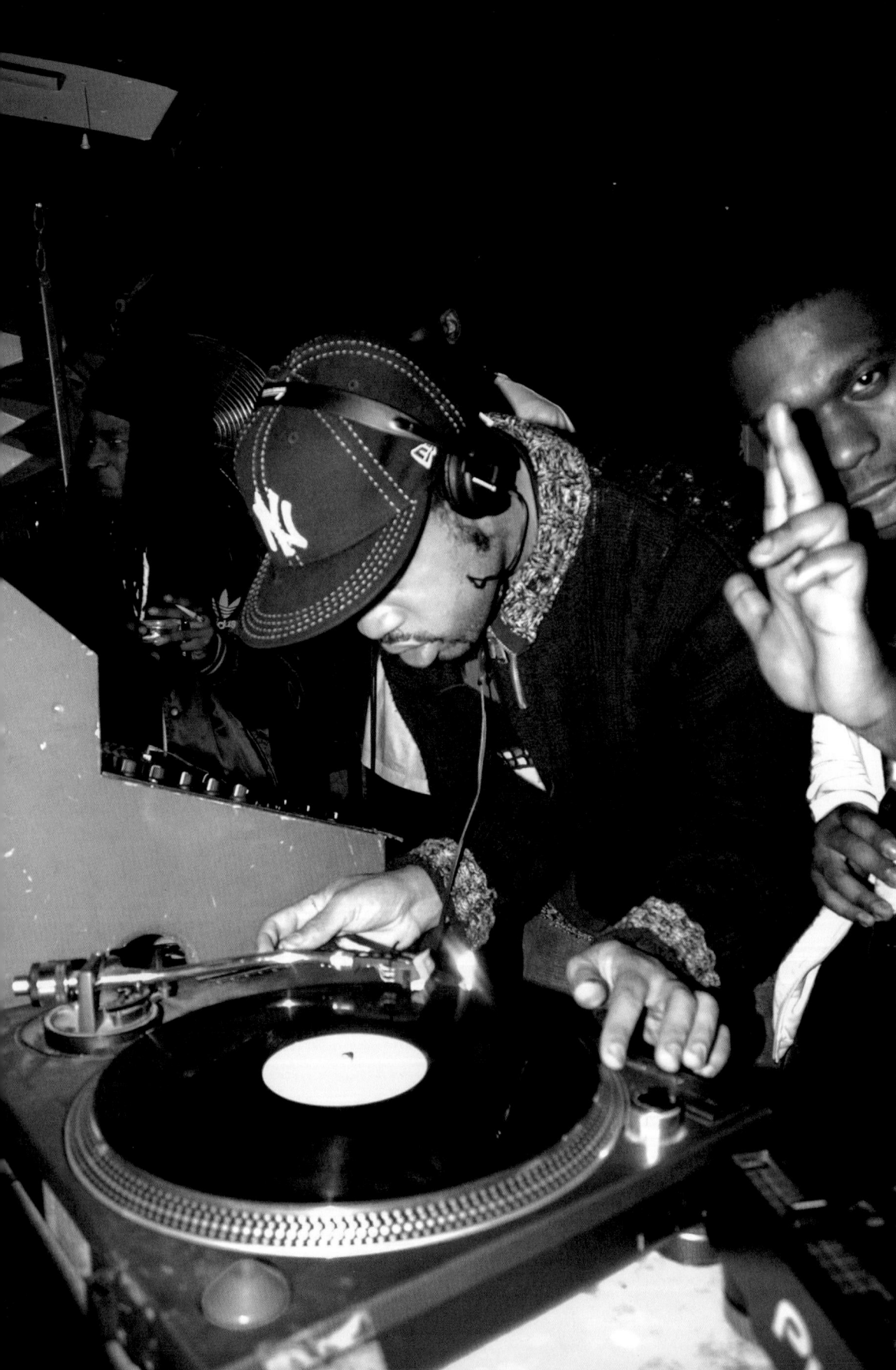

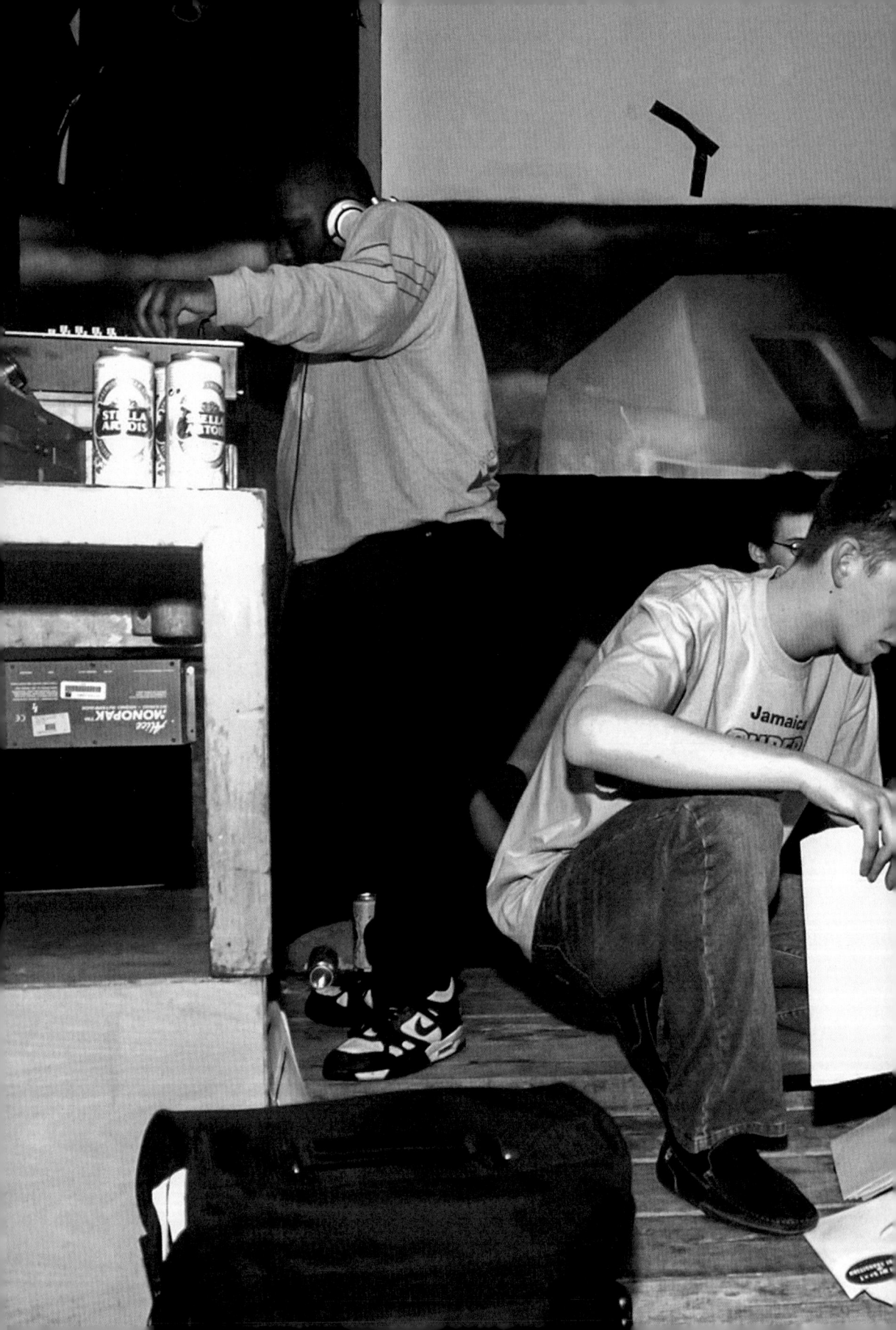

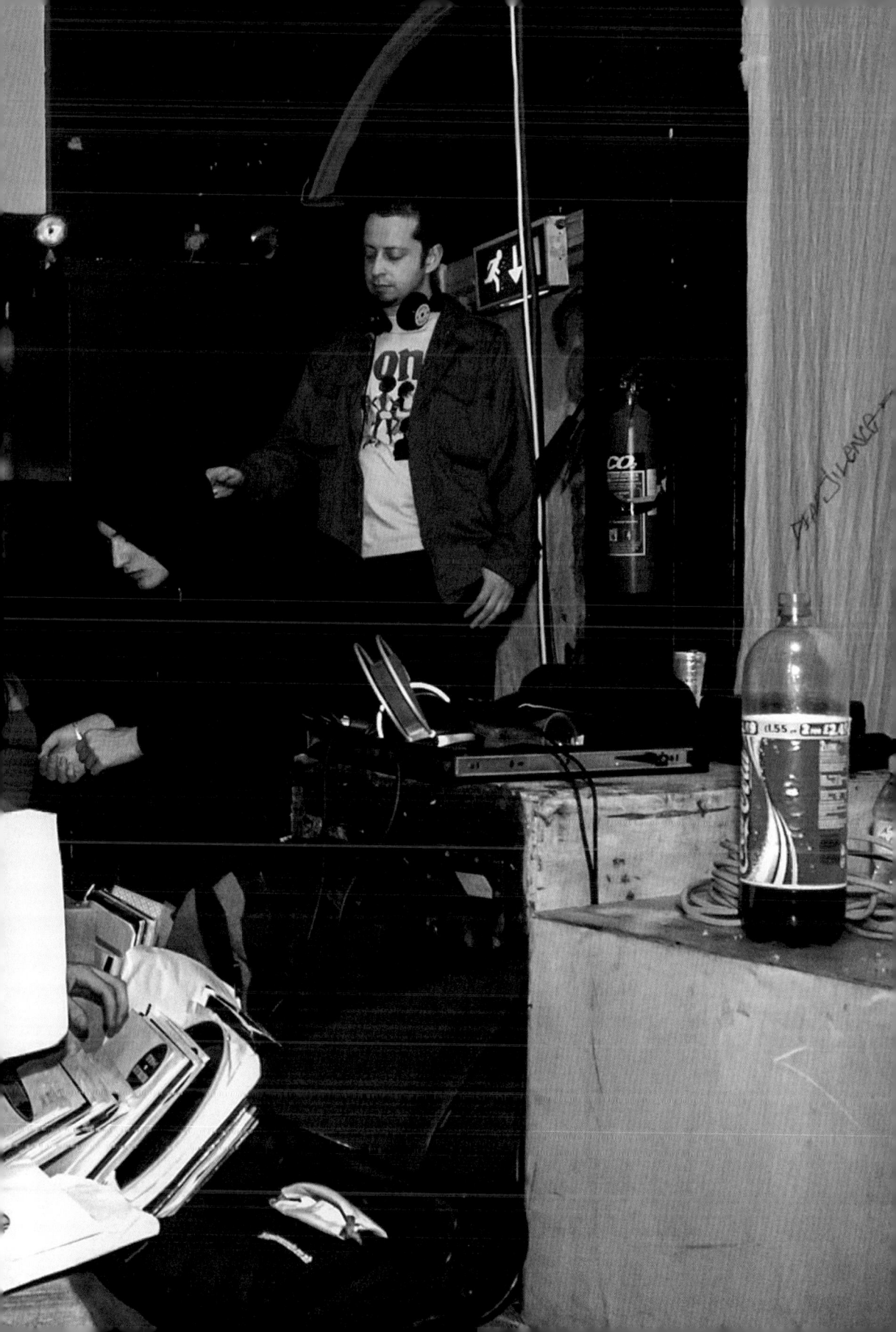

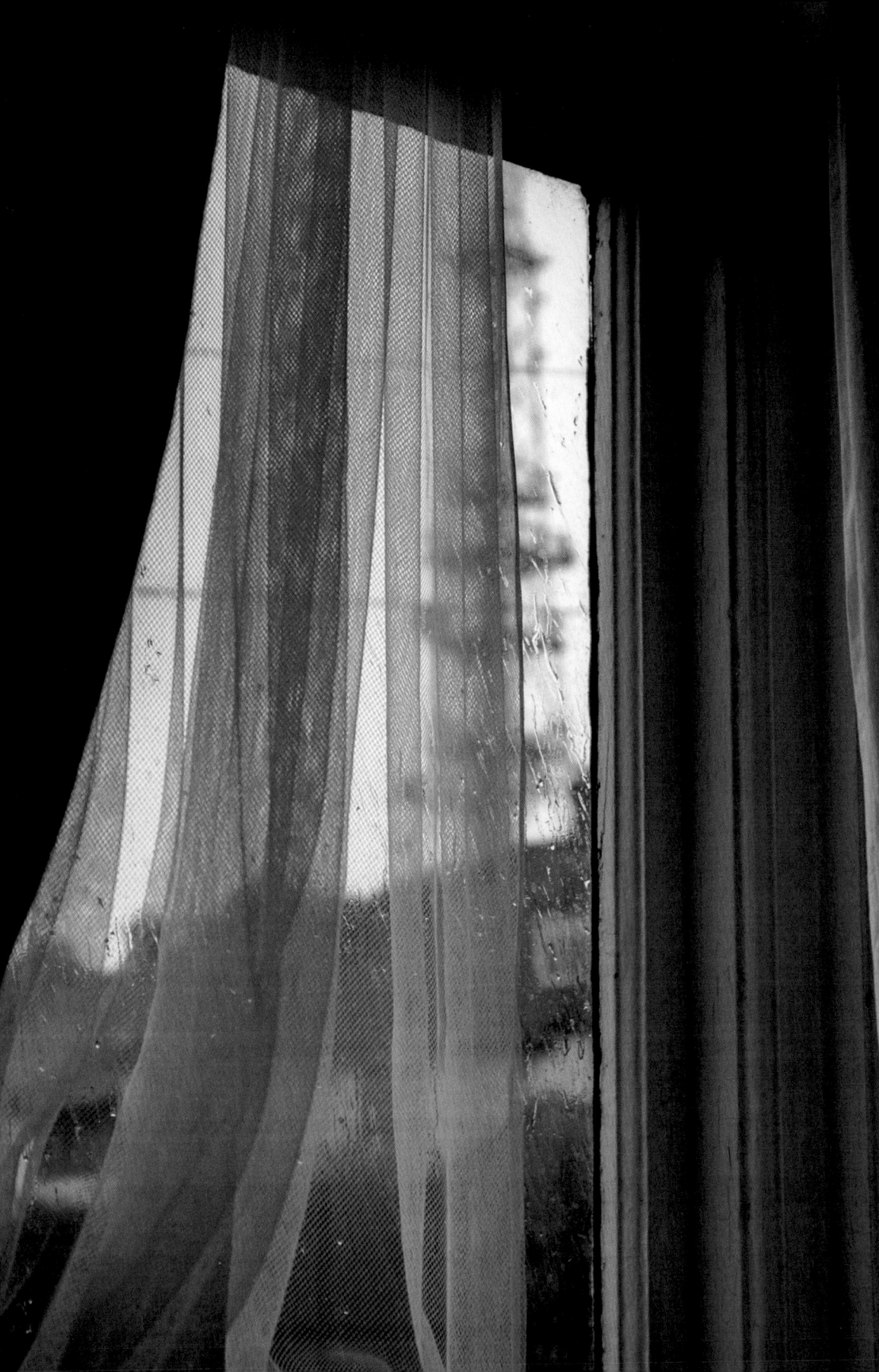

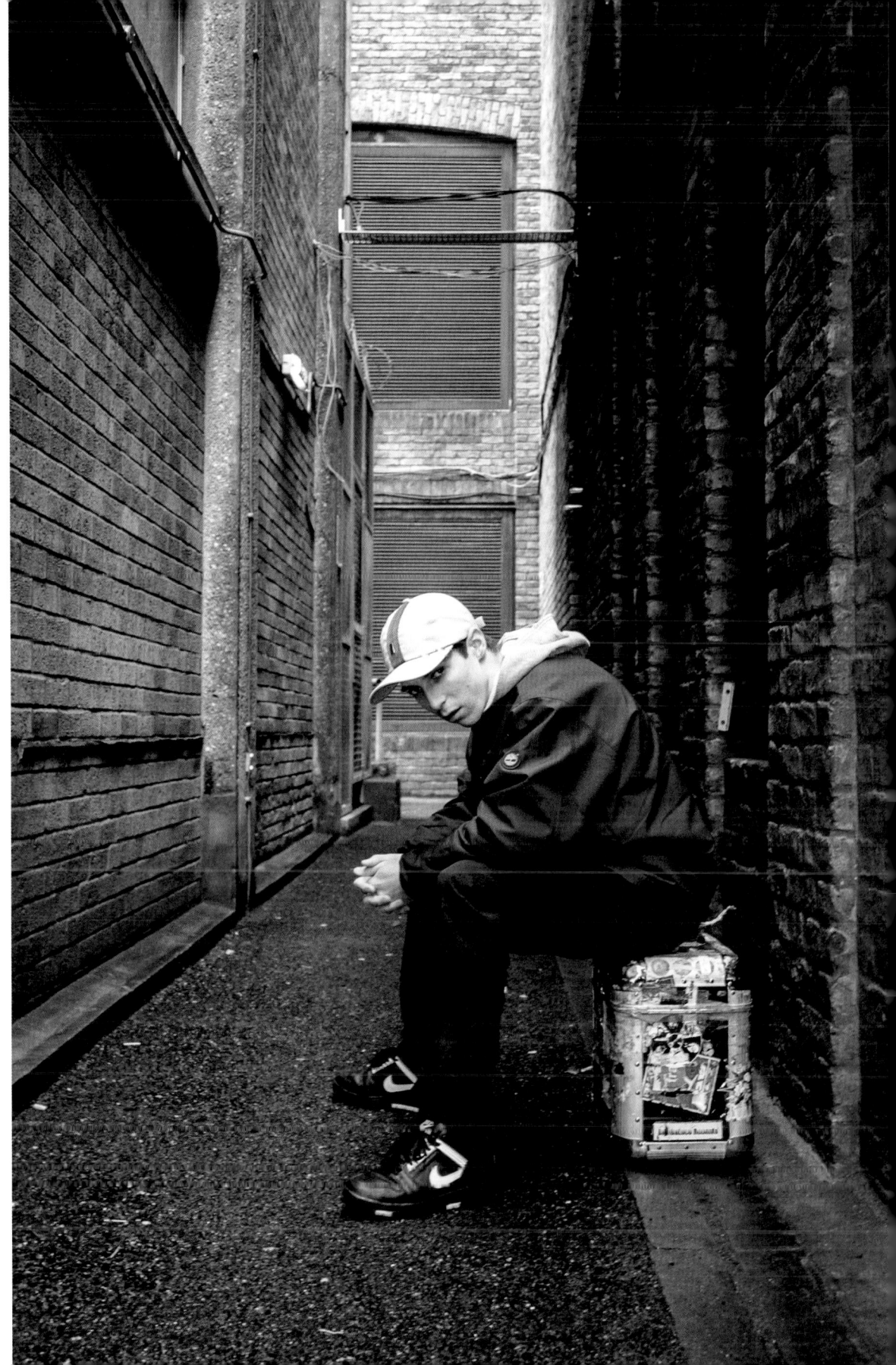

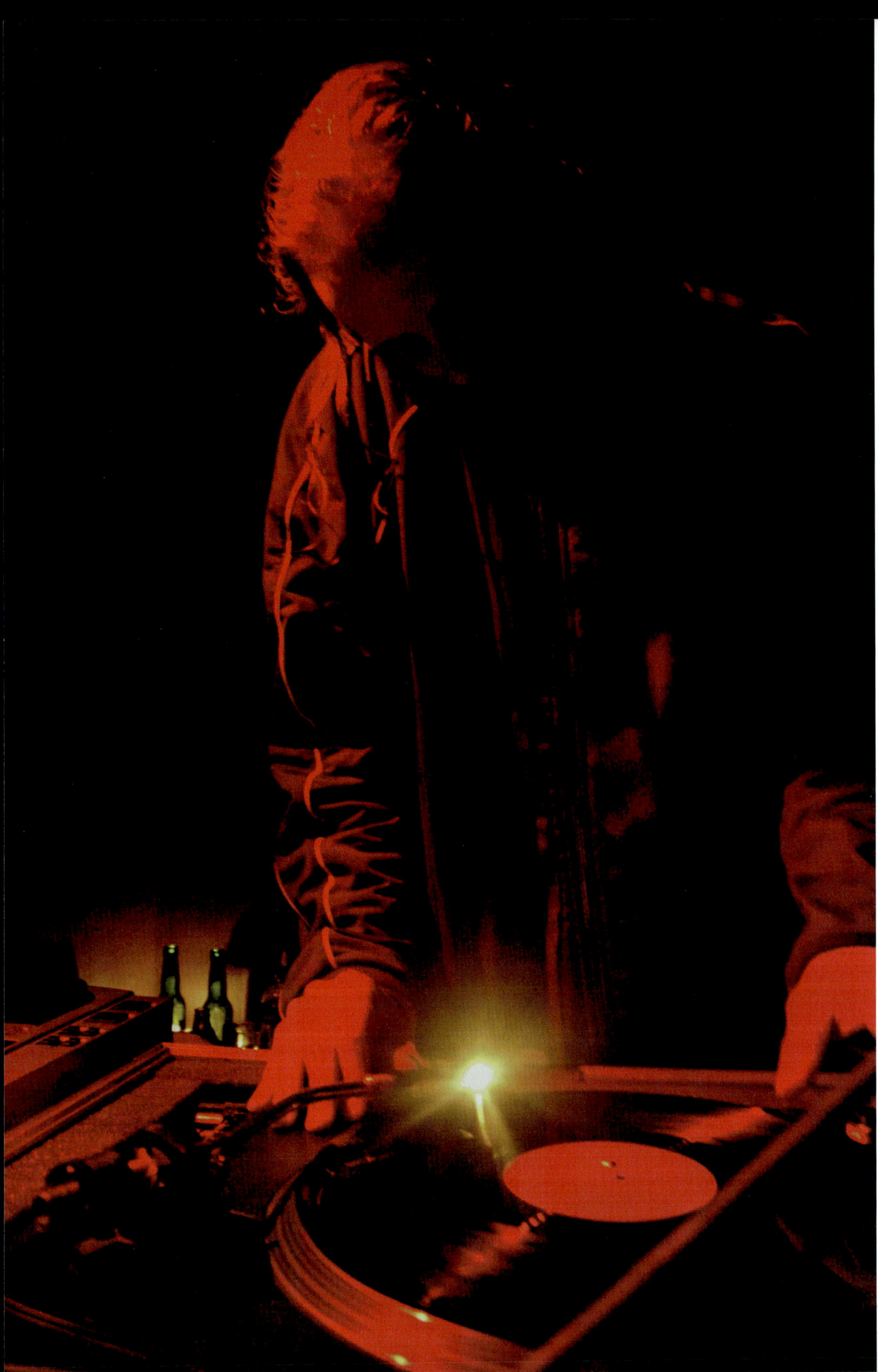

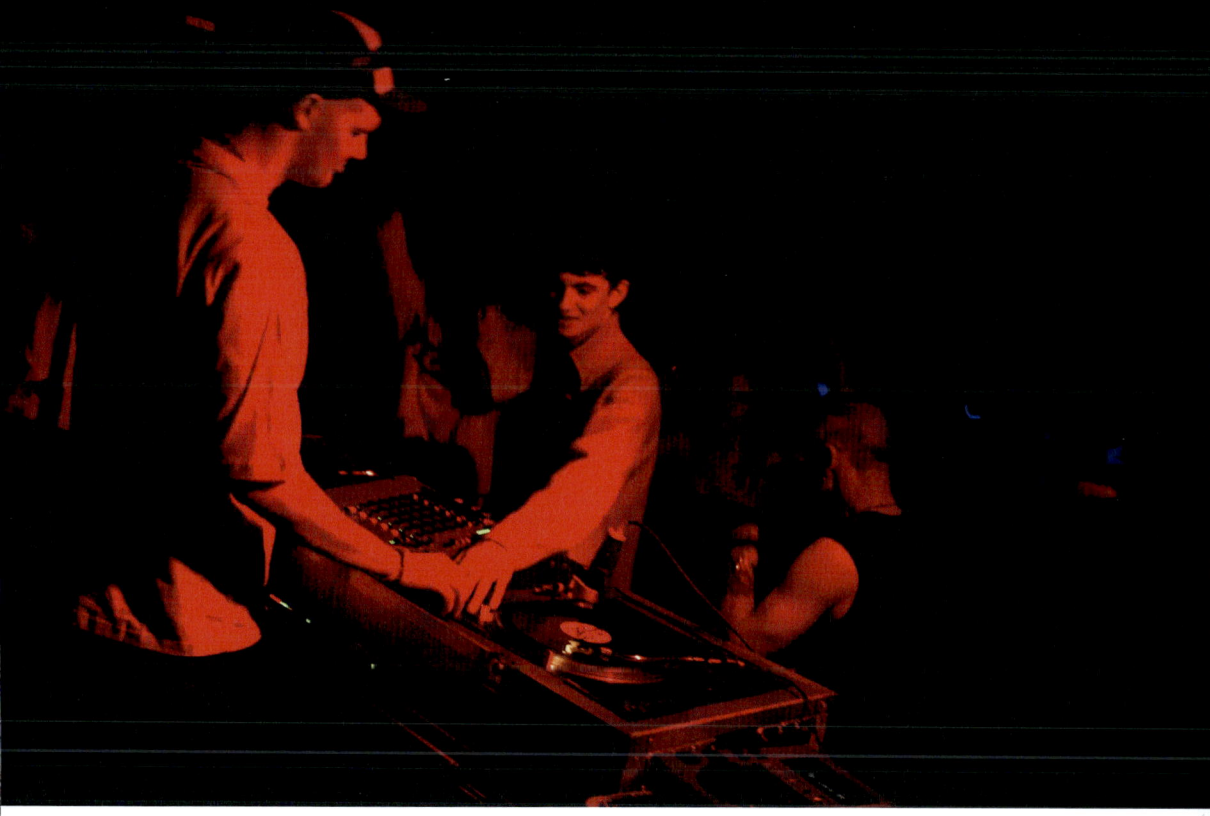

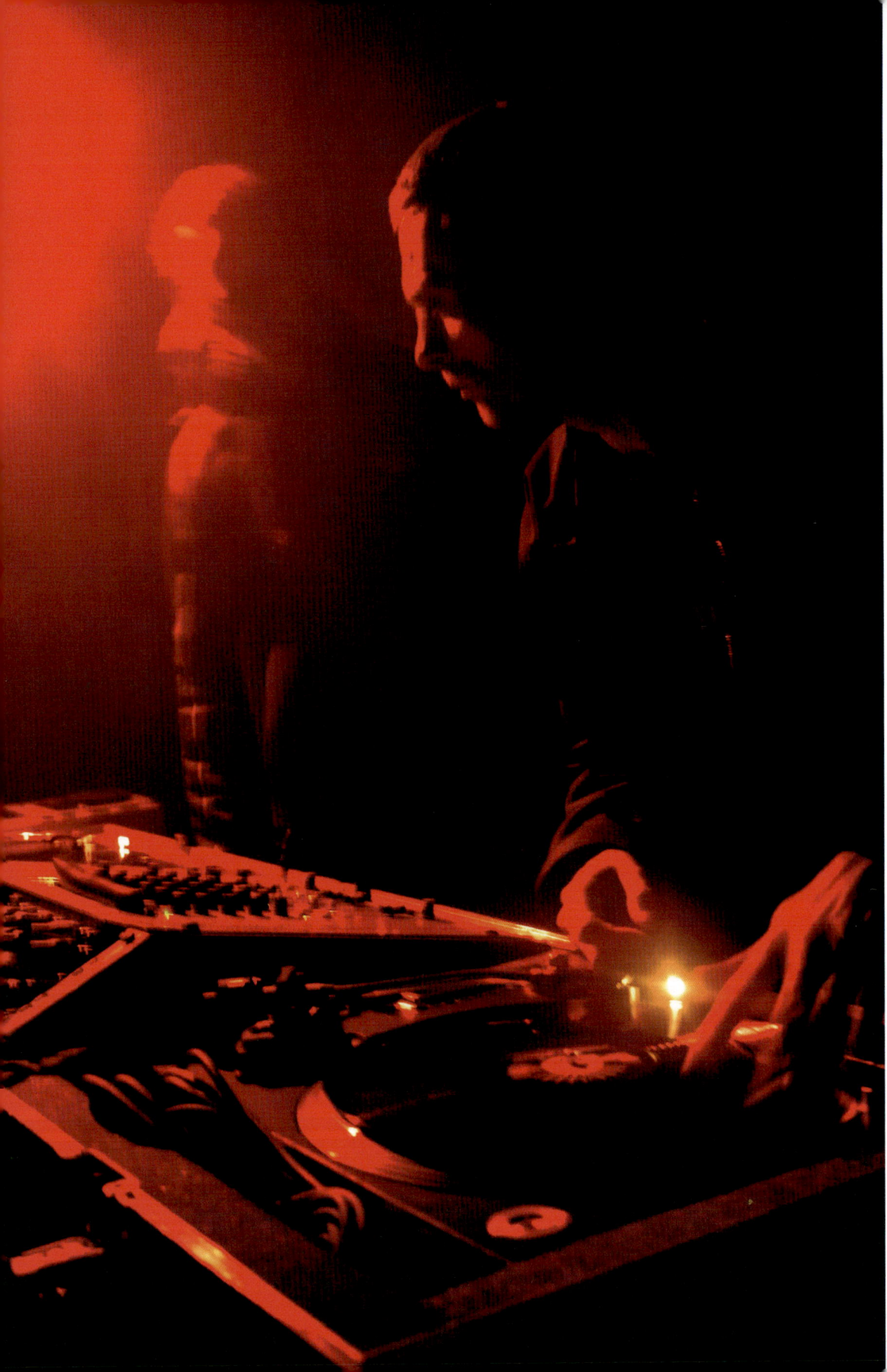

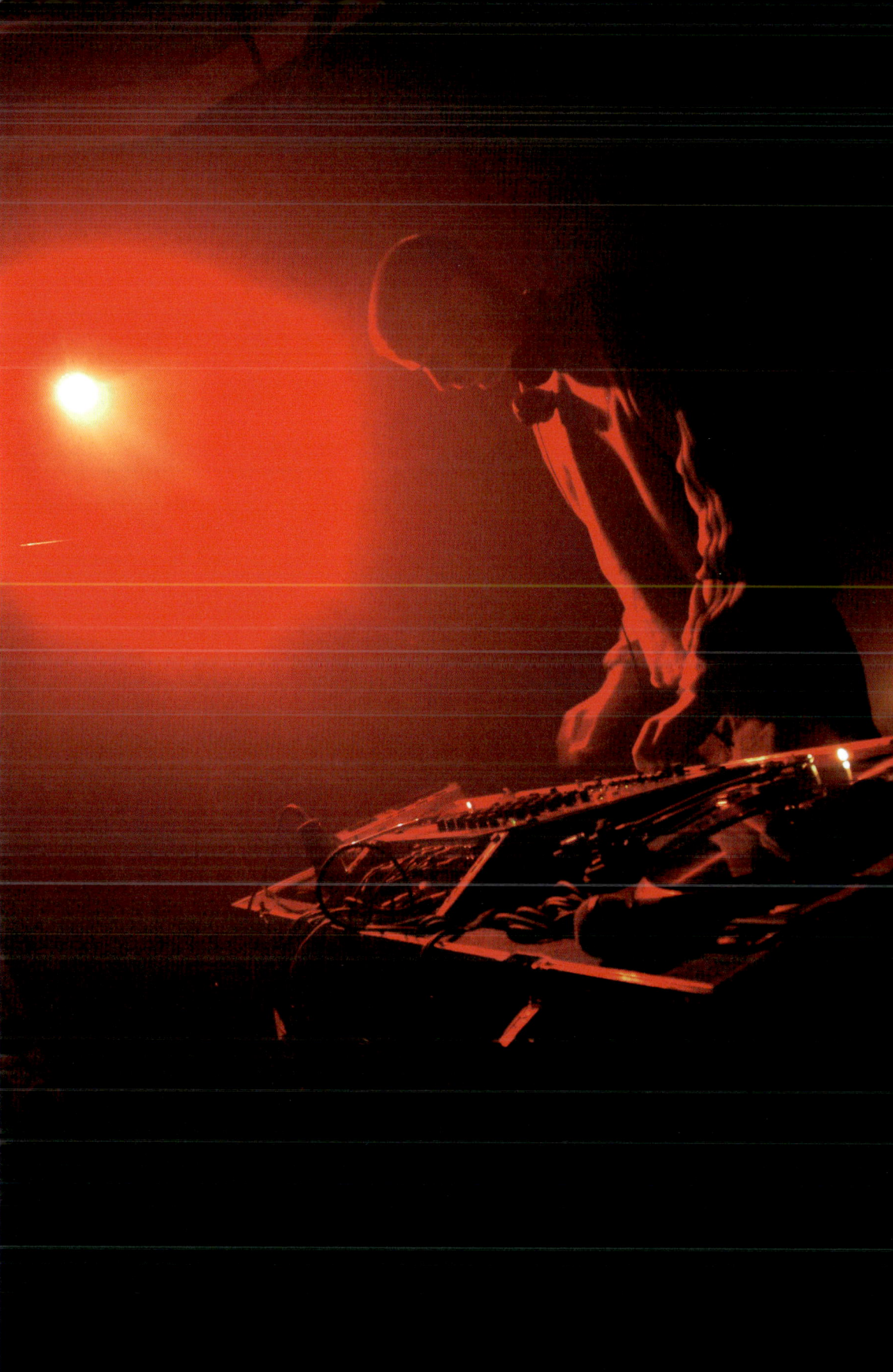

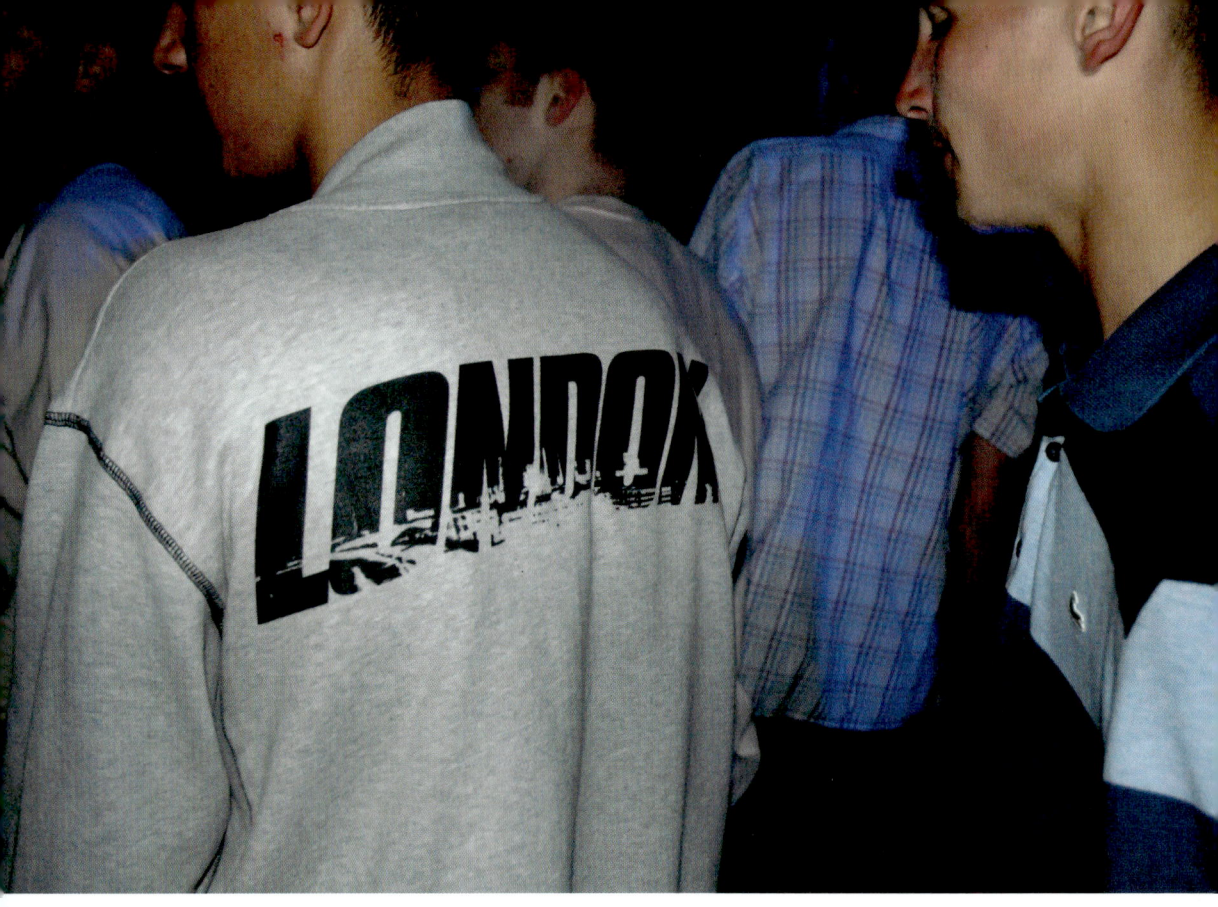

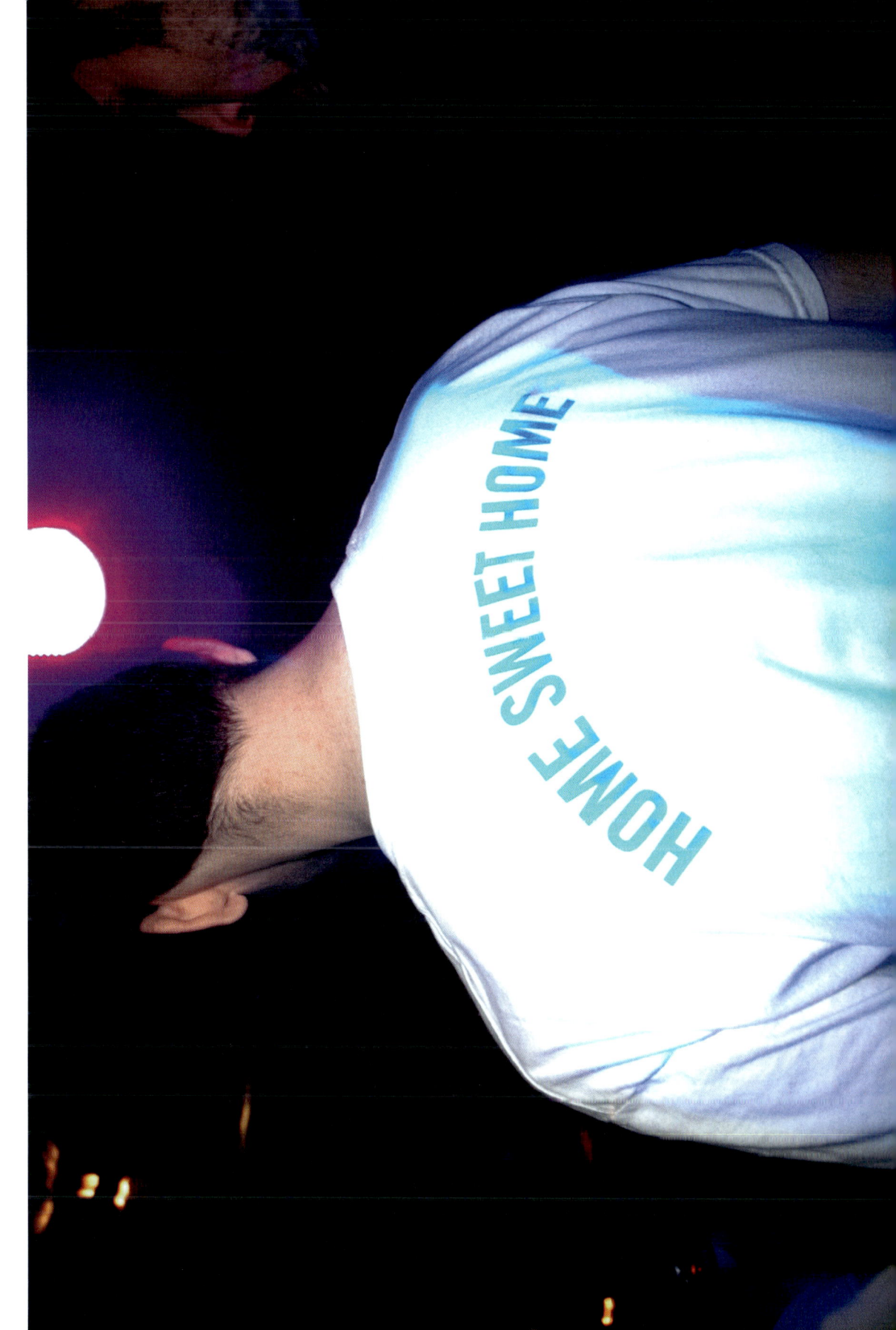

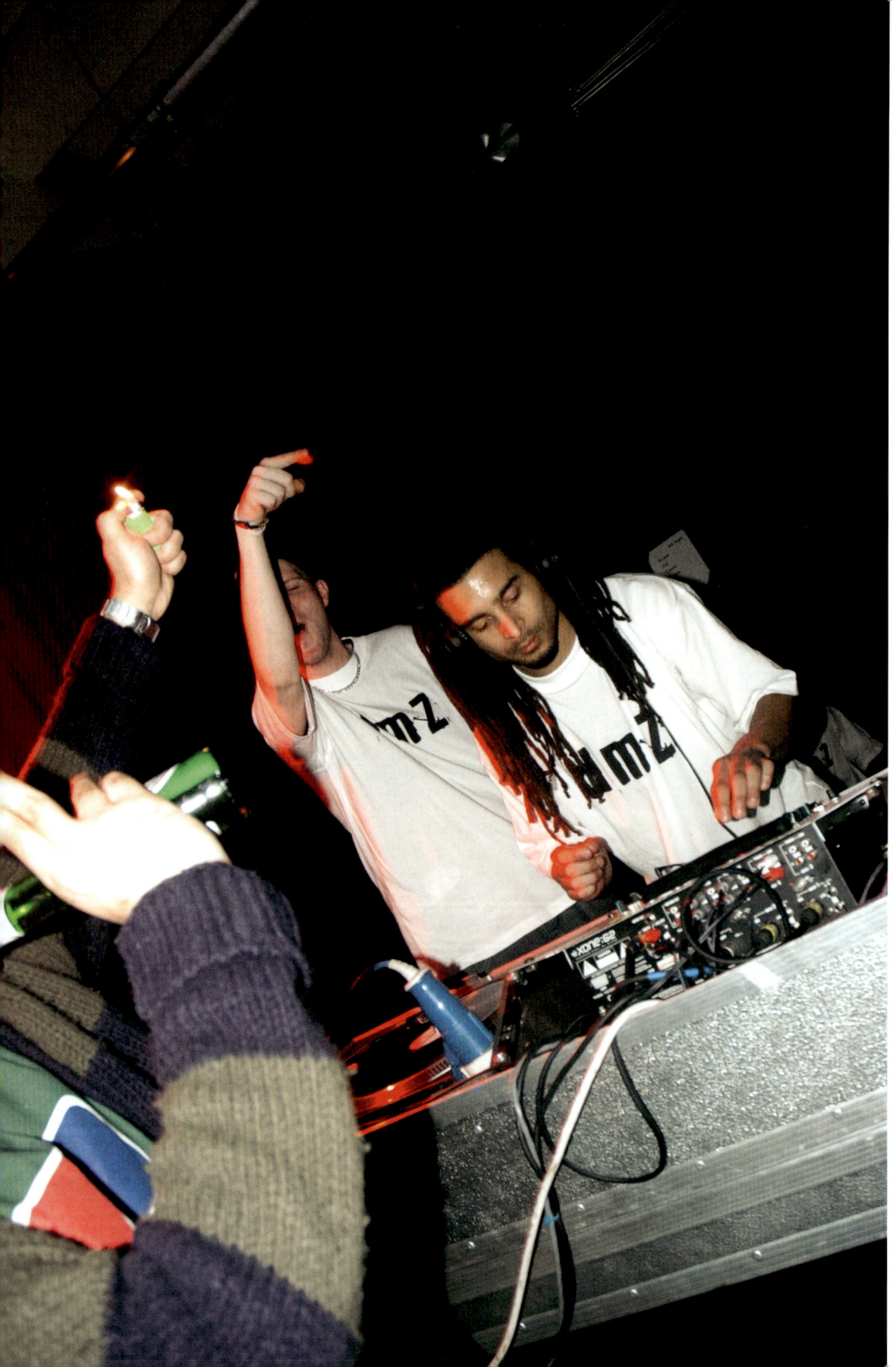

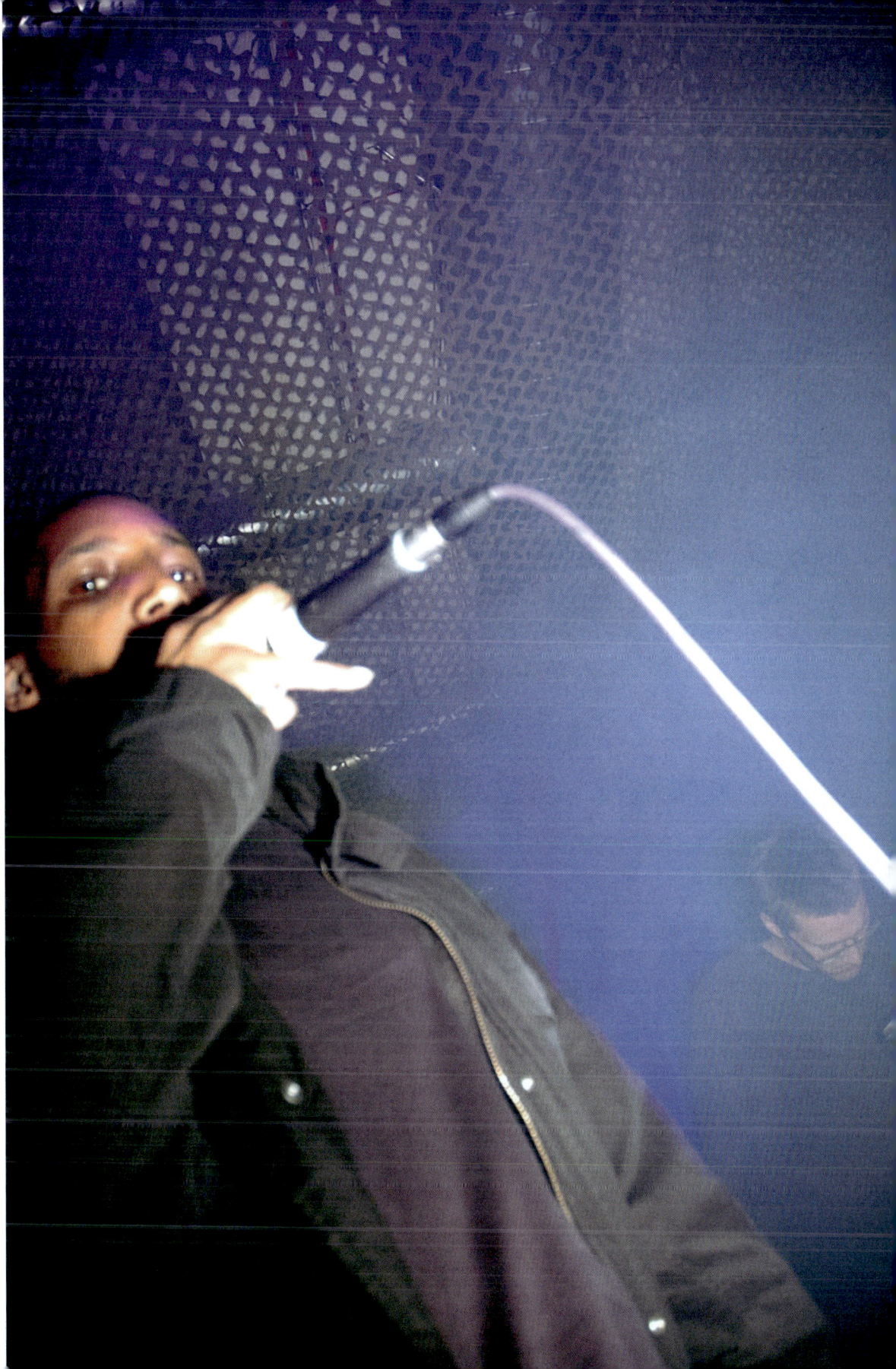

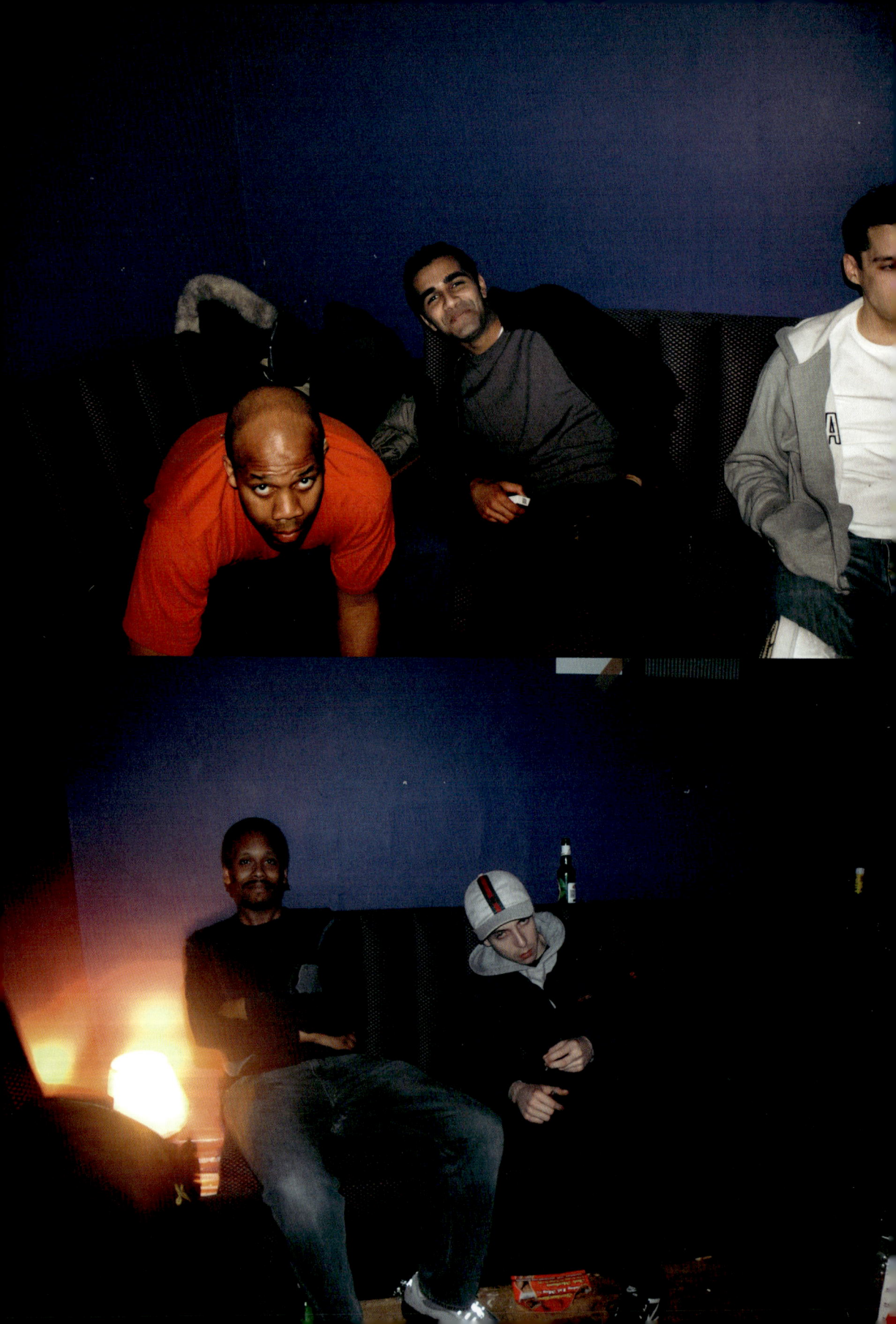

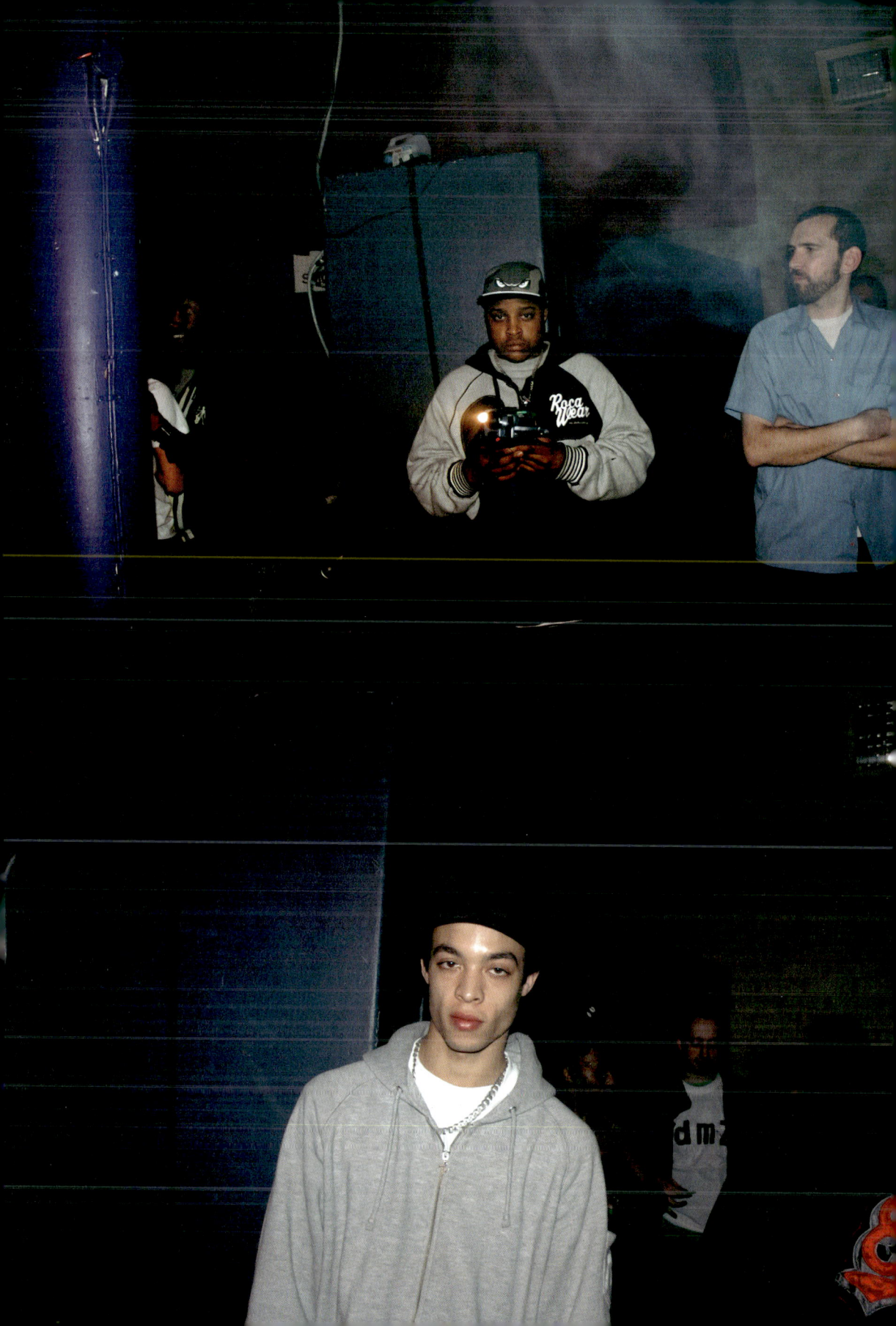

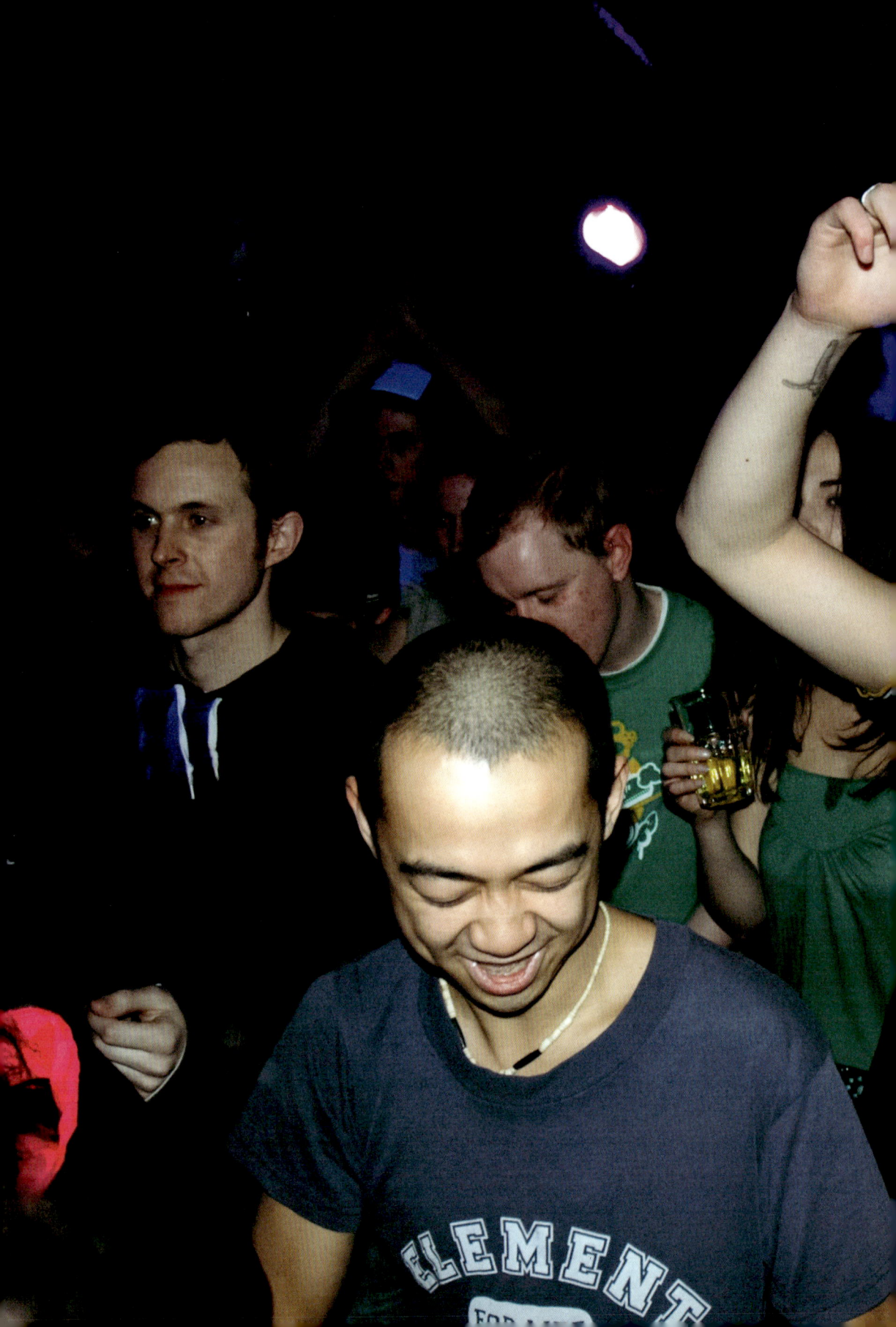

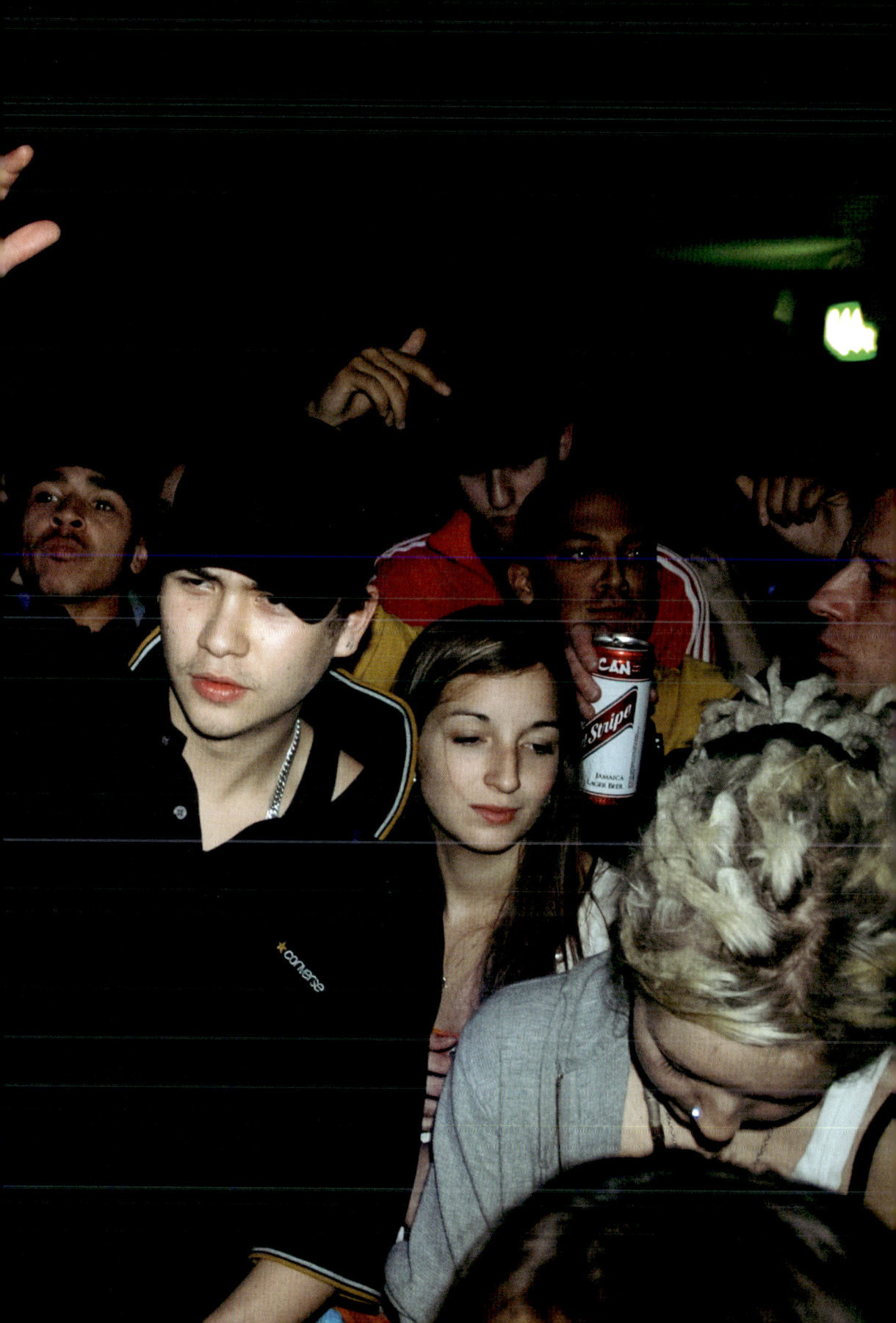

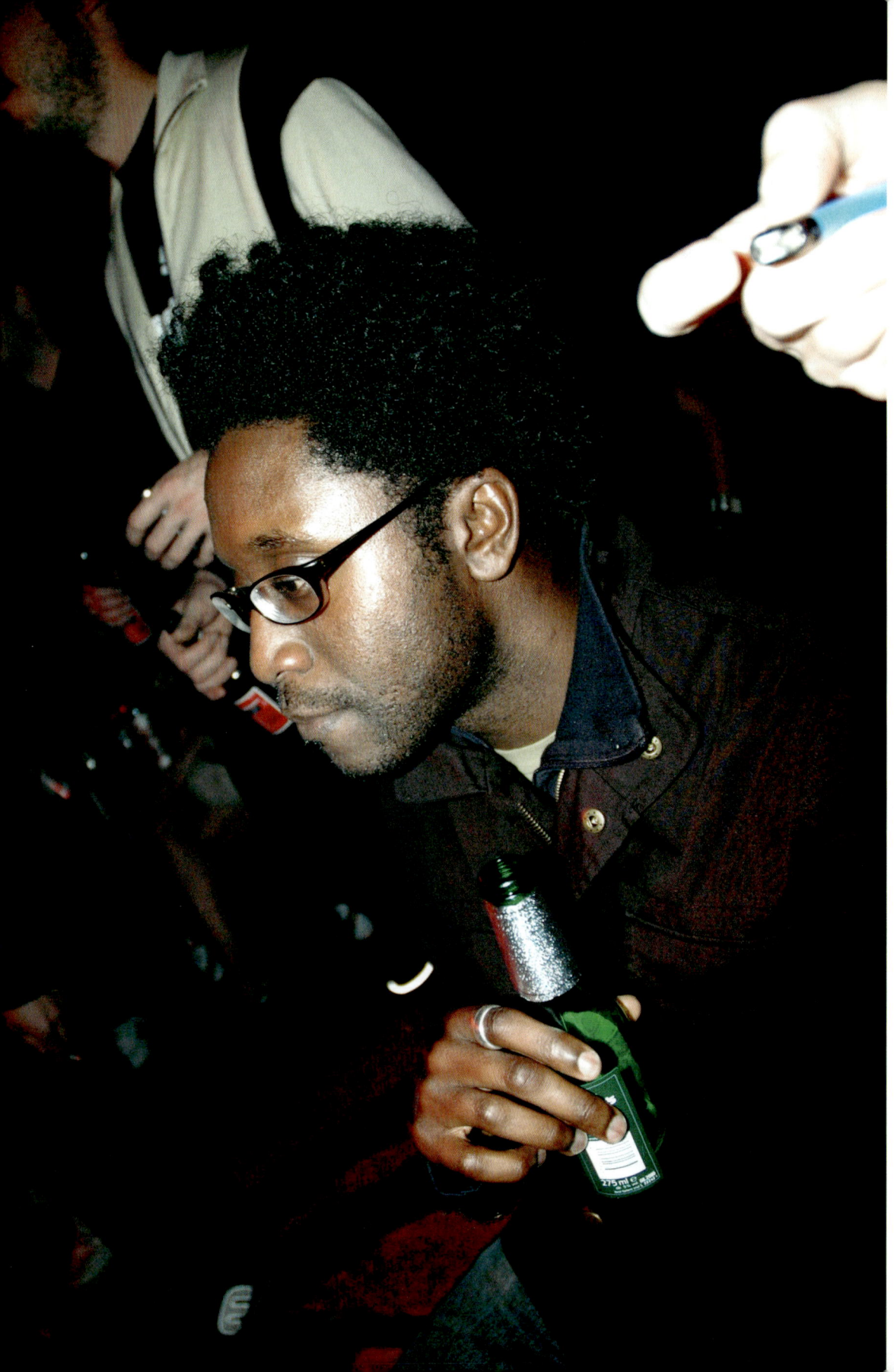

A Basement Of Opportunities

Charlie Dark on Plastic People

As a child of an immigrant, you are born into community. It's within your DNA and imprinted in your soul at every family gathering and with every morsel of food. It's no surprise that it seeps into your approach to business. A life spent navigating the opinions of aunties, uncles and extended family makes you hyper-aware of the power of listening and the magic that occurs when you bring people together and the bar of excellence is set high.

When people ask me what I do for a living I used to tell them I build, nurture and grow communities but if I'm honest the word "community" doesn't sit well with me anymore. It's become a buzzword for brands to sell products by people who've never really been part of a community but are great at pushing numbers around. So, if anything these days I'm more concerned with building movements that empower people to bring change to themselves and by doing so, the people around them. Movements that can exist without the help of outsiders and are self-sufficient, much like Run Dem Crew, which is the movement I'm most known for. An Urban Run Collective I founded in 2007, it has since morphed into a global movement much like the music and scenes that came out of the basement incubator we fondly refer to as Plastic People.

Nowadays the small basement with the red light is spoken about with an almost mythical tone

Nowadays the small basement with the red light is spoken about with an almost mythical tone. If the number of people who claim to have raved within its walls were true, perhaps it would never have closed its doors and would certainly have been ten times the size, but I digress.

My Plastic People story began with my good friend Acyde, whom I'd first encountered in another cultural hub of music, the legendary Blue Note club in Hoxton Square. Home to seminal nights such as Goldie's Metalheadz, James Lavelle's Mo Wax night Dusted and the Soundz of the Asian Underground with Anokha, it was the club that planted the seed for the resurgence in interest in Shoreditch and beyond. Nigerian-born and Hackney-residing, Acyde was next in line in a lineage of larger-than-life characters from West Africa who'd made Shoreditch their home in the days when warehouses were cheap, parties were thriving and the creative current that radiated through its streets was infectiously inspiring.

Once Plastic People departed from its original Oxford Street home, it was destined that it would cement its legacy in East London because a forest of West African creatives had already set up shop and the seeds of a creative community had already been planted.

From back in the late '80s, Wunmi, then of Soul to Soul, was tearing up the dance floor at the Bass Clef on Monday nights. This continued right through to Saturdays in its new incarnation as The Blue Note. The early frontline soldiers of the sound propped up the speaker stacks. Man like Ranx, who seemed to have the keys to every empty space in the area was among them. Tony Nwachukwu, Wale Adeyemi, myself, Acyde, and Ade Fakile - the driving engine behind the basement with the best sound on the planet - were also part of the scene. In that basement, every tune sounded amazing and the best DJs on the planet made it their home. Plastic was multicultural, everyone was welcome, and similarities were celebrated while differences were explored.

Acyde told me about a new club in Shoreditch run by a Nigerian guy who was open to giving people nights at a time when getting your foot through the

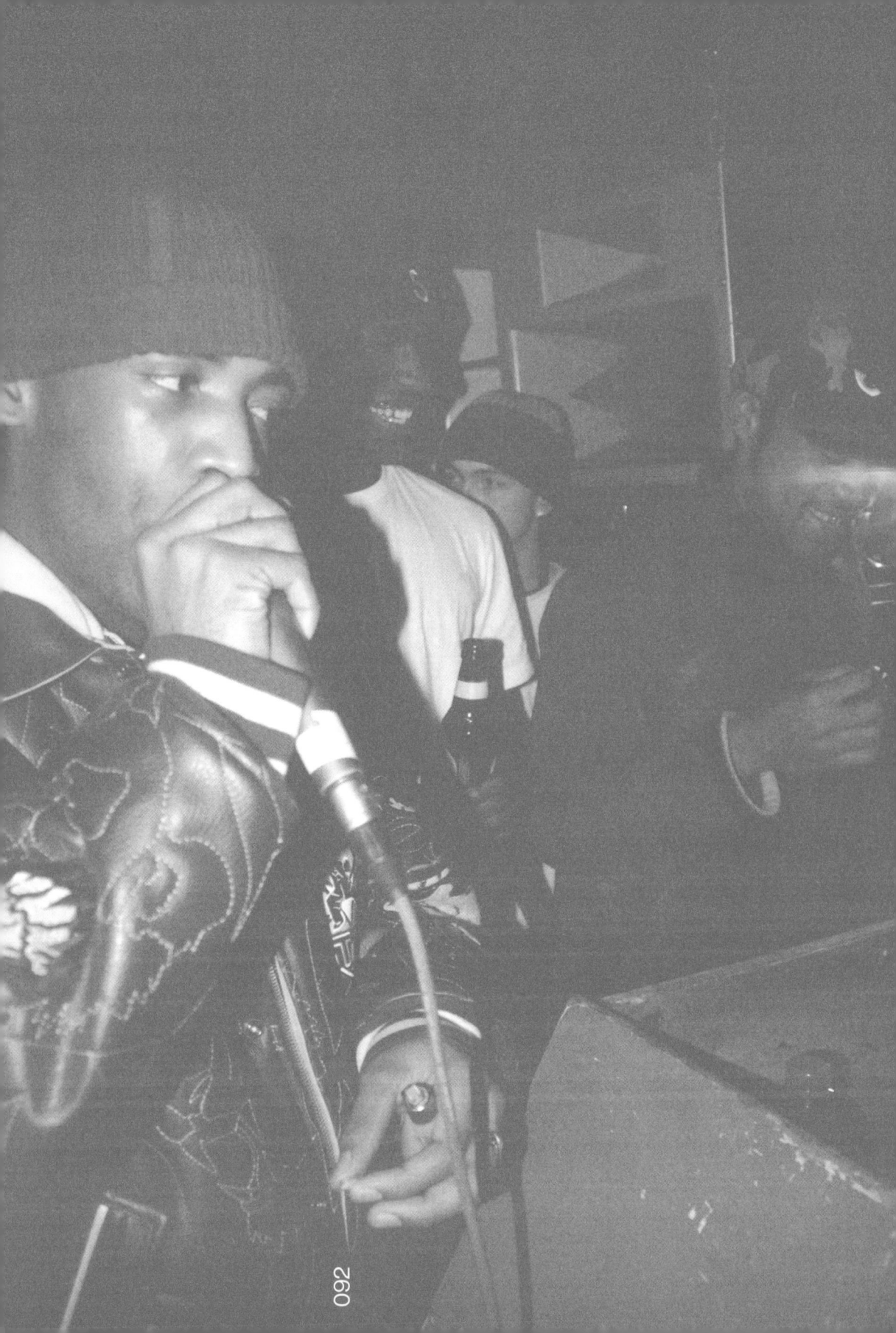

door was becoming increasingly hard if you weren't playing the commercial music of the times. We went down, met Ade, and a few weeks later we launched a monthly Sunday night that morphed into various nights run by myself and friends that ran throughout its opening.

Despite the plethora of quality nights at the club, Ade still gave smaller promoters chances to try out ideas knowing they had the potential to grow into something bigger. Like any great community leader, he saw the light in you before you flicked the switch and his track record as a curator was exemplary.

I always say that the sign of a great club is when producers from different scenes can be found hovering around the DJ box, even though the music is far removed from what they are making and Plastic was one of those places. A basement of opportunities where anything was possible, and even the most far-out or unknown was encouraged to grow roots.

Egos were left at the top of the stairs and the floor didn't care how many thousands of people you'd rocked the night before

Ade understood that the foremost rule of a great party is a roomful of different personalities united by an appreciation of sound and he spared no expense in building the best sound system he could and sharing its wonders with the best selectors he could find. Even if it meant interrupting a set to switch out the needles for better fidelity or dragging out the EMTs on a FWD>> night because he knew the dubplates would sound better through its circuitry despite Youngsta's protests.

In retrospect, we were spoilt at Plastic and the community ethos that amplified through the speakers is sadly missed during current times. It didn't matter who you were; egos were left at the top of the stairs and the floor didn't care how many thousands of people you'd rocked the night before - it was all about how you represented in the booth.

For a community to thrive it needs a leader with strong values, a clear vision and a manifesto that empowers its members and Plastic had all of that in spades. When the crowd started to change and the Saturday night requests became too much, Ade would have no qualms about refunding punters' money and escorting them out of the door if they ignored the signs to leave the DJ alone, fostering a community that policed the floor ensuring idiots didn't ruin the night or the flow of the music.

It's little wonder that so many great sessions came out of that building because, like all of the best communities, it encouraged people to come together to help each other be the best that they could be. You couldn't make weak music or cut subpar dubplates when you knew they were going to be played on the best sound system on the planet which meant the club was always on your mind whenever you sat down to create musical magic to be shared.

The Source
Jason Goz
on Mastering

33 ⅓

"My mission was to make the building shake when any of the tracks I had cut were played."

It started when someone turned up to cut a track by Horsepower's Benny III. It was different to everything else that was being made at the time. After a while there was a steady increase of people cutting similar music; it did not have a name but it did have bass. With my background I was happy to oblige.

Around 2005, well after the term "dubstep" was coined, Mala, Coki and Loefah started a night at Mass in Brixton. Mala was kind enough to give me guest-list for life and I used this opportunity to fine tune how my dubs and masters translated on their Funktion One rig.

My mission was to make the building shake when any of the tracks I had cut were played. A bit of knowledge, plus trial and error were used to get the results. Let's not forget that a vinyl record was not designed for that amount of bass so I had to set the lathe up differently in order to wrestle the grooves onto the discs. Some of the mastering techniques I learnt during those early days I still use today when mastering Bass music.

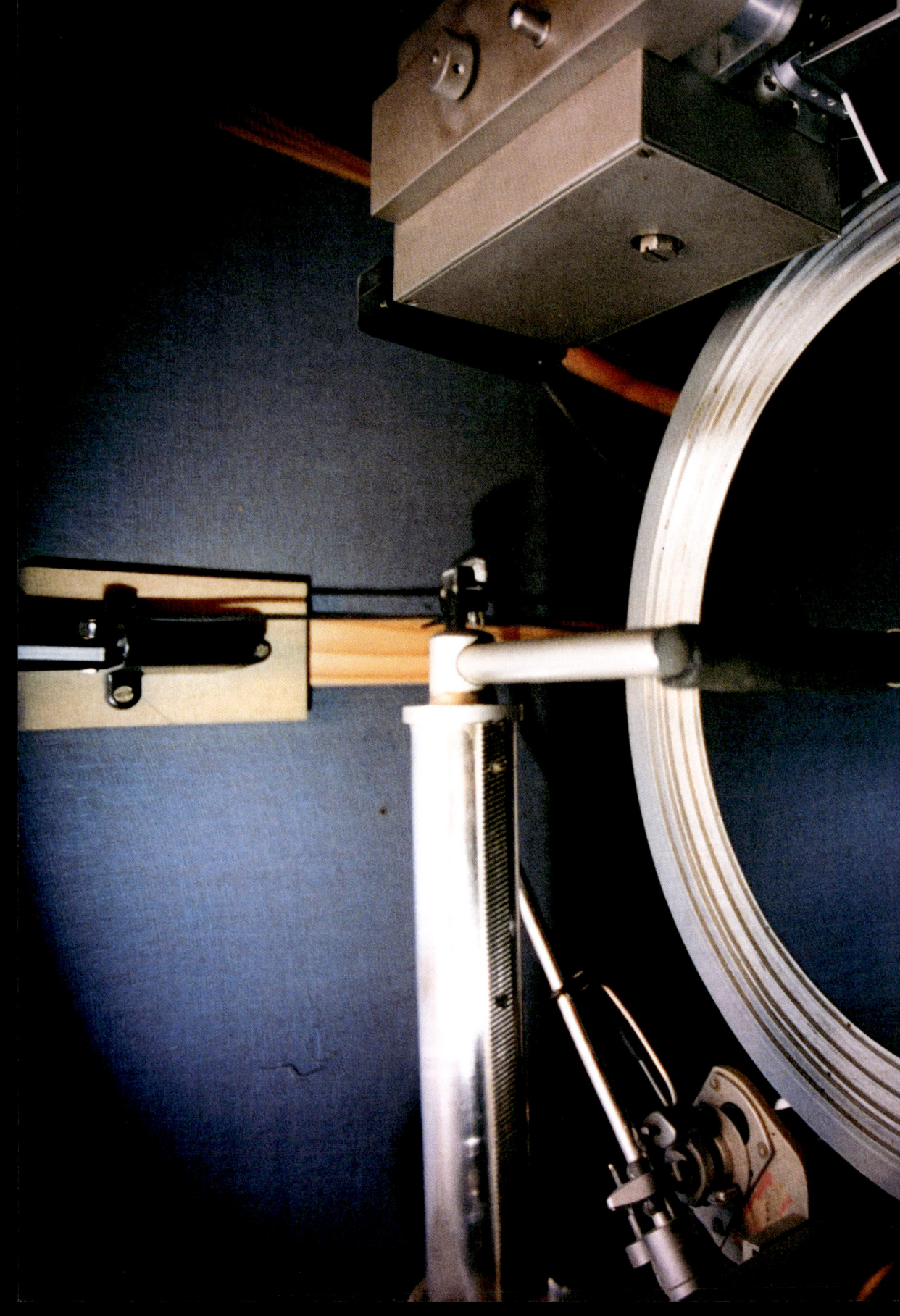

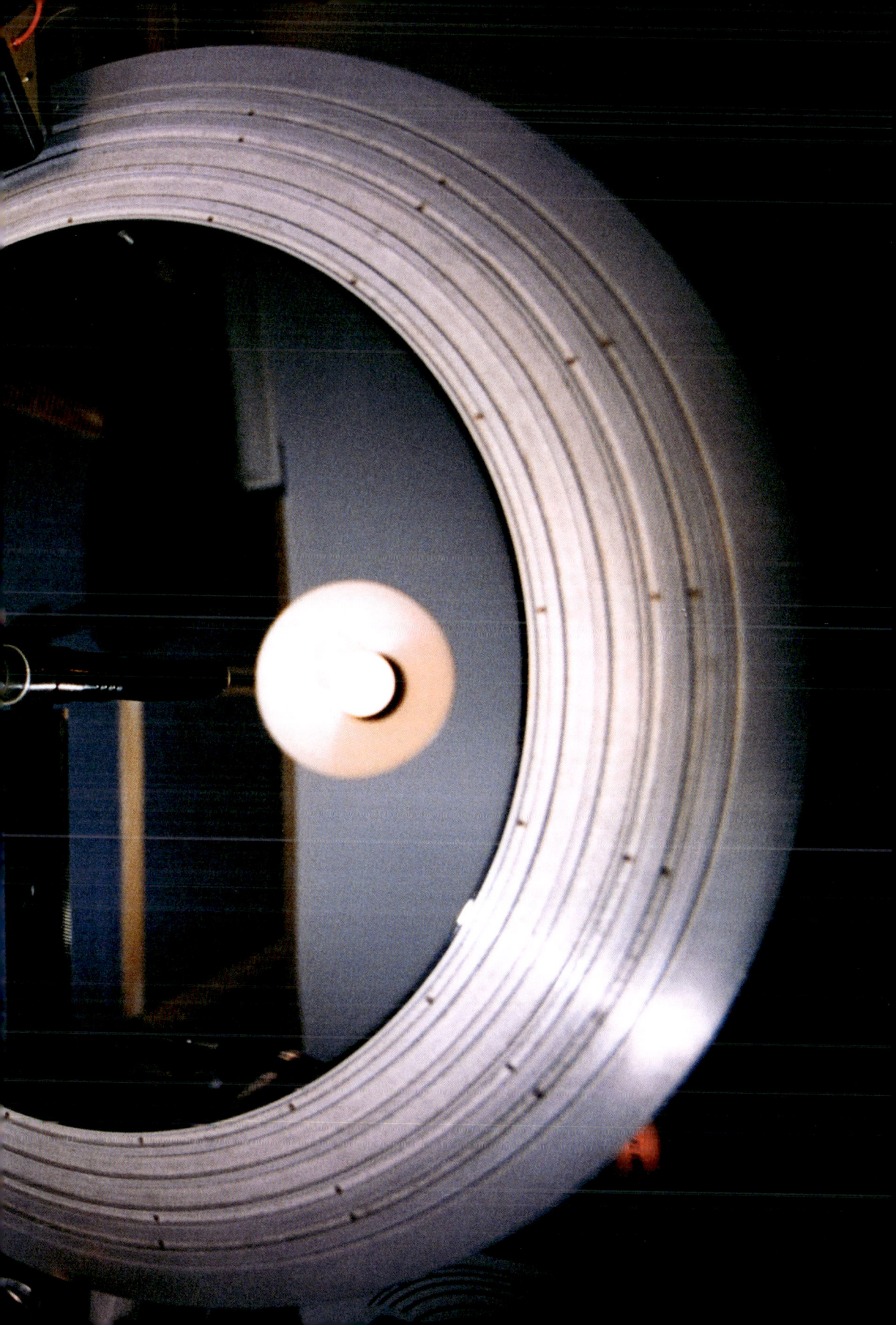

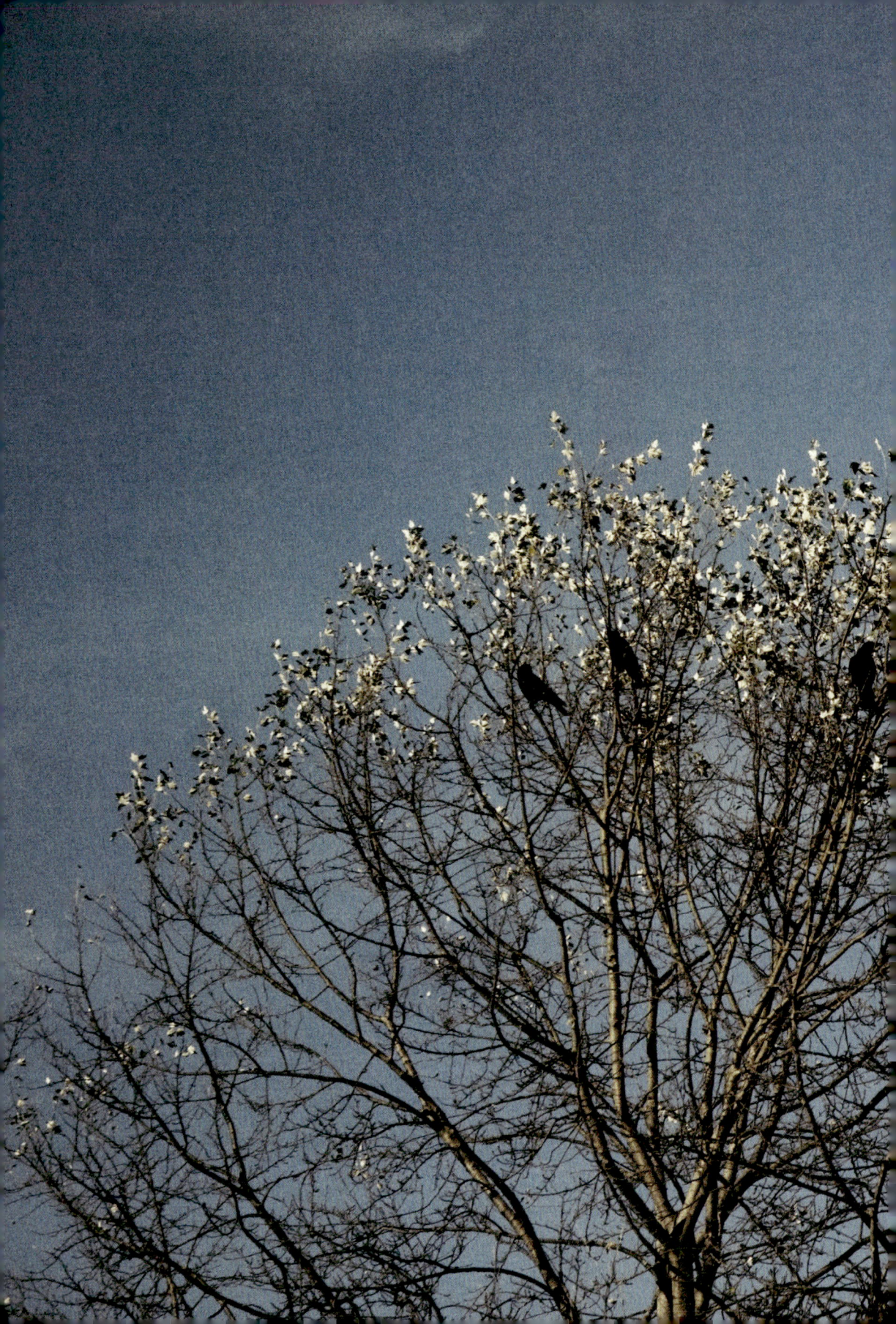

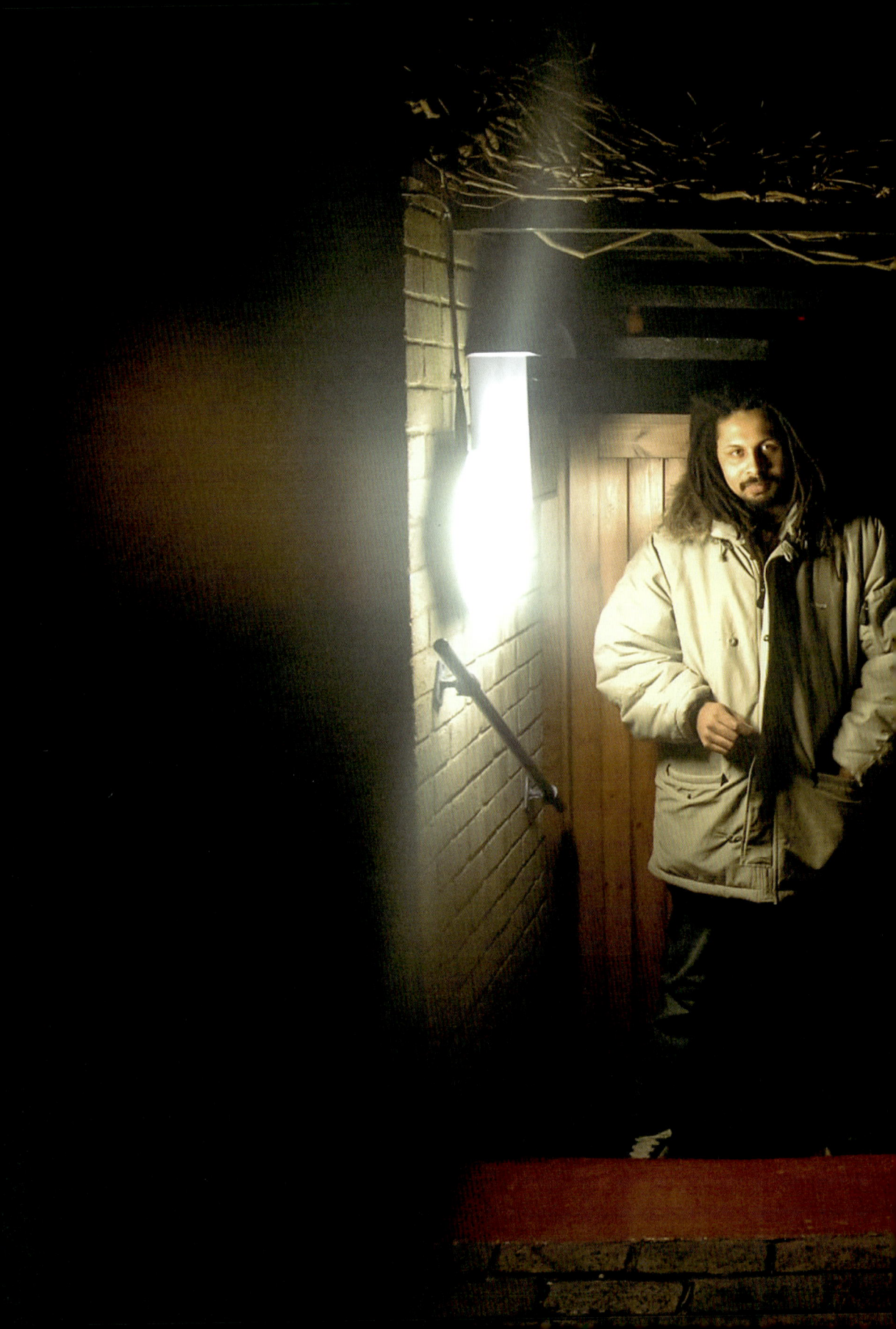

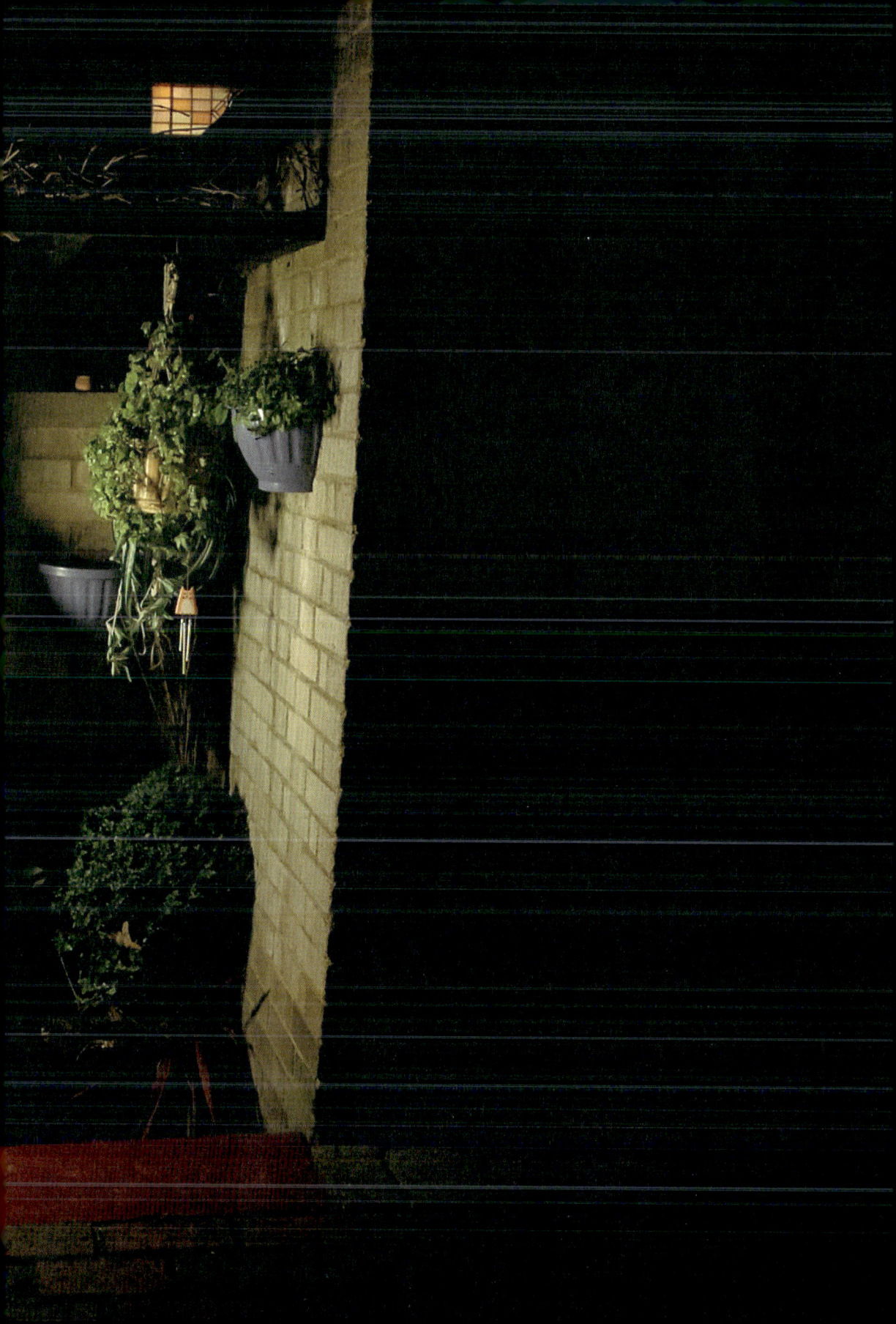

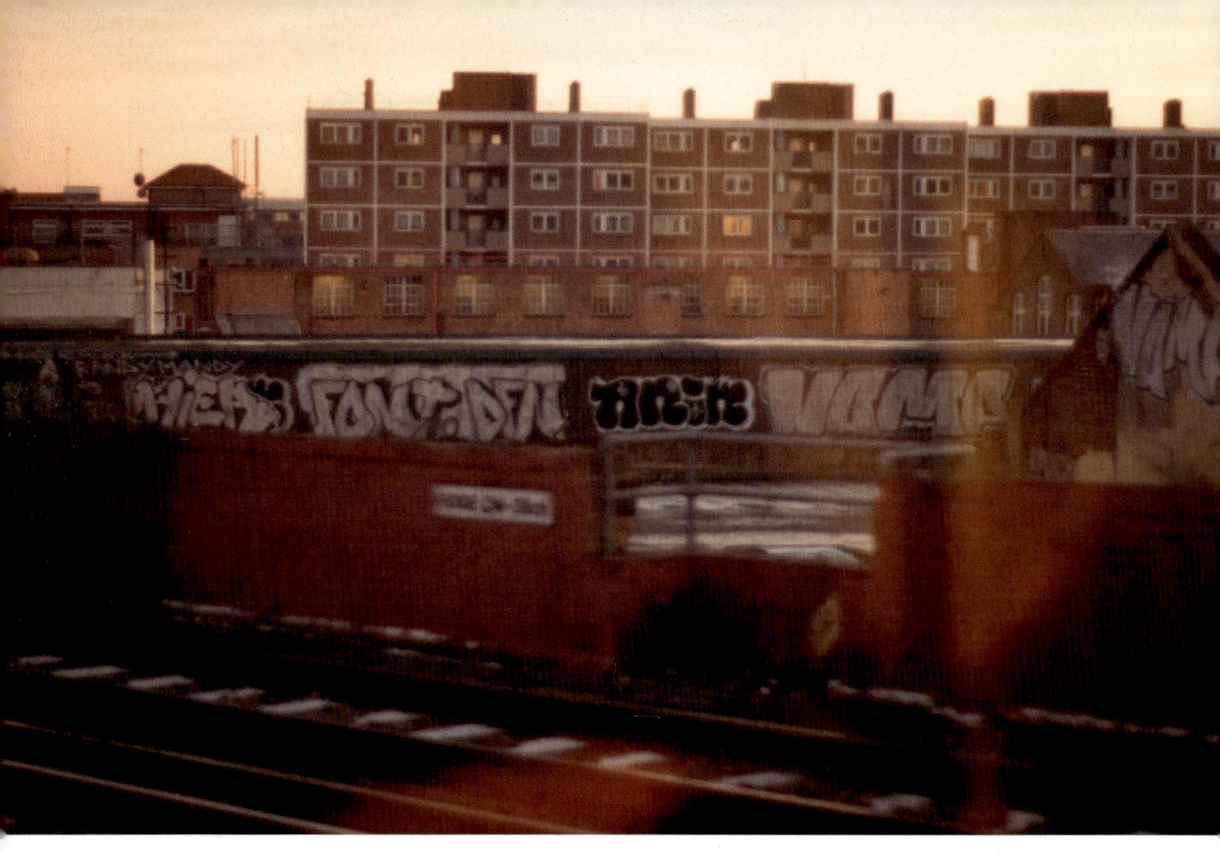

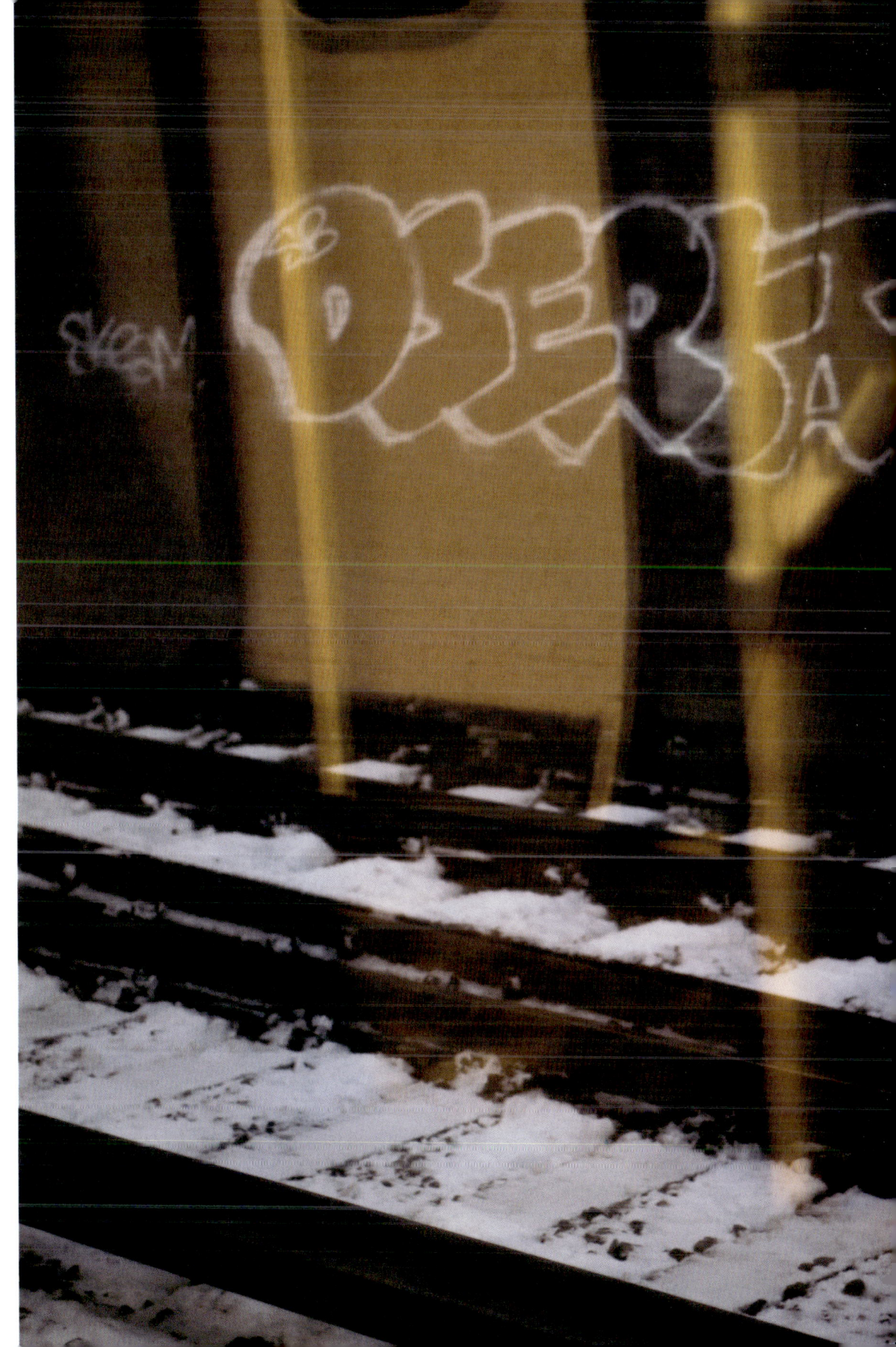

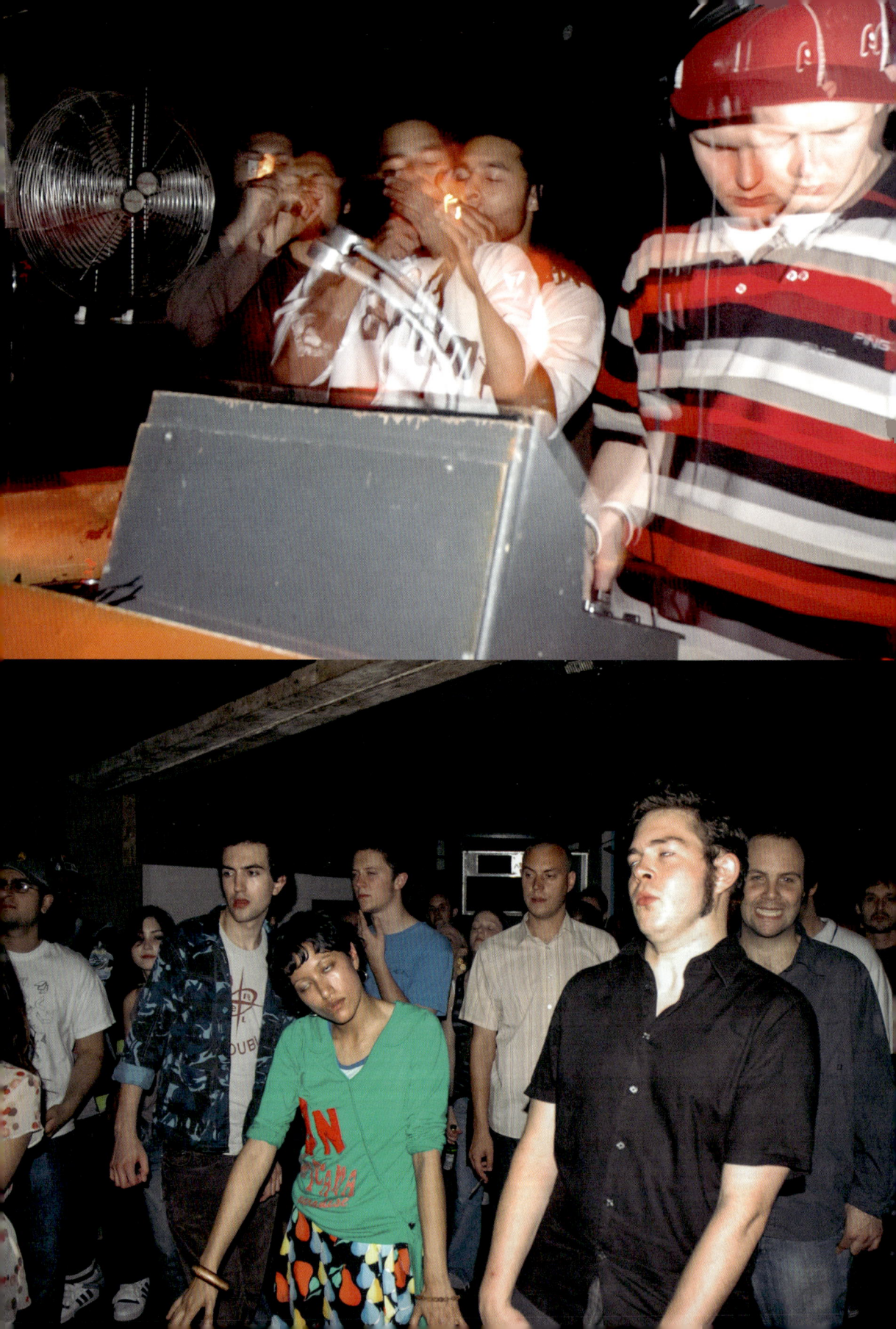

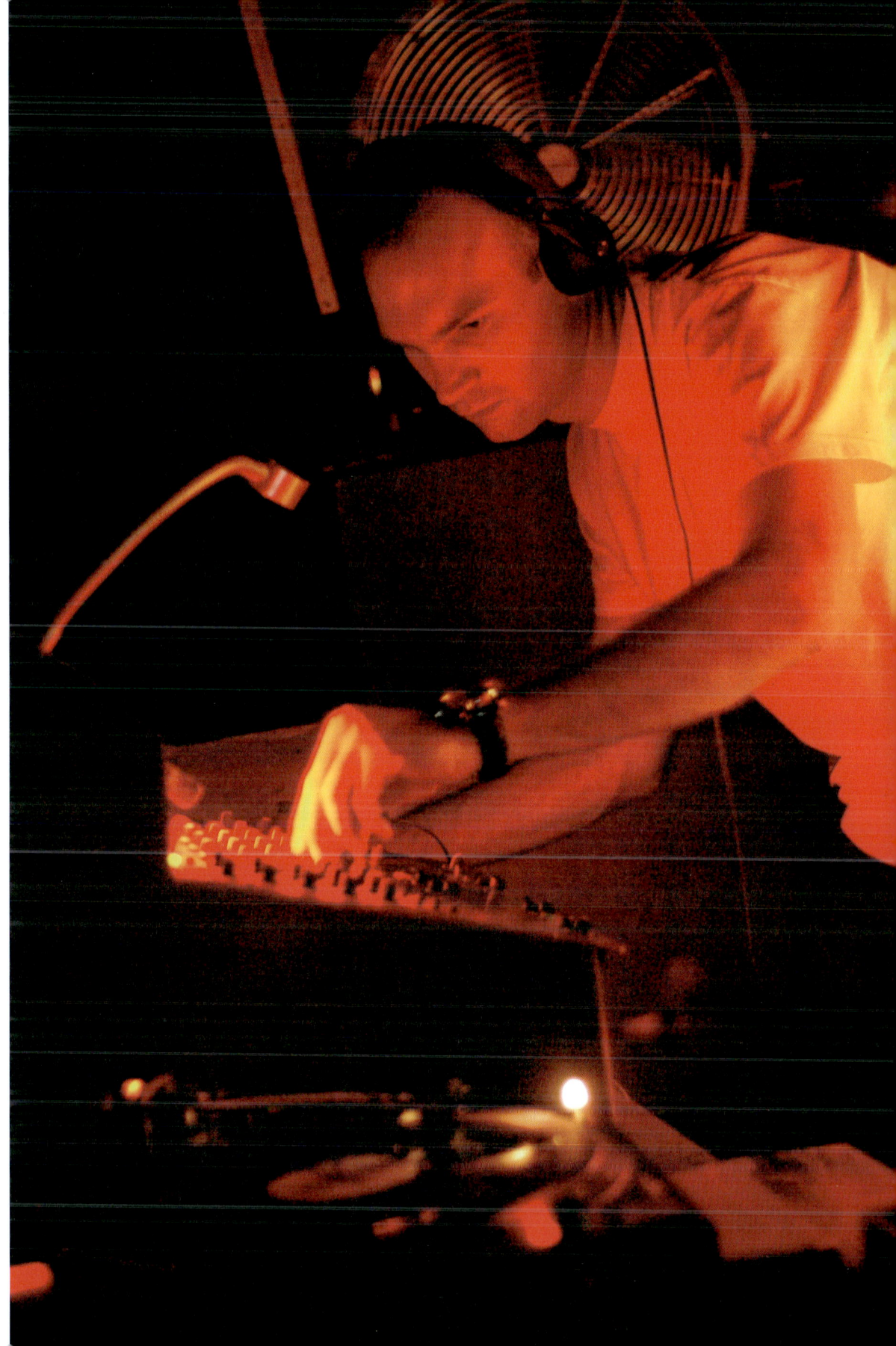

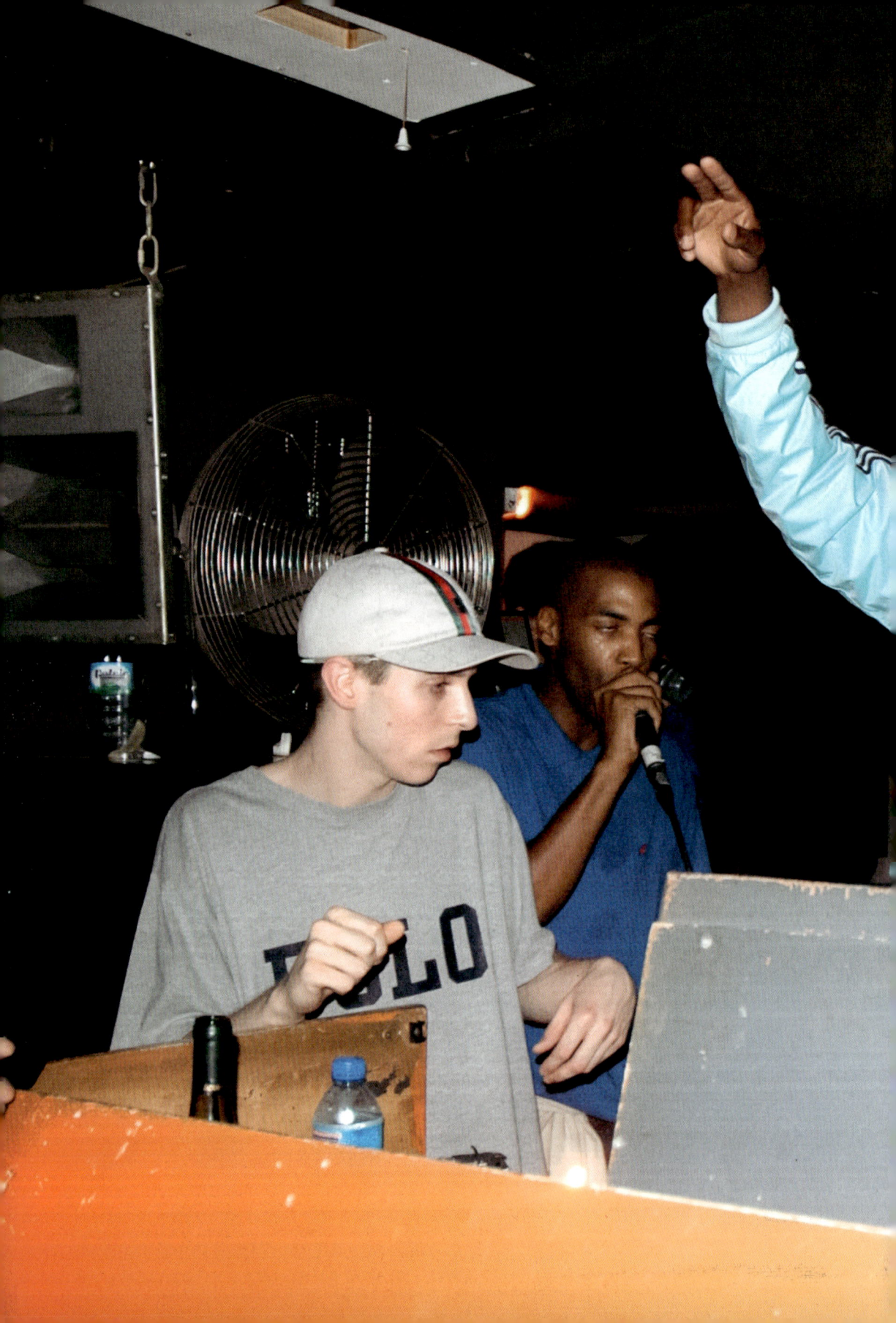

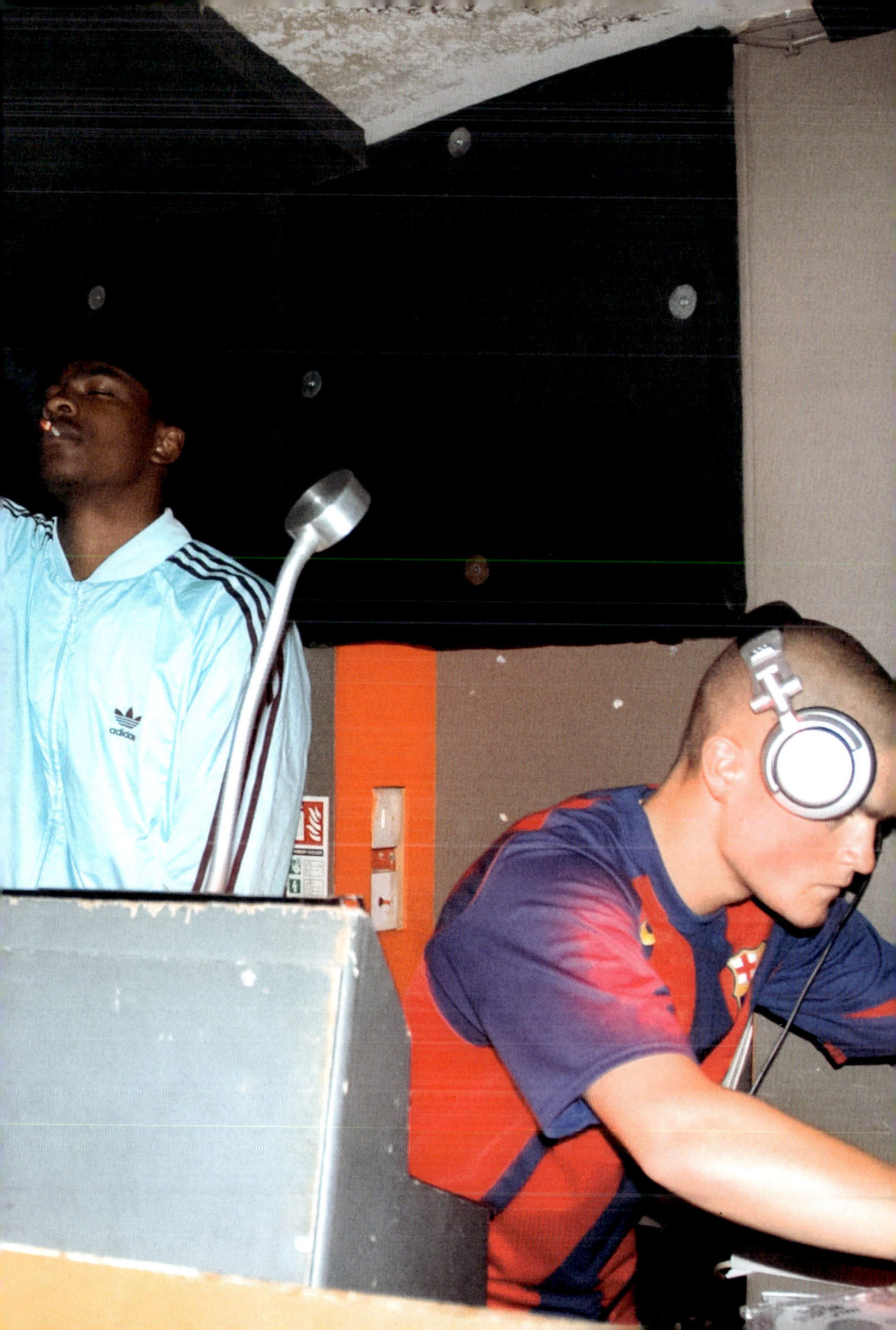

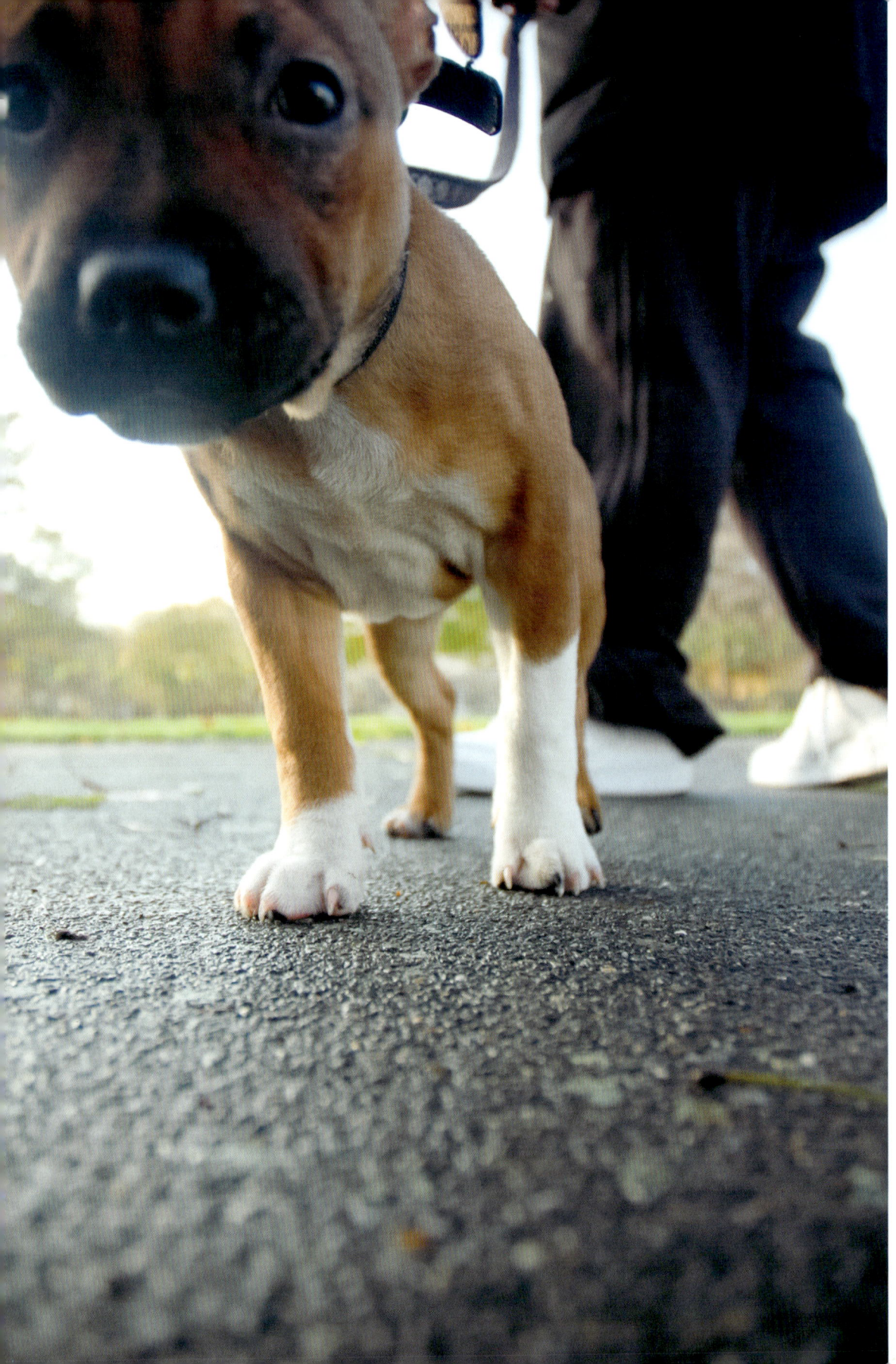

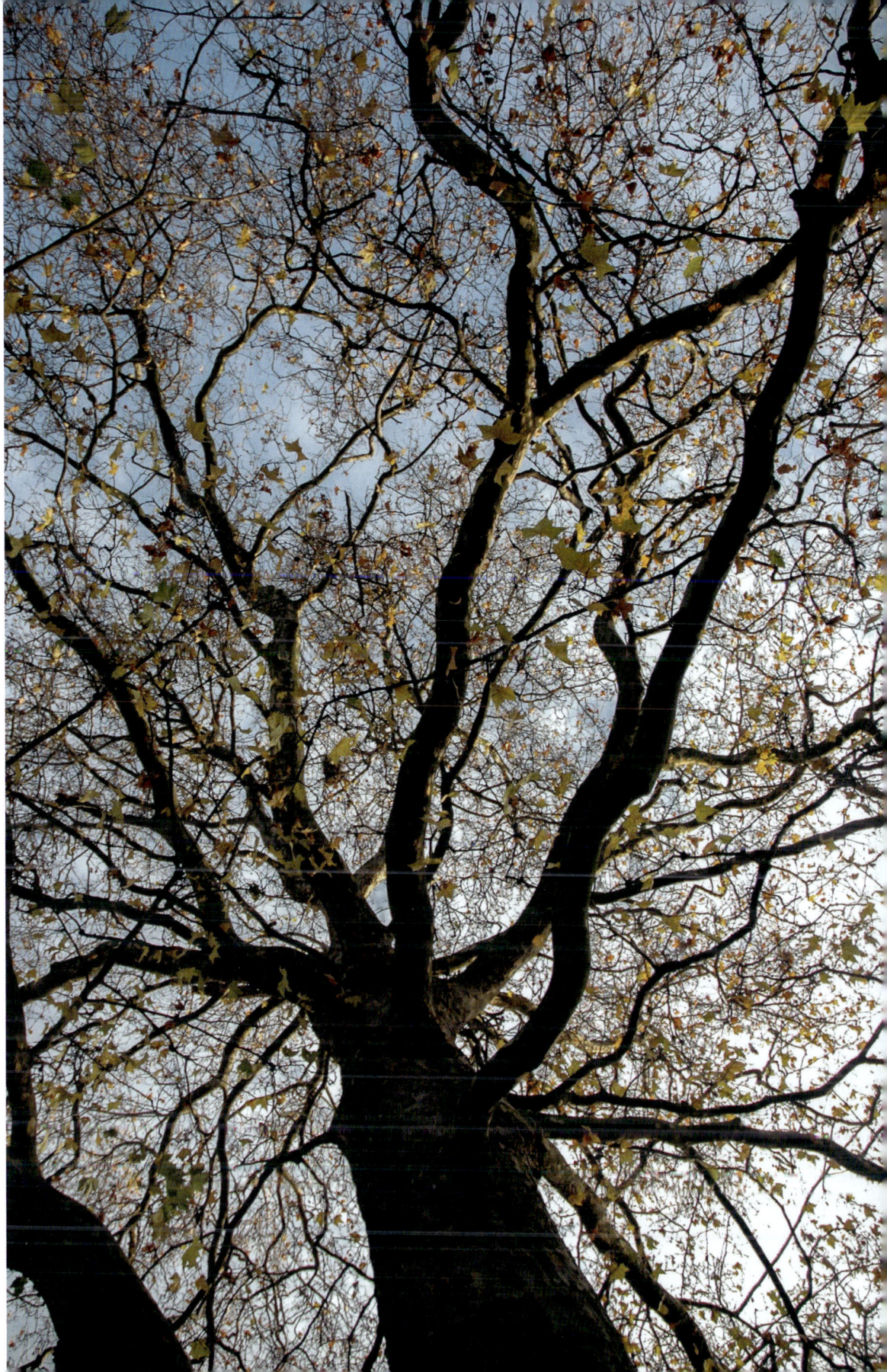

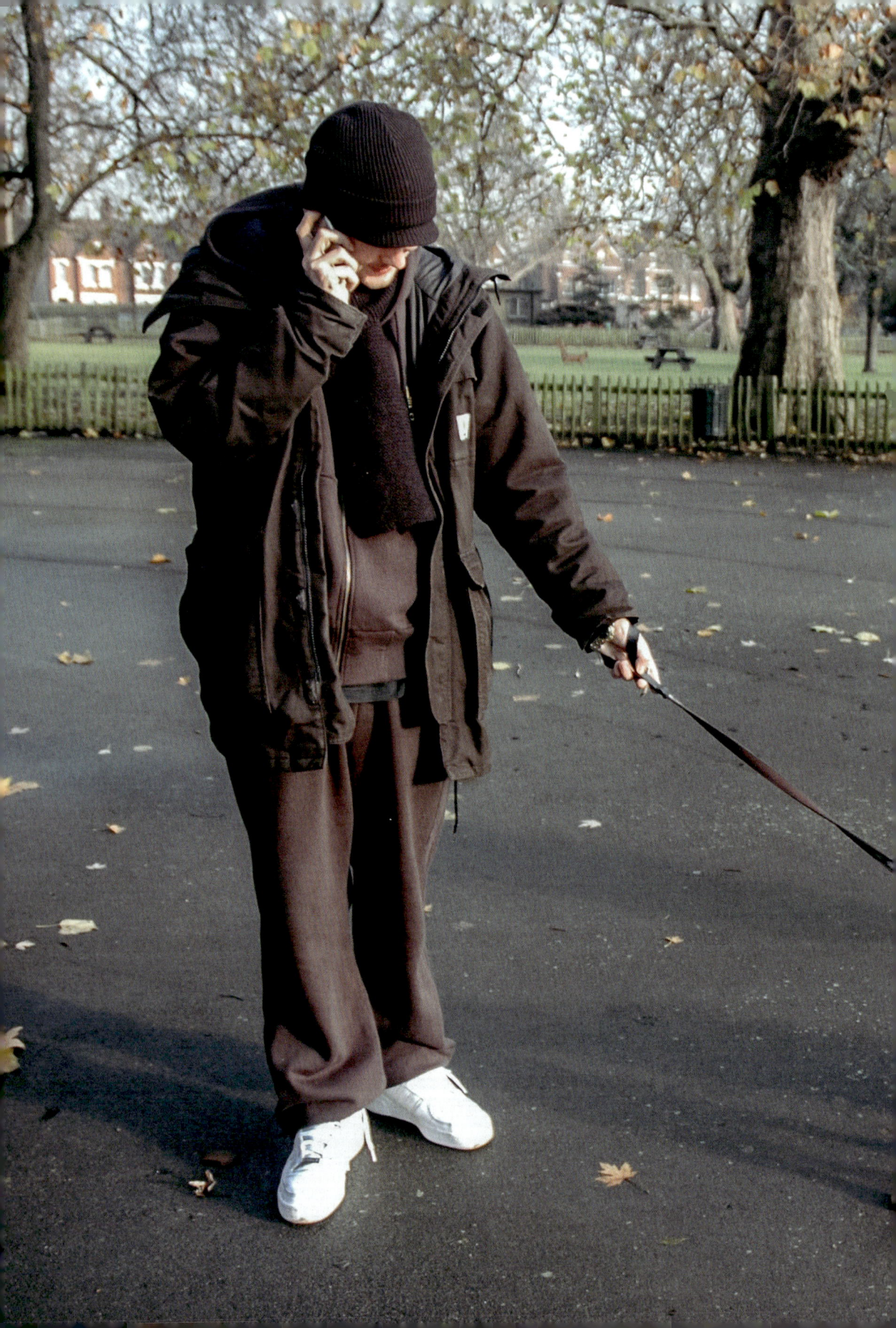

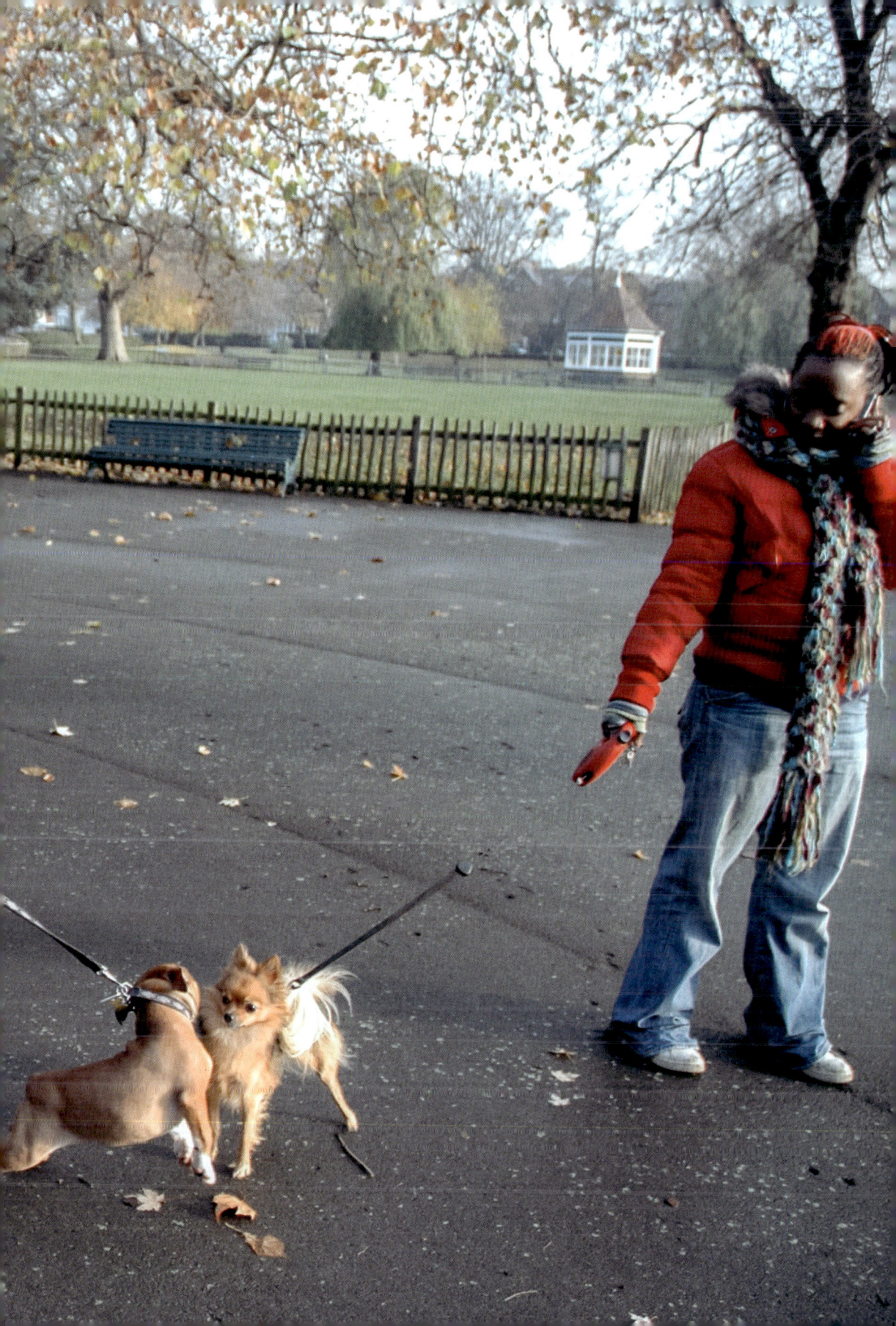

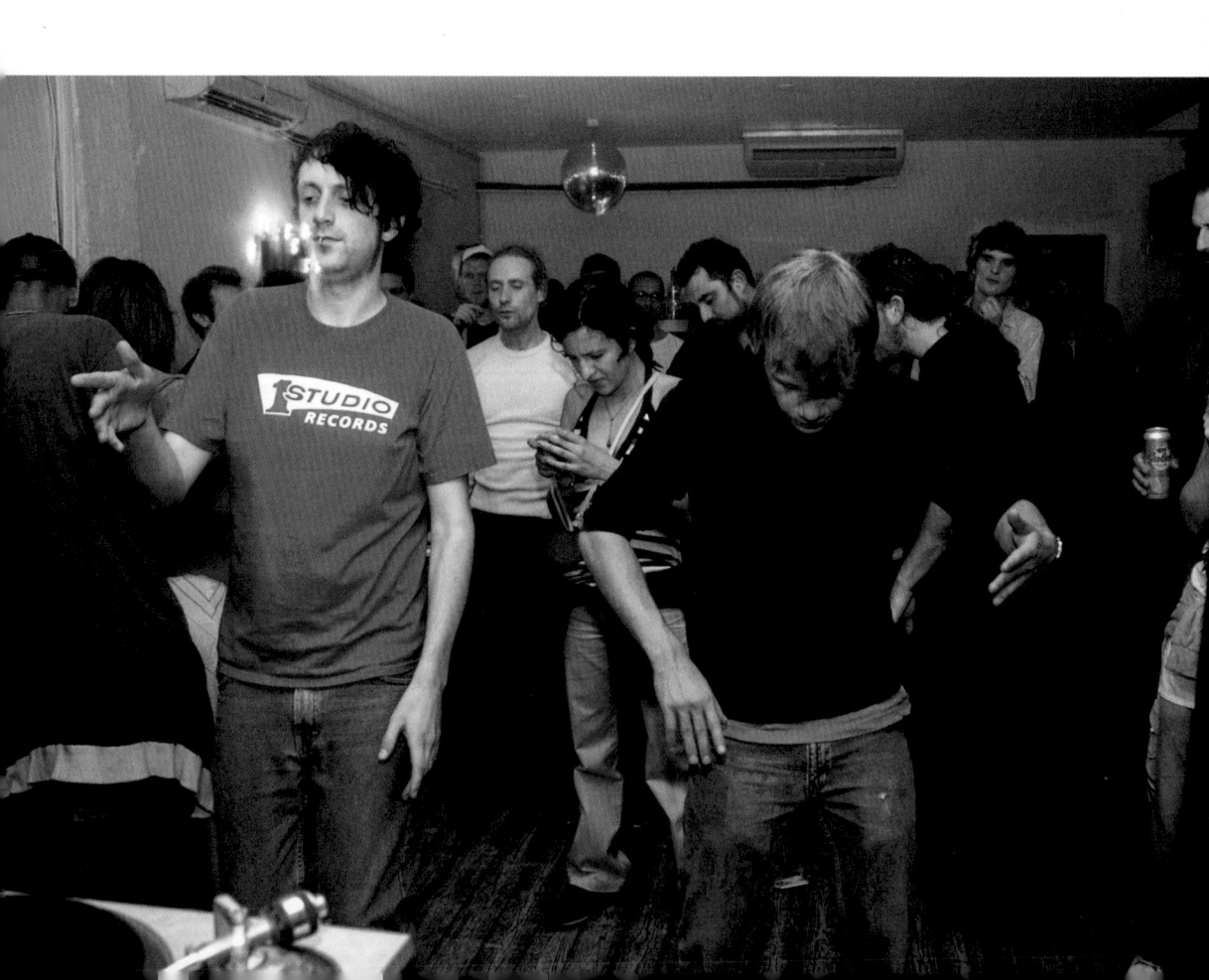

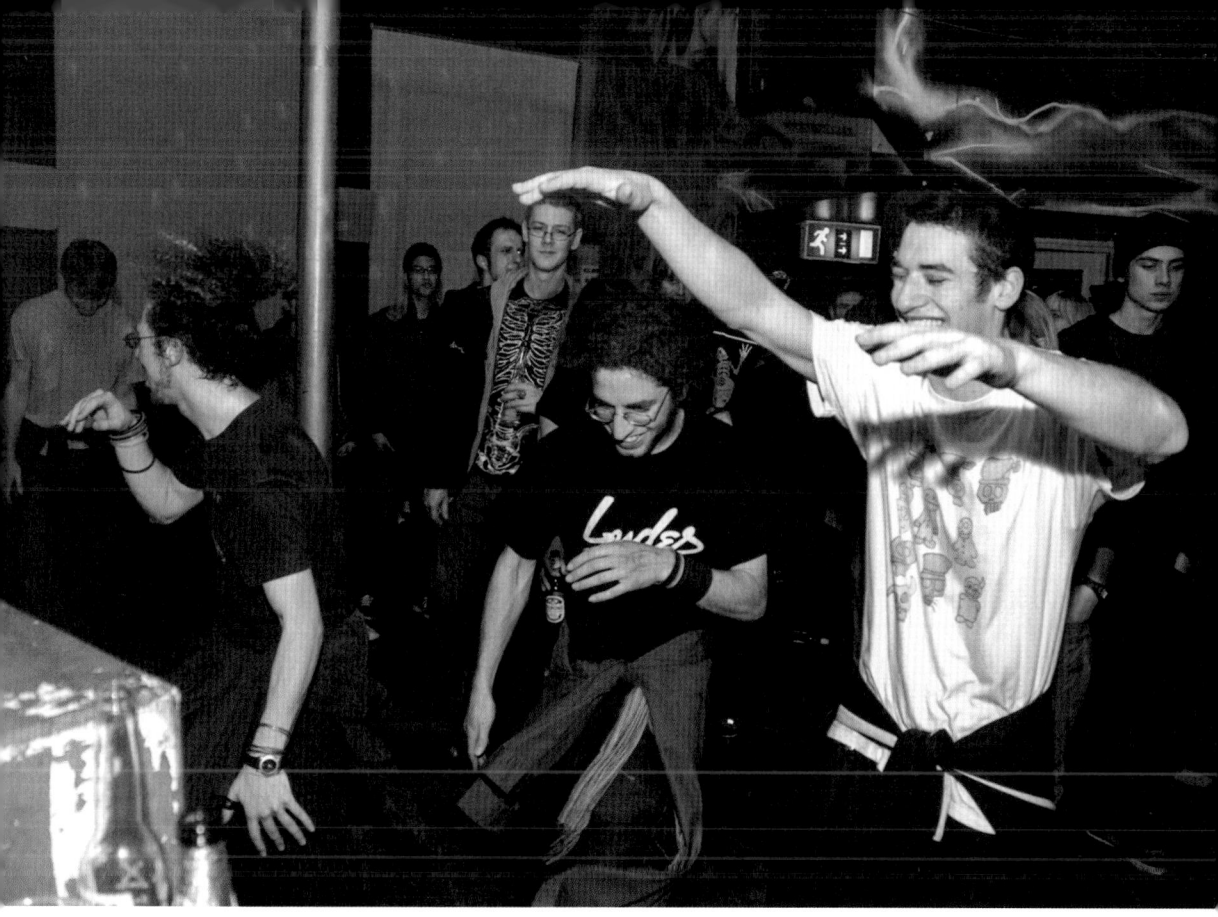

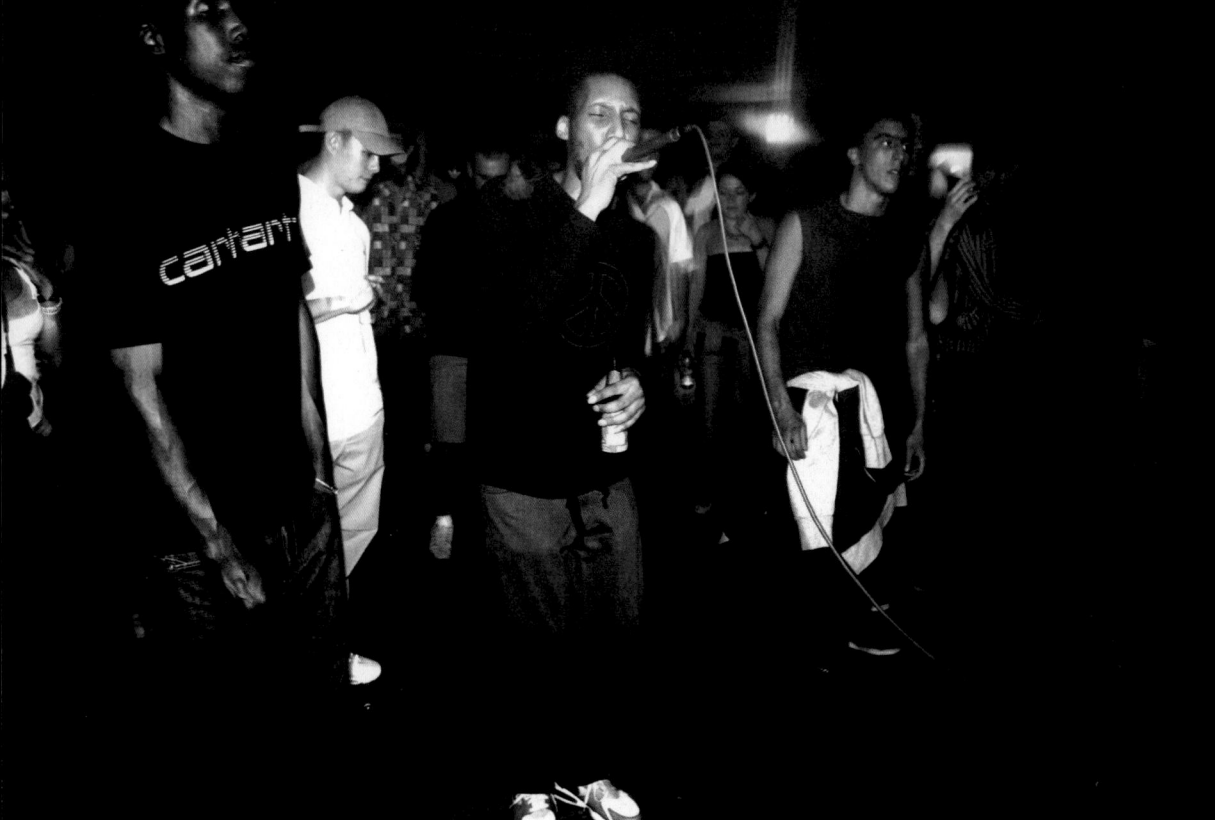

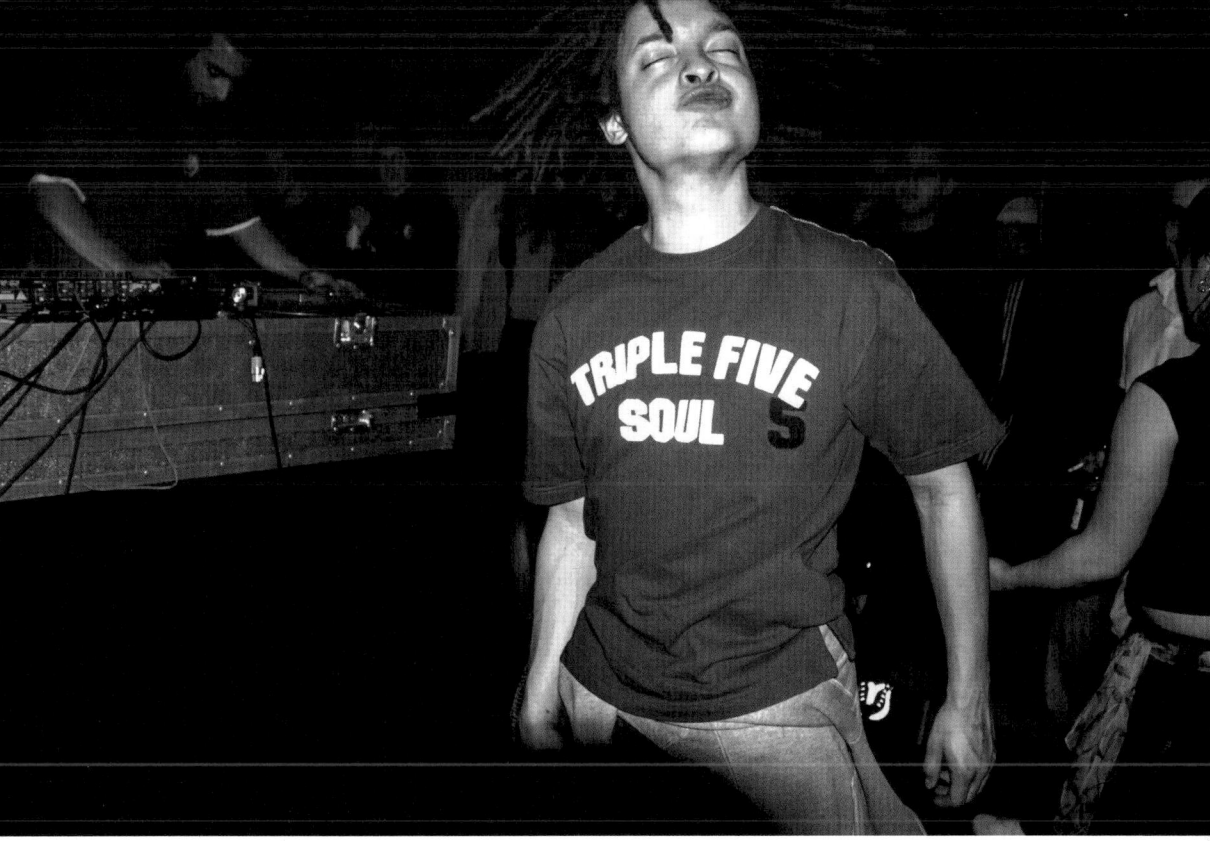

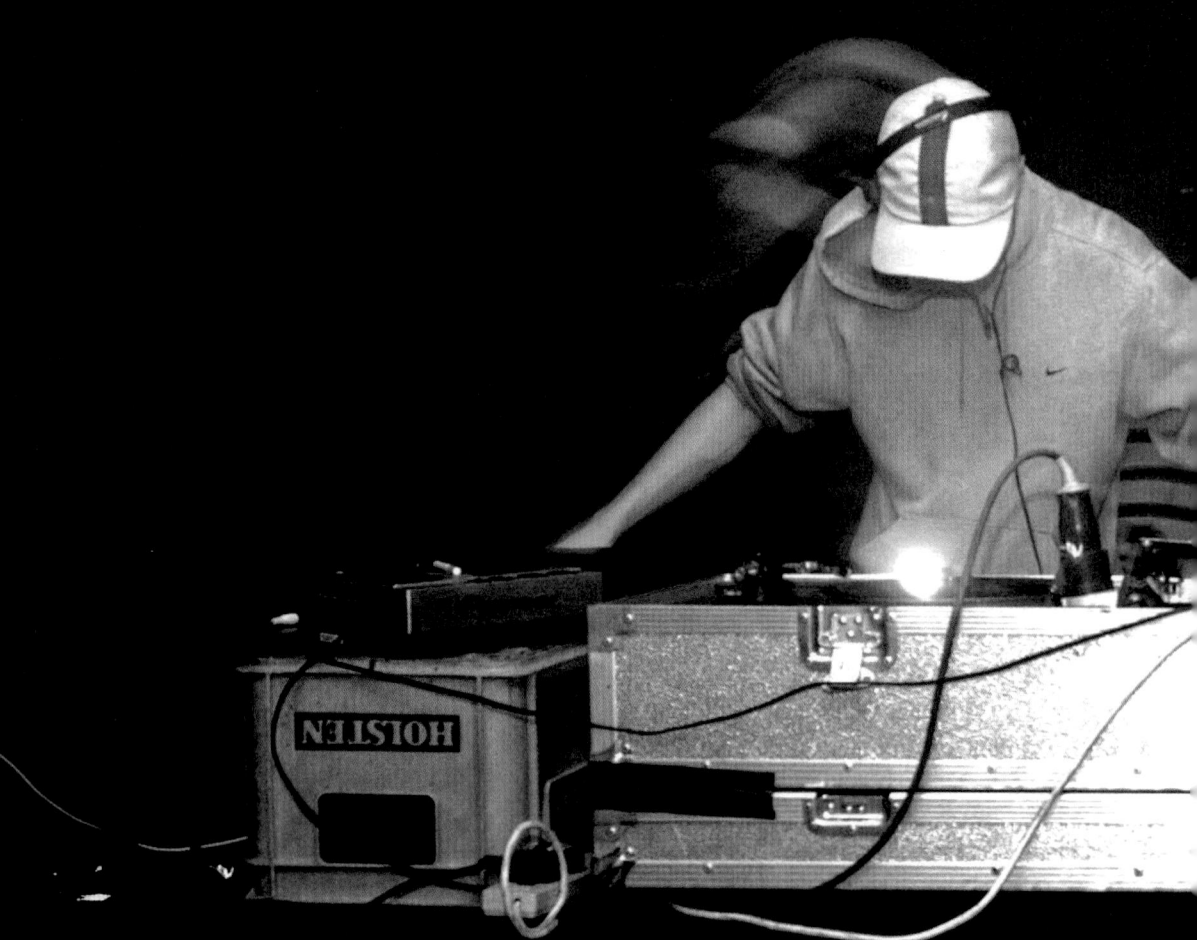

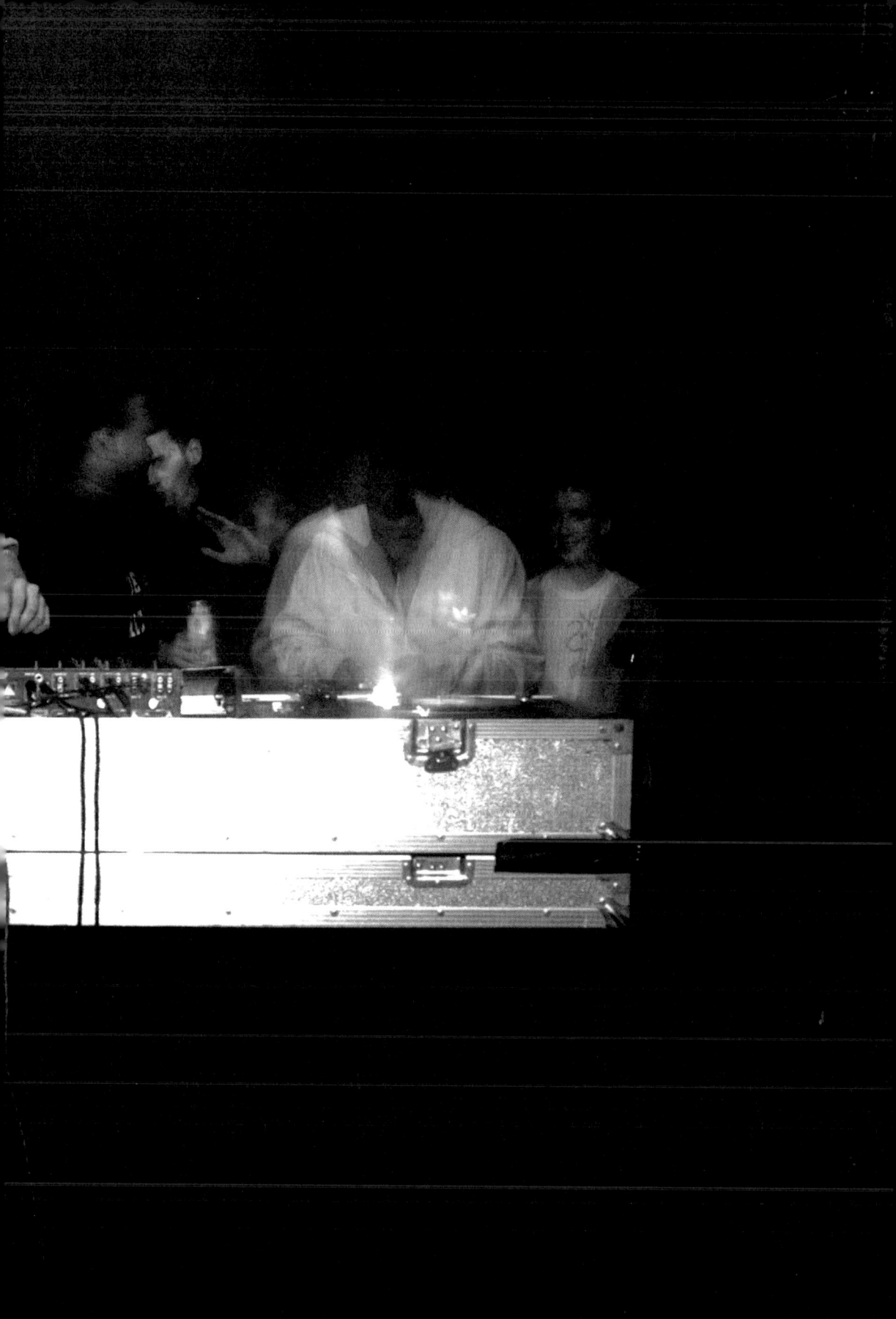

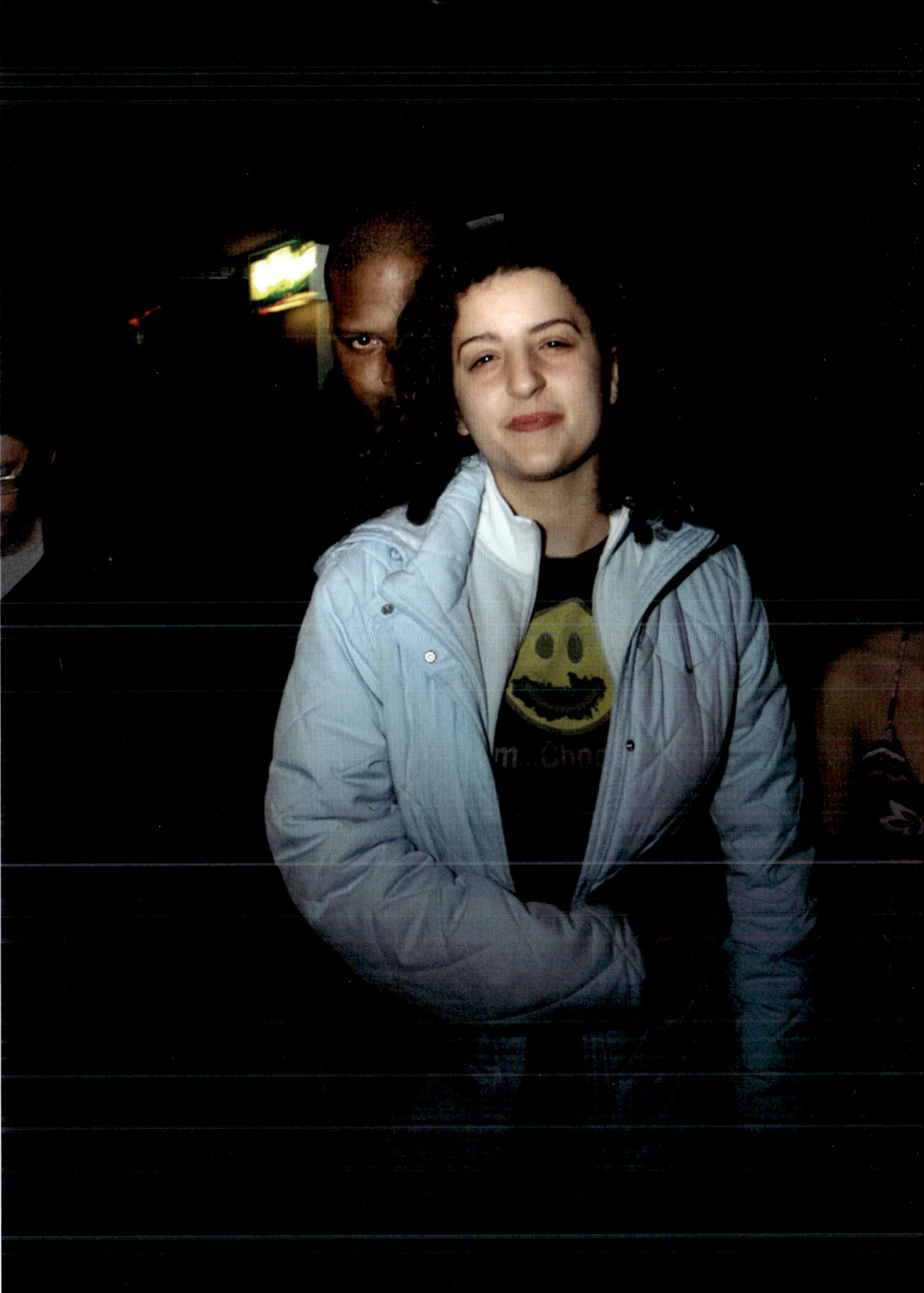

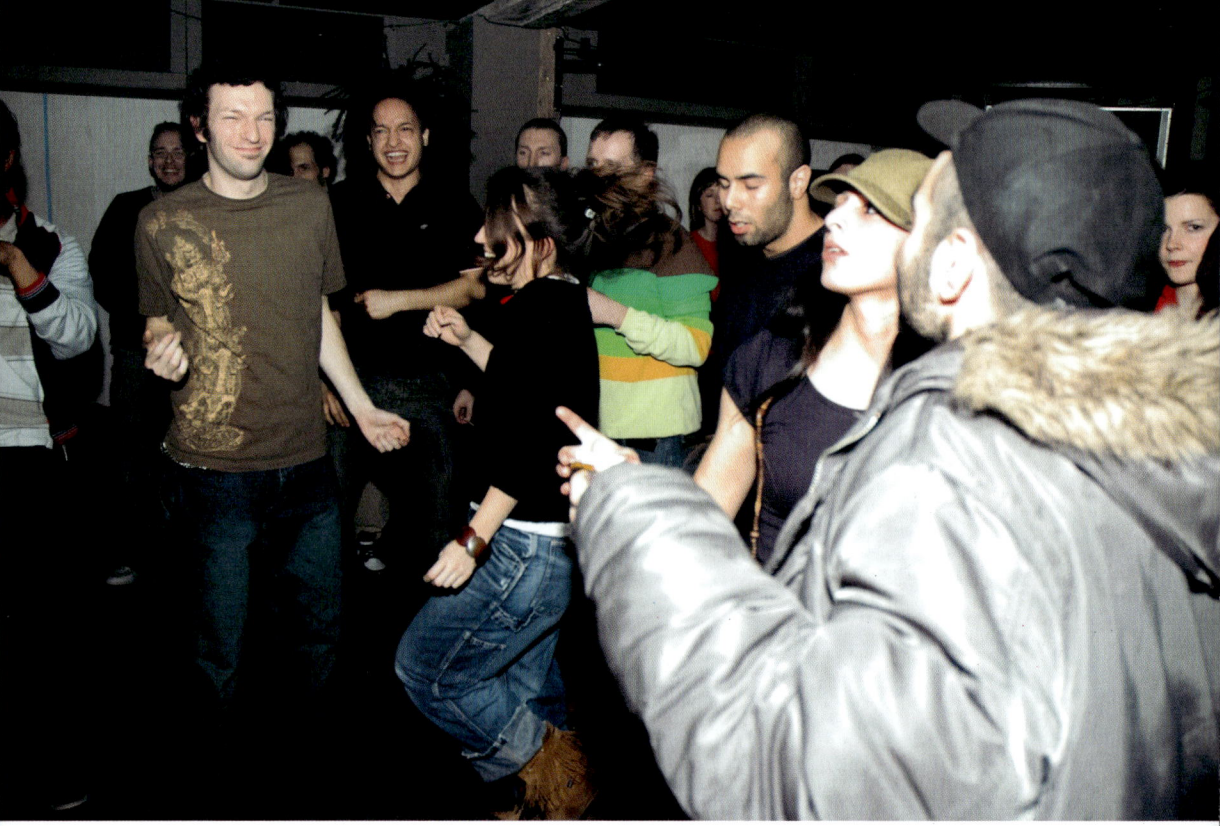

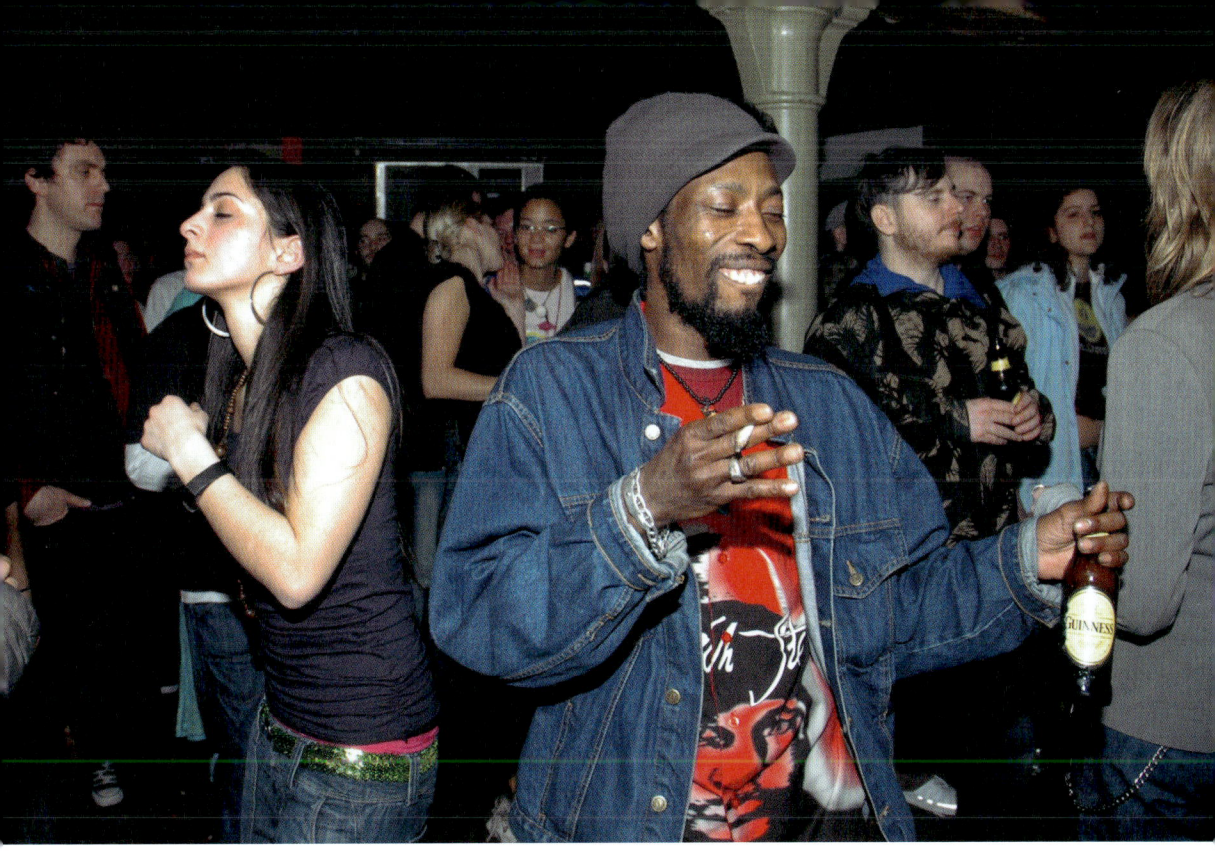

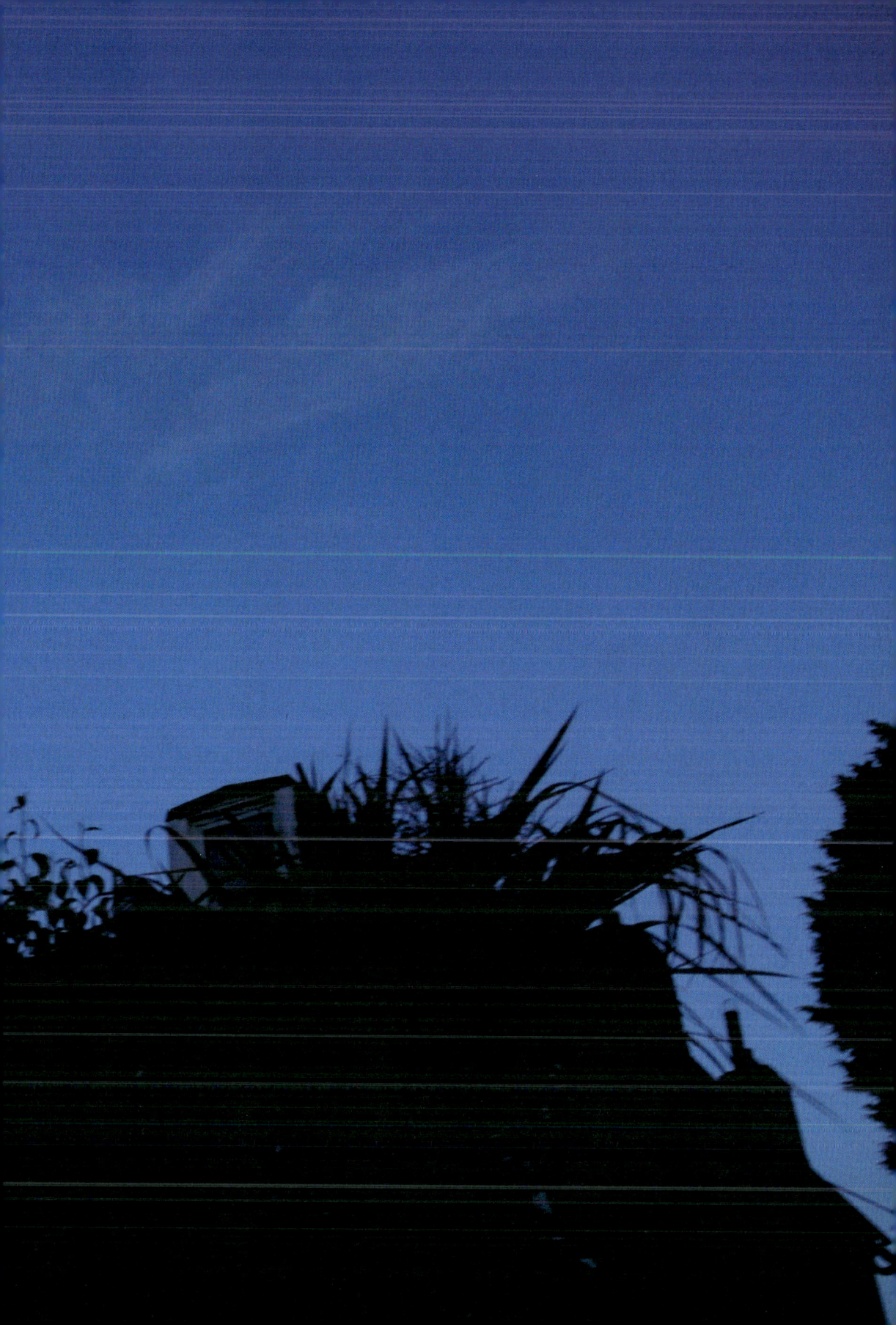

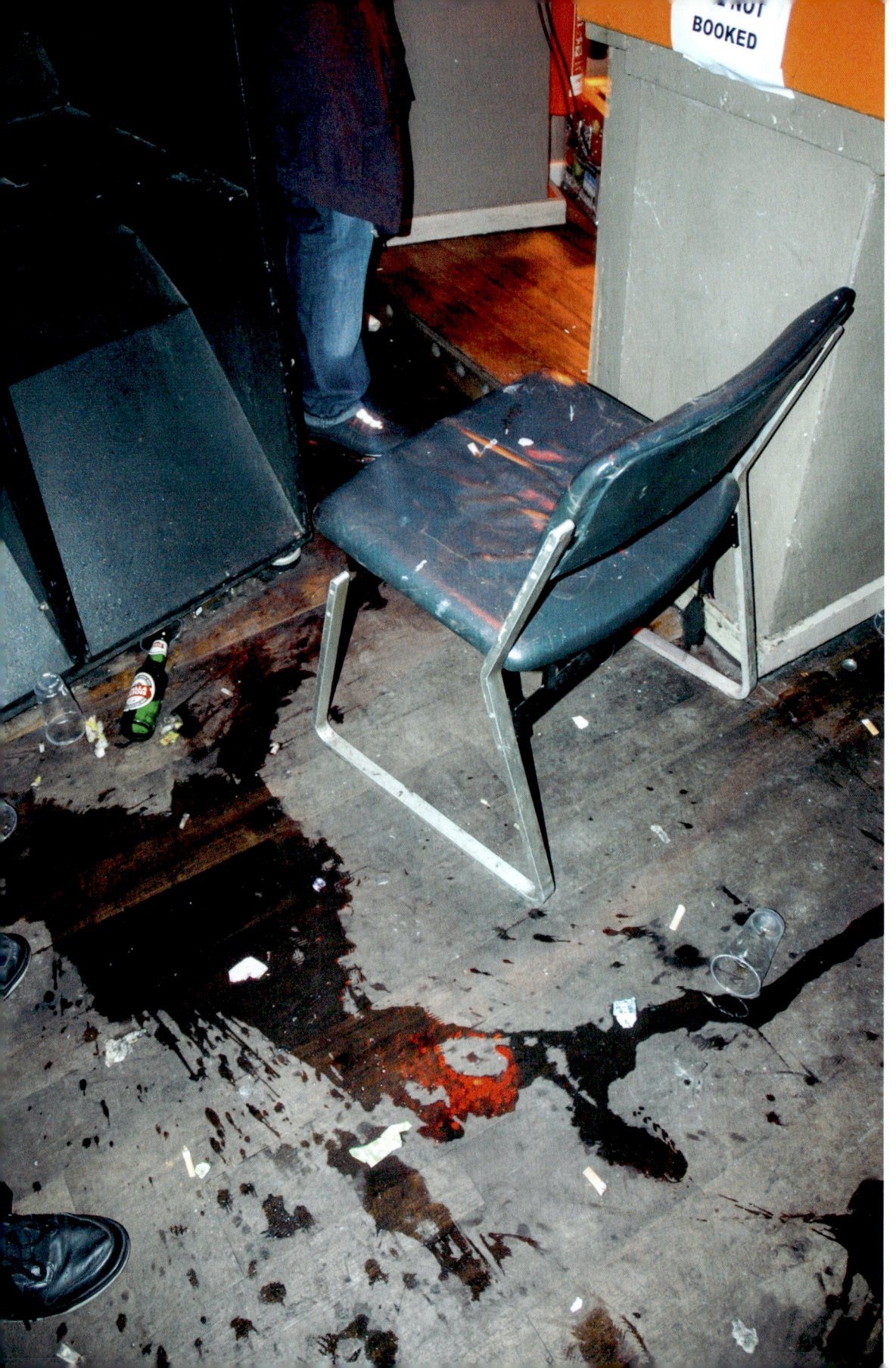

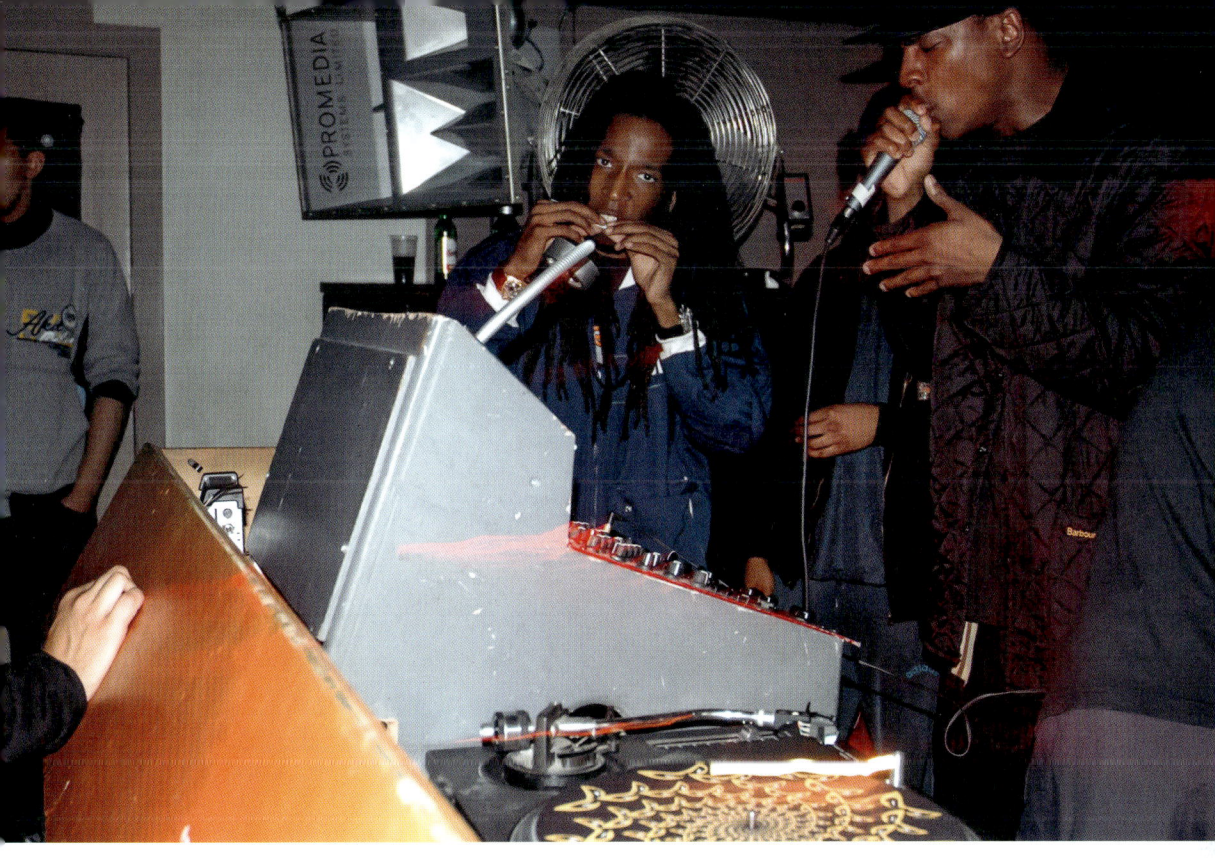

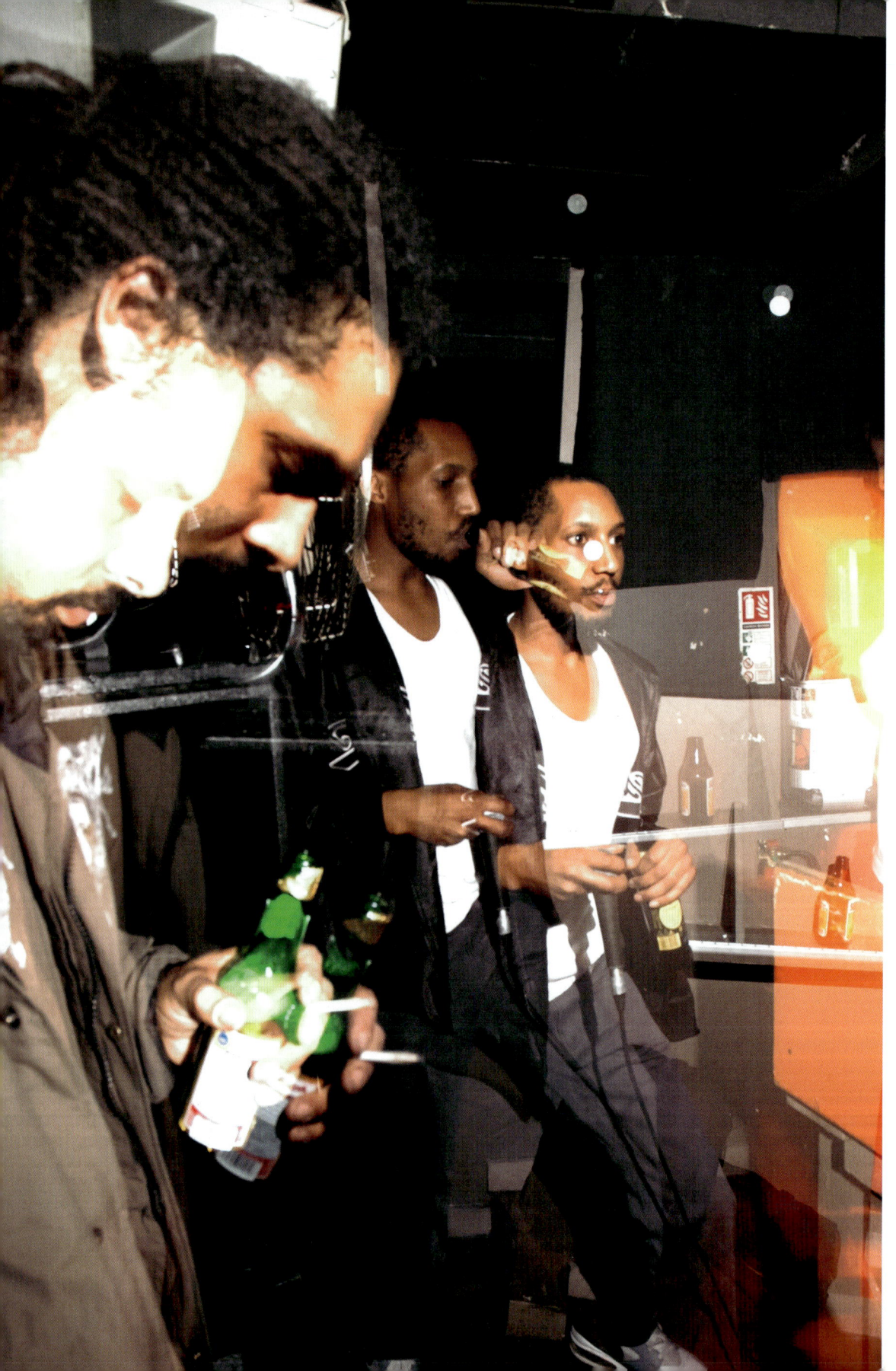

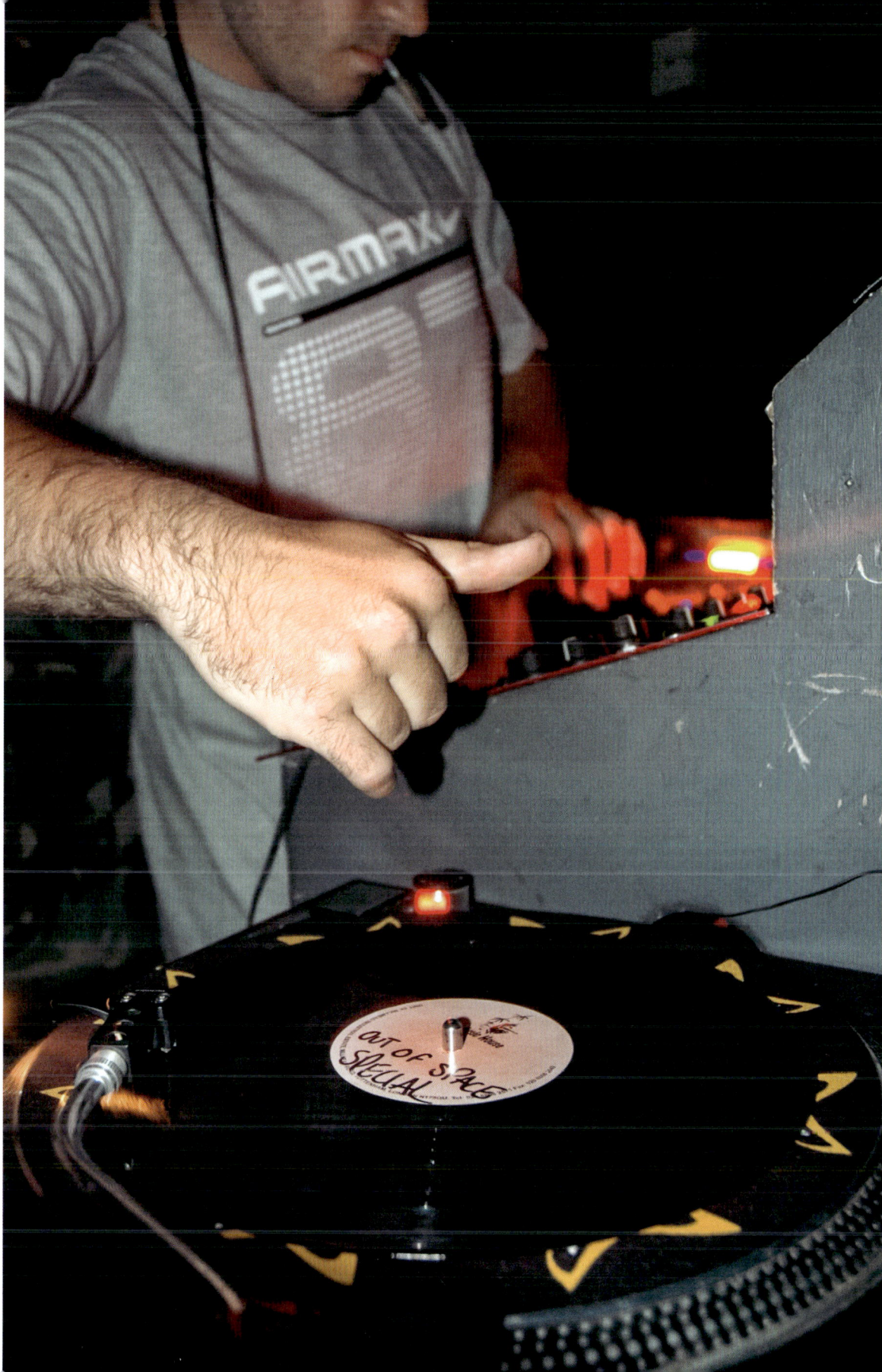

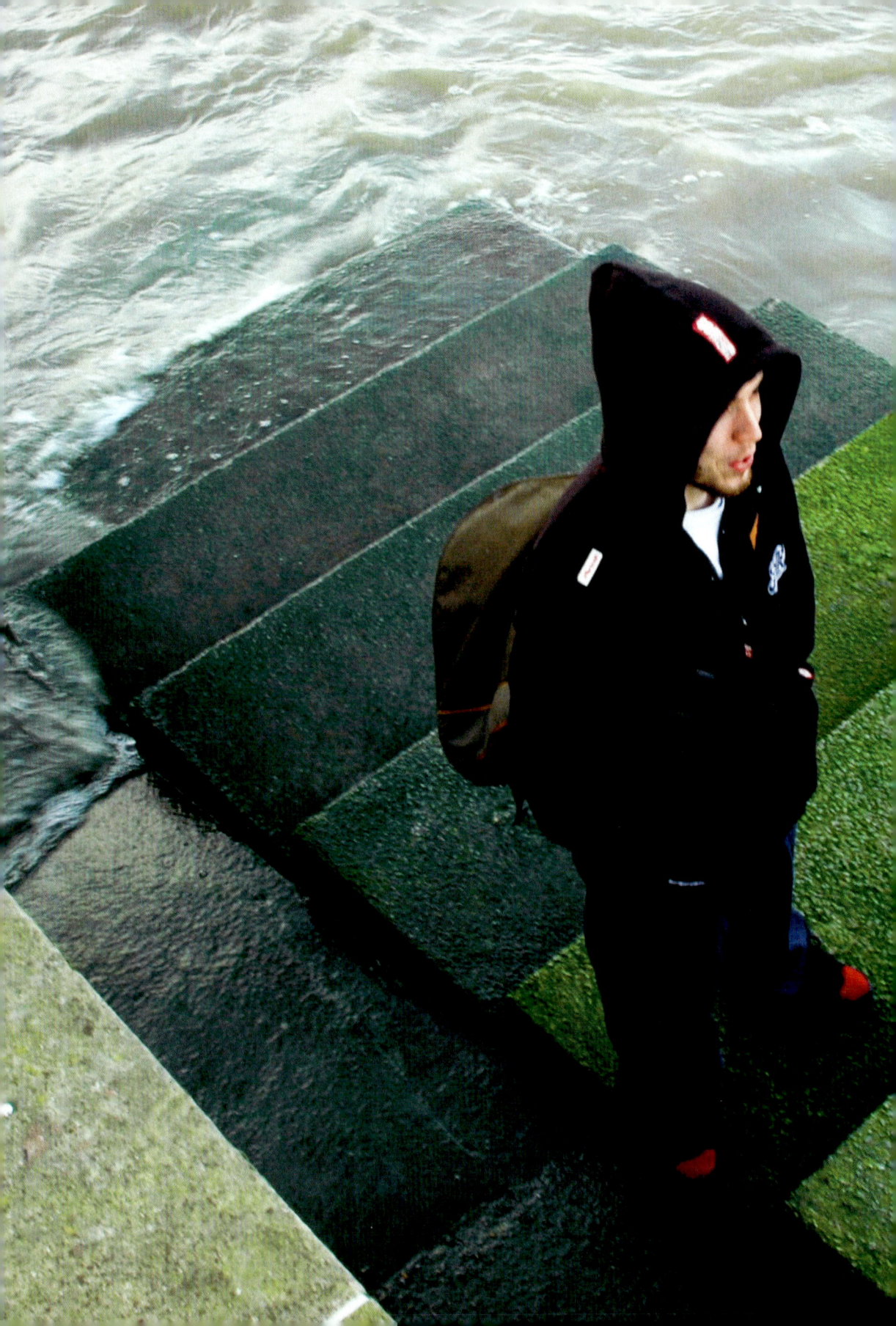

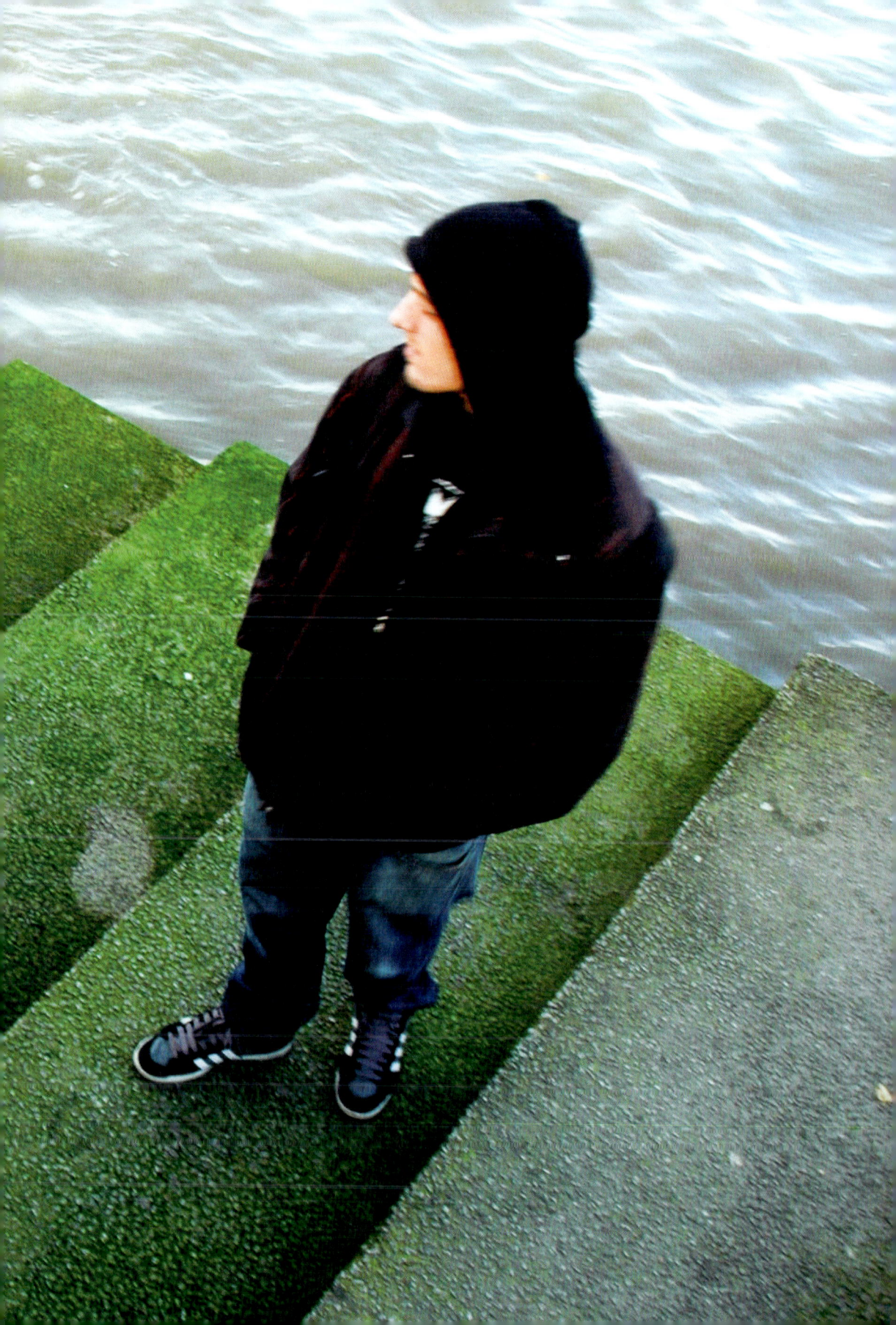

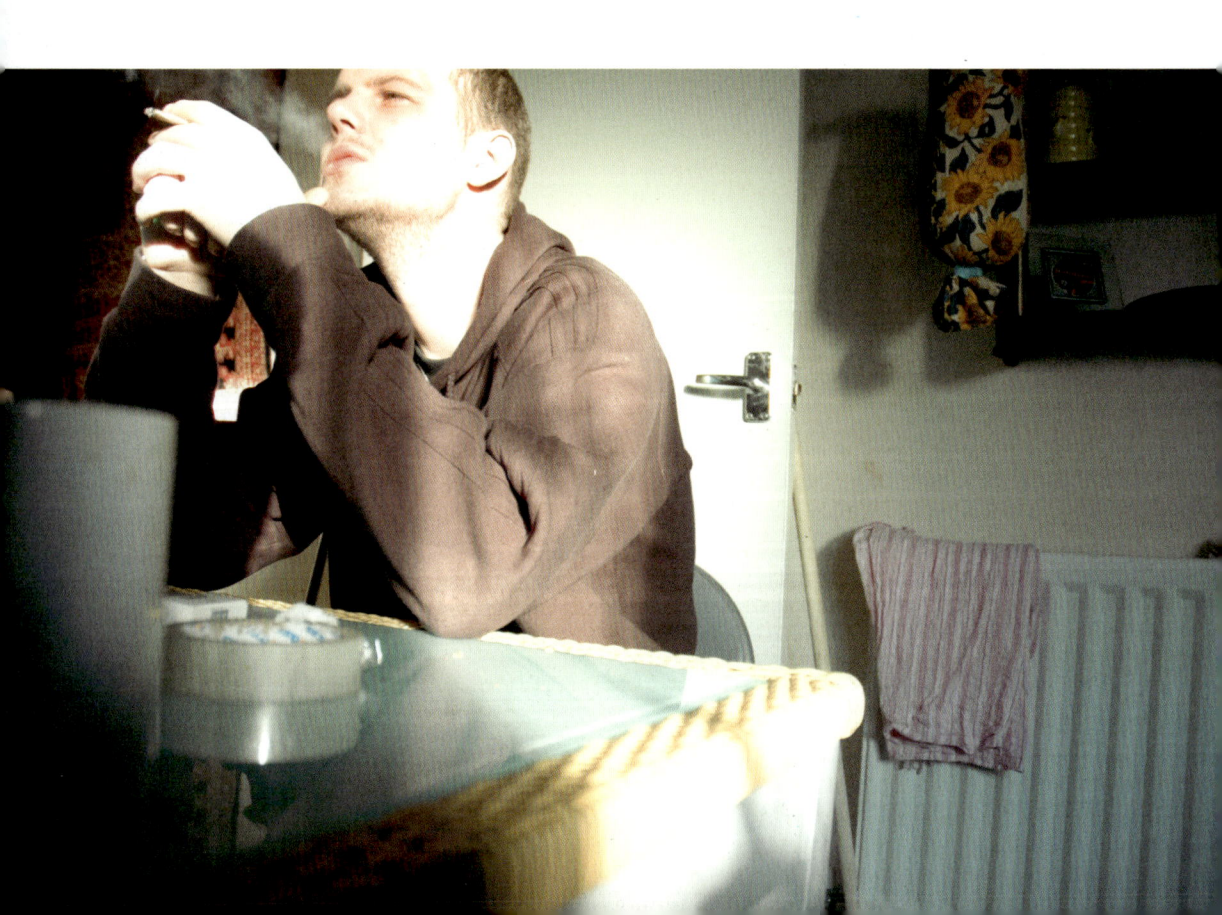

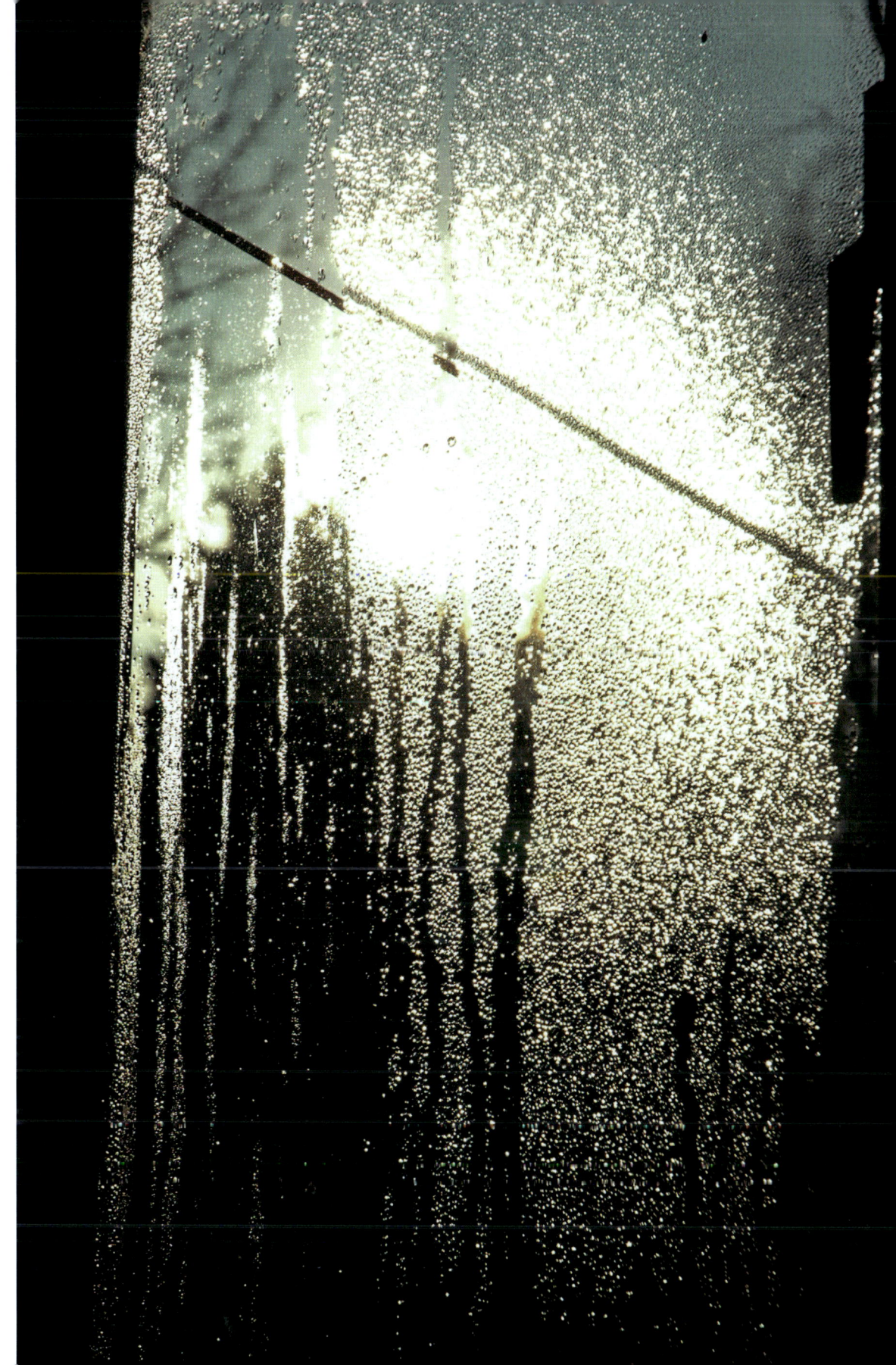

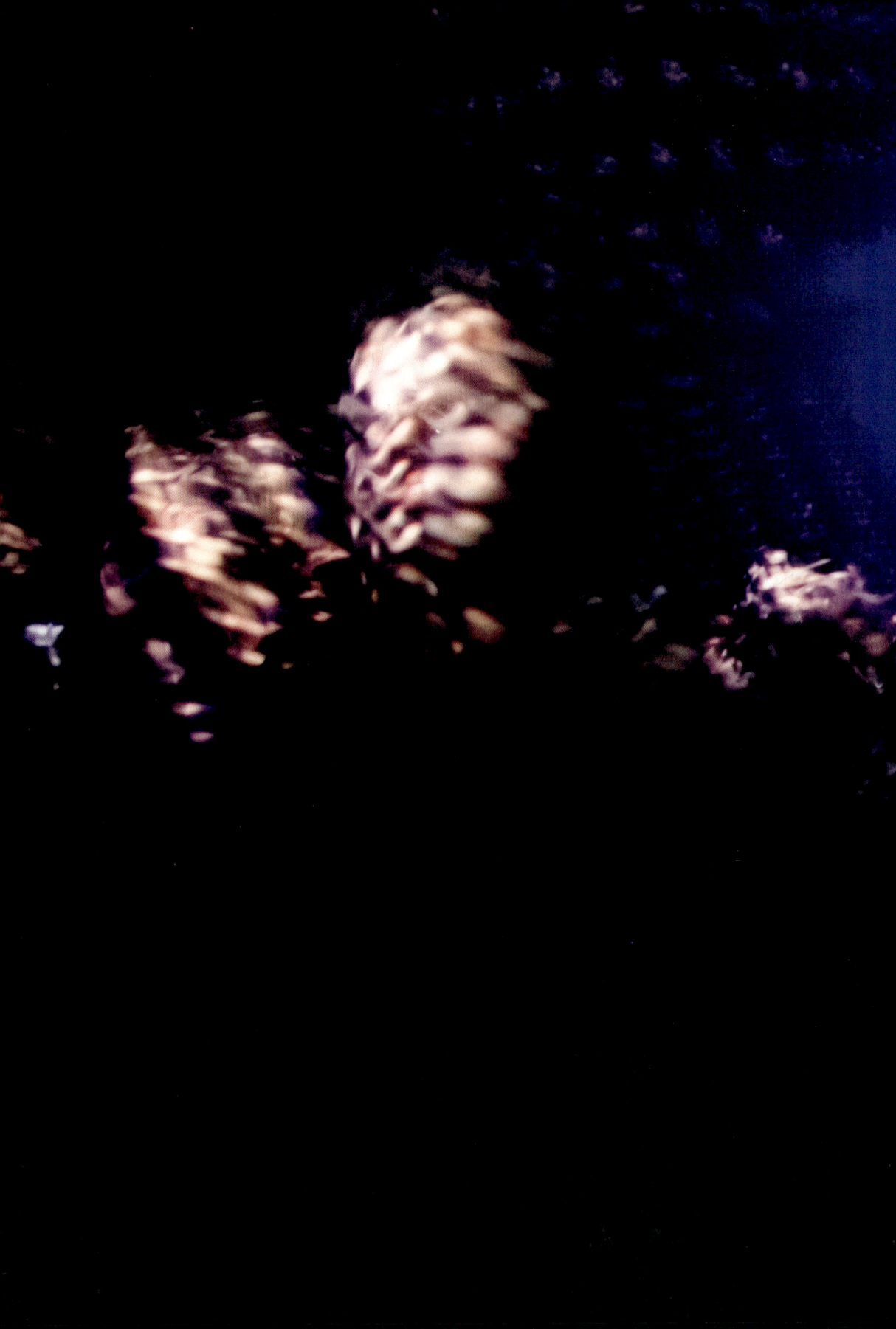

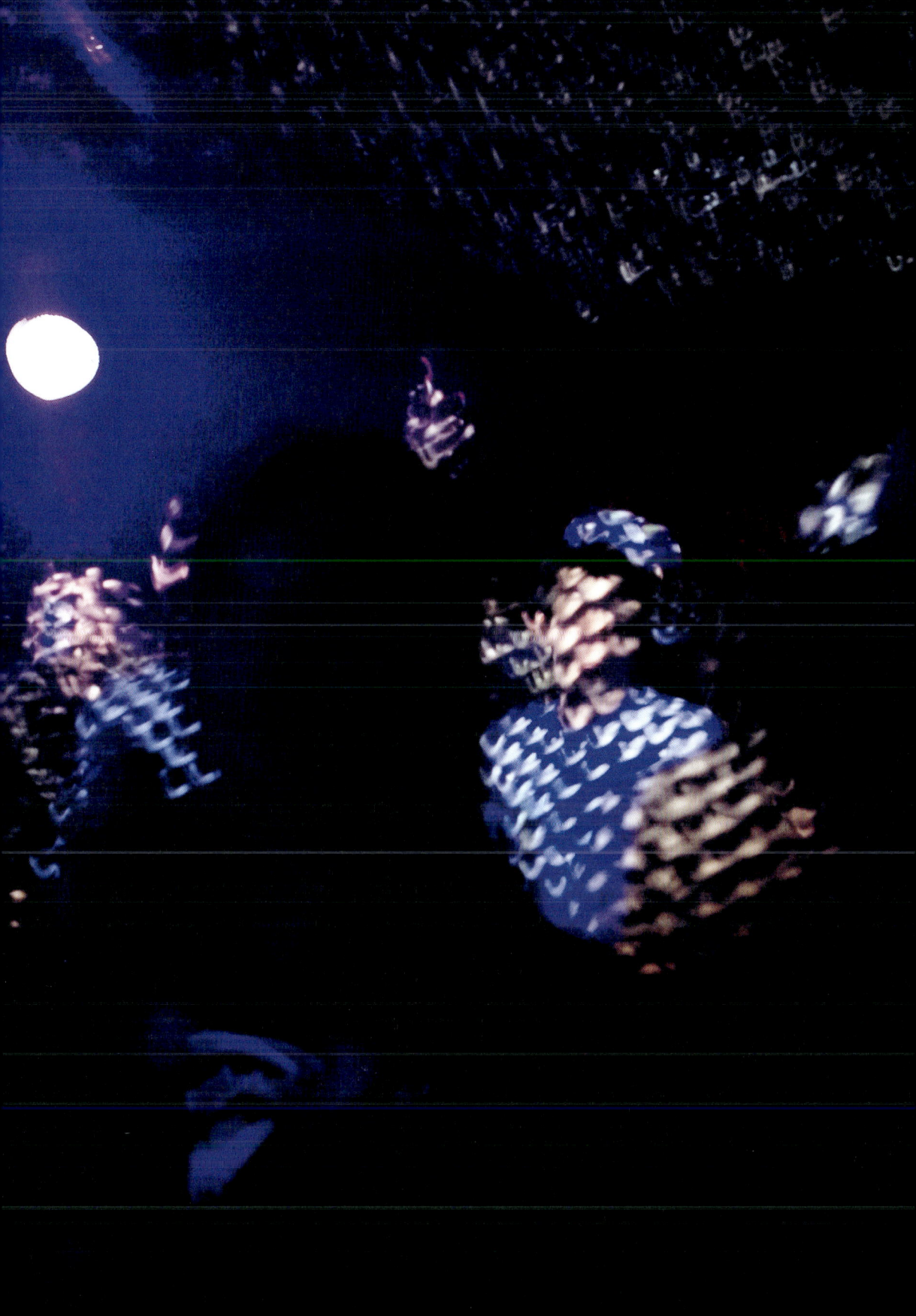

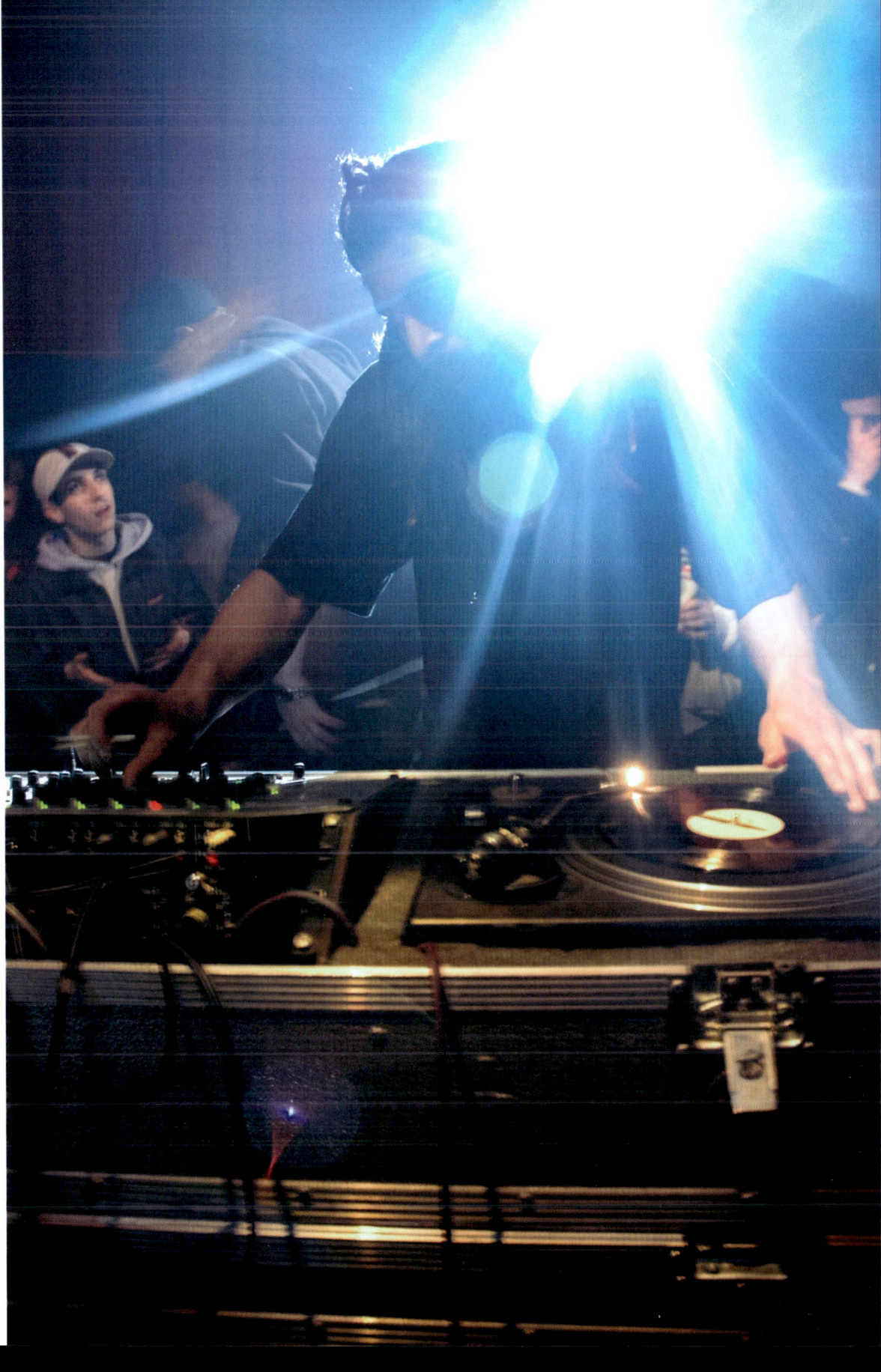

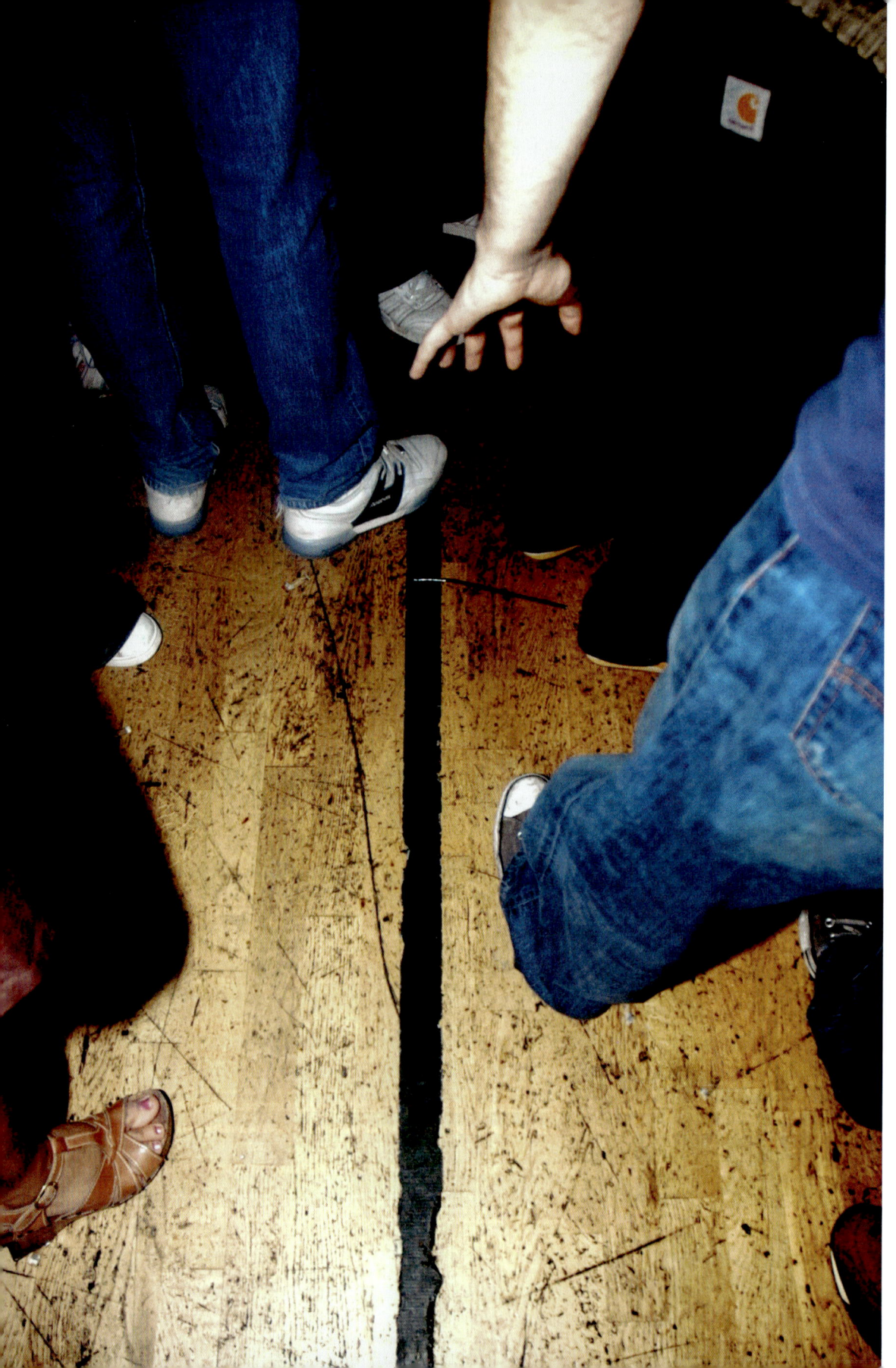

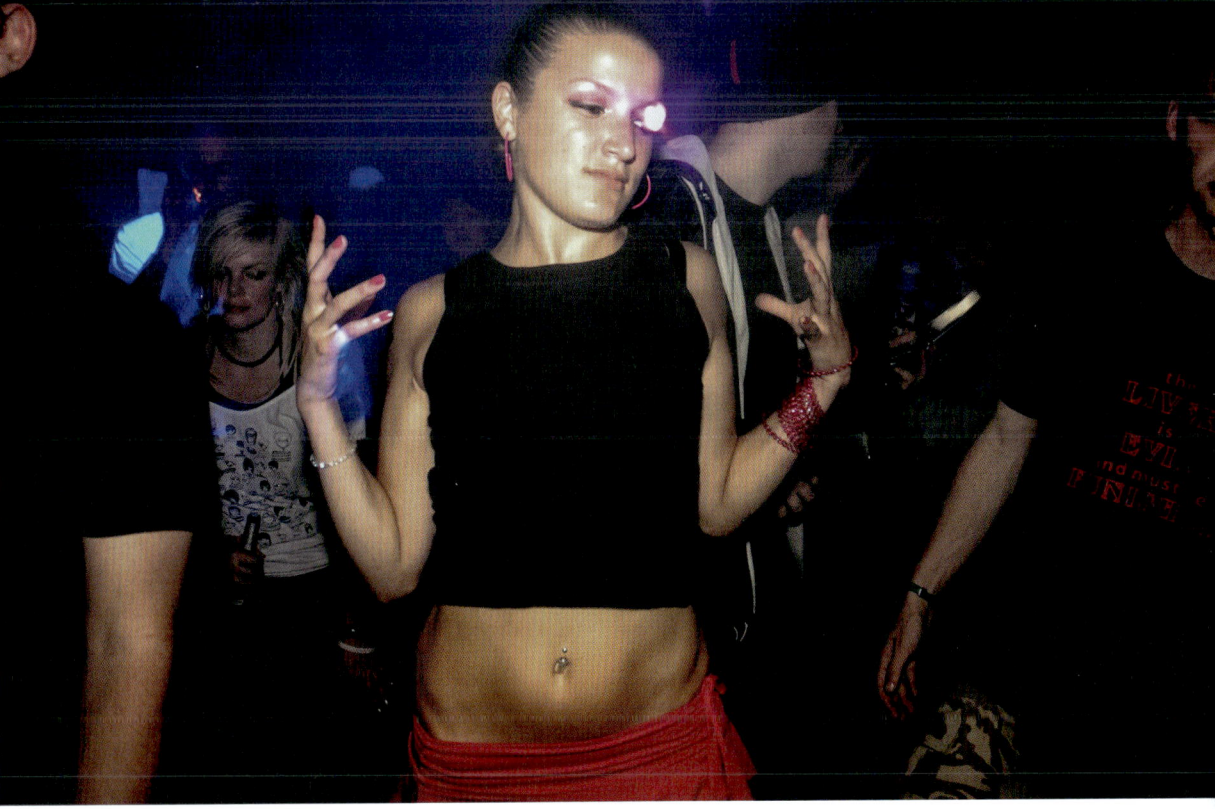

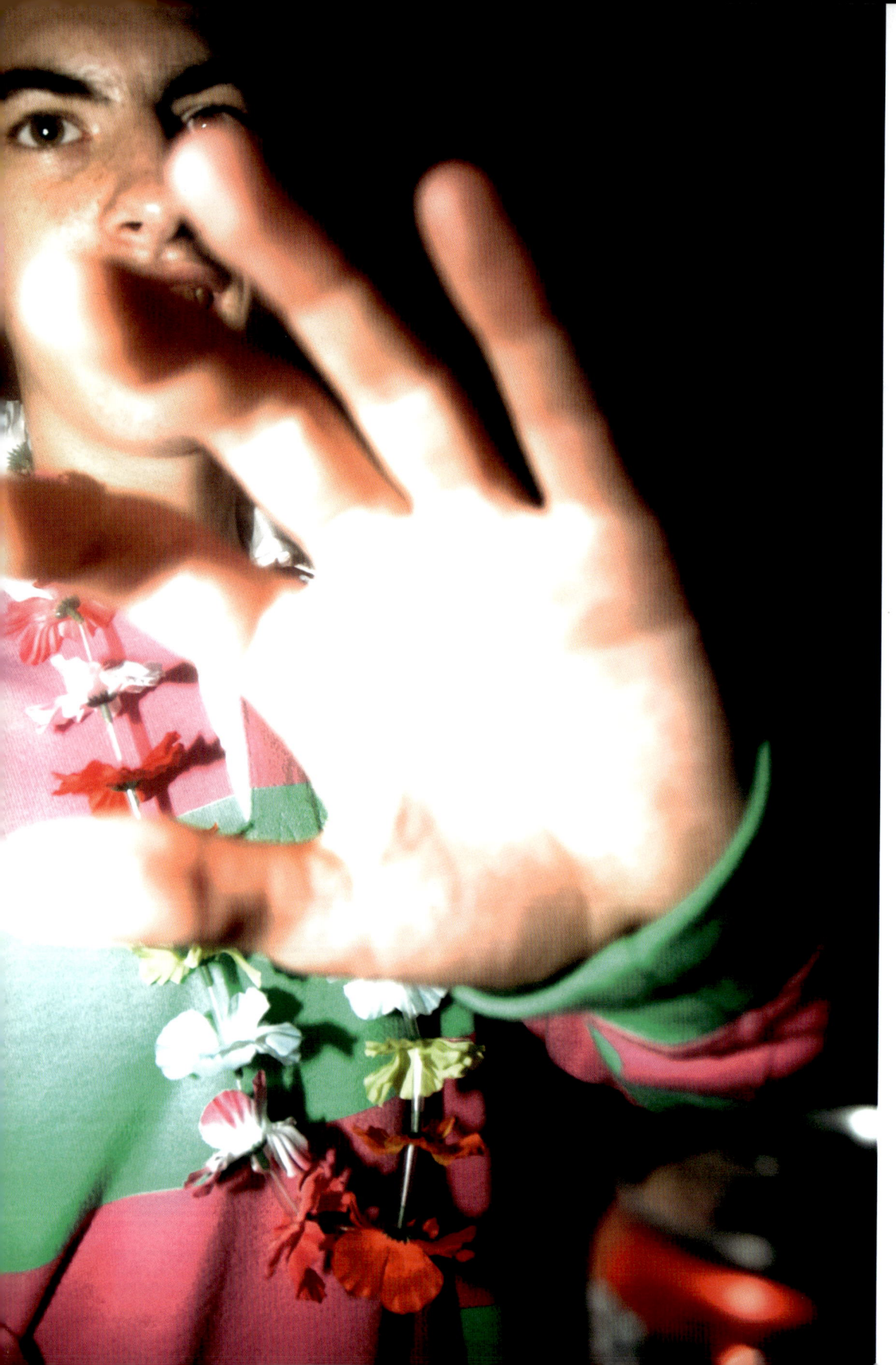

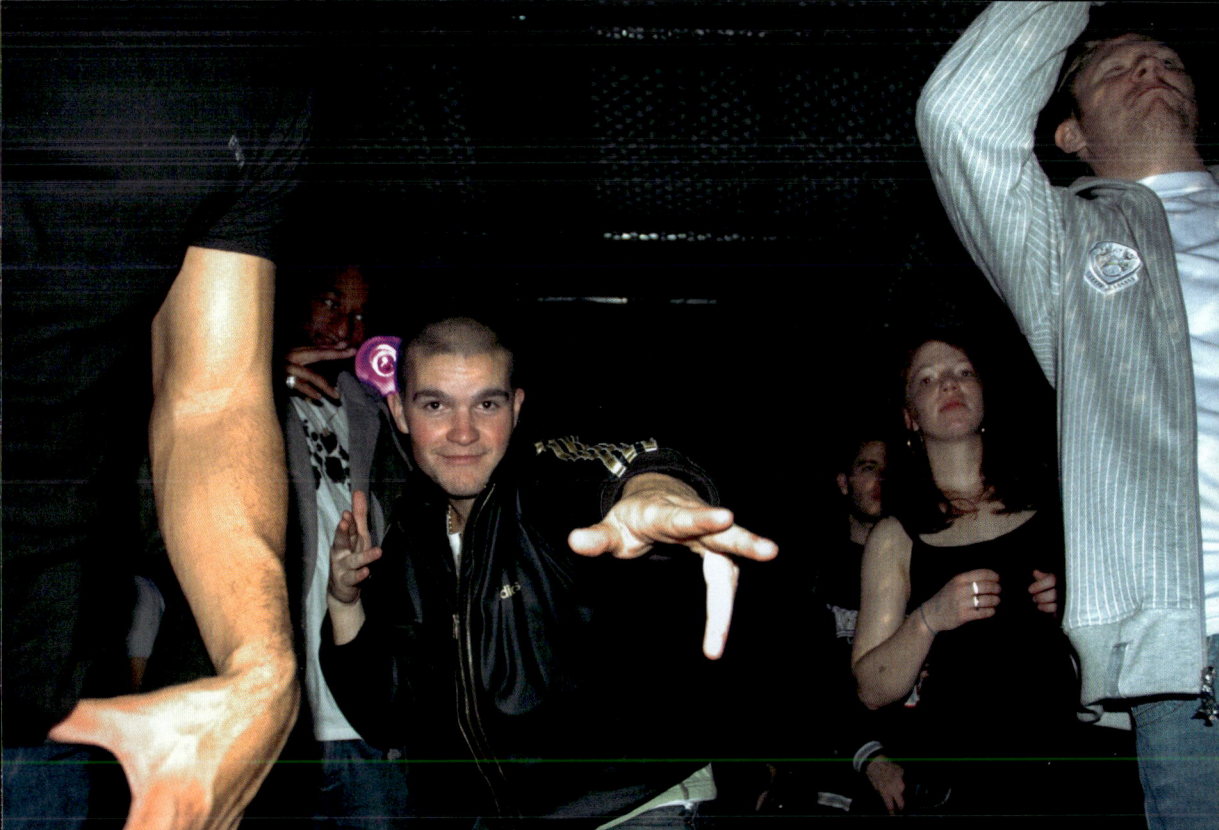

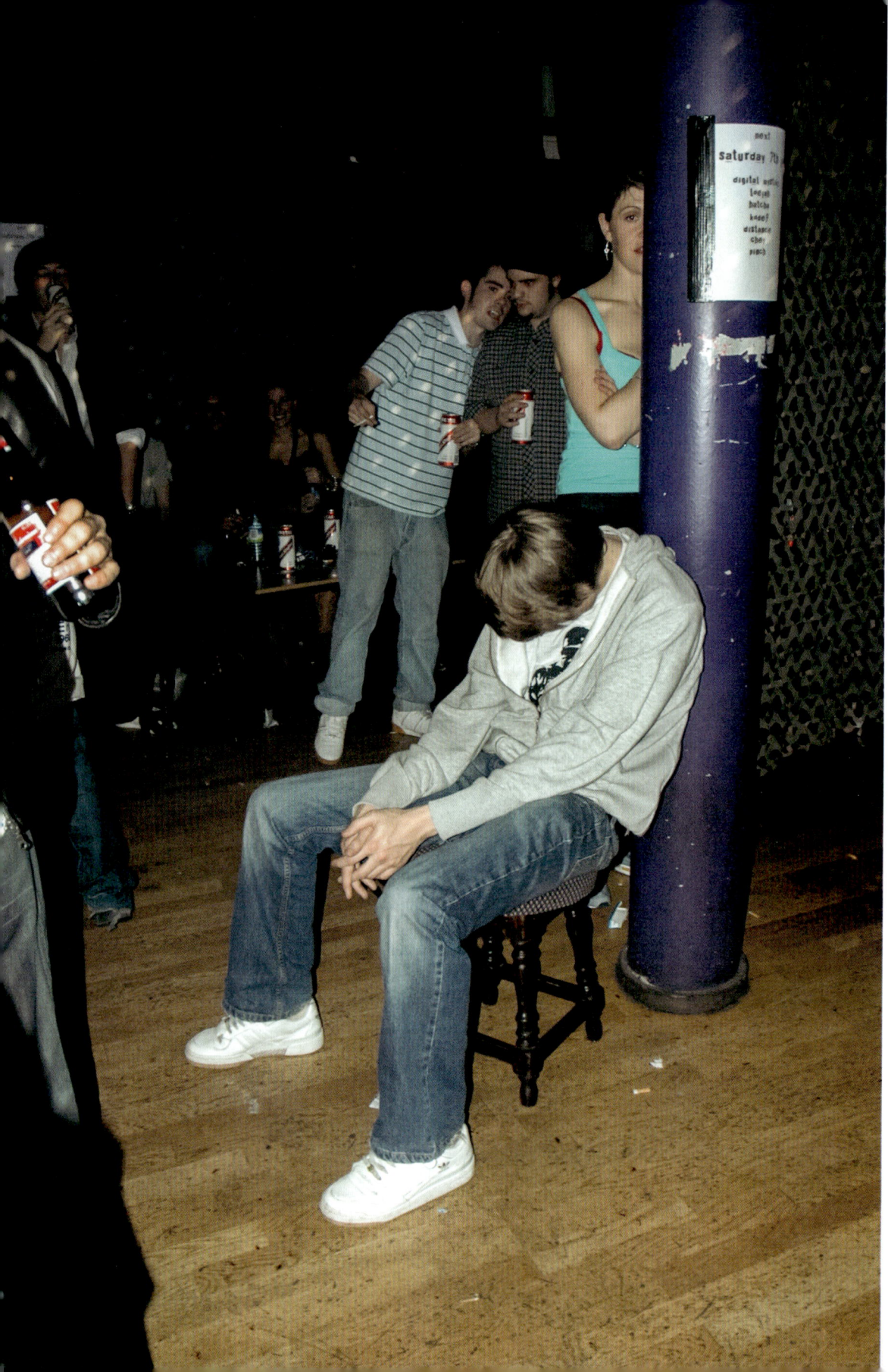

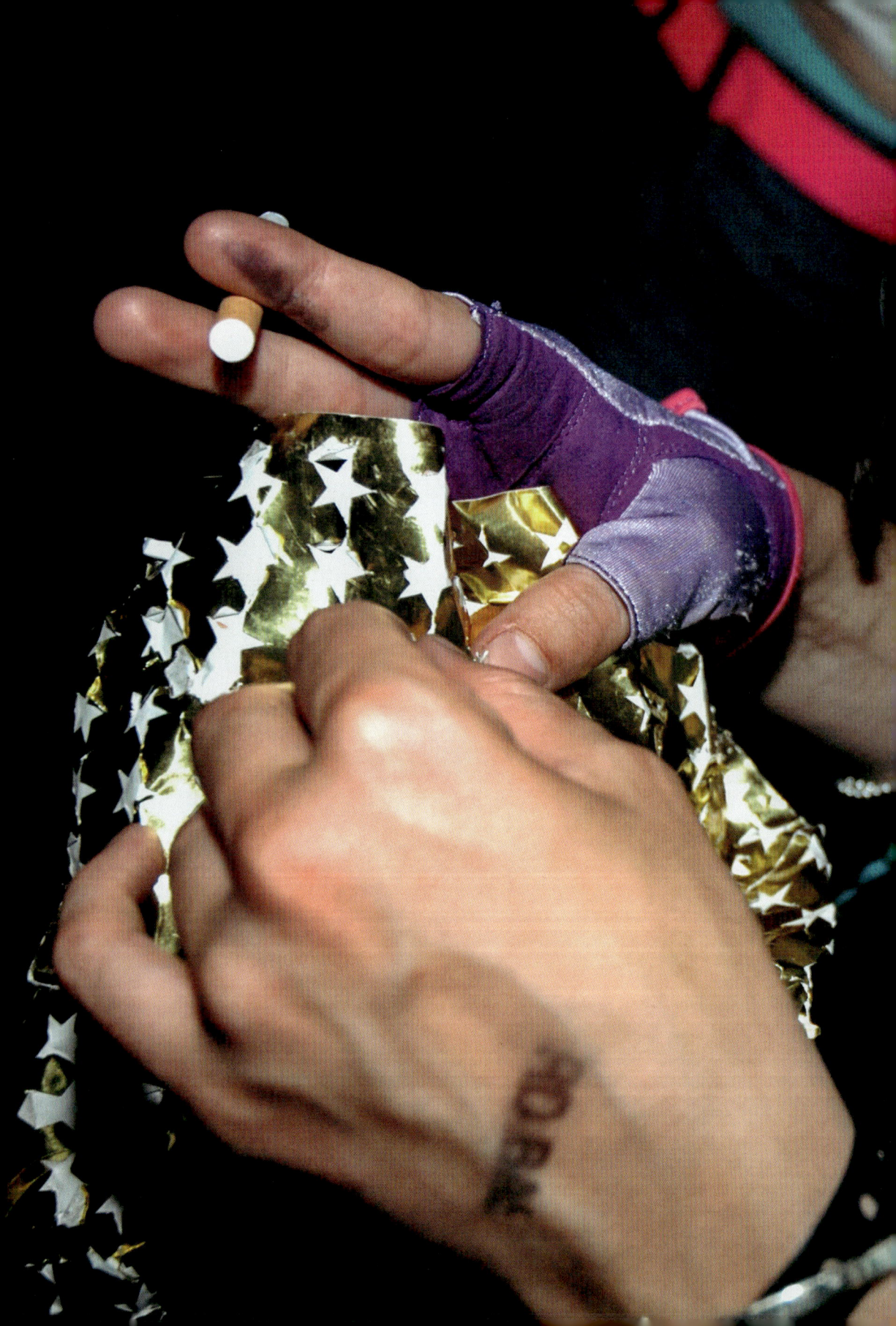

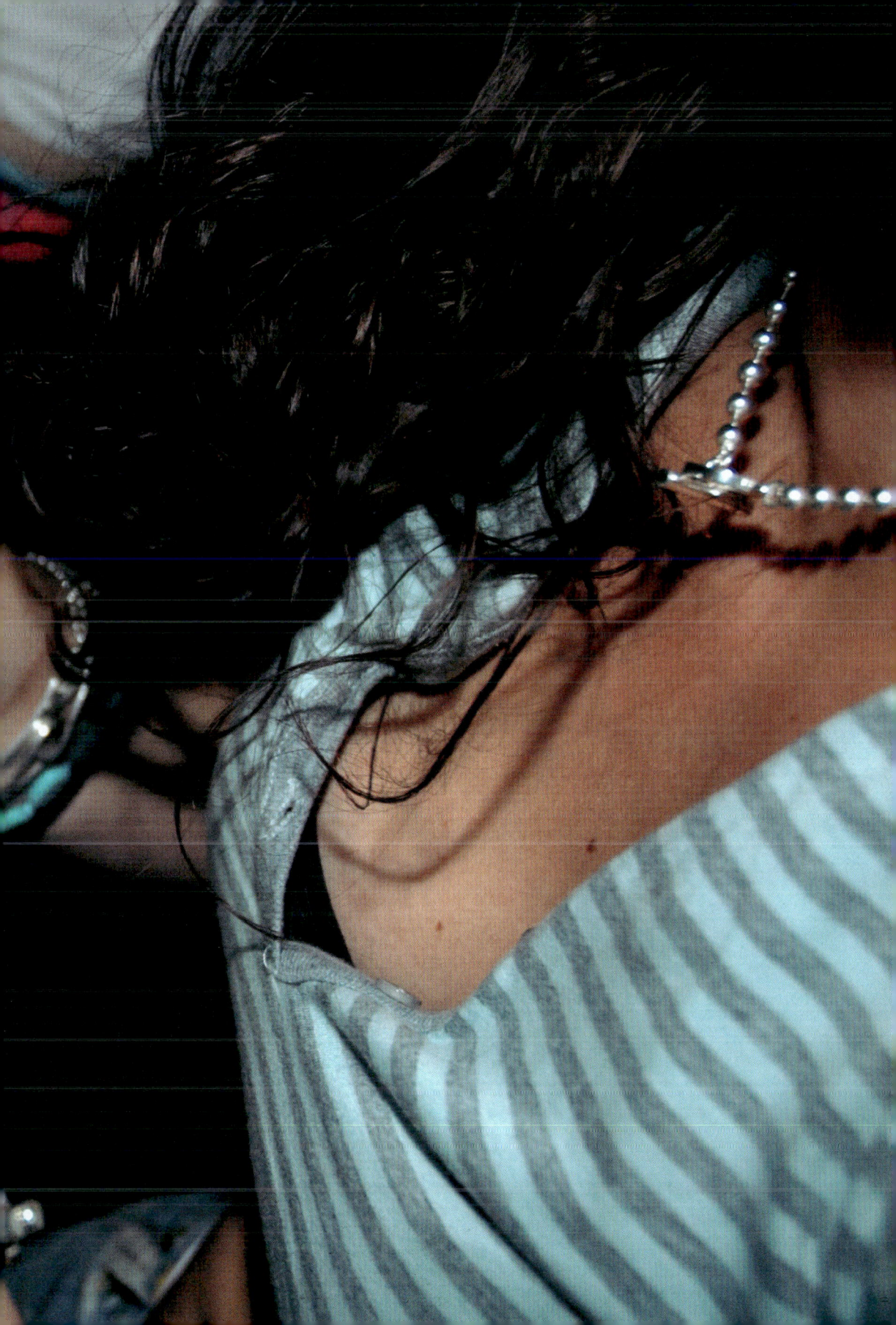

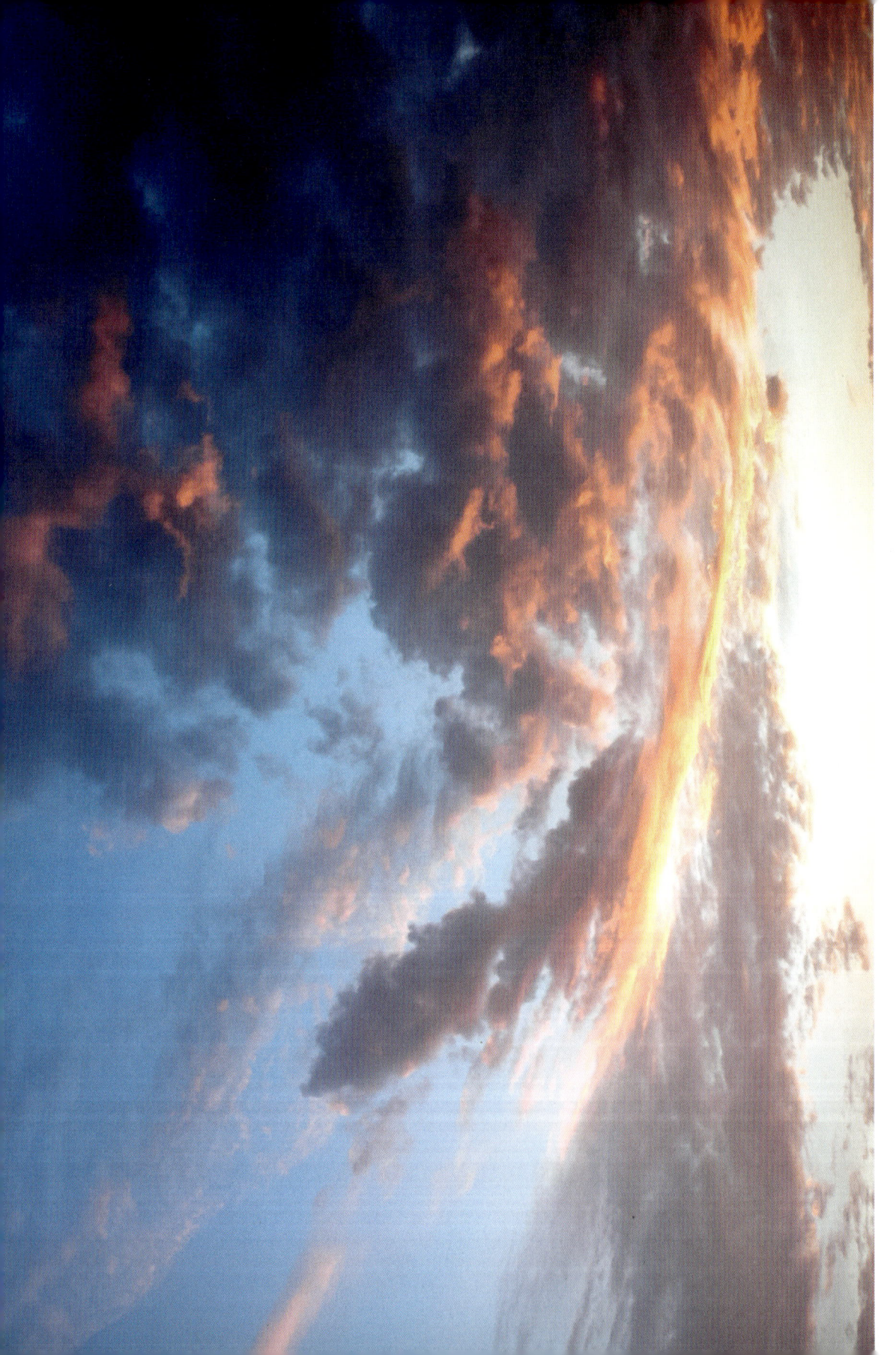

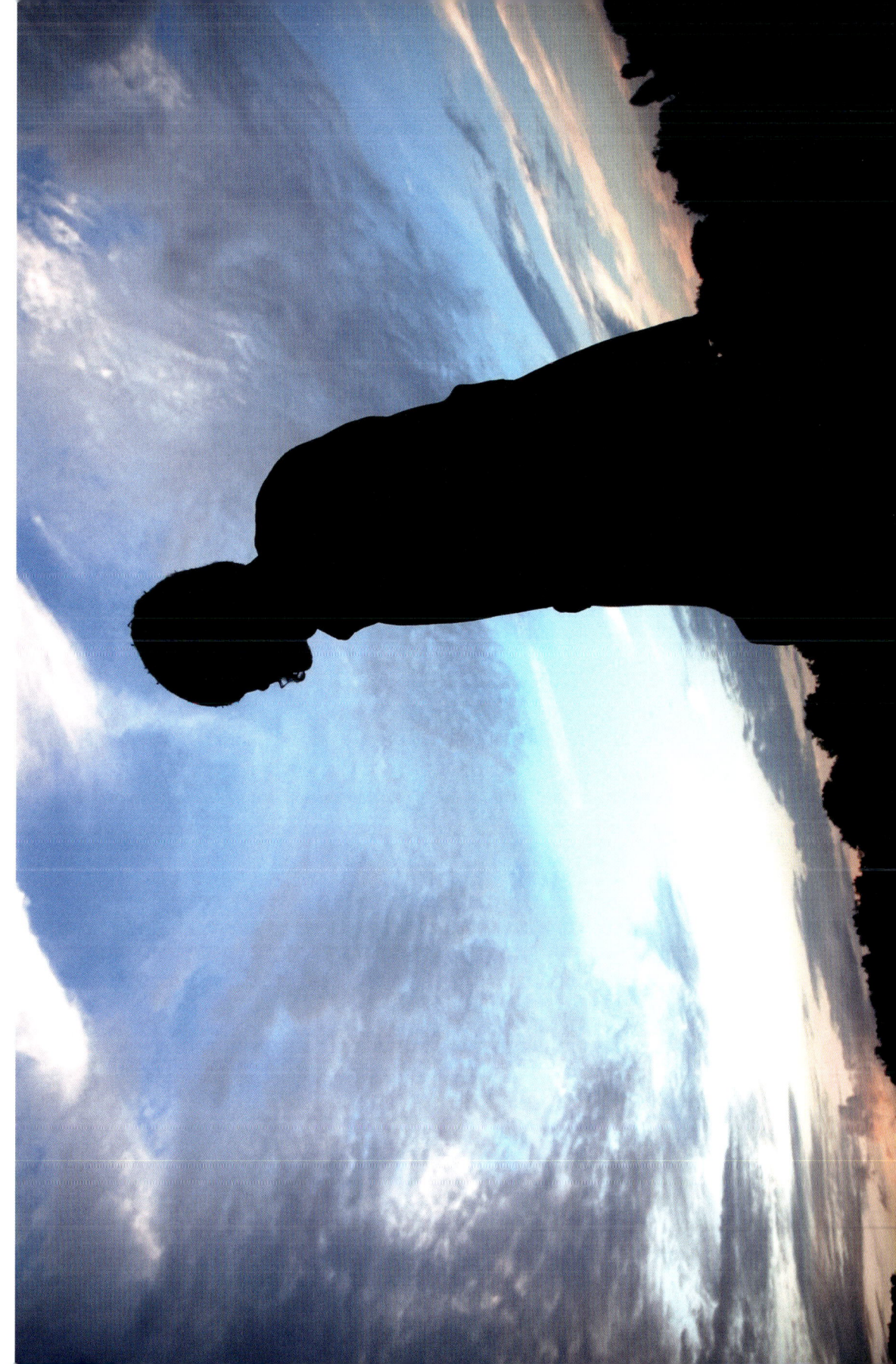

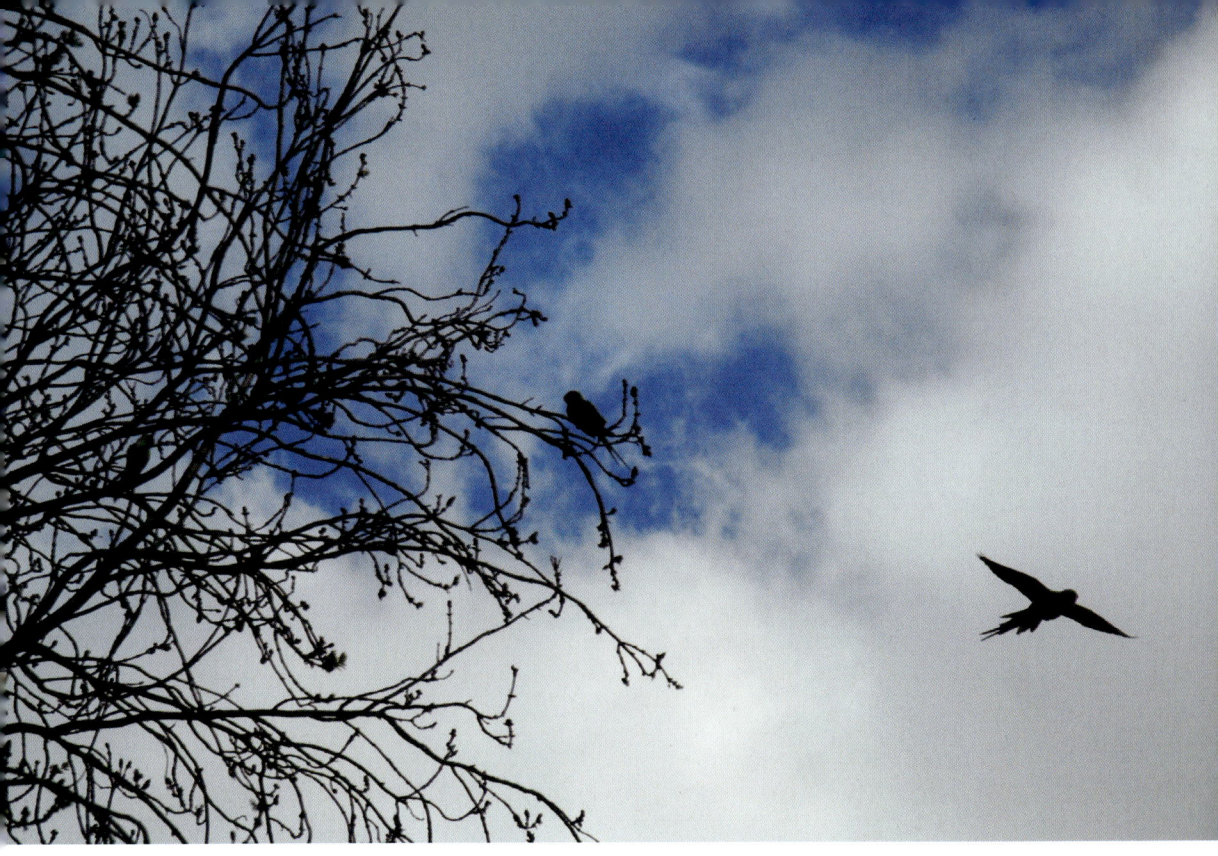

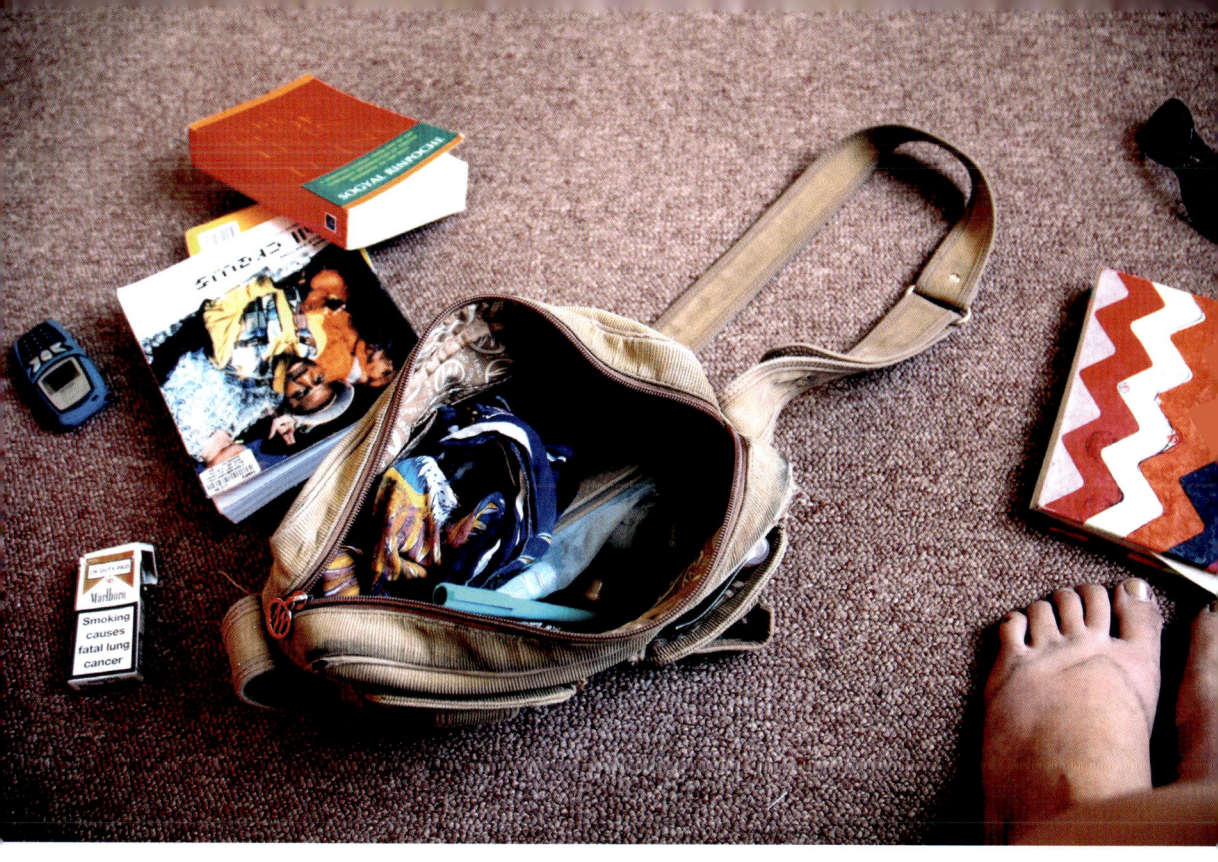

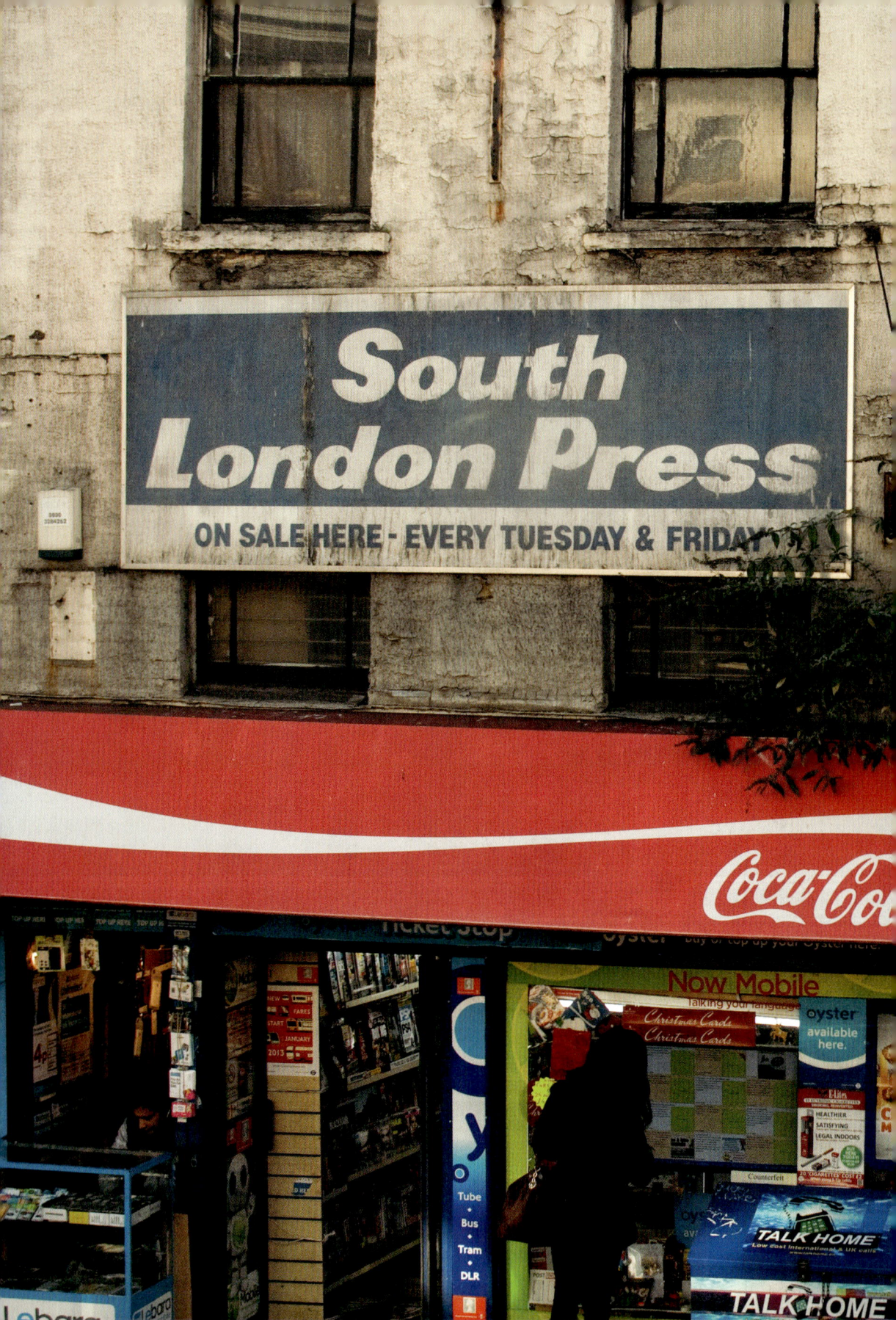

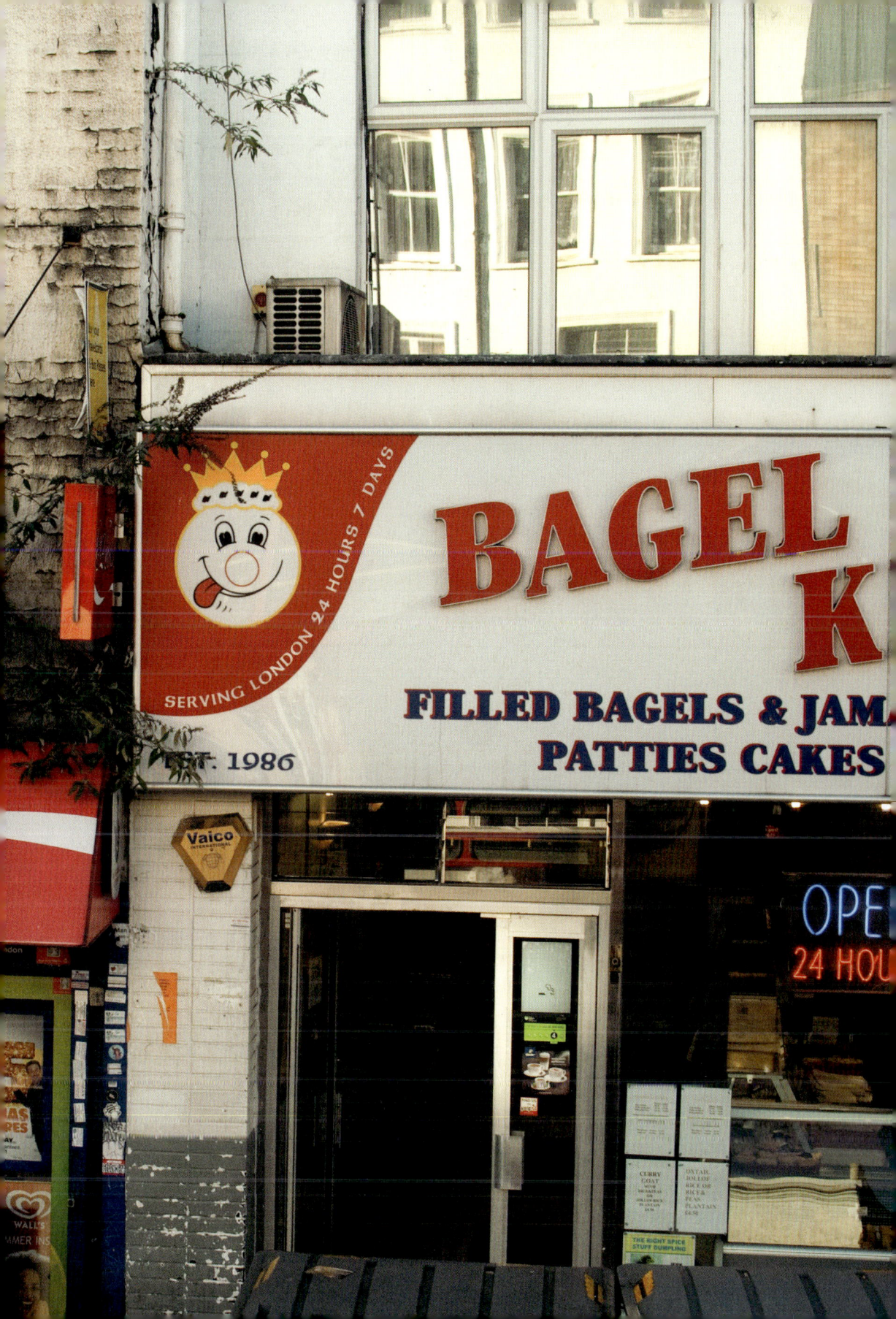

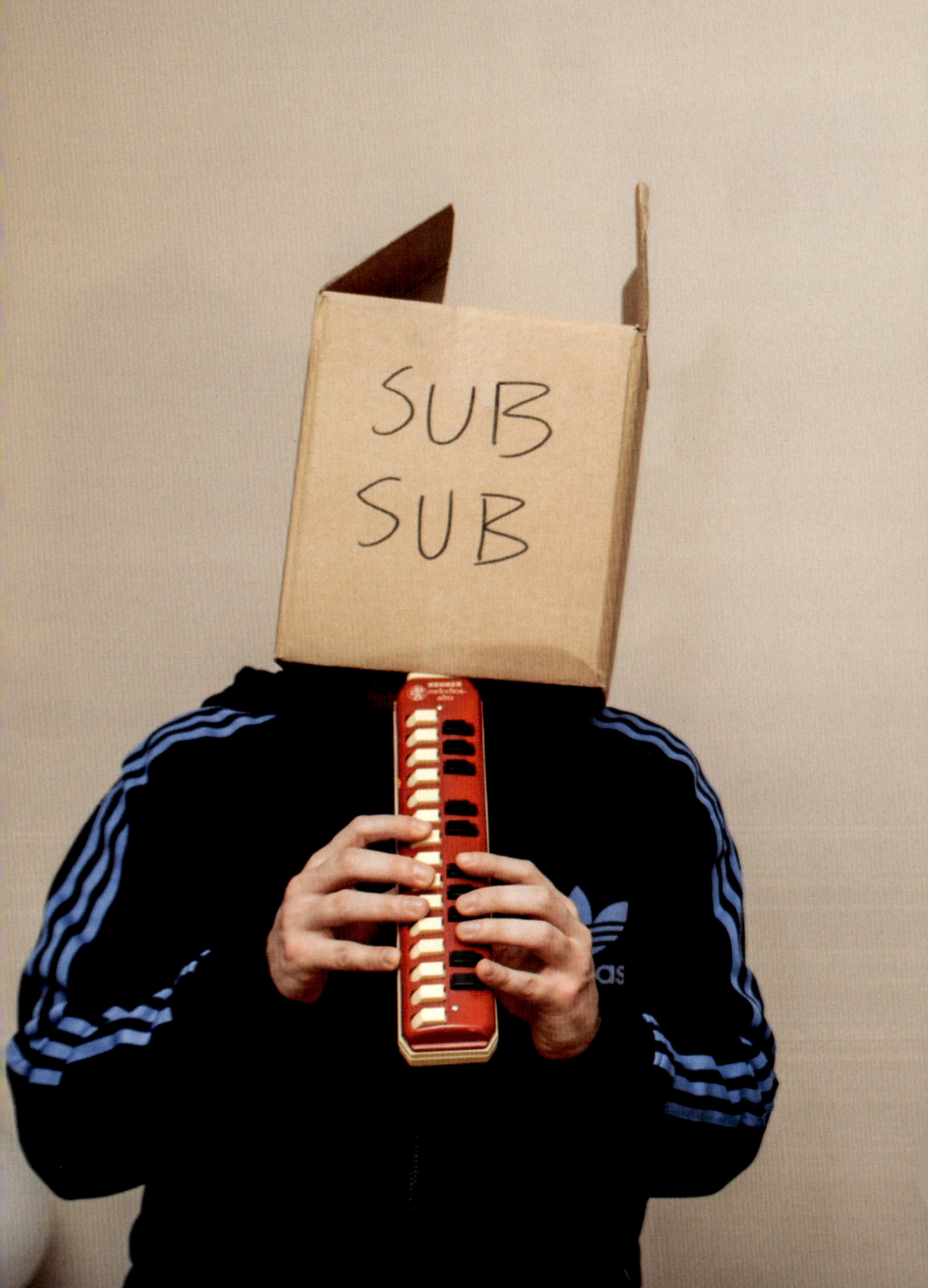

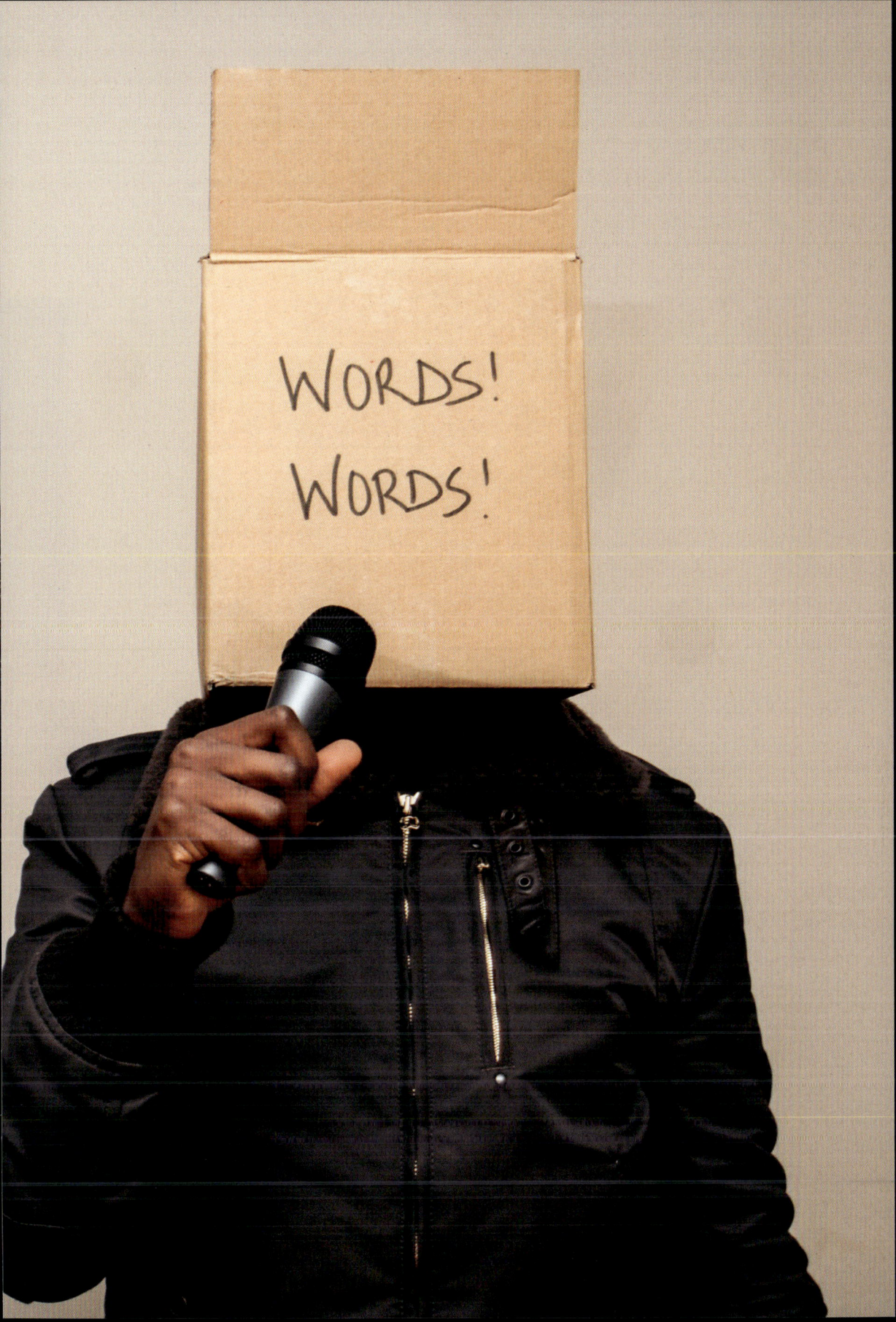

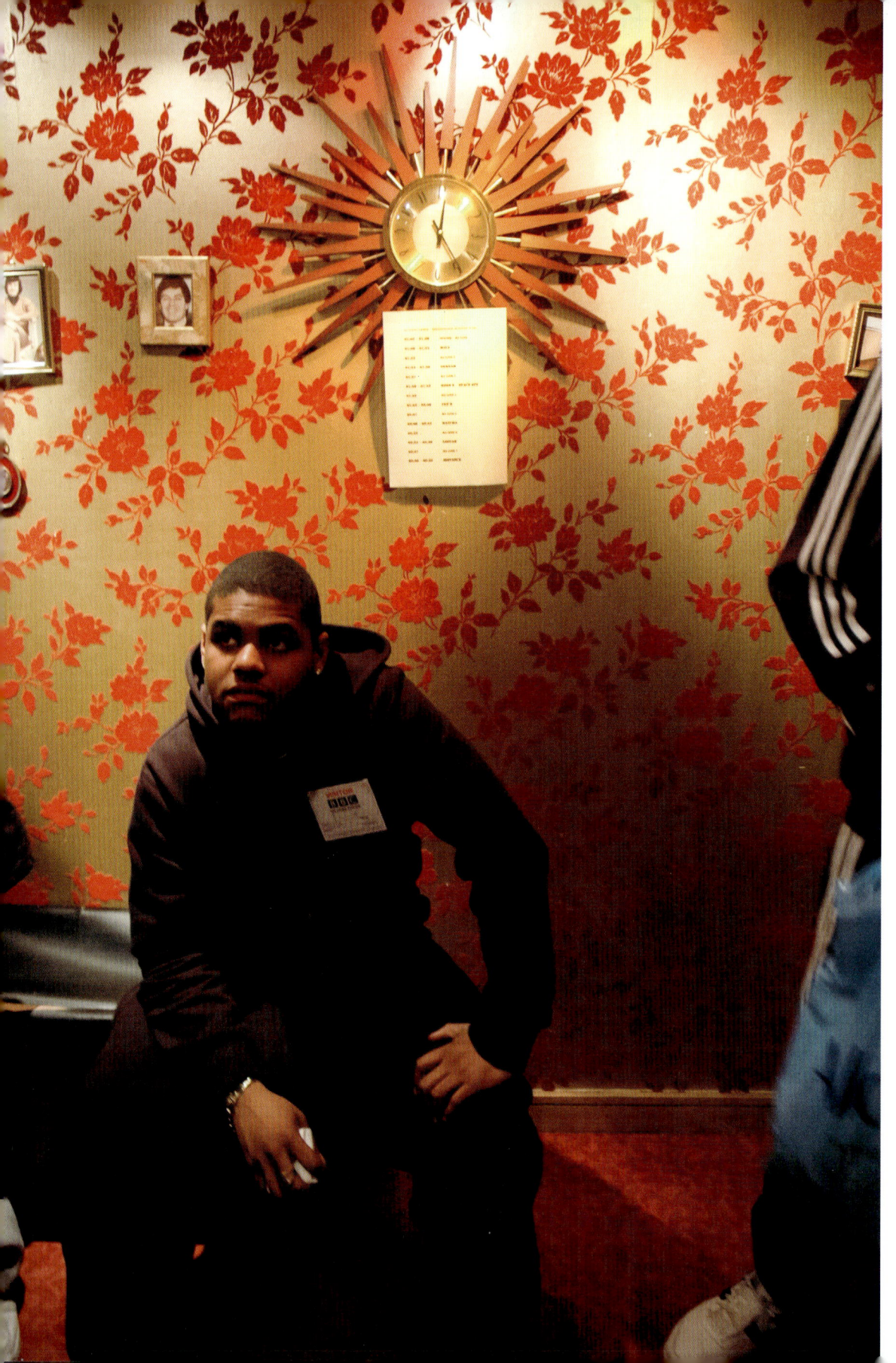

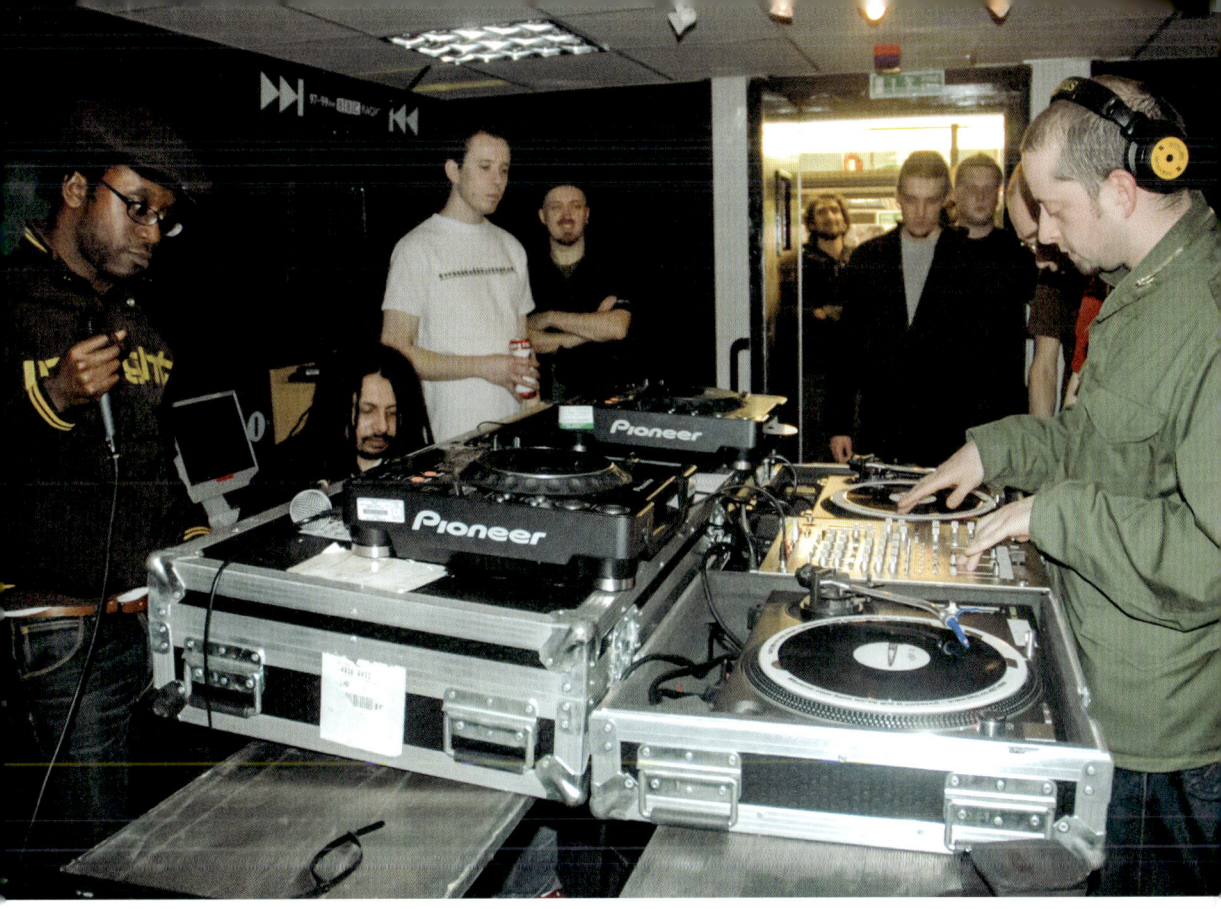

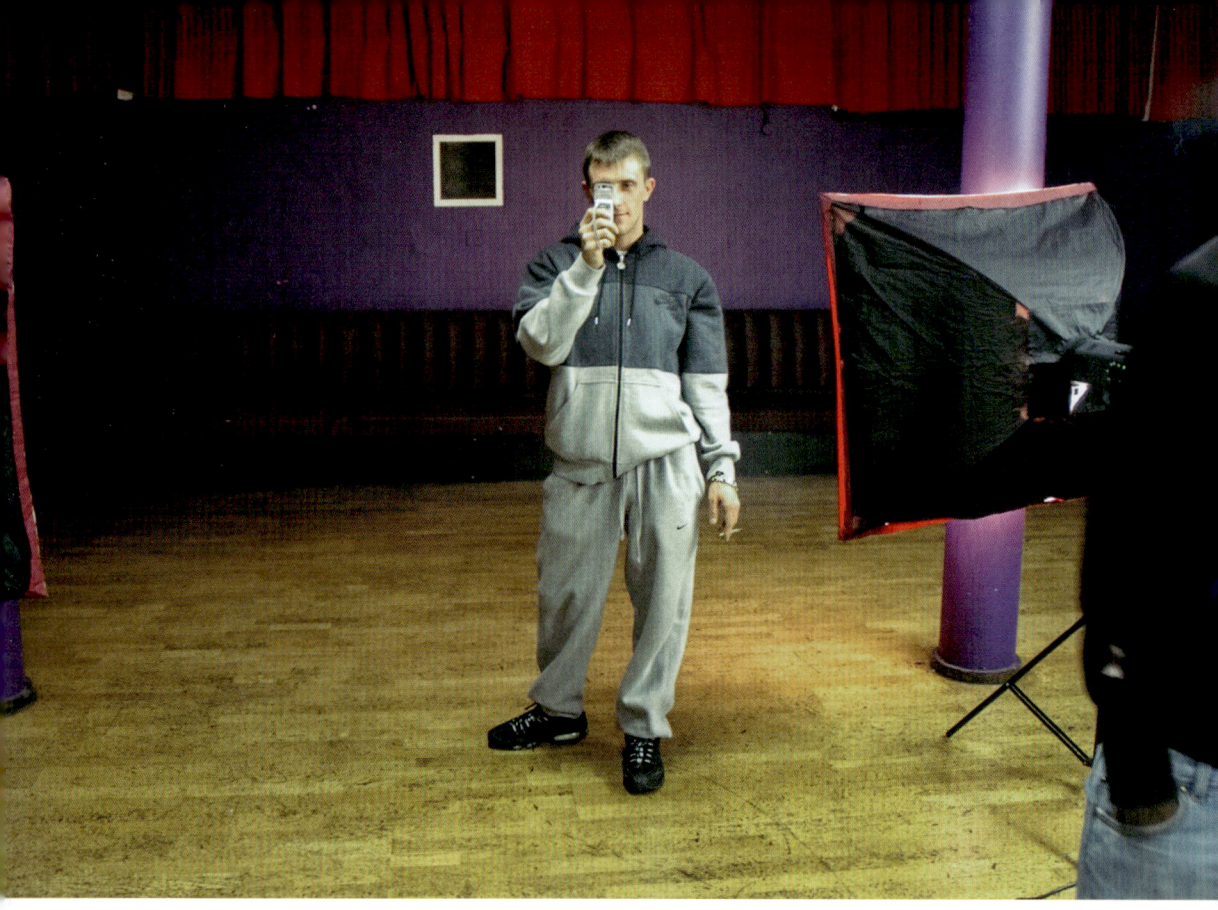

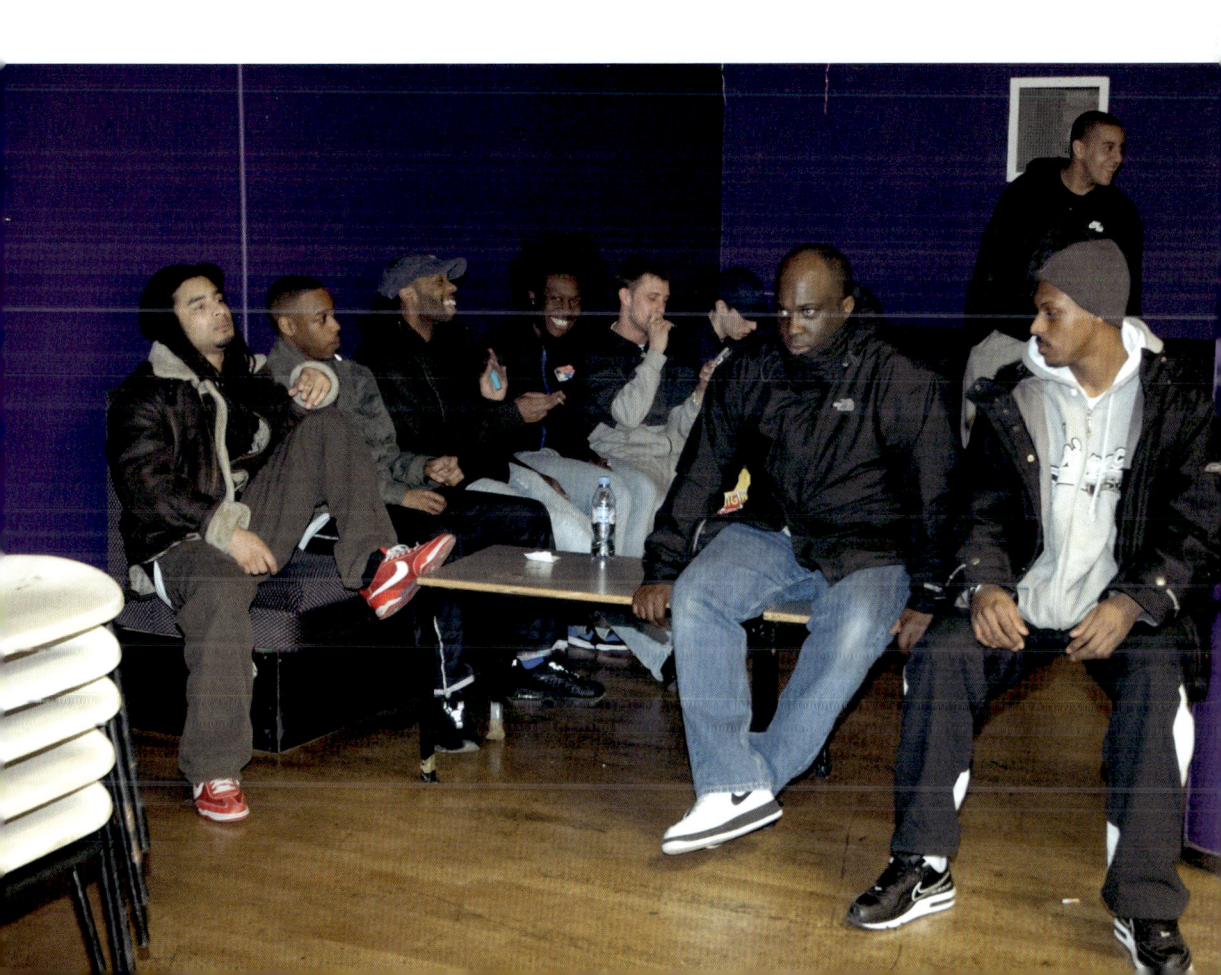

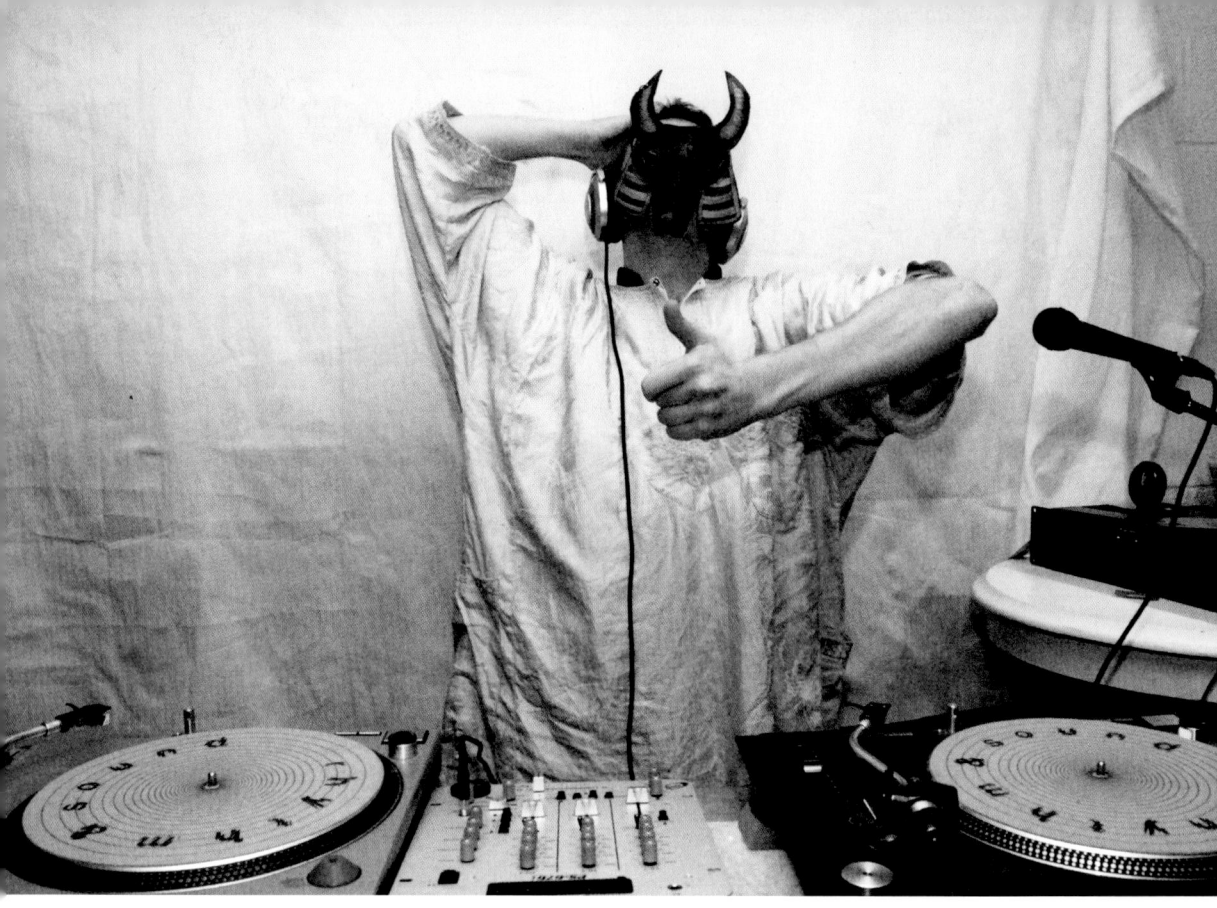

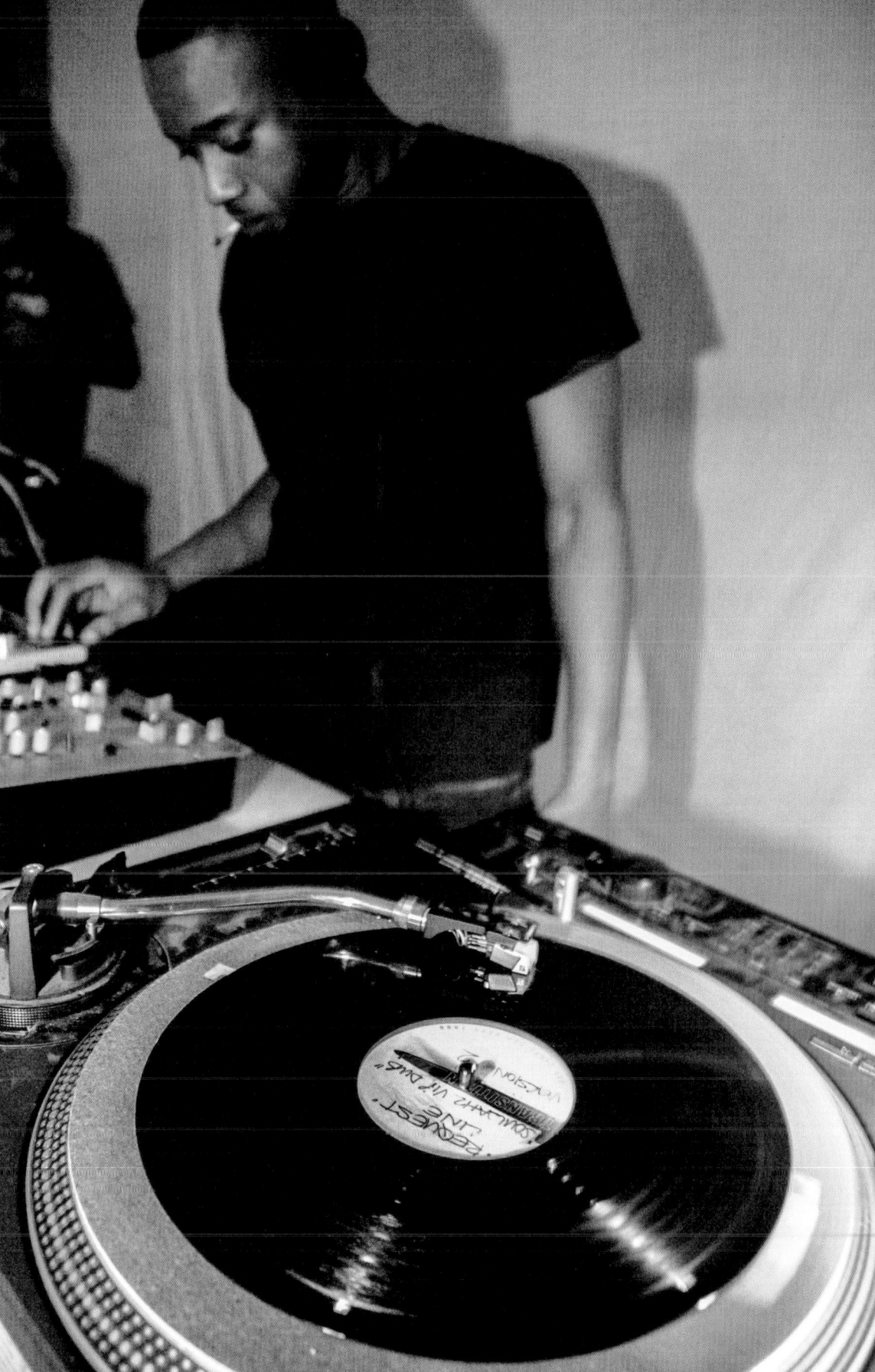

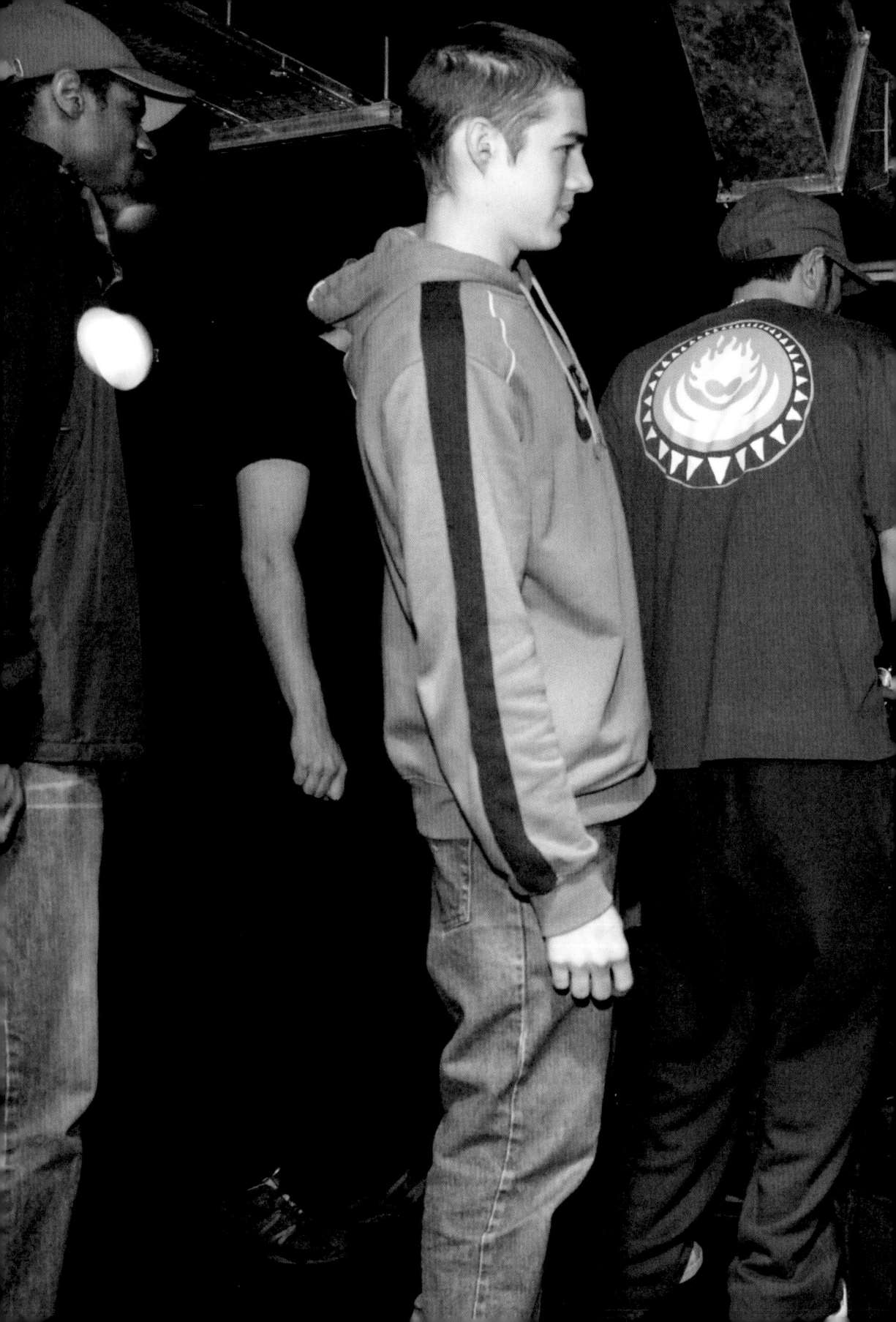

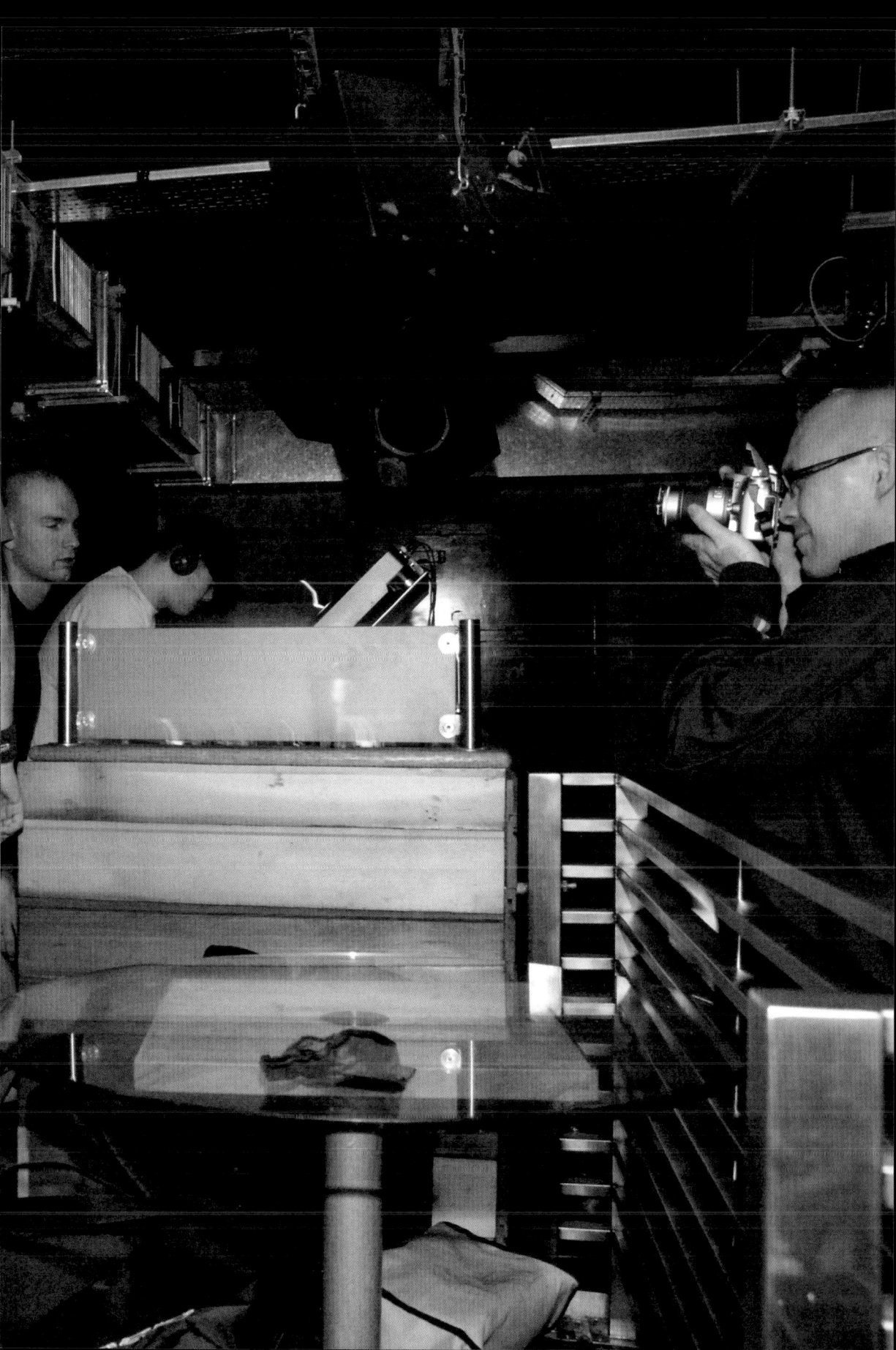

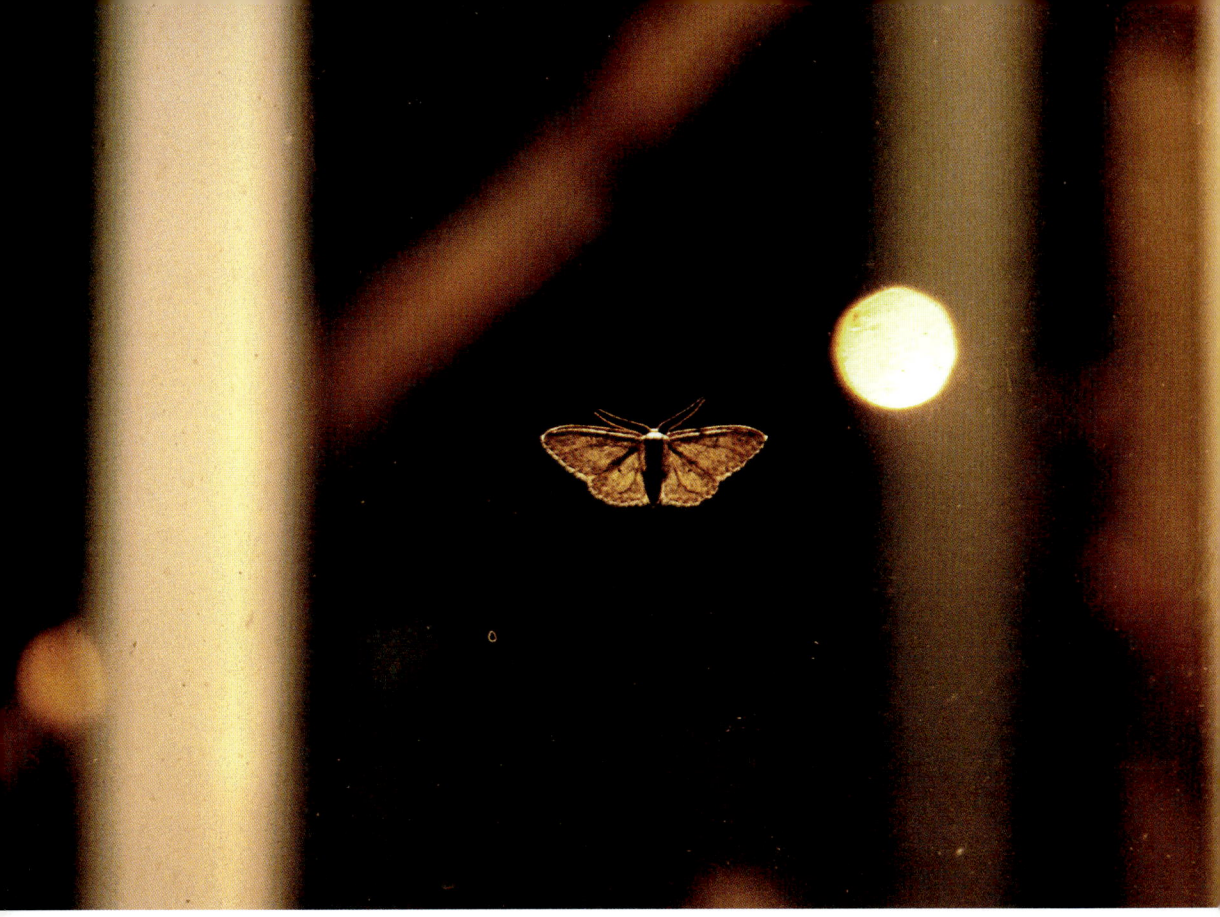

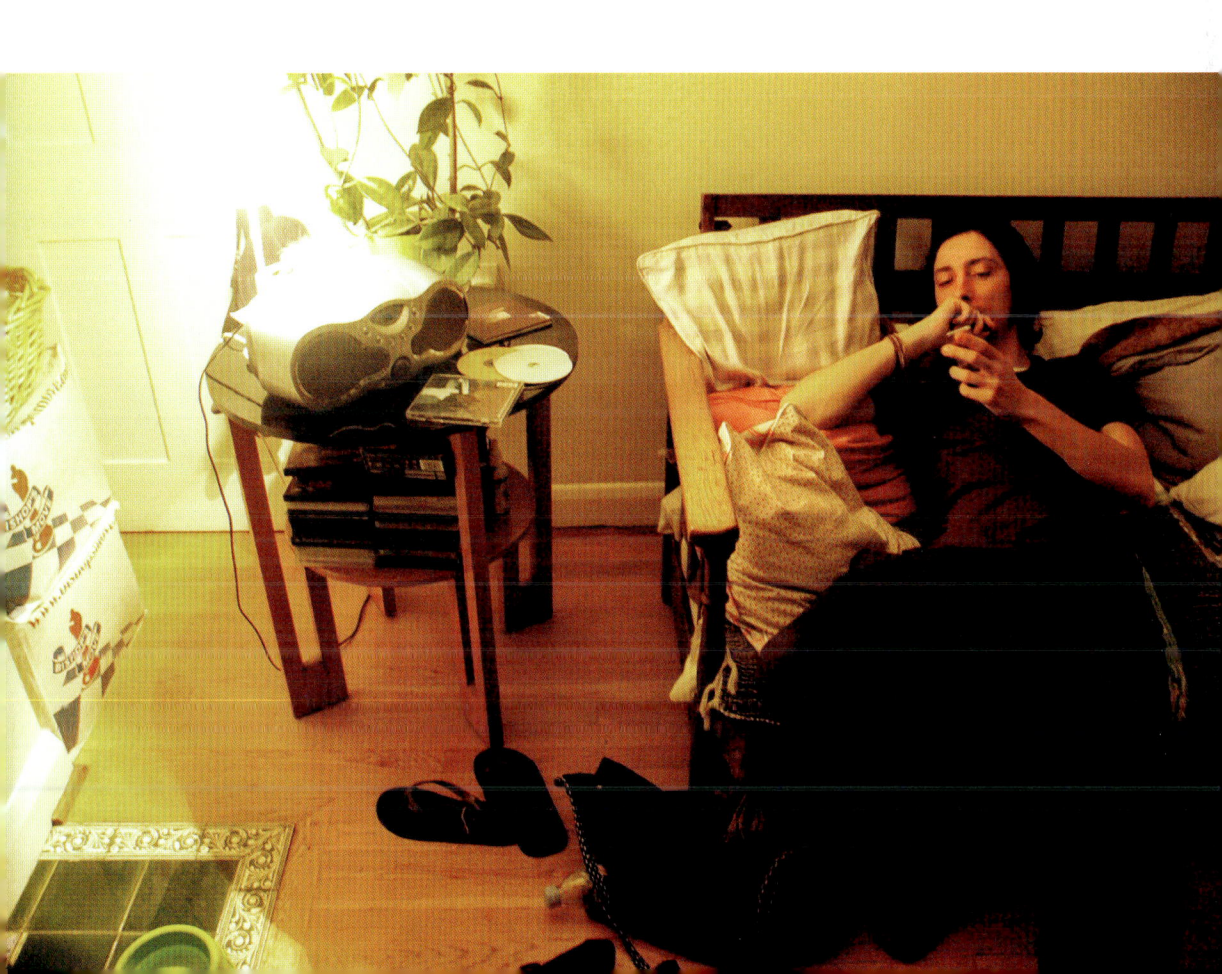

Where Are
The Women?
DJ Flight,[DF] Emma Warren[EW]
and Georgina Cook[GC]
in conversation.

GC   Natalie, this is funny as we're talking about women in the dance. Do you remember where we first met? It was a Red Bull Culture Clash, in the toilets.

DF   Yeah you were washing your hands and you turned to me and said "Who do you think really won that?" I was like "Well, I don't want to appear biased, but from where I was standing, the cheers did sound louder." And you went, "hmm," and that was it.

EW   Yeah, where are the women in the club? Well, sometimes we're talking to each other in the toilet. I had an important moment as a writer, also in the toilets at a club in Manchester, with a writer called Mandy James. I'd see her out and about – she was writing for proper magazines. I was washing my hands and she went, "Your writing's good, you could do this if you wanted to." I'd never had that sort of recognition. It felt extremely powerful for her to say that in the girls' toilets, on a night out.

"Immediately we're going straight to the way women support each other"

DF   And that's all it takes a lot of the time, whether it's spoken or a little email or a show of support on social media; it only takes that to spur you on.

EW   Isn't it interesting that immediately we're going straight to the way women support each other?

DF   Definitely. The first mixtapes that I recorded I gave to Kemistry and Storm for feedback. Kemi said she liked the way I put tunes together. And I said, "So do you think I should keep going?" And she said, "Definitely." And that sent me flying. Women have been the most supportive. Men have been quite supportive but not as publicly. Playing for Metalheadz was because of Kemistry and Storm and then Sara and Jo in the office. There have been a lot of times when women have been the catalyst.

EW   When people ask the question that has inspired this conversation – "where are the women?" – why do you think they can't see them? 'Cause if I close my eyes and imagine dance floors, from acid house all the way through, I can see women around me.

DF   Our stories haven't been covered anywhere near as much. And when they have, it tends to be the same names. Kate Theophilus said that when she was working on the Black Music Research project it was hard to get women in front of the camera to talk about themselves. Where we haven't been featured as much, women maybe don't think that what they say carries as much weight. When I'm interviewed, people always talk about the lack of women and issues around race. But they rarely ask my opinion on the music itself. And I've got a lot to say about the music. I've been around a long time, at pretty pivotal moments in the changing direction of sound and stuff.

GC A lot of the time when students ask me that question it's based on my archive. And to a certain extent, it's justified because the male presenting people in the images outweigh the female presenting people. So going by the images alone, there are holes. It was all men behind the decks at DMZ and FWD>>. I think Moxie was the only woman to play DMZ. Bash! was definitely a lot more gender-balanced though.

DF   I played at one.

GC Yeah I remember! Ari Up was there.

DF   Yeah and Nicolette and Mary Ann Hobbs.

EW   If you close your eyes and imagine those dancefloors again, is there any difference in terms of what you're seeing and the photos you would have taken?

GC I always try to be respectful of everyone that I photograph. Steffi from Deep Medi hated having her picture taken. I managed to get a picture of her twenty years later, a really nice portrait. Sarah Lockhart was also quite elusive. The only way I could change the way I photographed women would be to be more upfront about taking pictures of people. Maybe I would be more like Georg Gatsas and ask the women involved for portraits. Say, "Come on, let's do a portrait shoot."

EW   I have a distinct memory of when I started to go to clubs and then seeing the same clubs in i-D or The Face. I'd think,"I didn't see you there. You don't look like anyone I saw there." There was a disconnect between the people photographed and the people there. And that was really surprising. "Why don't you see what I see?" I don't think I've ever been on a dancefloor where everybody is masculine although they might have been skewed one way or another. What is the makeup as far as you see it?

DF   I guess it depends on the night. I've definitely been to events where it is male-heavy, like Renegade Hardware. The heavy and darker nights. Not to say there weren't women there though. Even when you look at photographs of events now, particularly if it's a venue with a stage at the front and a barrier; you might see a couple of women at the front raving it up but it's still male-heavy. It's a bit of a cliche that you probably find a more even balance at more soulful events. Sometimes with the jump-

EW   up style as well. But I don't like saying that because of the stereotype that women are only into the lighter styles, when we're all into really bass-heavy stuff. I think when drum & bass became so cold and dark sounding at the end of the '90s which coincided with the rise of UK garage, there was a mass exodus which left a lot of nights majority male. A lot of them are still that way.

EW   A lot of us like heavier sounds, we three are in that category. Is there something about us or is there something about that environment which means it's harder for women to discover that they like that kind of thing?

DF   It could be a bit of both. When I started going to record shops I would feel quite intimidated walking in. They're not that welcoming until you start speaking to people.

EW   Is that a kind of heaviness too?

DF   Yes. (laughing) Isn't it?

EW   Yeah. I'm thinking about the feeling of walking onto the dancefloor and the need to hold yourself a certain way. You can't just like wishy-washy walk into certain dancefloors, there's a need to be strengthened somehow. And that feels the same as the way you had to approach the non-dancefloor outposts like the record shop.

DF   Yeah, you kind of have to steel yourself. Let people know that you have a right to be there. It's like, okay, I'm into this. I'm gonna come into this space and you're gonna respect me as you respect everybody else in that space. But also, it partially comes down to having unwanted attention. I spoke to you about that for your book Dance Your Way Home, how I changed how I dressed when I went raving because I was fed up with unwanted attention, people grabbing my wrist and guys trying to speak to me when I just wanted to enjoy myself. So yeah, it is quite a big heaviness.

"If you look at the statistics of the cause of unsafety to women, it's boyfriends and husbands. So to apply "unsafety" to the dancefloor, it's a bit like, "nothing to see here.""

EW   Maybe in order not to present yourself as looking for that kind of attention, you have to have a certain amount of concentration. To be into the music, to zone in and zone out. But also it's a form of protection or signalling: "I'm not here for that. I'm here to be in the music, not out with you."

DF   Yeah, definitely. That probably influences the amount of women at certain nights. There are some places that are not the nicest because other people in attendance could prevent you from fully enjoying yourself.

GC There have been those exemplary nights where it has just been safe all round and you haven't necessarily had to think about how you hold yourself or what you wear or the codes basically. Like Plastic People. And I always felt pretty safe at Technicality regardless of the venue and Swerve and DMZ obviously.

EW   I'm interested in the way that safety has become such a big topic. Safety is almost more important than basslines. I have broadly felt safe in the specialist music environments I've been in. It's the non-specialist music environments where it's different. But if people are there for the music and the music's really good, the likelihood is, safety isn't a big issue. And actually, if you look at the statistics of the cause of unsafety to women, it's boyfriends and husbands. So to apply "unsafety" to the dancefloor, it's like we're looking in the wrong place. Not to say that people don't need to manage their behaviour.

GC There is this idea among some people that bass music is a masculine kind of sound. Why is that? Is it because of this idea that it's mostly men who make it, play it and attend the events? Or is there something inherent in the sound?

DF   I would say some of it is, but that would be specific labels or subgenres. But I think that it reflects the general sexism that permeates society. When you look at reggae and dub sound systems, there were barely any women involved. More women run sound systems now, which is great. But when you look at photographs or films of older sound systems, you rarely see women, so I guess that's continued.

EW   I think that people apply a gender lens over the sonic spectrum. If we think about the music that we're talking about, it's powerful music. It's strong. It's basslines, it's drums, it's often digitised horn sections. Sound that powers through. So if we're thinking about it on that spectrum of sweet to tough, we're talking about stuff that is more on the tough end. But that doesn't necessarily mean it can't also be sweet. Which makes me think, what is a masculine sound? Is this just about powerful sounds? And in the way that people who are gendered like men aren't often allowed to be soft, we who present as female are not really encouraged to be hard or tough, are we?

DF/GC   Exactly!

EW   So all of this dissonance isn't actually to do with the sound and what a human being likes to hear. It's to do with the connotation of the sound. And being part of powerful sounds is not considered to be ultra feminine, even though I don't feel any less feminine when I'm being compressed by a bassline.

DF   Exactly!

EW   That makes me also ask who is allowed to make the drum sound? Often instruments are gendered, aren't they? Who's allowed to have control of the powerful sounds, who are they made by and who for? I think there's something there to do with control and power and none of it is really to do with gender. It's all social, isn't it? It's not sonic. Maybe my body will respond differently to sound in its feminine shape on a cellular level. I don't know. What do you think?

GC   I agree, completely. These notions of what power is and who has it and how it's symbolised. But part of me believes that people who are gendered as men are a bit more competitive than women, based on experiences I've had. Which is probably social, not inherent. And maybe that comes out in the music sometimes. Like, how dubstep evolved, the early sound that I really loved. I loved the space in it, how you describe being compressed by bass. And all the different sounds were endlessly interesting. I feel like it got to a point around 2009, where it stopped being as varied. And it started eating itself. I imagined producers waking up and saying "I'm going to make dubstep today," rather than innovators, like Kode9, Loefah, Mala, Benga, Skream just making music that happened to fit into this wider community of sound. But some producers started to notice "Oh, the crowd really like this particular element of dubstep," what I call the 'Fighty Robots' or that wobble that Coki and Loefah were good at. And I feel like a lot of producers, most of them men, started to be like "Let's make tunes with that sound" and make it louder and faster. Almost like a competition to make the most fighty tune they could, which is the point I stepped out because I didn't want to feel like I was in that program Robot Wars! I feel like you can pick any genre of dance music and see a point where it becomes faster and more aggressive and not as outwards-looking. Maybe it's wrong to, but I associate that with a type of maleness.

"It's more accepted now, women having kids and continuing to work in music."

GC On a different note, I was just thinking that there's an element of women in the dance connected to motherhood. Because if you have a kid then nights out are limited. Me and a friend met a DJ at Sonar who had had a baby a few weeks prior. She was talking about her boobs hurting because she wasn't with her baby. And I remember thinking, "Gosh, what an amazing person."

DF It's more accepted now, women having kids and continuing to work in music. A couple of years ago, I saw a DJ bring her express milk thing to a festival, 'cause she didn't have her baby with her. I'd never seen any women doing that in my earlier days. I know there are quite a few women who did stop working in music once they had kids.

EW Partners make a difference too. I've had some really supportive partners but sometimes people don't want the women in their lives to be interesting because it's a bit embarrassing. "Rave Mum" is not a compliment and neither is being an interesting woman.

DF Yeah, I have a couple of ex-partners who weren't always that enamoured with what I was doing, even though they were in music as well. When people are not supportive it tends to have quite a big effect, doesn't it?

EW Again, that's to do with the power dynamic. But those of us that keep going, what a lot of benefit we get from it.

GC Do either of you think there's anything radical about being a woman in music?

DF At one time, I thought my being involved was quite radical because of the lack of black women in jungle as DJs or vocalists or MCs. But colourism is a part of it. Most of the black women in jungle and drum & bass work behind the scenes, as agents, label managers, promoters and most of them are darker-skinned black women. When you look at the black women at the forefront of the scene, the majority of us are light-skinned or mixed. When I was first DJing, I didn't pay too much attention to a lot of the obstacles, but as you become more entrenched in the music you notice things more. It's important to pay it forward as well. To shout people out, recommend people, give advice and help.

"I'm not supposed to know the things I know. I'm sorry, but I do."

EW   The way that I would respond to your question, Georgie, is to say that it's not particularly what women are supposed to do. At some point, we must have all decided that we weren't going to be the kind of women we were supposed to be and instead we'd be creative, busy, visible, interesting. I don't know about radical, but we would have decided long ago to live with being a bit anomalous. But it also means that you're constantly having to explain yourself. There's a gendered aspect to that as well. I'm not supposed to know the things I know. I'm sorry, but I do.

DF   Yeah, constantly having to prove yourself and give people reasons for your presence. Constantly having to reaffirm who I am and what I've done. Not so much in the last few years; the DJ Mag Best of British award is partly to do with that. But, people look at me in a different way, people that I've known since I was like 17 from Blue Note or at 16, going to raves. A lot of them are probably bored of still seeing me around and hearing me push for stuff via EQ50 and that. But when you have been around for such a long time, that's when people think, oh, okay, they are actually serious about it.

EW   Endless respect for what you have done with EQ50. It sends out such a good signal.

DF   We never remotely imagined where we'd be five and a half years later. We know that we've had a big effect on the number of women that are being platformed. It's incredible what we've achieved. It would just be nice if more of the men supported us publicly. Sometimes we get messages, "I love what you're doing," but okay, tell everybody else, support more women, you know, take action.

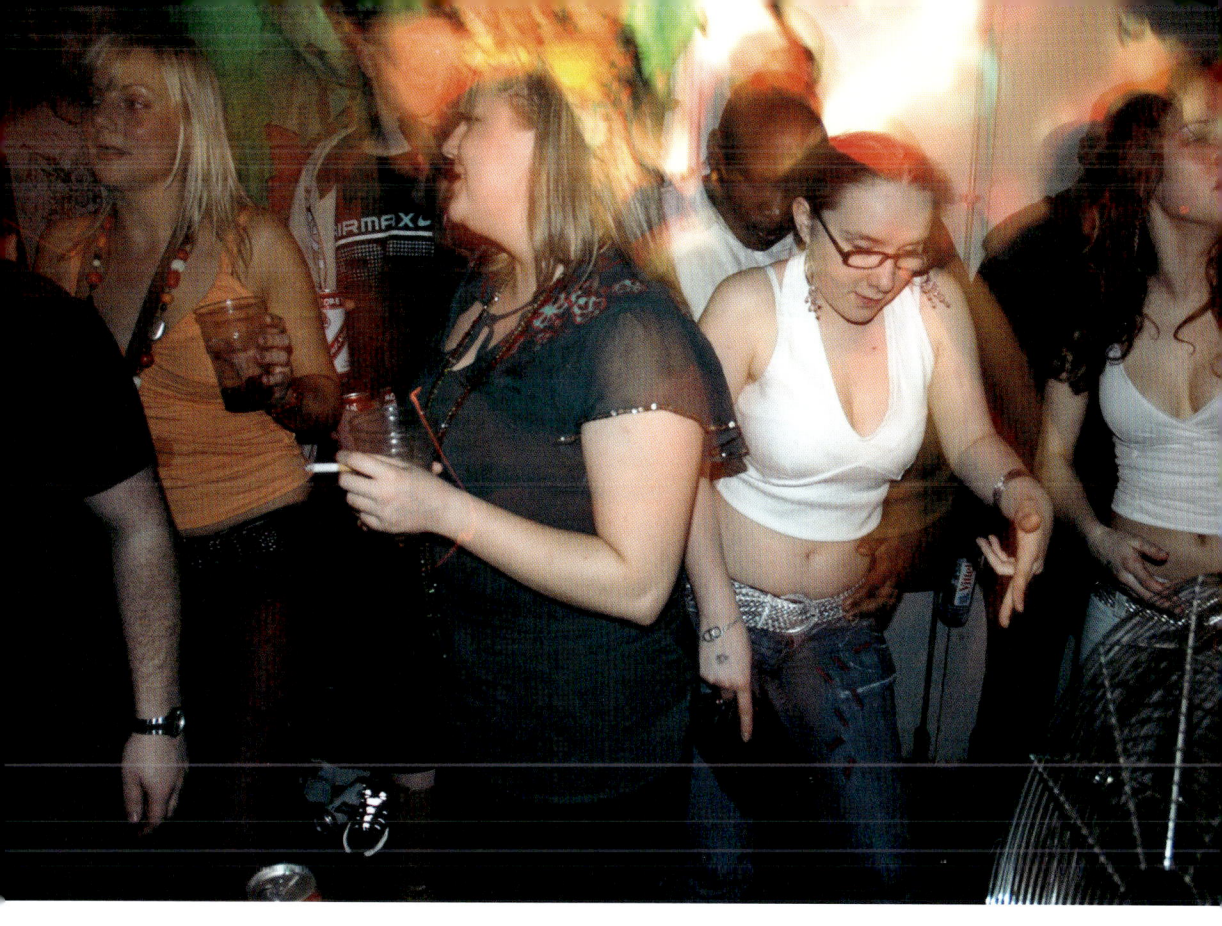

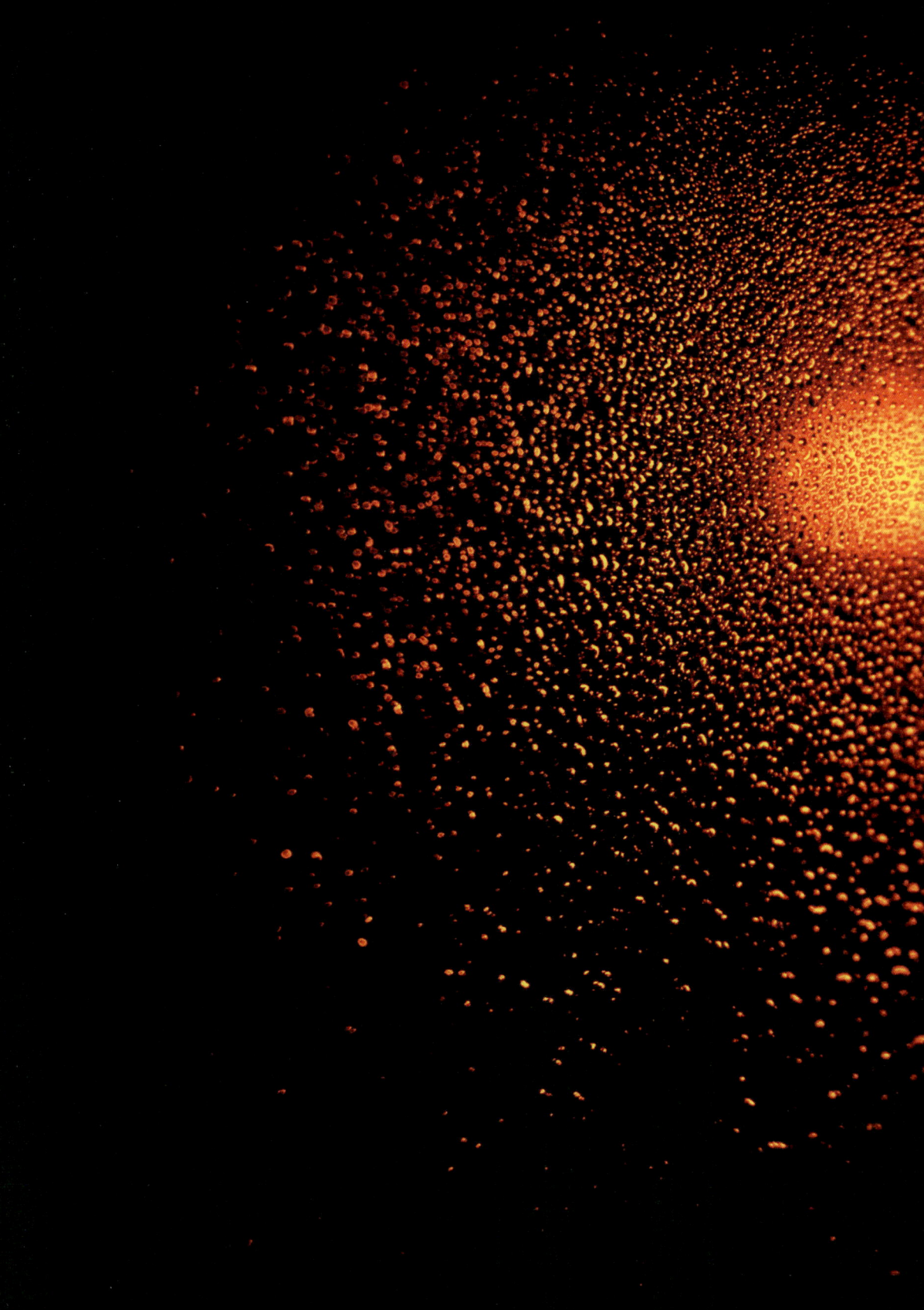

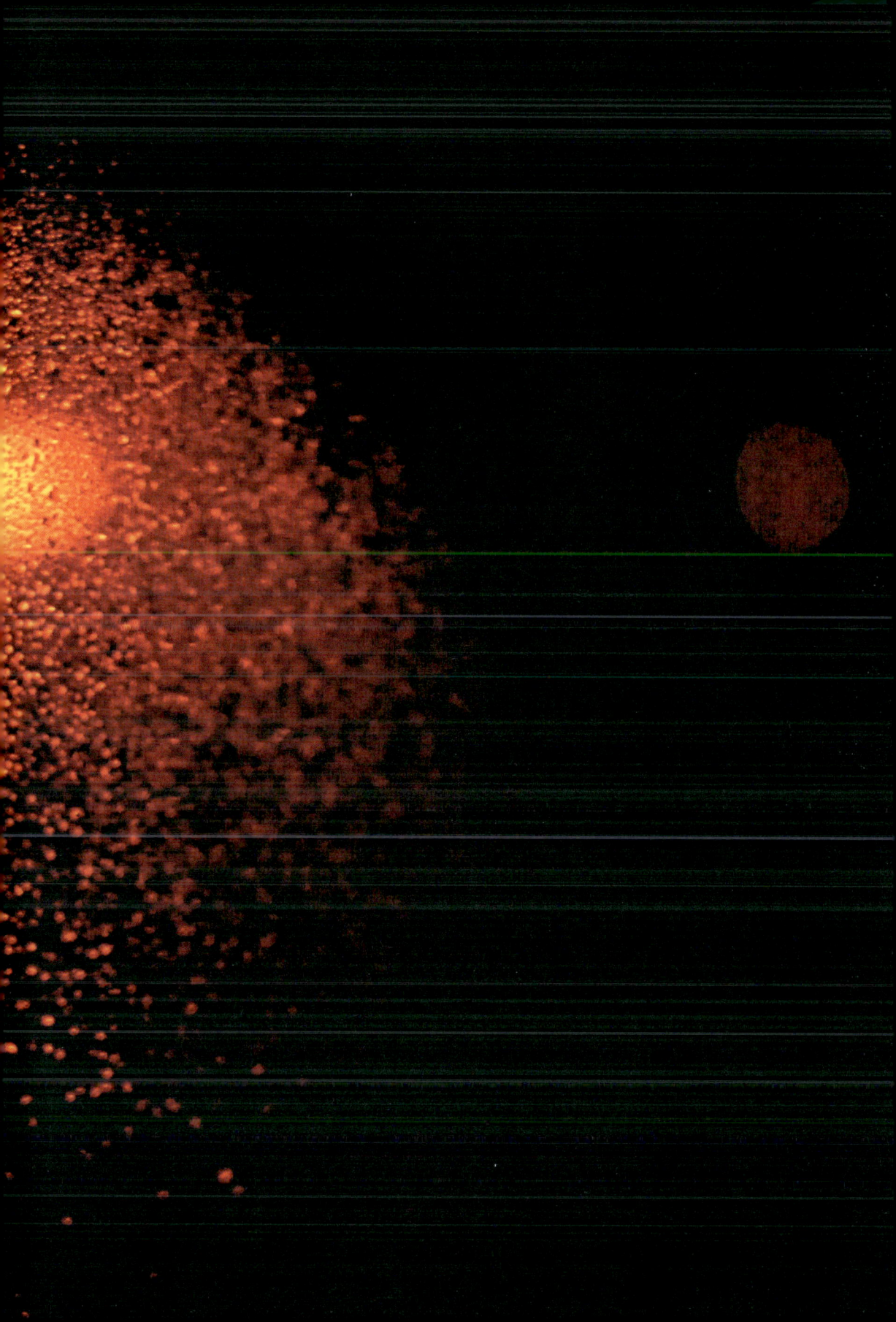

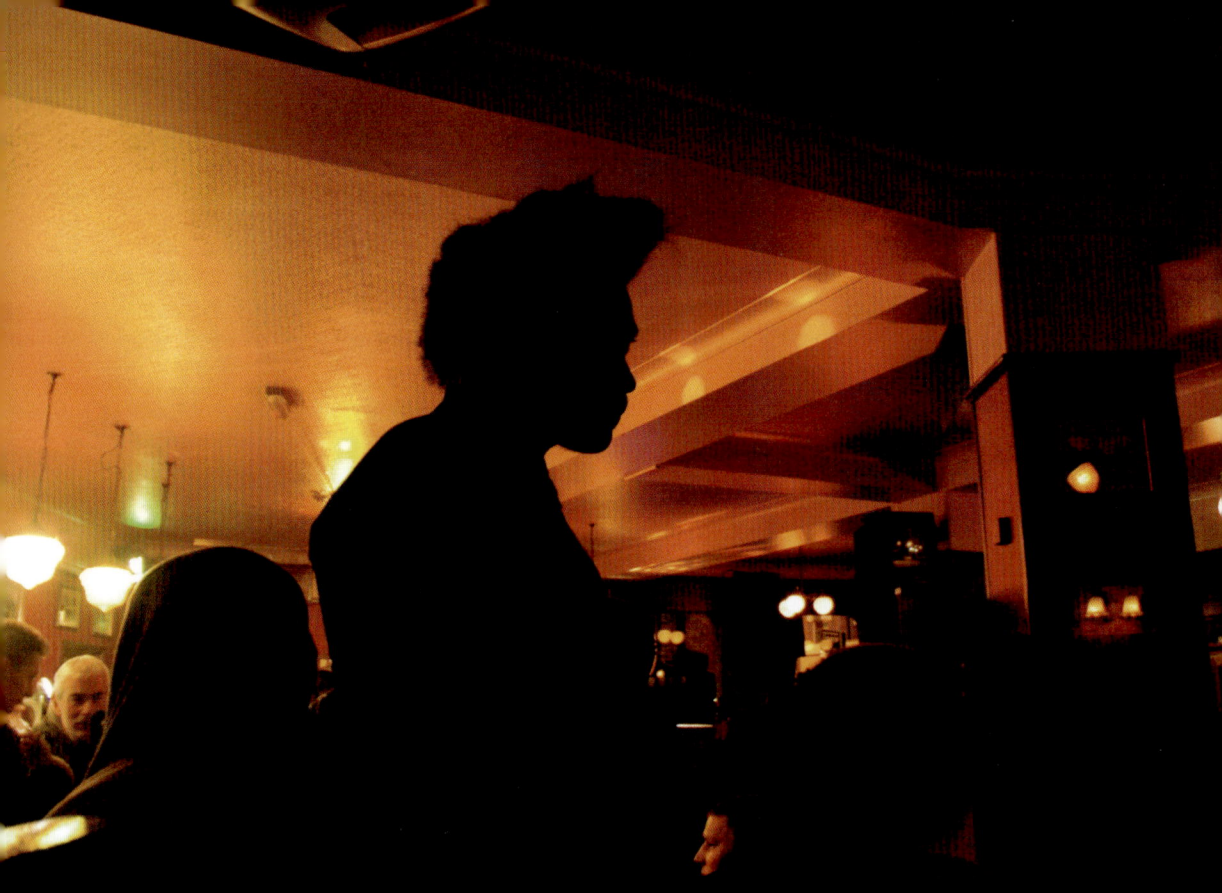

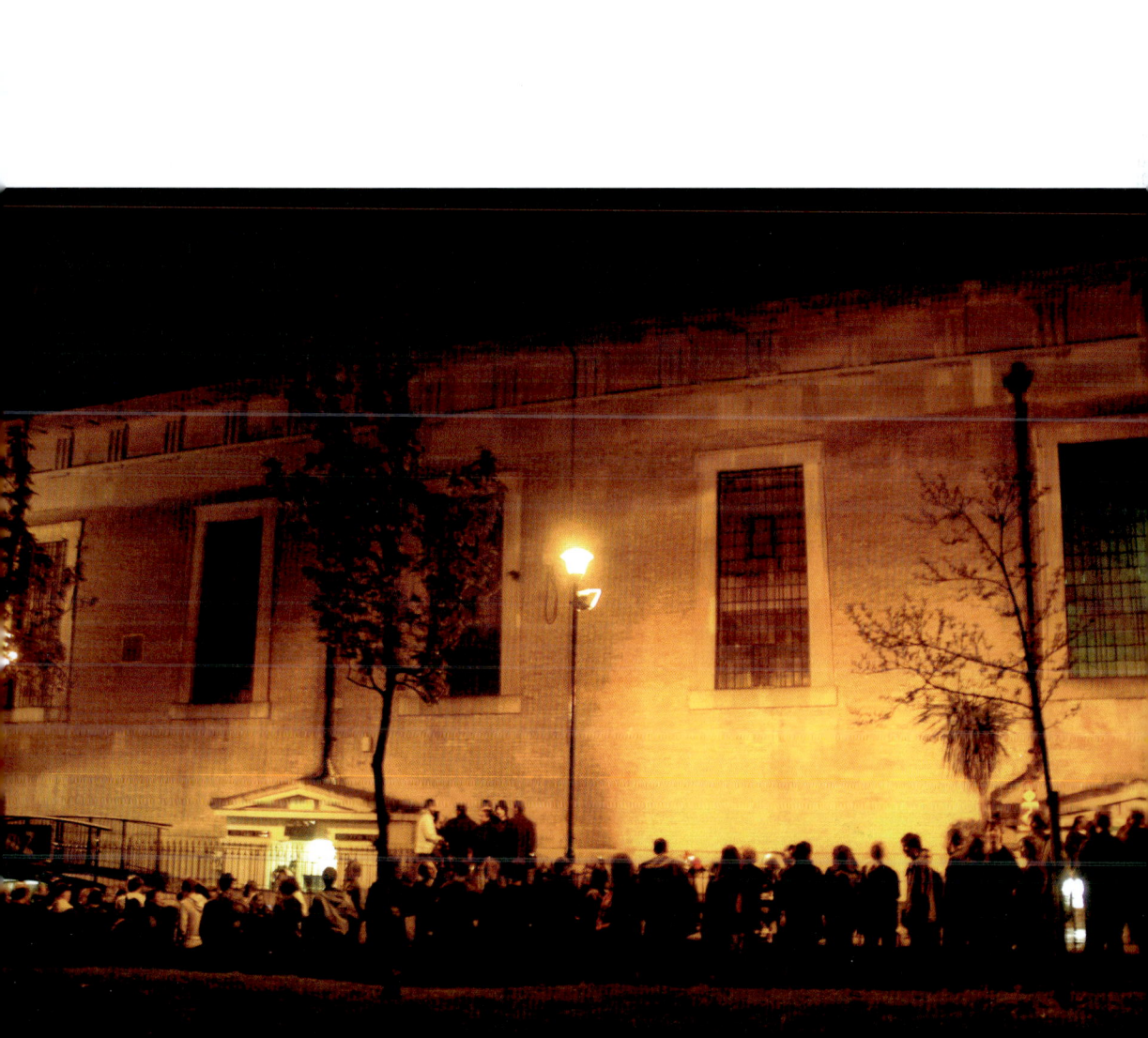

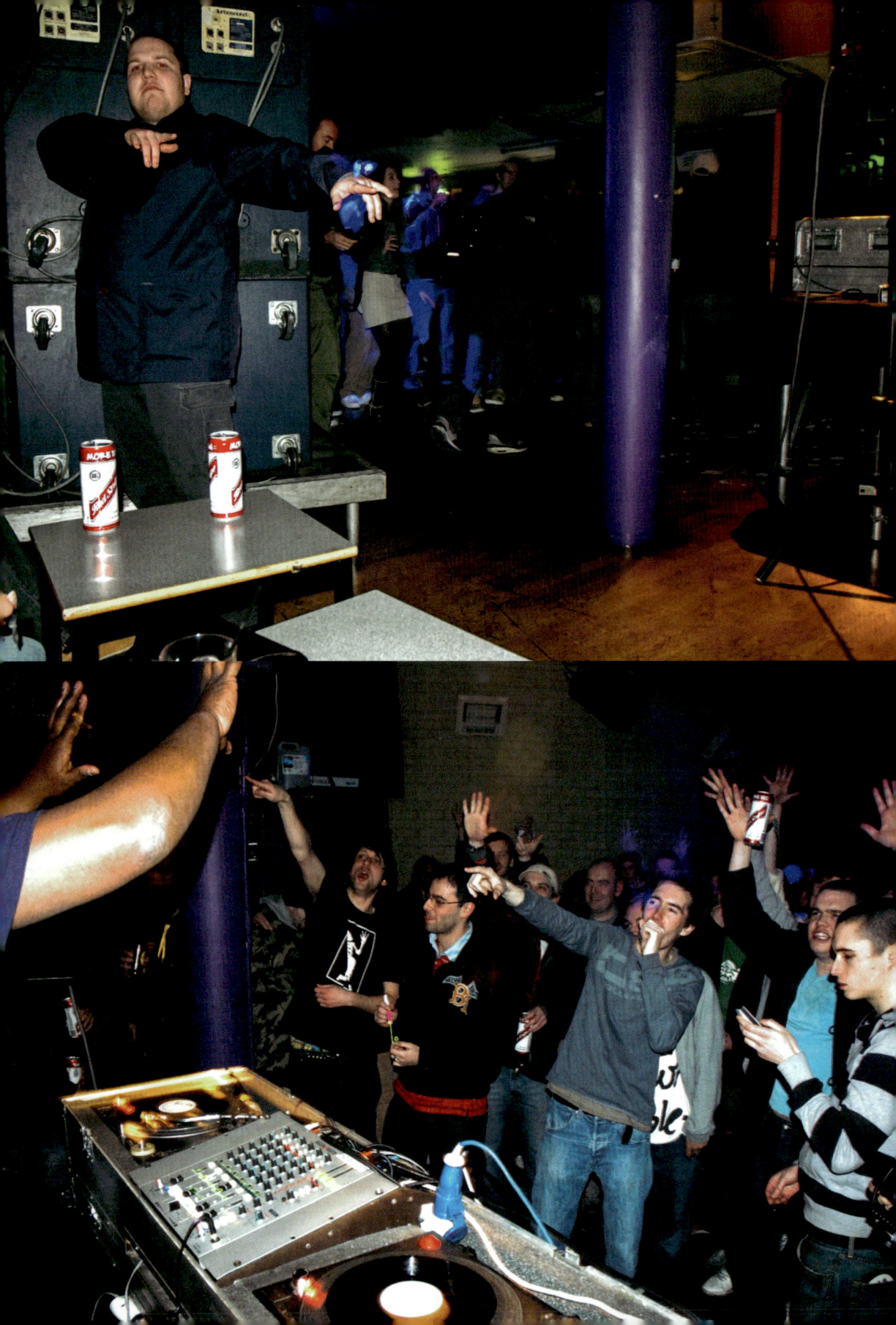

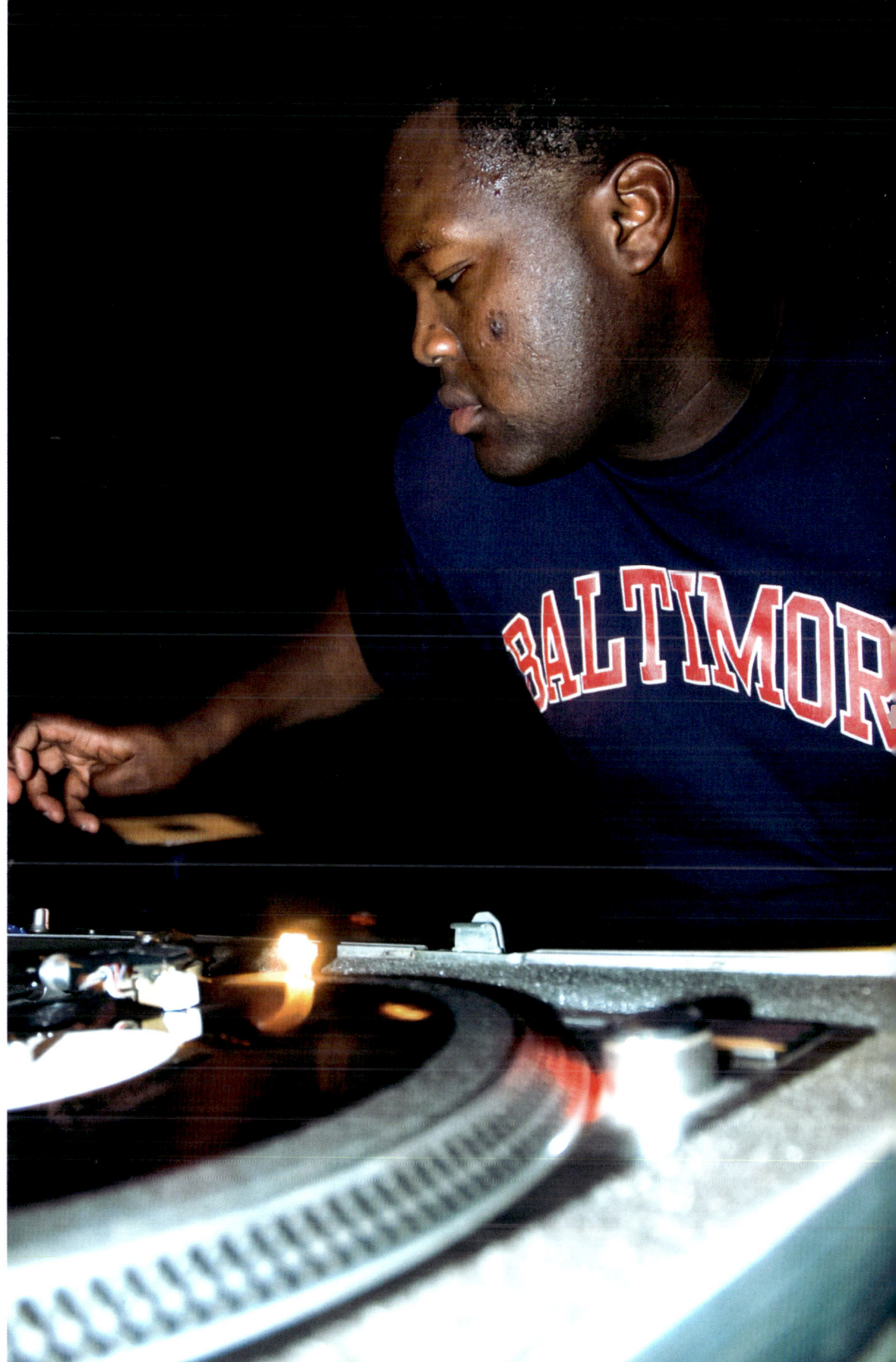

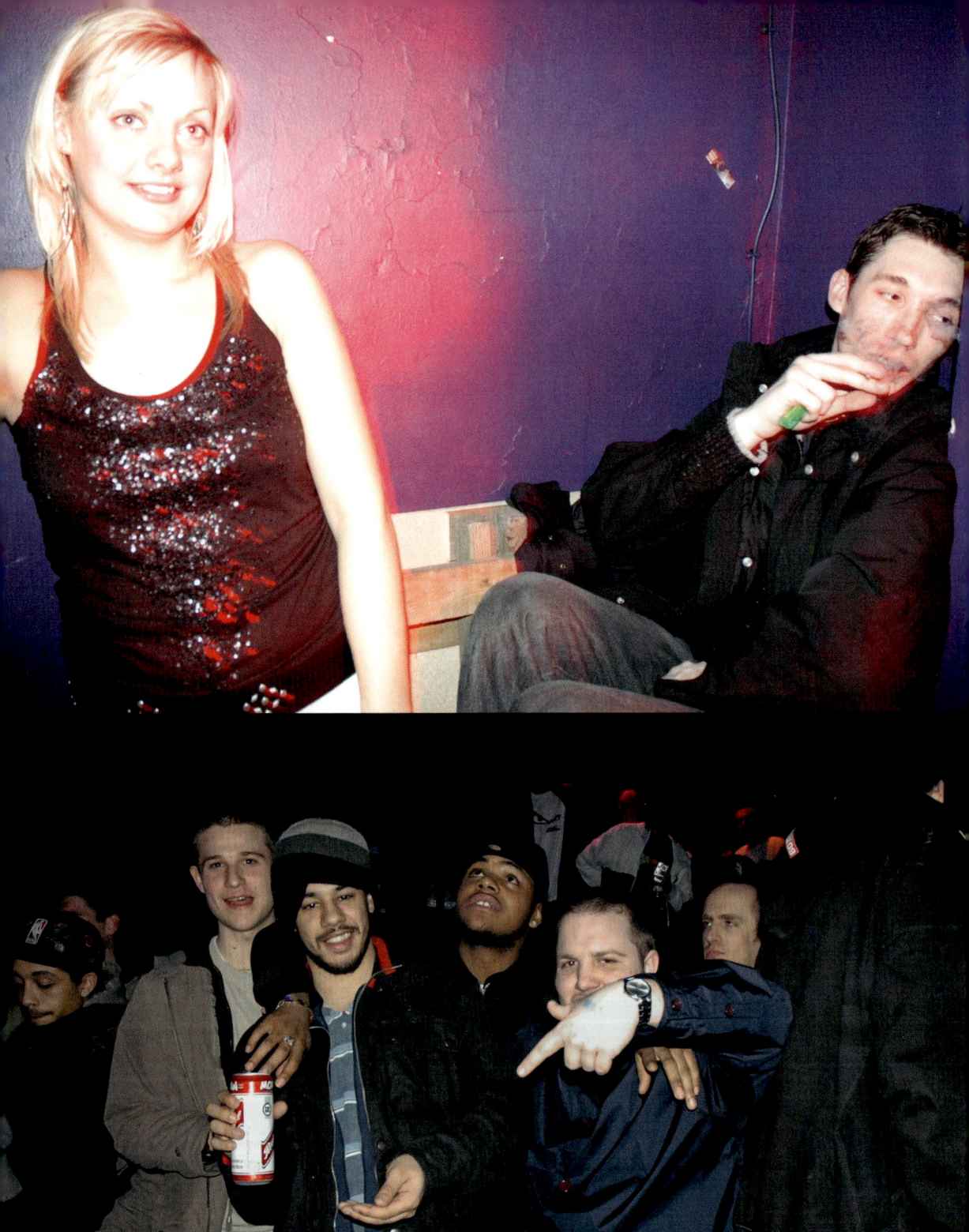

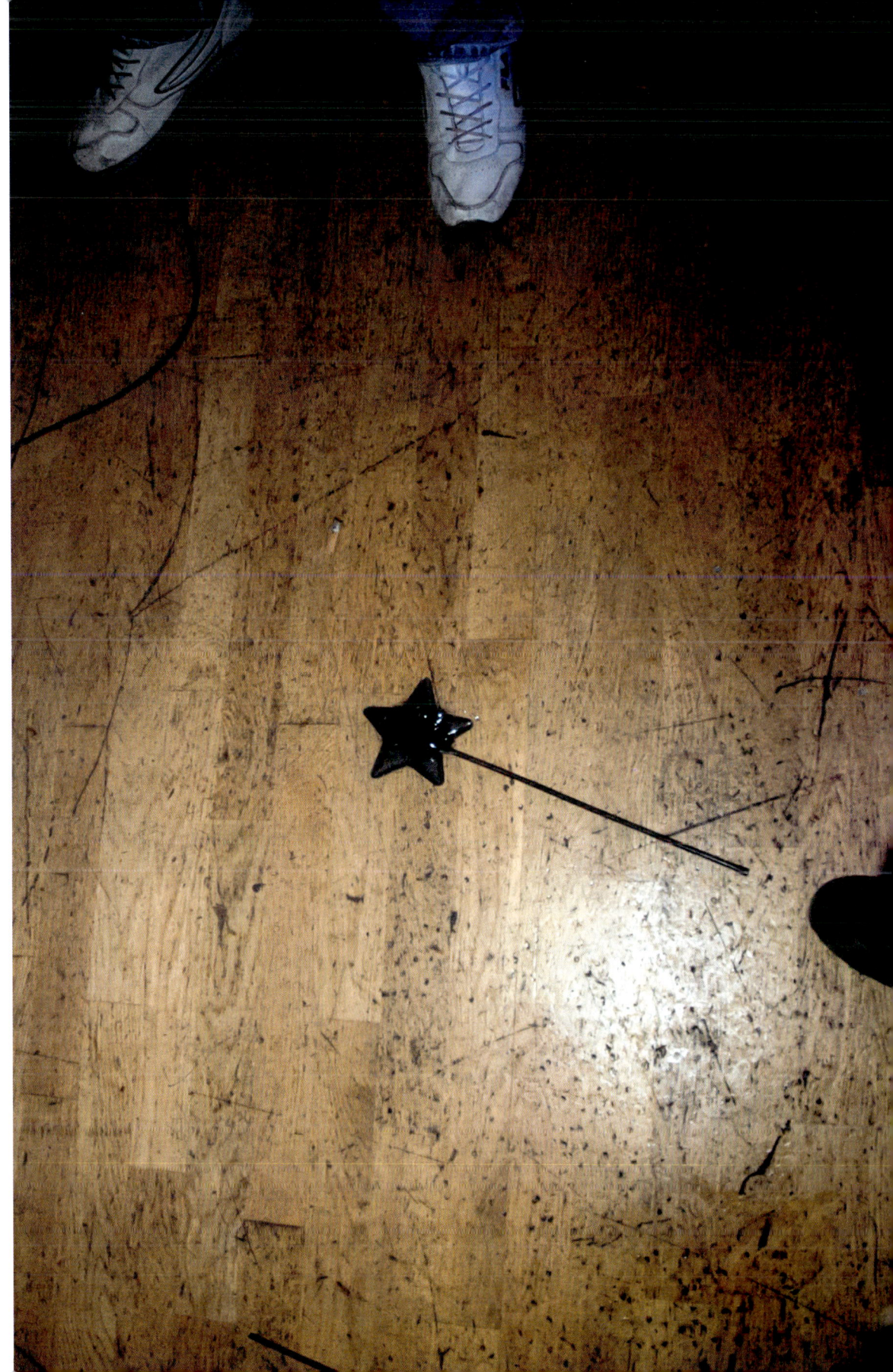

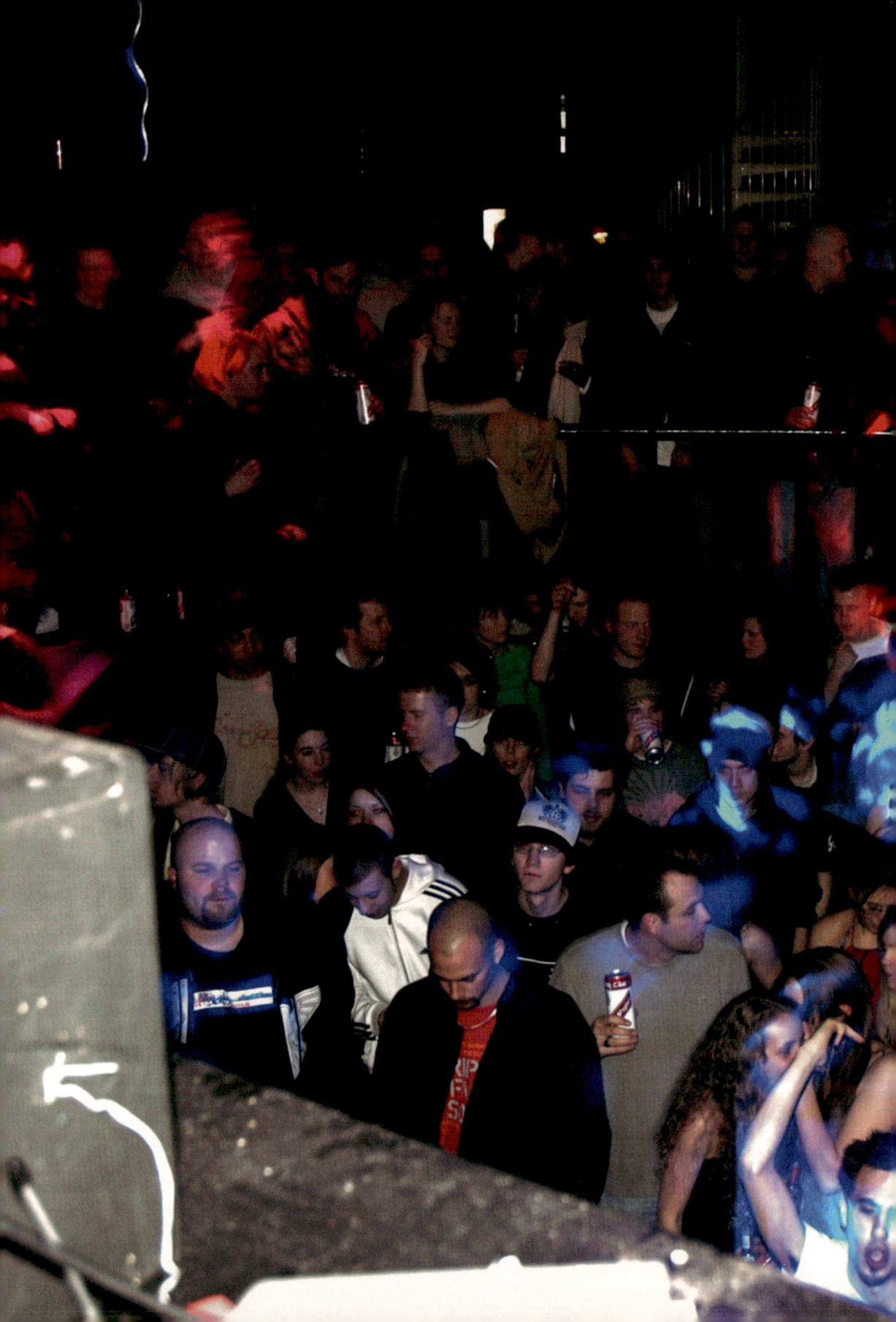

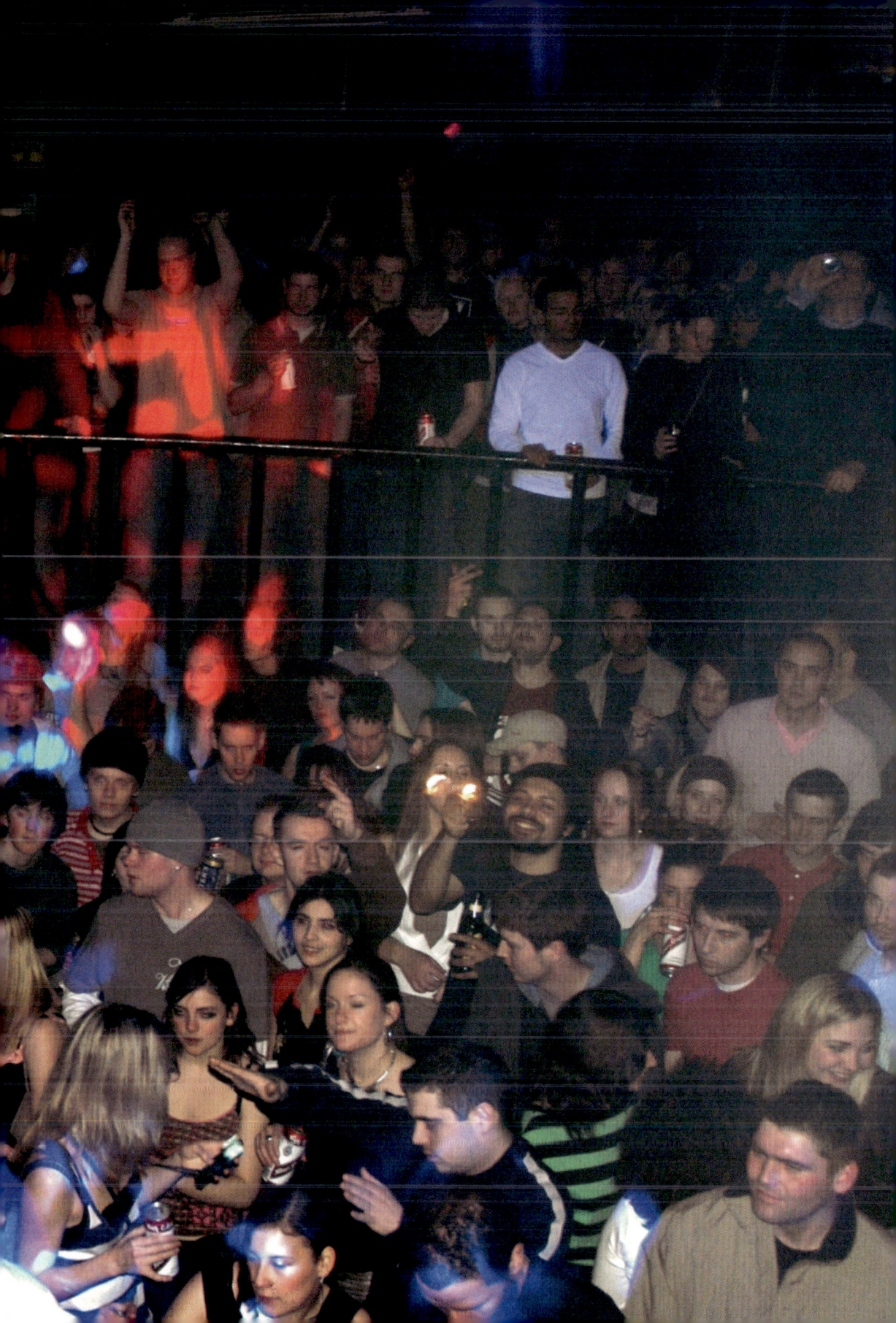

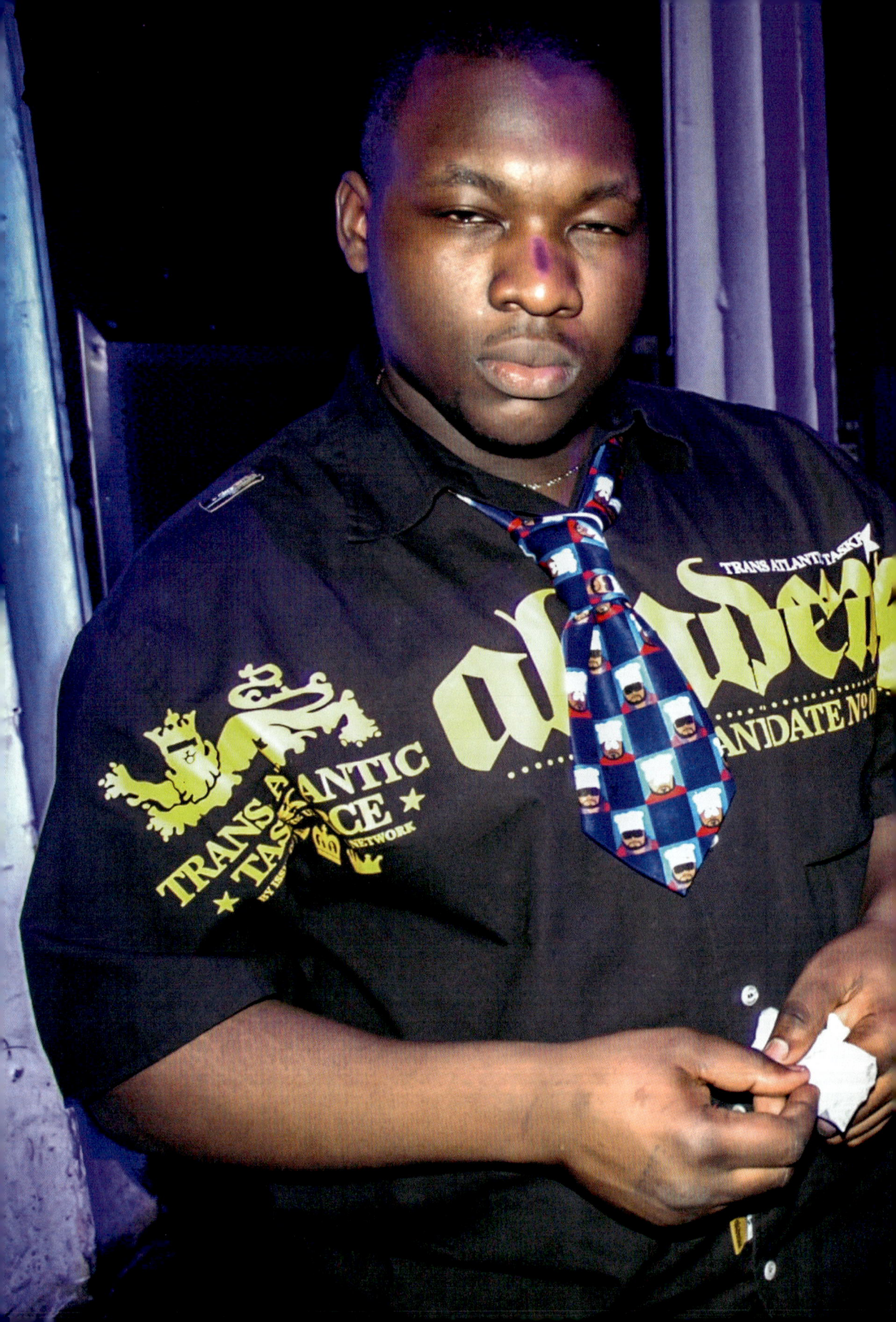

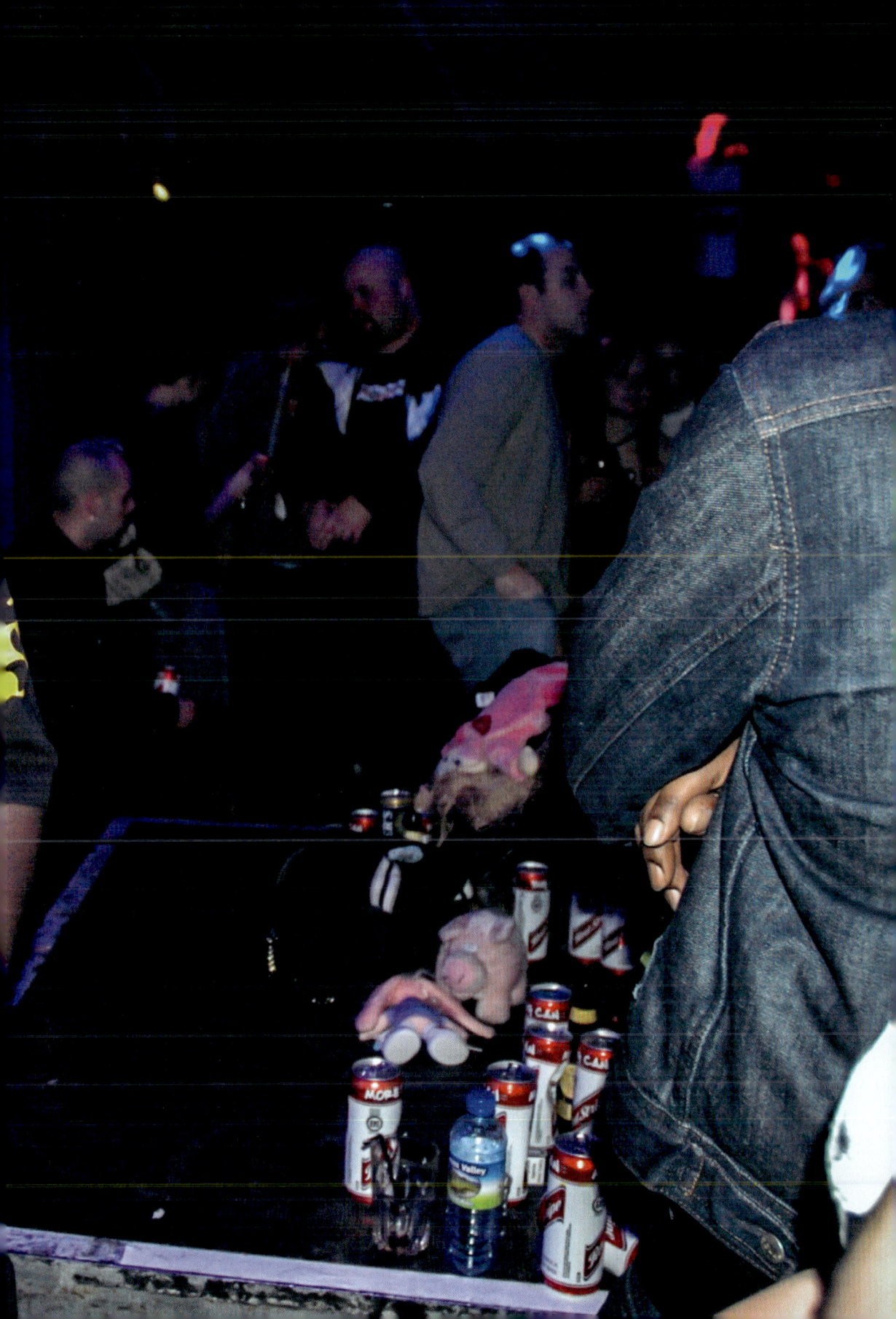

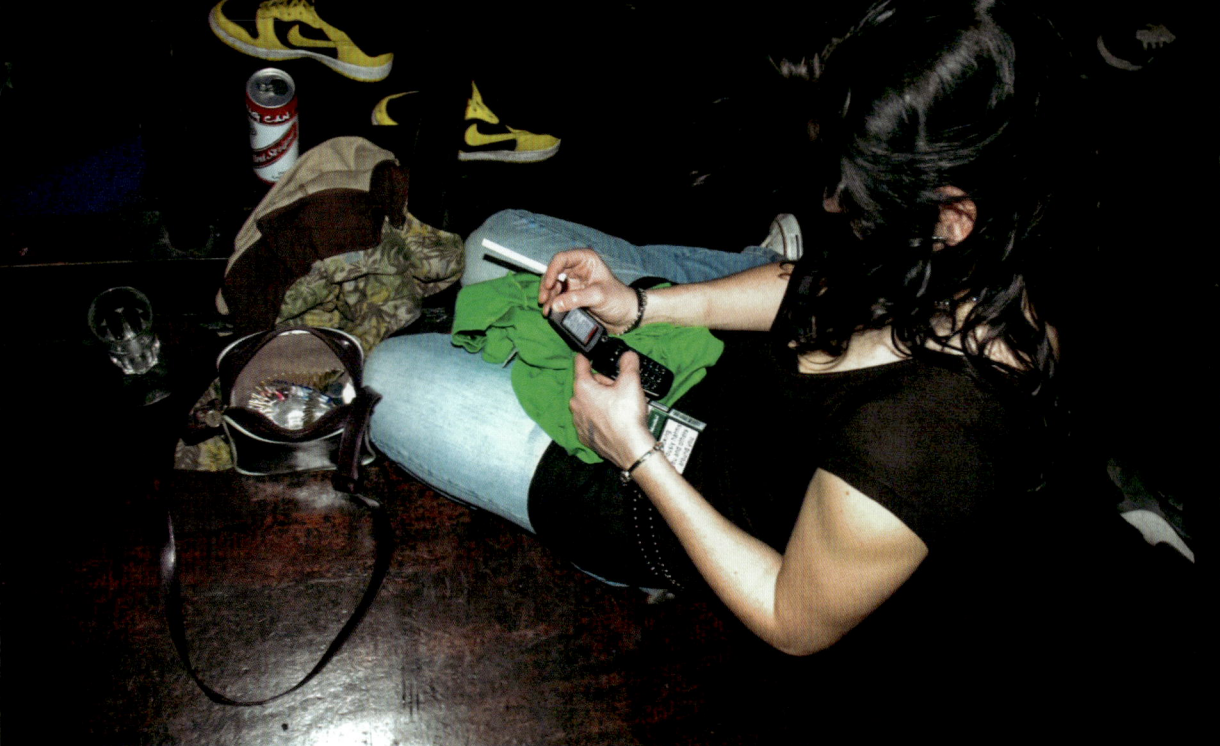

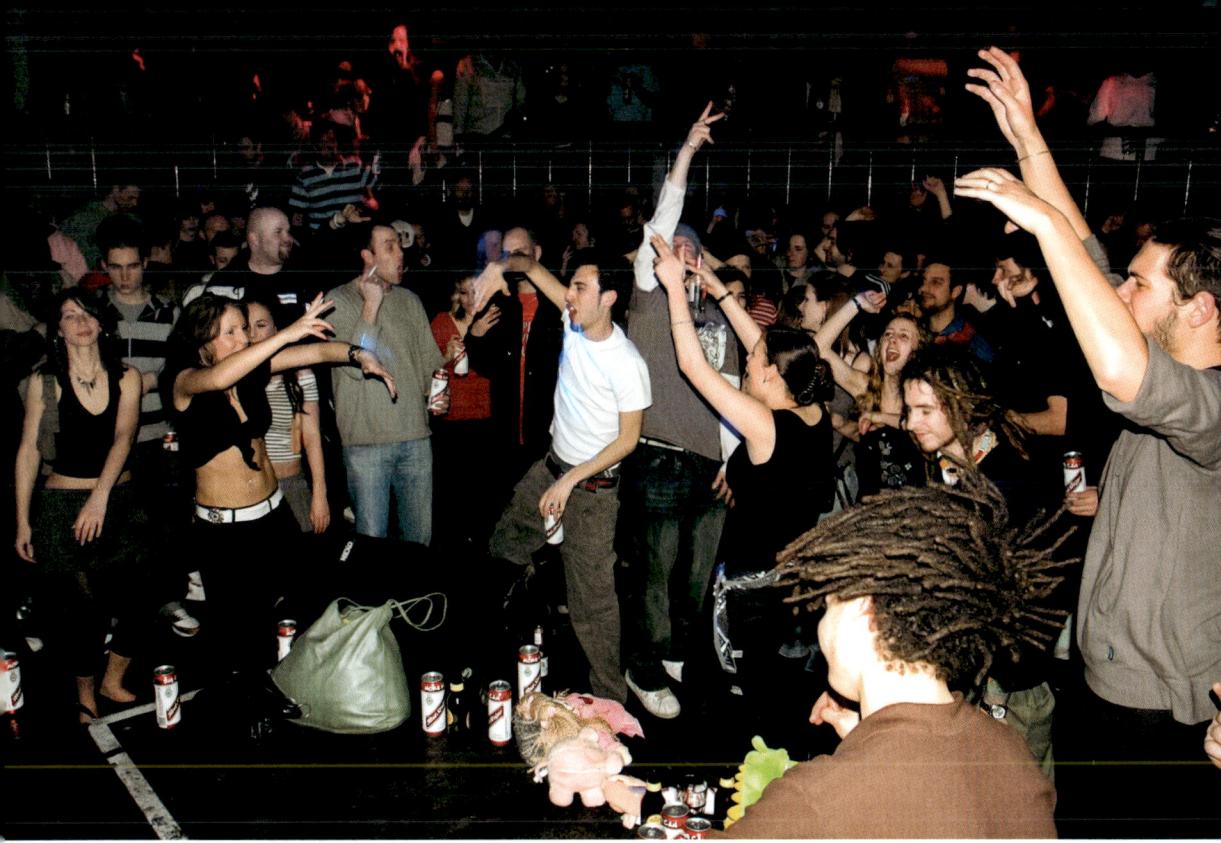

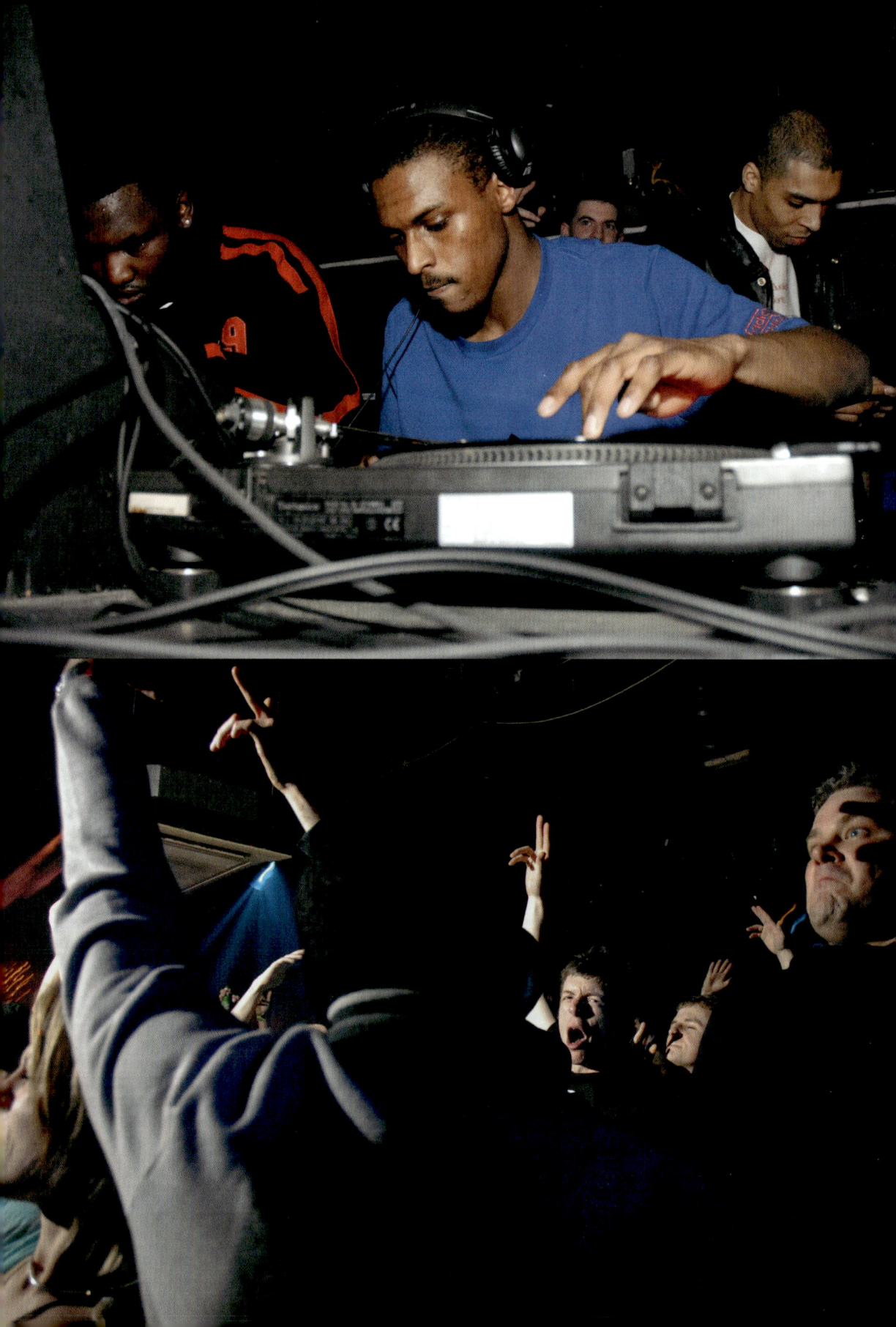

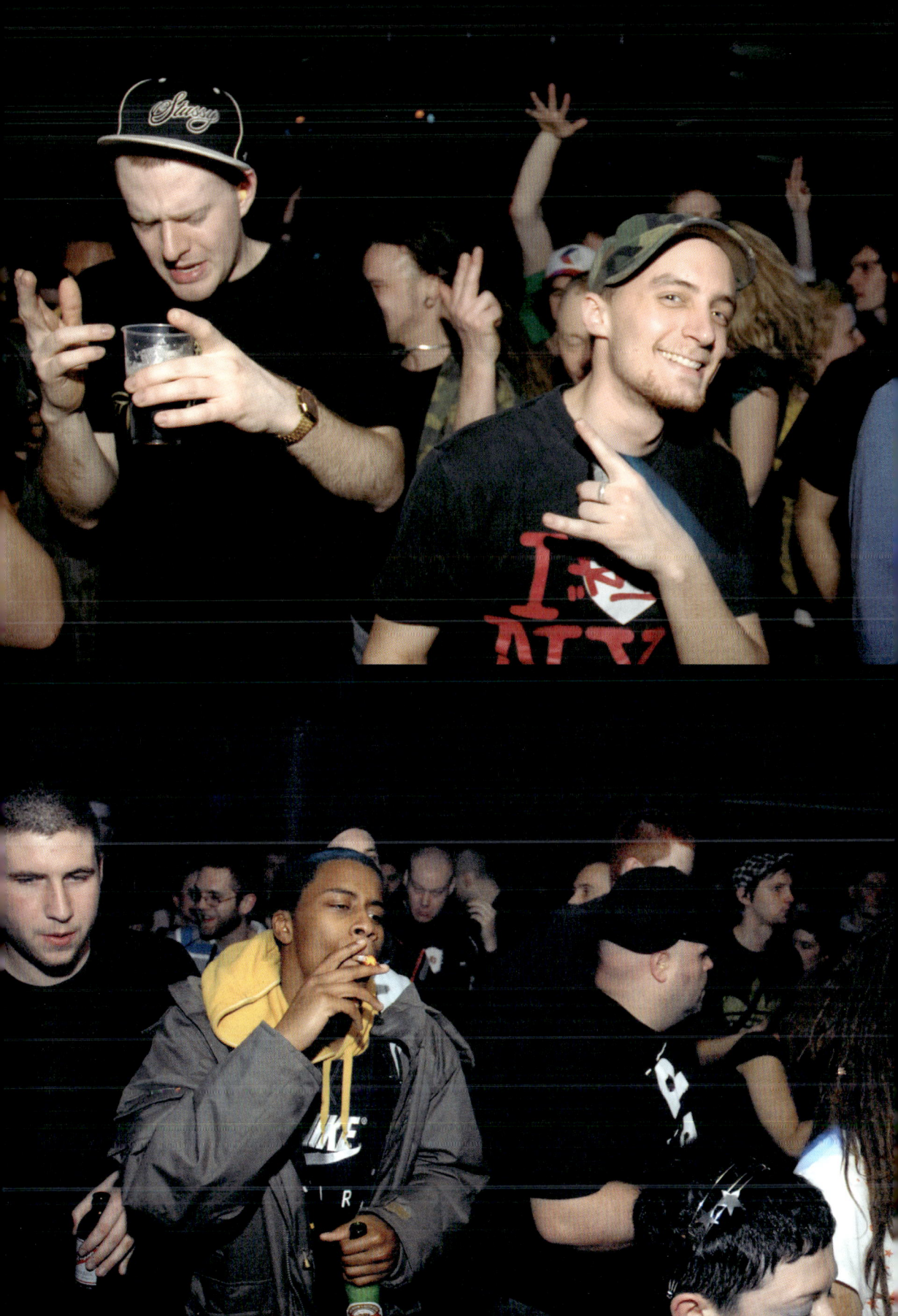

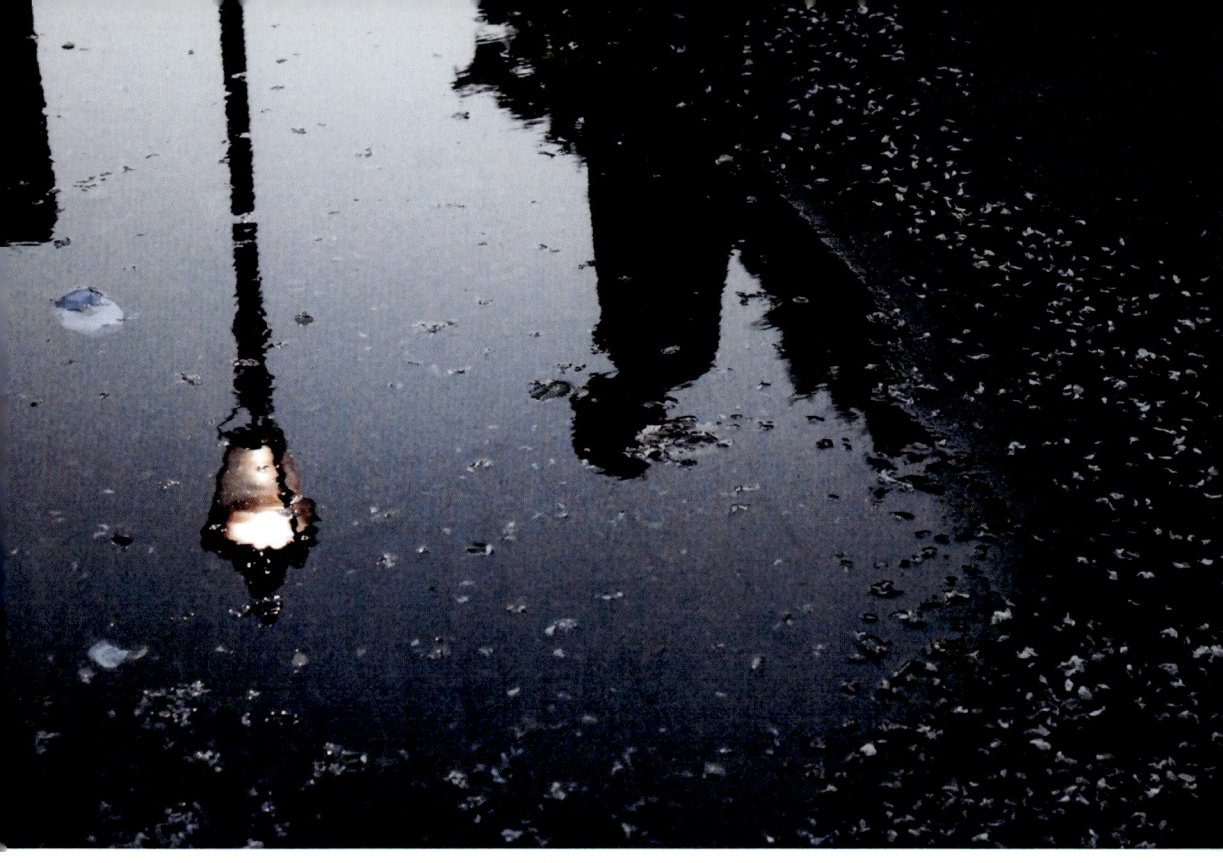

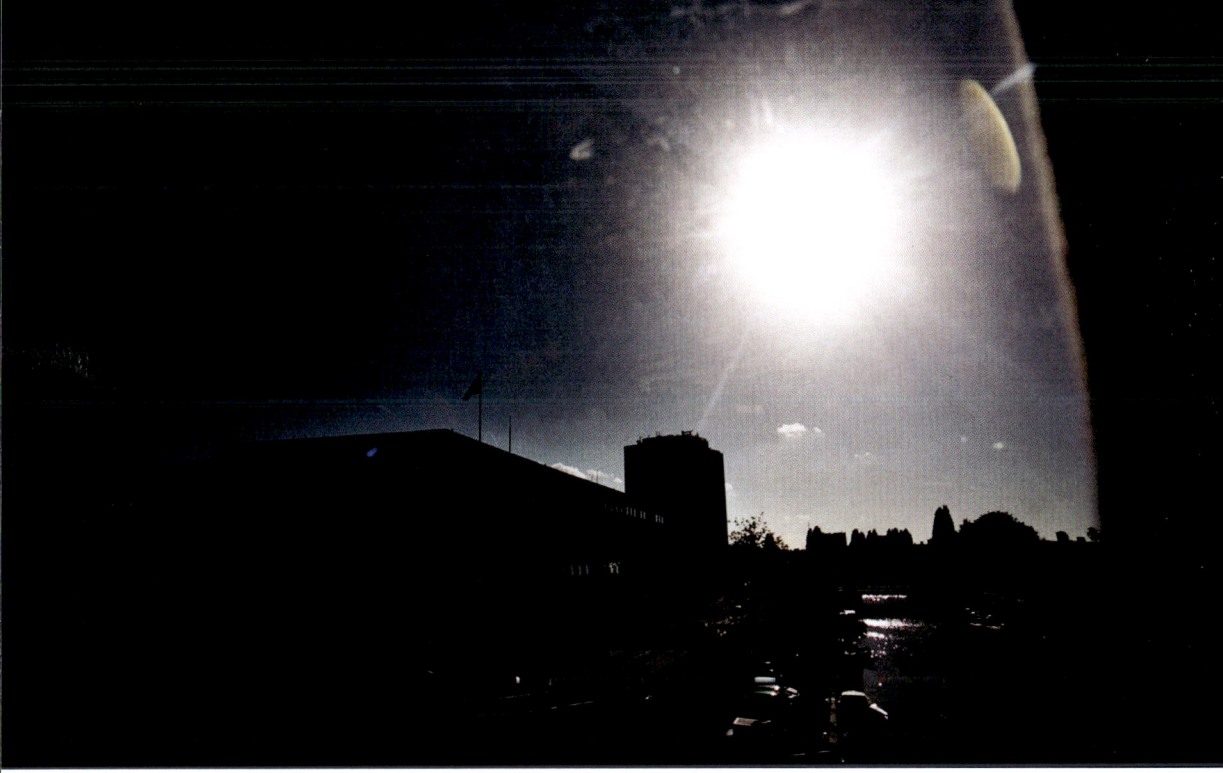

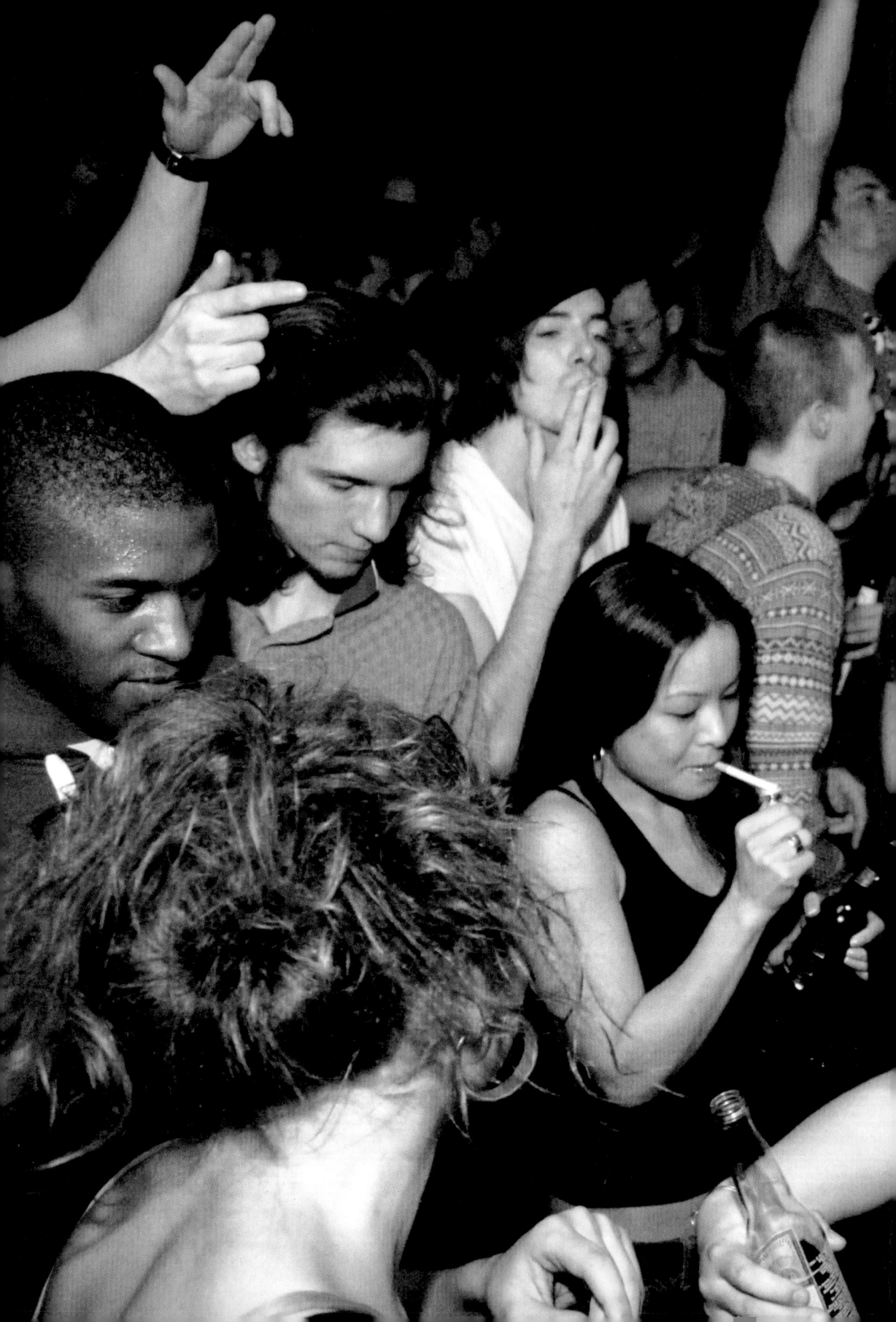

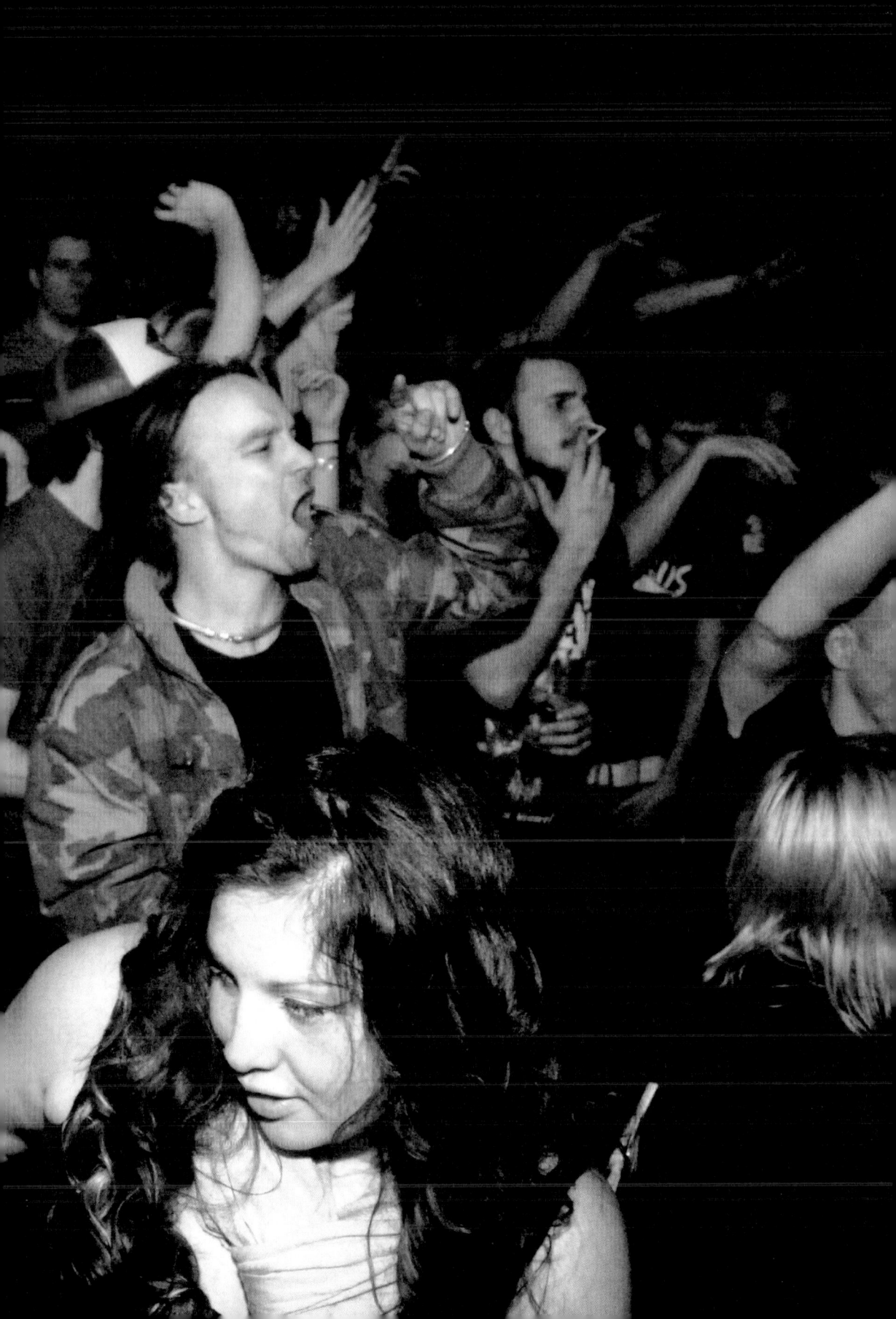

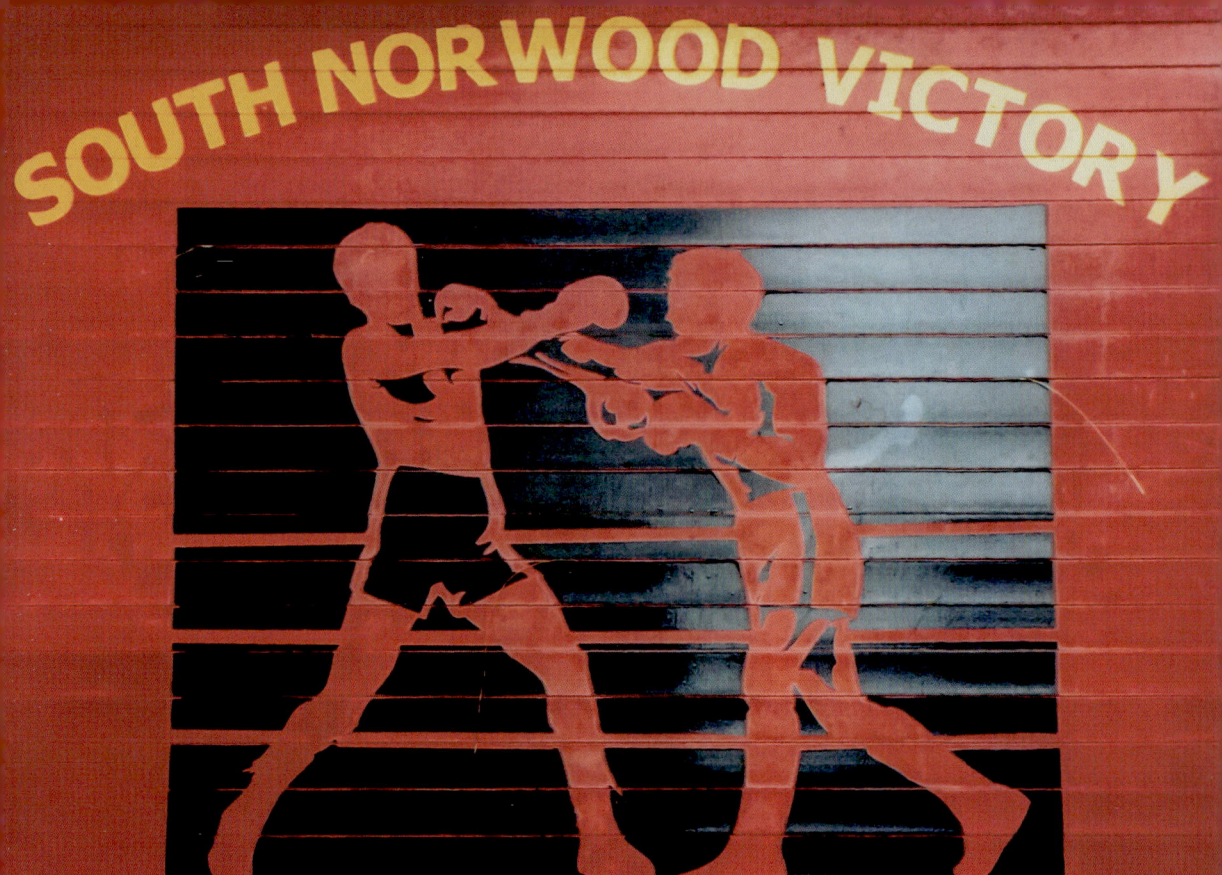

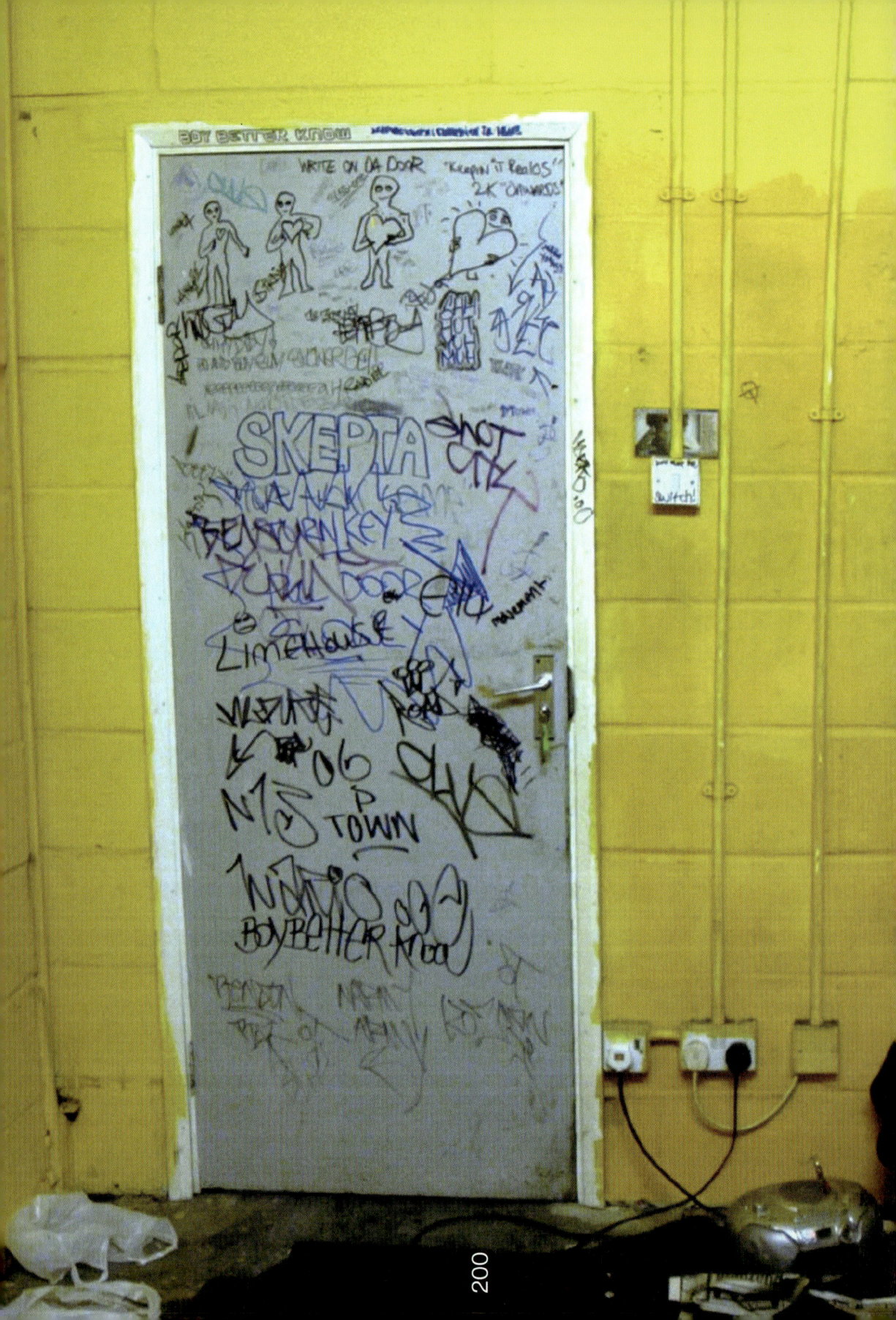

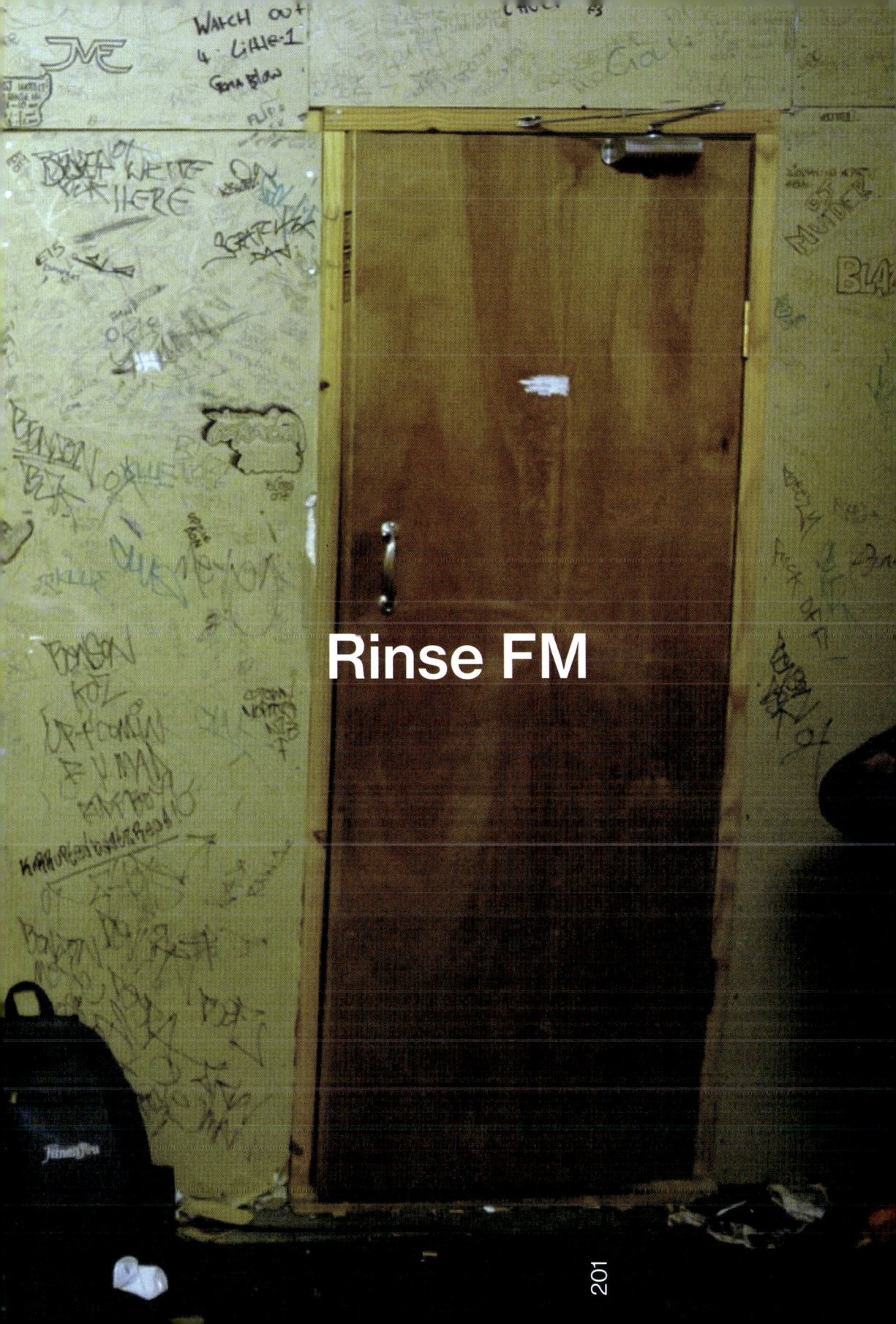

Rinse FM

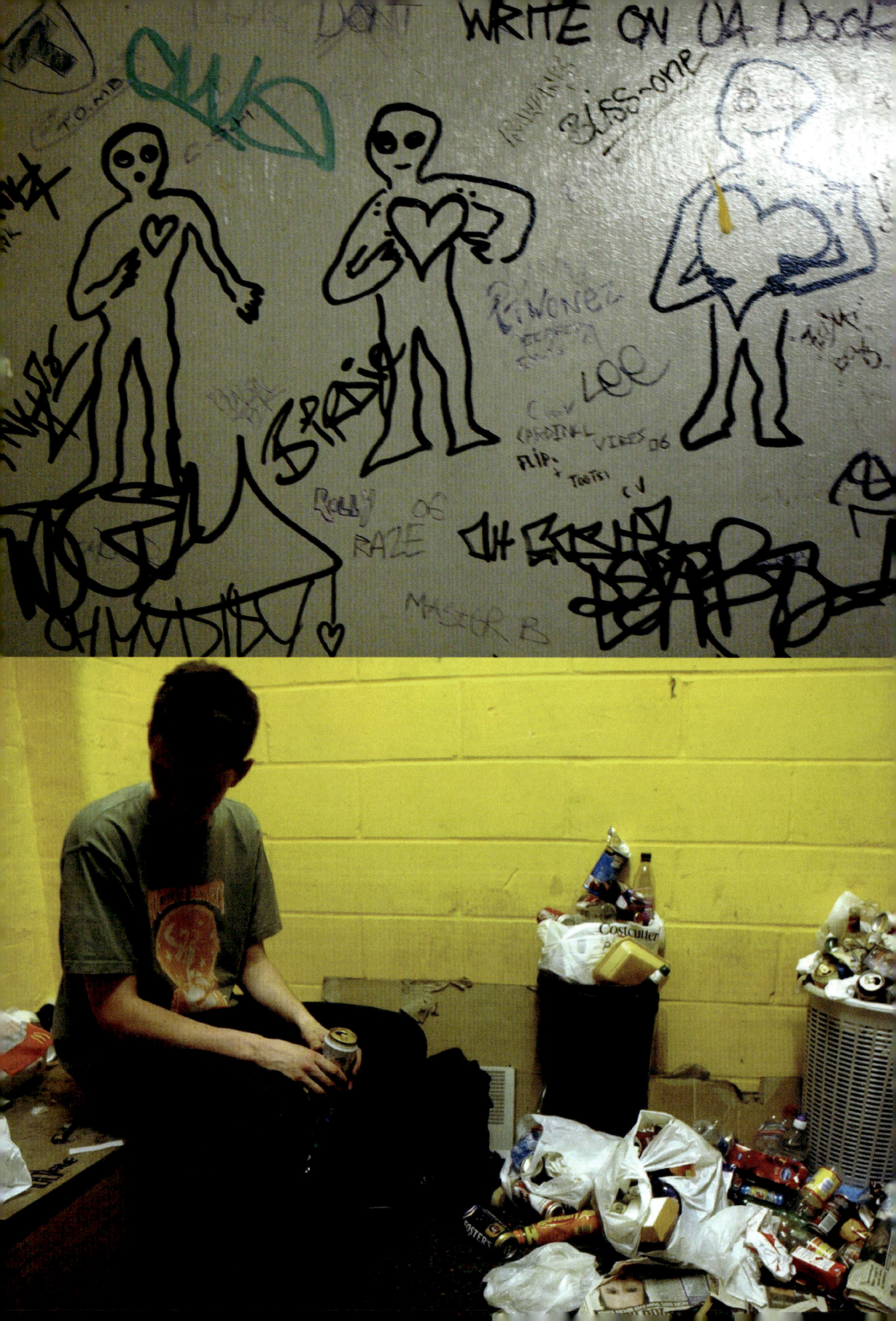

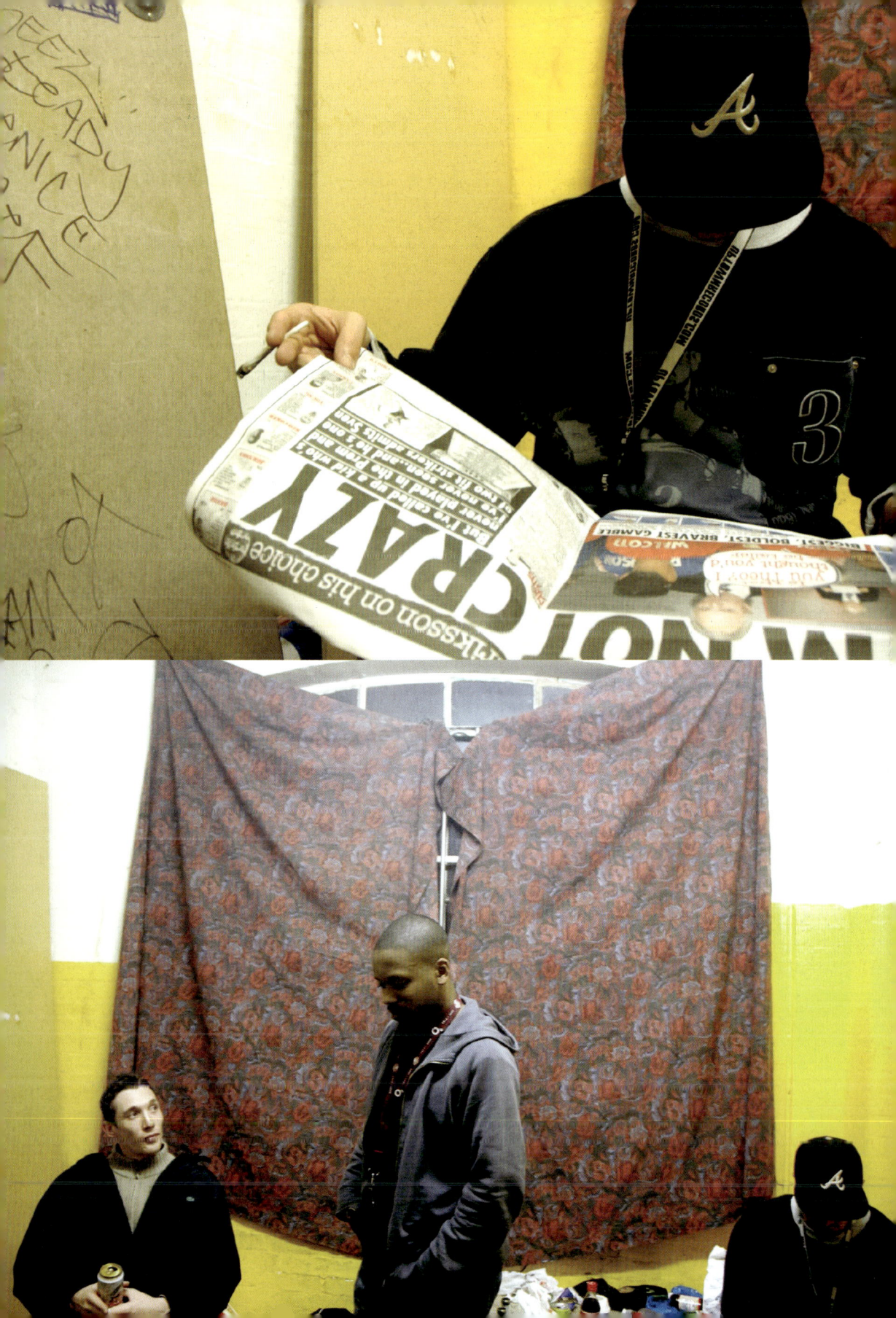

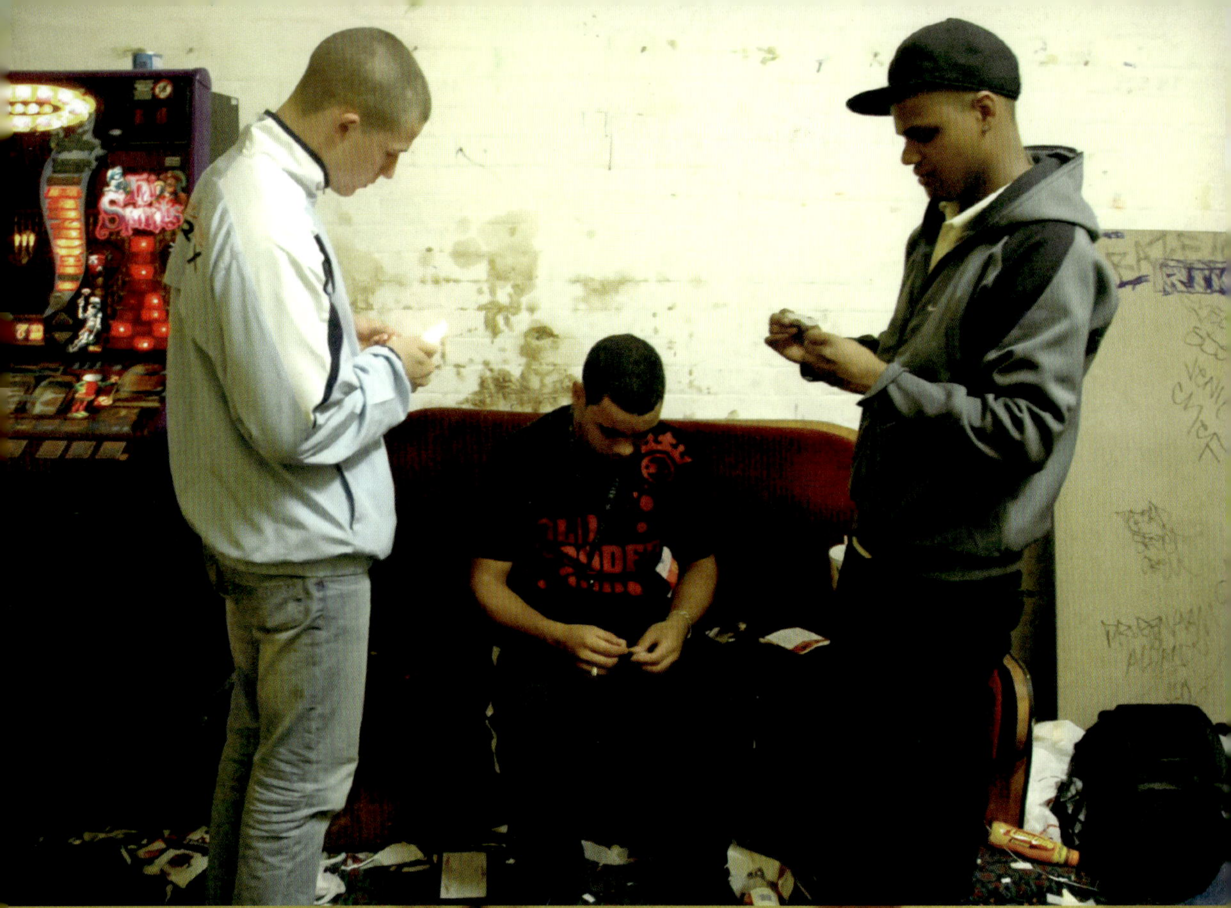

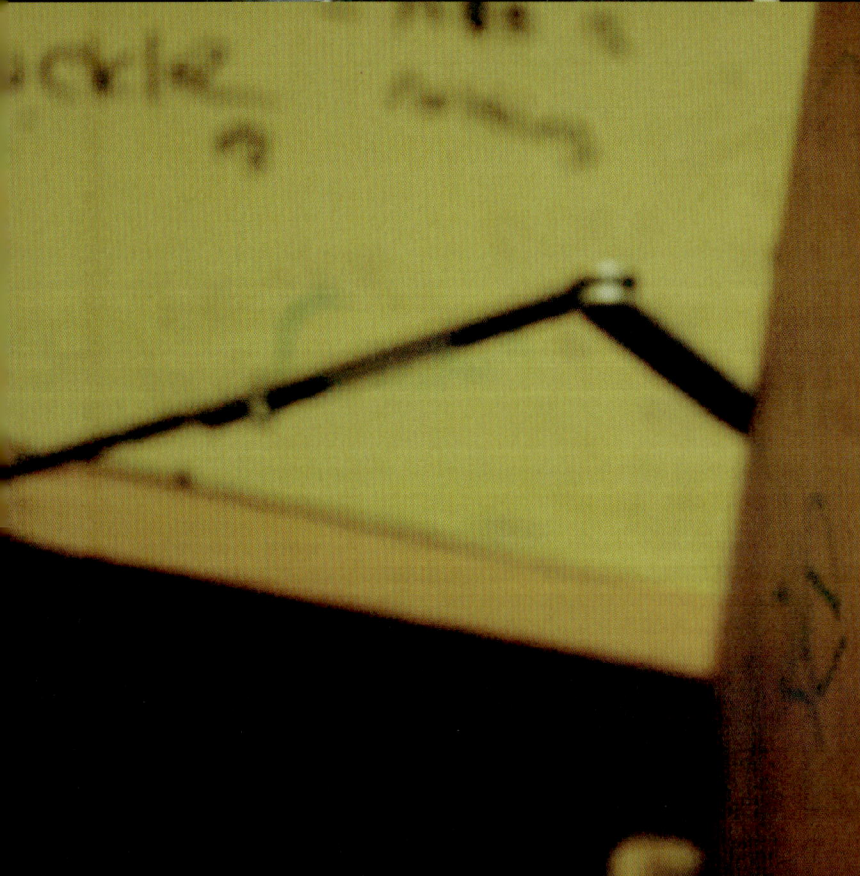

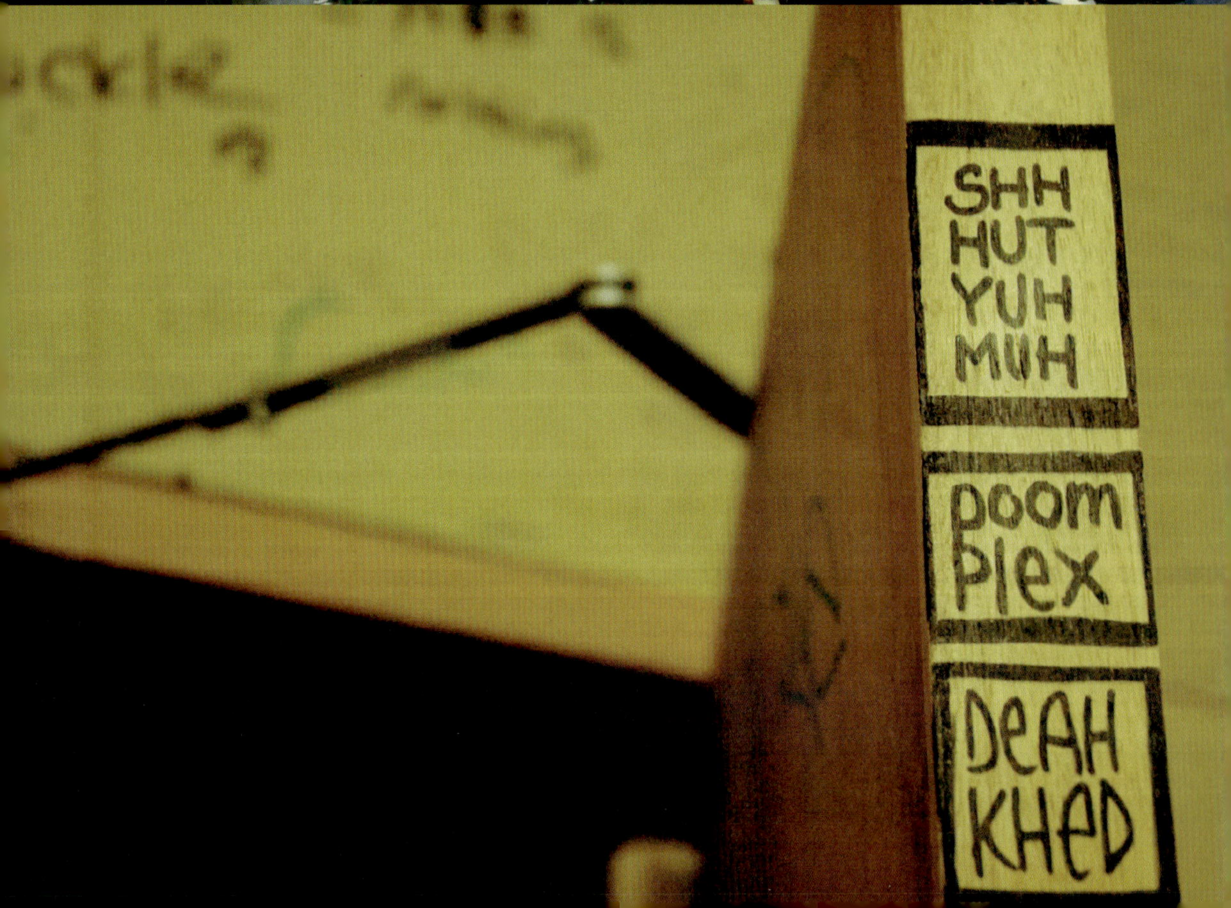

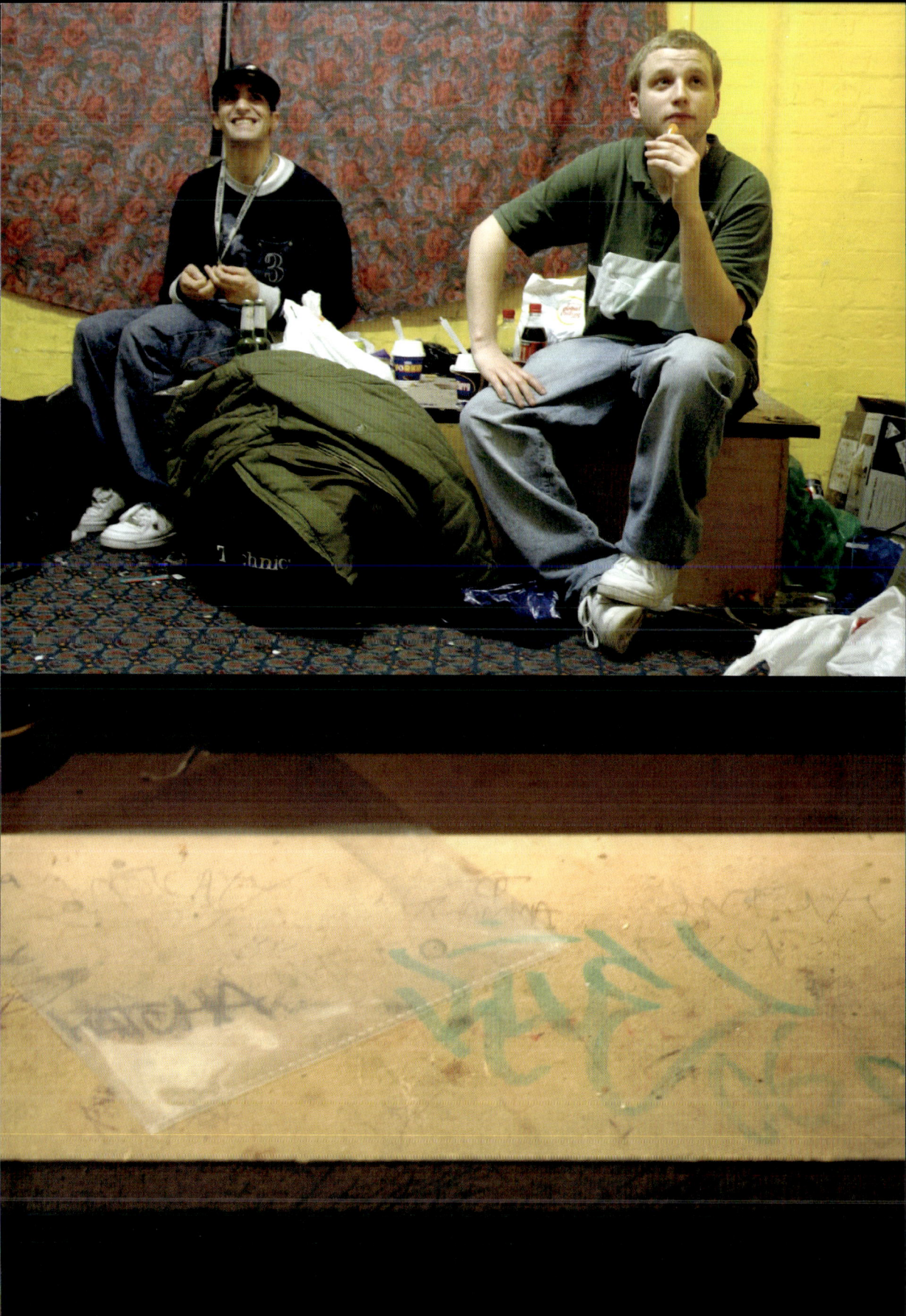

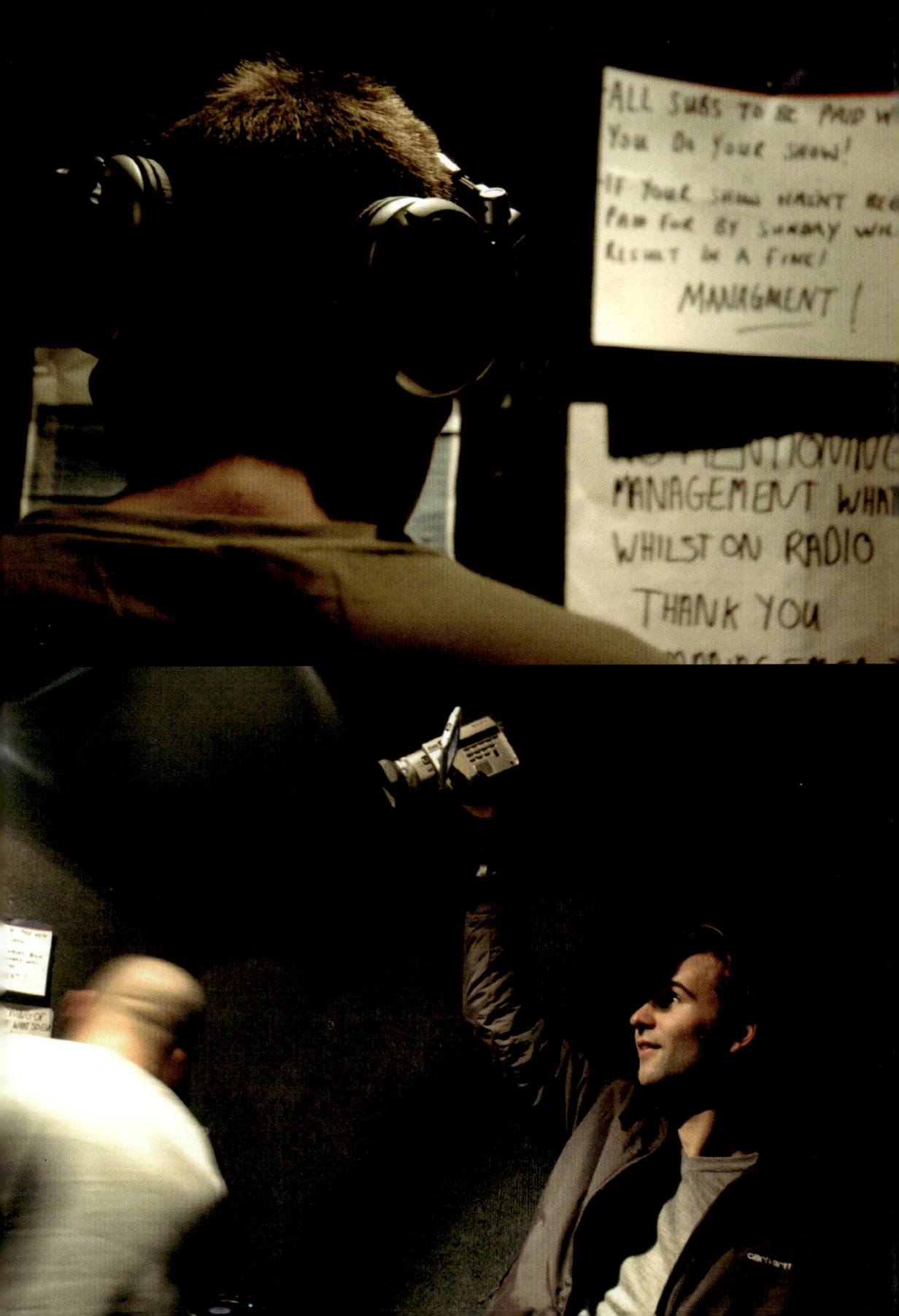

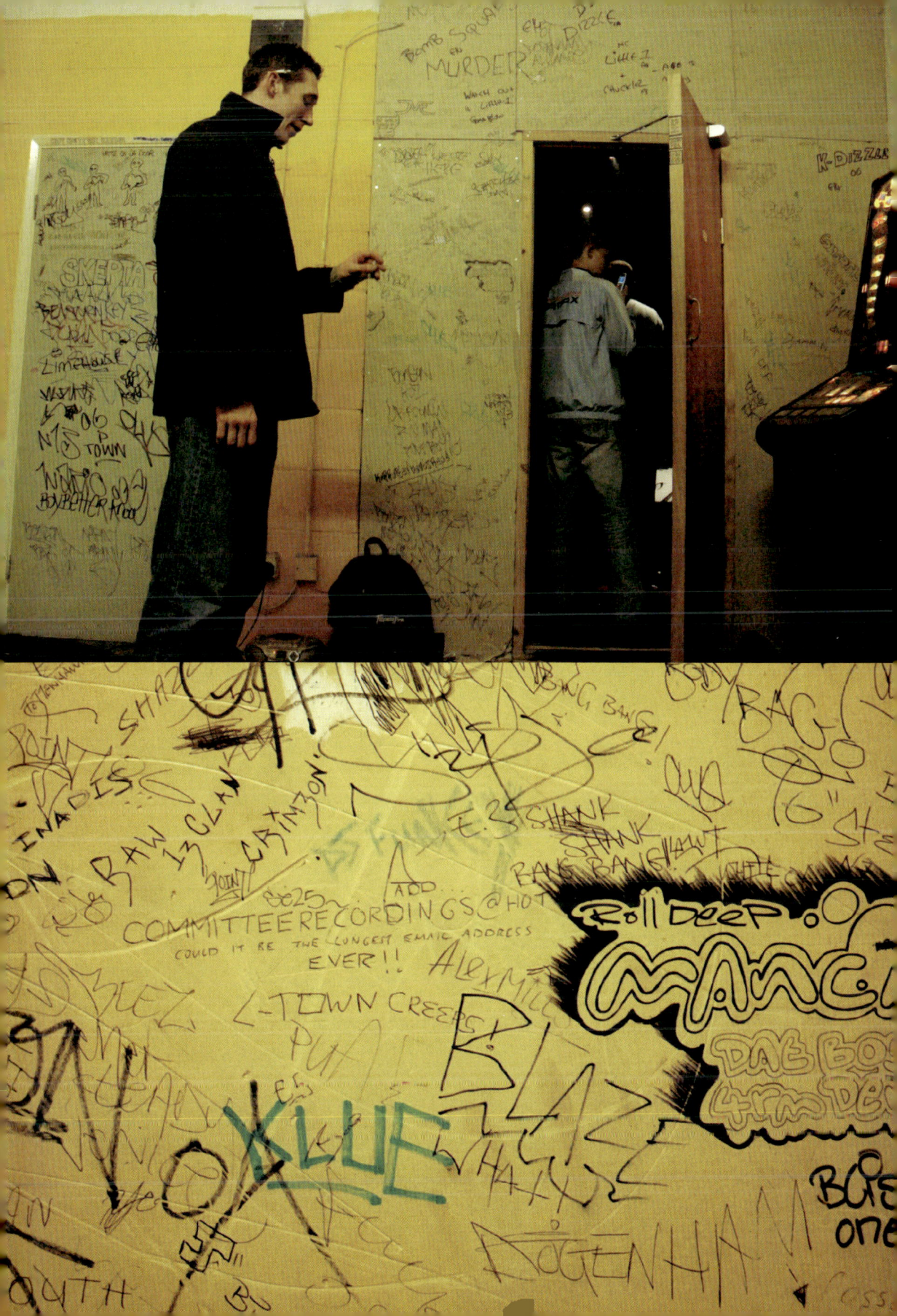

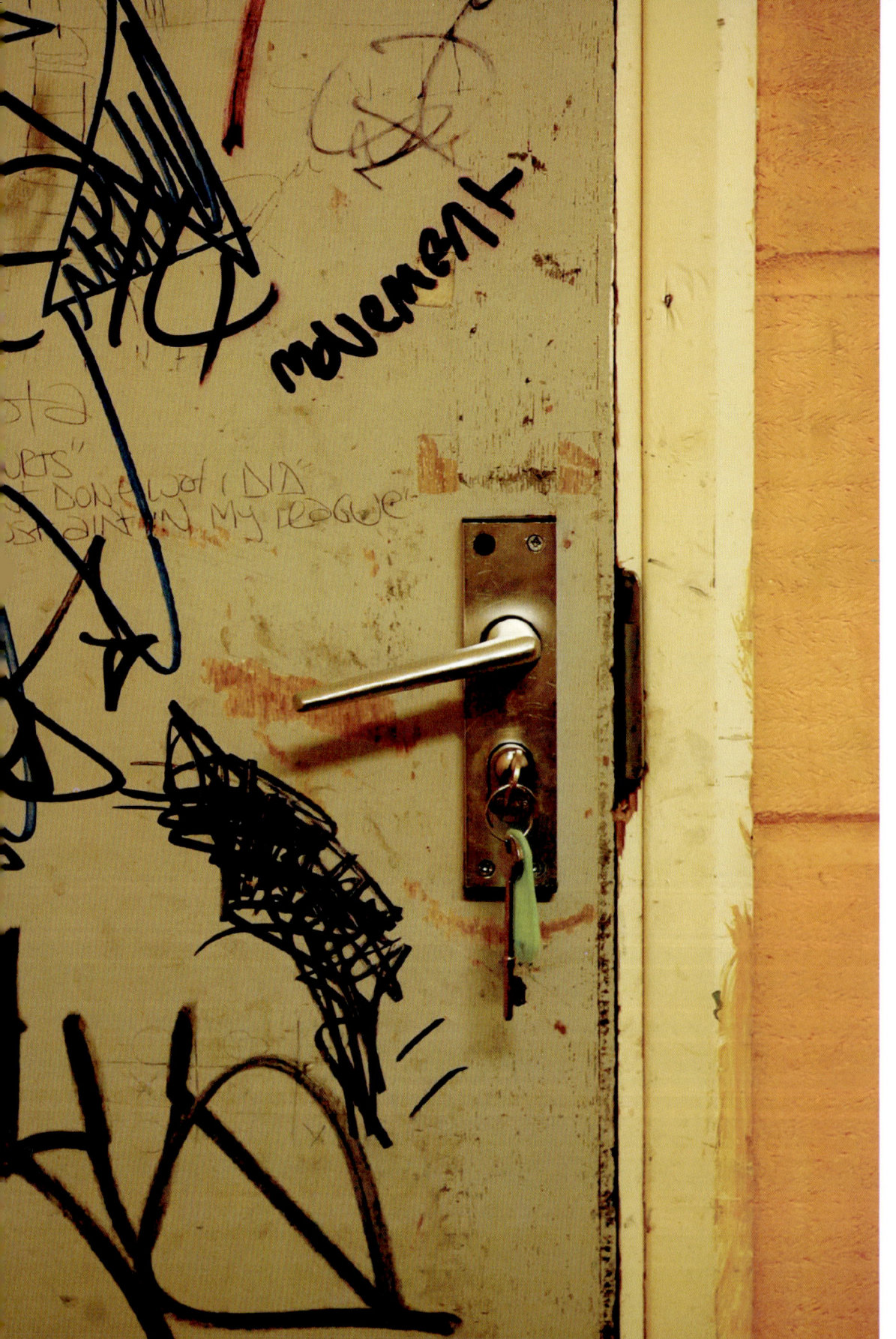

D.O.T.S Blog

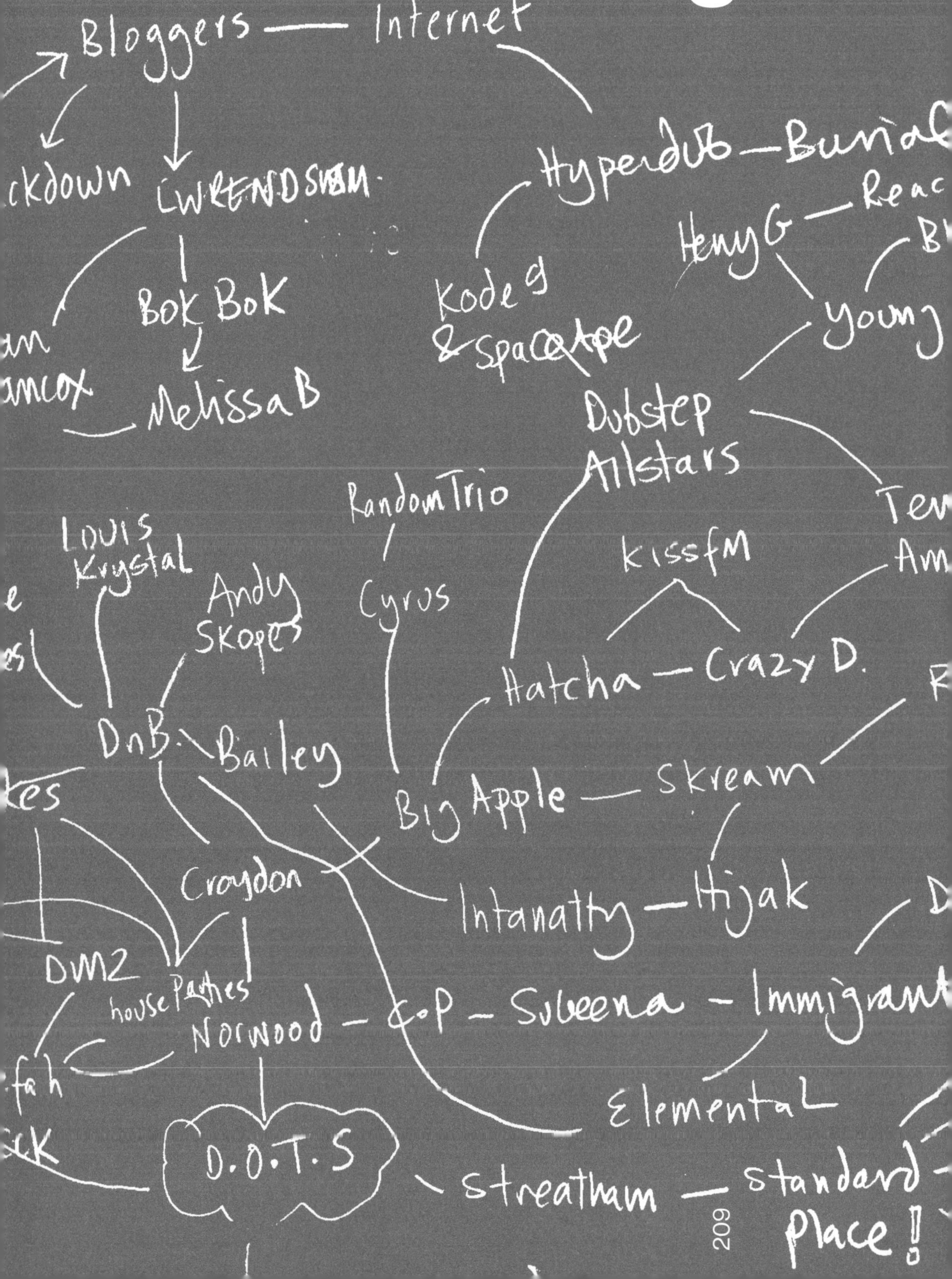

Bloggers —— Internet

Bloggers

ckdown

→ LWRENDSWM

Hyperdub — Burial

Heny G — Reac
B

Bok Bok

Kode9
& Spacape

Young

an
ancox

Melissa B

Dubstep
Allstars

Random Trio

Te
Am

Louis
Krystal

kiss fM

Andy
Skopes

Cyrus

Hatcha — Crazy D.

e
s

DnB Bailey

R

Big Apple — Skream

kes

Croydon

Intanalty — Hijak

D

DM2

house Parties

Norwood — Cop — Subeena — Immigrant

fah

Elemental

ck

D.O.T.S

Streatham — Standard
Place !

Interview: Digital Mystikz

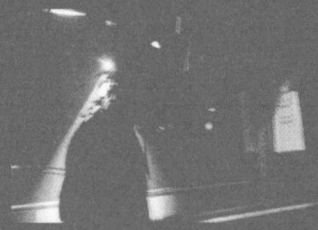

Mala and Coki have been tearing up the growing Dubstep scene since their first release on Big Apple Records The Pathways"- now somewhat of an anthem) and these days you'll rarely find yourself at a dubstep event without hearing the unmistakable basslines and samples of Digital Mystikz.

DIGITAL MYSTIKZ @ THE END
Originally uploaded by infinite.

Alongside like-minders Loefah and Kode 9, the Digital Mystikz successfully broke this indefinable sound out of the low-ceiling, low-light environments of many garage joints into the high-octane sheen of The End at last months Rephlex bash. I caught up with the South London Souljah's after a hard days work to chat about labeling, lack of sleep and the science of sound.

So, how do you guys find time for your music around the 9-5 day?

Coki: For me, it's more family life that keeps me away.... You get up, 9-5 you do your thing, come home and you've got a little kid to look after. Then it gets to about 9 o'clock, and I'm tired. There's really no time apart from weekends. That's when I try and do something.

Mala: Just don't sleep- I probably average 5 hours sleep, go to bed around three o'clock. What I do during the day and how it makes me feel is what goes into the music. It's my expression, my feelings, it's my release.

Coki: Expression is something that's needed in life like water is needed.

Sorry to flog a dead horse, but what's your reaction to the confusion surrounding garage genre handles? Do you guys make dubstep or grime? Does it matter?
C: Who ever produces a sound, it's their sound. You can't say that it comes under a certain label because that description is more well known. At the end of the day, the labels question shouldn't even be asked.

M: People are always gonna call it different things, I suppose it's more marketable that way. It is what it is. The person who wrote it, wrote it. Might come with a different sound on a different day, but it's come from the same person, so what do you call it then?

ABOUT ME

= INFINITE =
SOUTH LONDON, UNITED
KINGDOM

VIEW MY COMPLETE
PROFILE

www.flickr.com

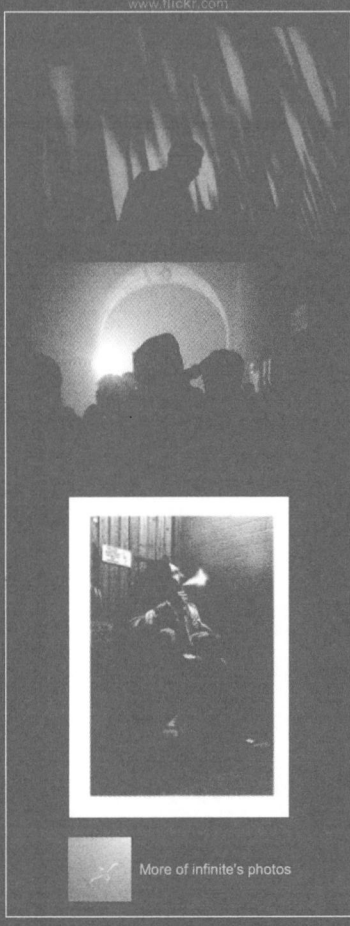

More of infinite's photos

PREVIOUS POSTS

ARCHIVED EVENT: TECHNICALITY, 1
   SEPTEMBER
ARCHIVED EVENT: Technicality July
Releases
Hear This:

C: **Wiley**, he was having the same problem.

Most Dubstep seems to be coming out of Croydon and South London. Is there a reason for this?
M: It's surprising that it's all around here. There might be people in other areas making something that would be called the same ting but it just aint getting heard. I dunno though... **Loefah, Hatcha, Benny III, Plasticman, Skream, Benga** are all round here. It's a weird one. It might be something the government put in the water round these parts!!

C: I guess what you're saying goes with the label thing. A couple of people come outta the same area, thier beats don't even sound the same really and truly.

What would you say are the greatest influences on your music?

M: I don't think about these things. It's a subconscious ting. As far as music, if I start saying one name, then I gotta say 'em all! I like all different kinds of music definitely. Vocals, instrumentals, traditional instruments, electronic shit, virtual shit... I just love sound at the end of the day. Sound and what you can do with it. People kinda take it for granted, but if you think about the science of sound, it's deep you know? It never fails to amaze me.

How do you two work as a collective?

M: [Smiles] What do u think? It's a natural ting for definite. We don't really think about it. [Looks at Coki], We don't think about a lot do we?!!

C: Obviously there's a process that we go through when we make a beat. We can't really describe it though. There's so many little things going on. It's endless.

Do you ever argue about beats?

M: Argue? Nah, sometimes you might think, "Can't really work with that!" It doesn't sound right to the ear.

C: It's like, "that no mek it boss."

M: So you come out and then you move on. You can't force anything. I don't just sit here and then all of a sudden I've finished something. It's a deep inner thing. That's why some people have hundreds of beats that they don't finish. Some things aren't meant to be finished.

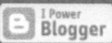

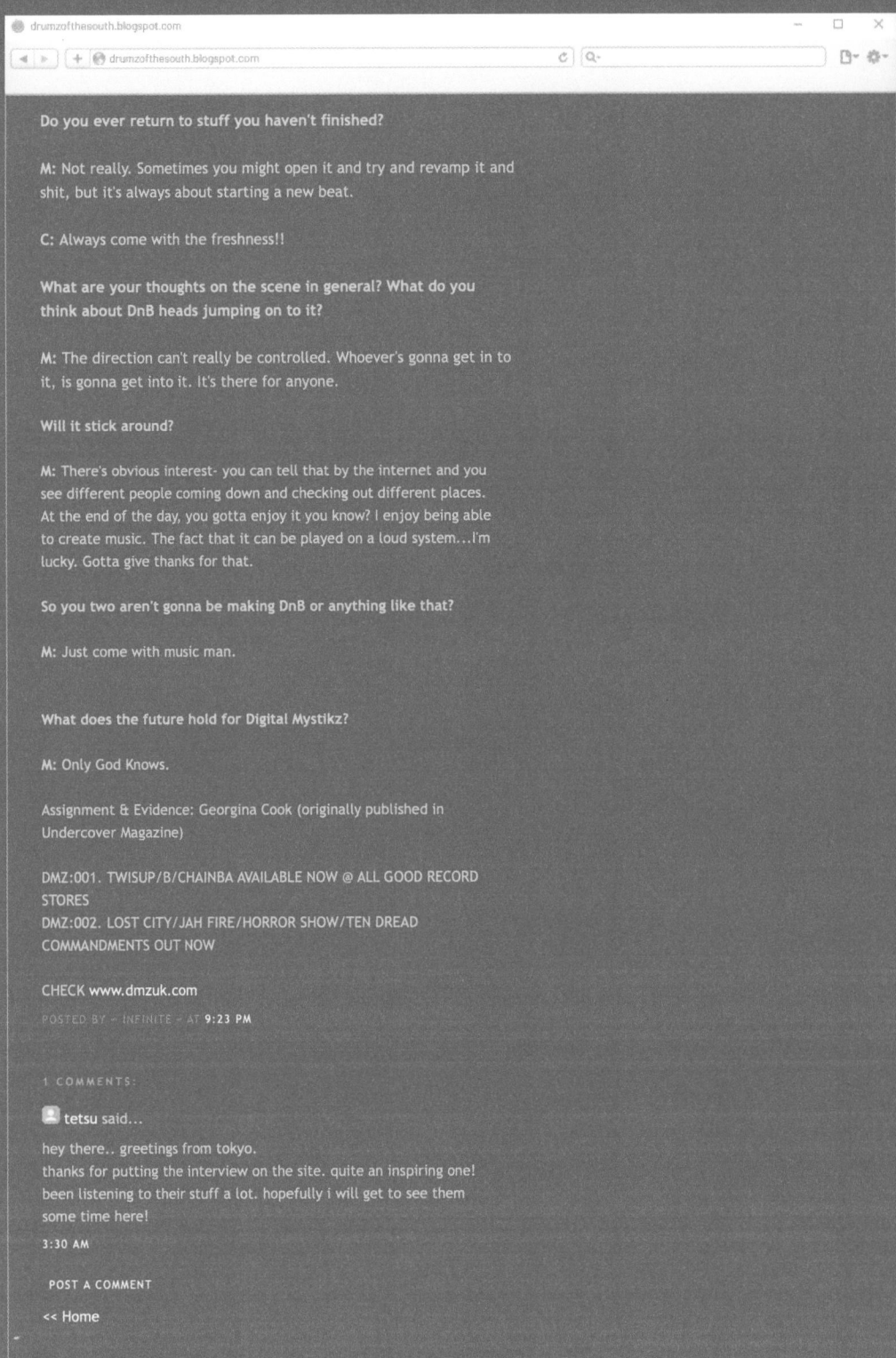

Do you ever return to stuff you haven't finished?

M: Not really. Sometimes you might open it and try and revamp it and shit, but it's always about starting a new beat.

C: Always come with the freshness!!

What are your thoughts on the scene in general? What do you think about DnB heads jumping on to it?

M: The direction can't really be controlled. Whoever's gonna get in to it, is gonna get into it. It's there for anyone.

Will it stick around?

M: There's obvious interest- you can tell that by the internet and you see different people coming down and checking out different places. At the end of the day, you gotta enjoy it you know? I enjoy being able to create music. The fact that it can be played on a loud system...I'm lucky. Gotta give thanks for that.

So you two aren't gonna be making DnB or anything like that?

M: Just come with music man.

What does the future hold for Digital Mystikz?

M: Only God Knows.

Assignment & Evidence: Georgina Cook (originally published in Undercover Magazine)

DMZ:001. TWISUP/B/CHAINBA AVAILABLE NOW @ ALL GOOD RECORD STORES
DMZ:002. LOST CITY/JAH FIRE/HORROR SHOW/TEN DREAD COMMANDMENTS OUT NOW

CHECK www.dmzuk.com

POSTED BY ~ INFINITE ~ AT **9:23 PM**

1 COMMENTS:

tetsu said...

hey there.. greetings from tokyo.
thanks for putting the interview on the site. quite an inspiring one!
been listening to their stuff a lot. hopefully i will get to see them
some time here!

3:30 AM

POST A COMMENT

<< Home

drumzofthesouth.blogspot.com — □ ×

◄ ► + 🌐 drumzofthesouth.blogspot.com ⟳ Q- 📄▾ ⚙▾

OCTOBER 09, 2006

The Art of Losing Things

Lost 2006:

3 phones (stolen)

-"Please leave a message after the tone"
-"Hello george, this is george. Please can you start chaining your mobile to your neck."

1 Camera (during Jamie Woon gig @ Cargo, East LDN) see here

- Photos of Woon gig (@ Cargo, East LDN)
- Photos of Diff'rent Strokes 2nd birthday party (@ Plan B, Brixton the night before)
- An inspiring 17 year old called Maja Jamba (@ Malc Fest, Catford, the weekend before)

Lighters
Socks
Pens

A silver bracelet from Mum (lost whilst carrying a snare drum up a hill in Palace, we'd had an argument the same day.)

Another silver bracelet, a gift from a travelling friend
Vintage pink leather belt (whereabouts known so therefore a loan to Lost?)

A friend (via telephone). Hopefully also a loan to Lost

A spangley black scarf (a tent at the Secret Garden Party)

A brown paper book of love letters, notes and sketches (Notting Hill Carnival)

White Woollen hat (somewhere in Marseille)

Found 2006:

2 pairs of gold and turquoise Puma's, perfect fit, very comfy. worn on many a dancefloor (last flat in Tulse Hill)

A tenner, put towards a wild/sketchy night at the 414 bar (pavement in Brixton)

Lighters
Socks
Pens (standard)

Pebbles, reminders of people and places (Brighton, Central London)

ABOUT ME

» INFINITE «
SOUTH LONDON, UNITED KINGDOM

Infinite is Photographer / Artist / Music Junky / Adventure Capitalist Georgie C. Drumzofthesouth is You, is Me is Them is We.

VIEW MY COMPLETE PROFILE

PREVIOUS POSTS

What is Maximal Minimalism anyway?
Beam me up Scotty
The City that never sleeps
The Soul Snatch Fundraiser
This flyer makes my eyes go funny....
XLR8ed
Familyar faces
Lady dubz
Night in shining armour!
Man can croon

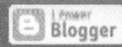

Subscribe to
Posts [Atom]

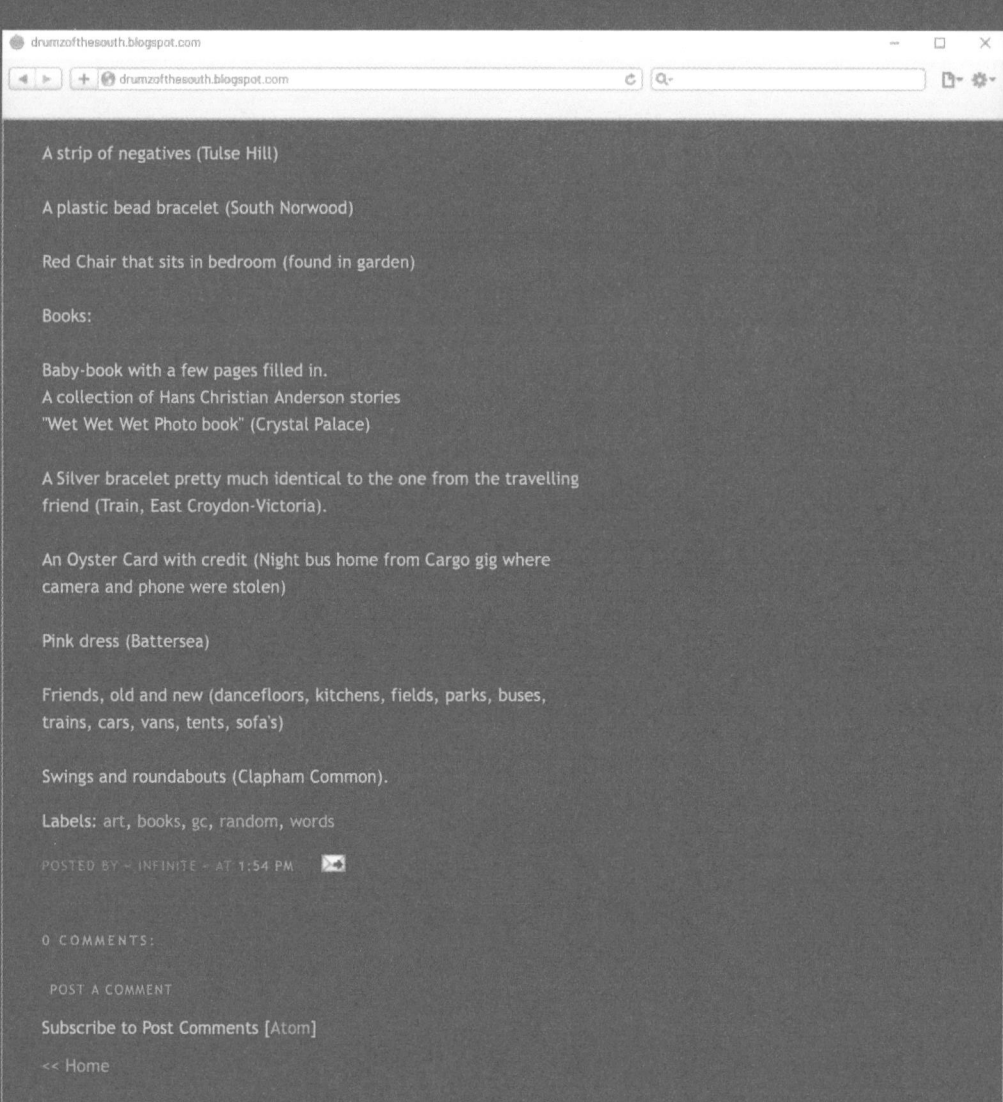

A strip of negatives (Tulse Hill)

A plastic bead bracelet (South Norwood)

Red Chair that sits in bedroom (found in garden)

Books:

Baby-book with a few pages filled in.
A collection of Hans Christian Anderson stories
"Wet Wet Wet Photo book" (Crystal Palace)

A Silver bracelet pretty much identical to the one from the travelling
friend (Train, East Croydon-Victoria).

An Oyster Card with credit (Night bus home from Cargo gig where
camera and phone were stolen)

Pink dress (Battersea)

Friends, old and new (dancefloors, kitchens, fields, parks, buses,
trains, cars, vans, tents, sofa's)

Swings and roundabouts (Clapham Common).

Labels: art, books, gc, random, words

POSTED BY ~ INFINITE ~ AT 1:54 PM

0 COMMENTS:

POST A COMMENT

Subscribe to Post Comments [Atom]

<< Home